THE FALL OF
ALTDORF

The Empire is beset as never before. In the north, the forces of Chaos have broken through the Auric Bastion, a mighty wall of stone and faith that had kept the invaders at bay. As the Emperor Karl Franz and his armies fight a desperate battle to turn back the tide, the Dark Gods hatch a plan that will bring ruin to the Empire. The foremost servants of the Plague Lord descend upon the city of Altdorf bearing Nurgle's greatest blessings with which to spread disease and disorder amongst the terrified citizens. Against them stand the exhausted and diseased remnants of the Empire's armies, their bodies weakening and faith waning. But other forces, both mortal and greater, converge upon Altdorf, for it is here that the first great battle will be fought in the war to end all wars.

WARHAMMER®
THE END TIMES

SIGMAR'S BLOOD
The Prequel to the End Times
Phil Kelly

THE RETURN OF NAGASH
Book One of the End Times
A novel by Josh Reynolds

THE FALL OF ALTDORF
Book Two of the End Times
A novel by Chris Wraight

THE CURSE OF KHAINE
Book Three of the End Times
A novel by Gav Thorpe

THE RISE OF THE HORNED RAT
Book Four of the End Times
A novel by Guy Haley

GOTREK & FELIX: KINSLAYER
Book One of the Doom of Gotrek Gurnisson
A novel by David Guymer

DEATHBLADE
A Chronicle of Malus Darkblade
A novel by C L Werner

Read about the birth of Sigmar's Empire

• TIME OF LEGENDS: THE LEGEND OF SIGMAR •
By Graham McNeill
BOOK 1: HELDENHAMMER
BOOK 2: EMPIRE
BOOK 3: GOD KING

WARHAMMER®
THE END TIMES

THE FALL OF
ALTDORF

CHRIS WRAIGHT

BLACK LIBRARY

To Hannah, with love. Also with special thanks to Phil Kelly, Matt Ward and the GW Studio for developing the End Times storyline, and to Graeme Lyon and the BL editorial team for invaluable help on turning it into a novel.

A BLACK LIBRARY PUBLICATION

First published in 2014.
This edition published in 2015 by
Black Library,
Games Workshop Ltd.,
Willow Road,
Nottingham, NG7 2WS, UK.

10 9 8 7 6 5 4 3 2 1

Cover artwork by Paul Dainton.
Map artwork by John Michelbach.
Internal artwork by Alex Boyd and Slawomir Maniak.

See Black Library on the internet at

blacklibrary.com

Find out more about Games Workshop
and the world of Warhammer at

games-workshop.com

Printed and bound by CPI Group (UK) Ltd, Croydon, CR0 4YY

The world is dying, but it has been so since the
coming of the Chaos Gods.

For years beyond reckoning, the Ruinous Powers have
coveted the mortal realm. They have made many attempts to
seize it, their anointed champions leading vast hordes into
the lands of men, elves and dwarfs. Each time, they have
been defeated.

Until now.

In the frozen north, Archaon, a former templar of the
warrior-god Sigmar, has been crowned the Everchosen of
Chaos. He stands poised to march south and bring ruin to
the lands he once fought to protect. Behind him amass all
the forces of the Dark Gods, mortal and daemonic. When
they come, they will bring with them a storm such as has
never been seen. Already, the lands of men are coming to
ruin. Archaon's vanguard run riot across Kislev and make
inroads into the north of the Empire. The once-proud
country of Bretonnia has fallen into anarchy. The southern
lands have been consumed by a tide of verminous rat-
men. And in the trackless forests of the Empire, there are
whispers that another ancient power is rising. The Great
Necromancer, Nagash, has returned to the world, and none
know if his armies of the dead will stand against the hordes
of Chaos, or fight beneath their banners.

The men of the Empire, the elves of Ulthuan and the dwarfs
of the Worlds Edge Mountains fortify their cities and prepare for the inevitable onslaught. They will fight bravely and
to the last. But in their hearts, all know that their efforts
will be futile. The victory of Chaos is inevitable.

These are the End Times.

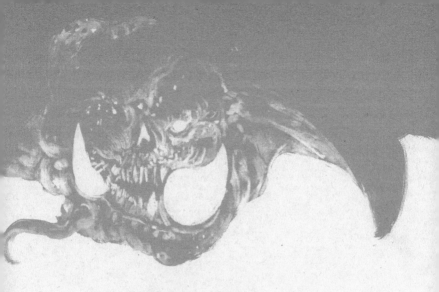

PART ONE

Heffengen
Late Winter 2524-2525

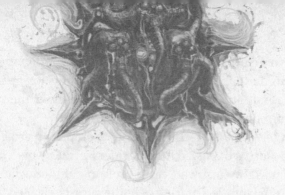

ONE

The tent's walls flapped in the cold west wind, making the fires in the torches spit and gutter. Its lone occupant knelt on mud-slick grass, bowing his head before a makeshift altar. A rich red cloak hung, rain-heavy, from his armoured shoulders. His gauntlets were crossed on the hilt of a proffered sword, thrust naked and point-down into the earth in the knight's fashion.

His eyes remained closed. He was un-helmed, exposing a lean, noble face lost in prayer. His hair was close-cropped and mottled with the marks of the battlefield – mud, blood, lines of old sweat.

The altar was small, and had been carried with his baggage ever since his first days as a squire. It was made of rosewood, with a carved representation of twin griffons facing one another across the battered top face. It was a cheap thing, in truth. He could have had it replaced with a gold-plated one by now, or employed priests to pray on his behalf, but he had prayed before that same altar for thirty-two years, and was not about to change now. Not today, of all days.

'My lord Heldenhammer,' he whispered, his breath steaming

in the dawn's chill. 'As I have ever been faithful, remember Your servant this day. I fear no death, no pain, no trial, if it be in Your service. I admit only one fear: to prove unworthy of the sword I bear, the armour I wear, the men I command.'

From outside the tent, the noises of a preparing army could be heard – horses being led to their riders, artillery pieces being hauled across the furrowed earth on iron-rimmed wheels. He could hear the muffled roaring of battle-priests, rivalled only by the parade-ground shouts of sergeants and captains.

He had heard such sounds all his life. Ever since childhood, the instruments of war had been around him. In that, if in no other way, this day was little different.

'When I slay, let it be in Your name. When I face the darkness, let it be in Your name. And when the hour comes, and when my service ends, let it be that I reflected honour to You in the time that I was given.'

Rain started up again, drumming on the already sodden canvas. The downpour would make the earth well with water, hampering the charge of the warhorses.

'Let it be,' he prayed, near-silently, 'that no man has cause to doubt my devotion, and that they will say nothing more of me, after I am gone, but that I fulfilled my vows.'

He opened his eyes, and stood stiffly. He took up his sword and sheathed the blade, then made the sign of the comet across his breastplate and bowed a final time. As he did so, the wind whipped around the tent-walls, brushing ice-cold rain under the skirts.

He reached for his helm, held it loosely in his left hand, and turned to the entrance flaps.

Outside, they were waiting for him.

Schwarzhelm glowered massively in the drizzle, his heavy broadsword already unsheathed, his great beard dank and draggled. Huss stood in his shadow, scarce less brutal in mien, moisture running in trickles down his bald pate. The boy Valten was beside him, grasping Ghal Maraz one-handed as if it weighed less than a stick of straw. Helborg stood apart, magnificent in his war-plate, steel-clad, hard and hawk-like.

Behind them were the generals, the warriors, the foot soldiers, the knights, the halberdiers, in white and red and yellow and chequered black and carrying the serried weapons of the Empire in readiness.

As one, they raised those blades.

'*Karl Franz!*' they roared.

At that, the Elector Count of Reikland, the Prince of Altdorf, the Bearer of the Silver Seal and the holder of the *Drachenzahn* runefang, Emperor of all Sigmar's holy inheritance between the Worlds Edge Mountains and the Great Sea, nodded in acknowledgement.

'Gentlemen,' he said. 'Let us begin.'

Heffengen, like all towns in the upper Ostermark, was fortified. Thick stone walls enclosed its tight streets of wattle-and-daub dwellings, overlooked by steep tiled roofs. Those walls, though, had been left to rot by a neglectful burgomeister, whose body now swung from a high gibbet over the gates.

Perhaps the burgomeister had done the best he could. Perhaps the plague or the heavy draft of fighting men had made his job impossible. It hardly mattered now – an example had to be set.

With the walls in their state of disrepair, Karl Franz had decided that a defence of the town itself was impossible. In any case, the army he had mustered would have struggled to fit inside, and so the coming battle would be fought on the plains, out in the open, under the rain and the watchful eyes of whatever gods deigned to observe.

Squalls continued to drive hard from the north-west, bearing more moisture with them. The land stretched away to a steel-grey horizon, glistening with standing water atop soft black earth. A few blasted trees hunched over here and there, dark against the water-heavy sky.

Karl Franz had drawn his forces up on the wastelands a mile north of Heffengen's limits. The battlefield was bounded on the east by the deep cleft of the Revesnecht river as it snaked north towards the greater flood of the Talabec. Over to the west, open ground slowly gave way to the straggling fronds of marginal forest.

The enemy would come at them from the north, just as they always did. They would sweep over the moors, fresh from their slaughter at the Auric Bastion, tearing up sodden ground under brazen hooves. The hounds would come first, loping with jaws agape; then the cavalry on their red-eyed mounts; then, striding on cloven hooves, the armoured behemoths with spiked helms and skulls hanging from blood-glossed armour.

Their formations would be ragged, powered onward by lust for slaughter. The one defence, the only advantage possessed by mortal men, was discipline. Just as had been the case for a hundred lifetimes, raw mania would be met by ordered lines of Imperial steel.

General Talb had petitioned hard for the honour of guarding the eastern flank. His ranks of Ostermarkers stood in place, arranged into squares of halberdiers and pikemen. They were supported by units of gunners and swordsmen, including a contingent of mercenary ogres who towered over the warriors around them. Huss had taken his fanatics with him to bolster Talb's lines, though the warrior priest's presence alone was worth more than all the zealots he brought with him. Valten, as ever, accompanied his mentor.

Karl Franz had watched them go. It remained uncomfortable to see the holy warhammer borne by hands other than his own. Gelt had counselled against it from the start, but the decision had not been his to make.

What brought you down? thought Karl Franz, ruminating on

Gelt's disgrace and departure. *Pride? Weakness of will? Or just, like so many before you, despair?*

So much had changed, and in so short a time. The mighty defensive bastion Balthasar Gelt had raised across the Empire's northern borders had been breached at last, freeing the hordes of the Wastes to pour into Ostermark like blood fountaining from a wound. The strain of maintaining it had turned the Gold Wizard's mind in the end, damning him to association with fallen souls he would not have so much as spat on while sane.

Gelt had not deserved his sudden fall from grace, not after the service he had rendered, but then so many did not deserve the fates that had befallen them, and there was no leisure to mourn them all.

You could have fought here with us. Your spells might have turned them back.

'You will not ride out,' grunted Schwarzhelm.

Karl Franz smiled. His bodyguard had been fighting solidly for weeks, first on the Bastion, now as part of the long retreat south from the breach at Alderfen. He was caked with grime, much of it flecked amongst the curls of his immense beard.

'The choice is mine, Ludwig,' he reminded him.

'Ludwig is right, my lord,' said Helborg. 'They wish to draw you out. We may fall in battle, you may not. You are the Empire.'

You are the Empire. Those words always gave Karl Franz a cold twinge of unease, though he had heard them many times before.

It was a comfort, though, to hear his two lieutenants in agreement. Such had not always been the case.

'The judgement will be mine,' Karl Franz said, firmly. 'As ever, Sigmar will guide.'

The three of them stood at the very centre of the Empire battle lines, set some way back from the front ranks. Ahead of them was arrayed the main force of Reiklanders, decked in white and red. Three whole regiments of the Palace guard had been assembled, flanked by greater numbers of regular troops. Like the

Ostermarkers to the east, the halberdier squares formed the backbone, supported by ranged weaponry – bowmen, hand-gunners, light artillery pieces. The elite of the entire army, the Reiksguard cavalry, had formed up to the left, waiting for their lord Helborg to join them. Proud banners bearing the Imperial griffon and black cross of the knightly order hung limp in the drizzle.

It looked solid. Rows and rows of steel glinted dully in the grey light, close-serried and well-drilled. Sharpened stakes protruded from the earth in steed-killing lines, dripping dankly in the morning mist.

'And Mecke?' asked Schwarzhelm.

The west flank was held by Lord General Mecke of Talabheim, whom Karl Franz thought was an ambitious bastard with an unseemly enthusiasm for the coming slaughter. Still, his men were as disciplined as any of the others, and he had numbers. The red and forest-green livery of his infantry squares was just visible to the west, part-shielded by fringes of foliage. The greater part of the artillery pieces were there too, lodged on higher ground and with a commanding vantage over the open field.

'He knows his business,' said Karl Franz. 'Nothing more to be done, now.'

Helborg wiped a sluice of rainwater from the visor of his hawk-winged helm. Karl Franz could see he was anxious to be gone, to saddle up and join his men. That man was only truly happy on the charge, his runefang in his fist and the thunder and crash of arms around him. He would have made a poor statesman, so it was fortunate he had never been charged with that role. Killing suited him better than bartering.

'I can smell them already,' said the Reiksmarshal.

Karl Franz turned his gaze north. Beyond the furthest ranks of the central defence, the land ran away, bleak and empty. Eddies of rain whipped across the mud.

'You should go, Kurt,' said Karl Franz.

Helborg pushed his cloak back, drew his sword and saluted. 'This day will see the line restored.'

Always confident, always brash.

Karl Franz acknowledged the salute. 'Should we lose the field–'

'We cannot lose,' muttered Schwarzhelm.

'Should we lose the field, they will press for Altdorf. We discussed what is to be done then.'

'Middenheim is closer, and stronger,' said Helborg, repeating what he had argued in the war council two days ago. 'I still think–'

'I have spoken,' said Karl Franz, holding the Reiksmarshal's gaze calmly. 'These are desperate times. I have no faith in electors, wizards have proven themselves unreliable, and I barely understand Huss's motives.' He smiled, clapping an armoured hand on Helborg's shoulder. '*We* are the Empire. *Men*. Altdorf is the key. It always has been, and they know it too.'

Helborg looked, for a moment, like he might argue the point. Then he bowed. 'It matters not – we will drive their bones into the earth. Here is where the tide turns.'

'Well said,' said Karl Franz. 'Now go in faith.'

'Always.'

Helborg strode off. As the Reiksmarshal walked down through the ranks, attendants hurried after him. Soon he would be mounted, blade in hand, poised at the forefront of the Reiksguard's formation.

Schwarzhelm stayed put. His unsmiling eyes strayed over to the stockade behind them, where Deathclaw had been chained. The griffon's scent penetrated through all the others – a wild, bitter aroma, suggestive of raw meat and frenzy.

'I know what you're thinking, Ludwig,' said Karl Franz.

'Listen to Kurt, if you will not listen to me,' grumbled the old warrior.

Karl Franz laughed. 'I don't know what to worry about more – them, or the fact you're both speaking with one voice. It's almost as if Averland never happened.'

Schwarzhelm's face did not so much as twitch from its mask of belligerent certainty. His trials in the south were almost forgotten now, washed away by the greater war of the north. Combat with an enemy he understood had restored him to his former self, it seemed.

He looked about to say something else, no doubt some plea for the Emperor to remember his place at the rear of the army, and not to go charging off into the fray like some avatar of Sigmar reborn. Such counsel was Schwarzhelm's duty, of course, just as it was Karl Franz's prerogative to make his own damned mind up.

In the event, Schwarzhelm said nothing. Any words he might have uttered were snatched from his lips by a clamour rising up out of the north. It started off low, like the growl of beasts at bay, then picked up in volume, carried by the skirling winds and wafted across the empty land.

Soon it was a *howl*, a mass of screaming and roaring. Drums underpinned it, making the standing waters shiver. The northern horizon darkened, as if storm clouds had boiled into existence in defiance of the law of nature.

Then Karl Franz saw the truth – the clouds were birds, thousands of them, flocking unnaturally. They blotted out the meagre sunlight in a fast-moving scab of ragged black, sweeping out of the mist and circling clear of arrow-range.

The howling continued, muffled by distance for the moment, but that would not last. All along the Empire lines, sergeants bellowed at their men to hold fast, to grip their halberds ready, to remember their vows, to take no damned backward step or their bones would be first to feel the crack of the maul.

Schwarzhelm's grizzled face tightened. His burly hand crept automatically to the hilt of his great blade, the *Rechtstahl*, the famed Sword of Justice.

'Here they come,' he murmured.

Karl Franz heard Deathclaw's agitated growling from behind

the stockade. The war-griffon was eager to tear at the foe. The beast might not have to wait much longer.

'Unto death,' he breathed, feeling the weight of the runefang at his belt. 'Never yield.'

The enemy charged under the shadow of crows.

The birds wheeled and dived across the Empire defences, cawing maddeningly. Detachment captains forbade the wasting of arrows against such fodder, and so the birds were left unmolested to crash and flap into the waiting soldiers. They clawed at faces and fingers, and soon the halberdiers were flailing at them, their exposed flesh running with lacerations.

Runners broke out of the mist next, hundreds of them, isolated and without formation. From atop his mount, Helborg watched them come. No Imperial gunner opened up at them yet, giving the runners an unimpeded charge at the Empire positions. They careered mindlessly, limbs cartwheeling, eyes staring. Some were naked and daubed with inks across their snow-pale flesh; others were riddled with disease, their eyes staring and red-rimmed. All were lost in battle-fury, triggered by the poisons they had been fed by their shamans.

Helborg curled his lip in disgust. The first of the baresarks hurled themselves into the outer lines of pikemen. He saw one skinny lunatic impale himself on the stakes designed for the cavalry, and writhe there in a kind of wild-eyed ecstasy. Others slammed into the waiting defenders, and the halberds rose and fell, slewing up tatters of plague-sick gore.

Helborg felt his steed twitch under him. The warhorse knew what was coming, and was eager for it. Cold wind, still laced with fine rain, hissed up against its barding, chilling the muscles beneath.

'Easy,' he murmured, keeping a light hold on the reins.

More runners emerged from the mists, screaming as they came. They charged down the centre of the battlefield, ignoring the flanks. Still the handgunners restrained themselves, letting the infantry squares deal with the threat as it emerged. The real enemy was still to show itself.

It did not take long. Norscans strode out of the grey haze, rain bouncing from thick, bronze-lipped armour. They carried heavy axes, or mauls, or gouges, or double-bladed swords with obscene daemon-headed hilts. Some had helical horns twisting from their helms, others tusks, or spikes, or strips of flayed skin.

As the mist flayed into tatters around them, the front rank of Chaos warriors broke into a lumbering charge. There was still no formation to speak of, just a broken wave of massive bodies, swollen and distended by disease and mutation. War horns, carved into crude likenesses of two-headed dragons and leering troll-faces, were raised amid the throng.

The Norscan infantry brought the rolling stink with them – like charnel-house residue, but thicker and more nauseating. It seethed across the battlefield, pungent and inescapable, making mortal soldiers gag and retch. Even before the first of them had entered blade-range, the Empire's defensive formations began to suffer.

'First rank, fire!' came the cry, and the first squads of hand-gunners opened up. A second later, and the long rifles sent a curtain of shot scything out. A few Chaos warriors stumbled, borne down by those coming behind and trodden into the mud.

After frantic reloading, the gunners opened up again, then again, taking aim as soon as they could, and the air became acrid with the drifting stench of blackpowder. The great cannons opened up from Mecke's western position, booming with thunderous reports and driving gouges into the emerging horde. They were more effective: dozens of warriors were dragged to a bloody ruin by the iron balls.

Even the thickest plate armour was no defence against such

disciplined fire, launched in wave after wave. Norscans and bare-sarks alike were blasted apart, their armour-shards spiralling into the swooping flocks of crows. One huge champion, antler-horned and clad in overlapping iron plates the width of a man's hand, took a cannonball direct in the throat, severing his head clear. He rocked for a moment, before the momentum of the charge dragged his body under.

It still was not enough. The howling screams became deafening as more warriors strode onto the battlefield. Soon the cacophony was so loud that it was impossible to hear the shouts of the captains. The earth reeled under the massed treads of iron-shod boots, and the northern horizon filled with the rain-shrouded shadow of thousands upon thousands of Chaos fighters.

By then the foremost of the Norscans had caught up with the baresarks, and they crashed into the static defenders. Most detachments initially held out as the battle-blinded enemy charged straight into thickets of angled halberds. Every impact, though, drove the defenders back a pace, until gaps began to form. Halberd-shafts snapped, arms were broken, legs slipped in the mire, and the squares buckled.

The blood would flow freely, now. The preliminaries were over, and the hard, desperate grind had begun.

'Reiksguard!' roared Helborg, raising his blade *Klingerach*, the fabled Solland runefang. Rain bounced from the naked blade. 'On my word.'

Behind him, he heard the stamp and clatter of five hundred knights prepare for the charge. They drew their swords in a glitter of revealed steel, flashing against the darkening pall ahead.

Helborg looked out, tracing a path into the storm. A mass of Reikland halberdiers stood to his right, the artillery positions and Mecke's contingent to his left. The knights would charge through the gap, emerging into the Chaos hordes just as the last of the cannon volleys rang out. After that, the fighting would be closer, grimier, harder – just as he liked it.

'For Sigmar!' he roared, brandishing his sacred blade in a wild circle before pointing the tip directly at the enemy. 'For the Empire! For *Karl Franz!*'

Then he kicked his spurs in, and the mighty Reiksguard, driving on in a wedge of ivory and black, thundered into the heart of the storm.

TWO

Karl Franz strode up the wooden steps of the stockade, his armour clanking, and Schwarzhelm followed him up.

The Emperor could hear the incessant chants of the warrior priests. Huss had taken the best of them with him to the front, and those left behind to lead the prayers to Sigmar were the old and the wounded. Their dirges, normally strident with martial vigour, sounded feeble set against the horrific wall of noise to the north.

The Emperor reached the stockade's summit, where a fortified platform rose twenty feet above the battle-plain. Standards of the Empire, Talabheim, Ostermark and Reikland hung heavily in the drizzle, their colours drab and sodden. Guards in Ostermark livery saluted as he approached, then withdrew to allow his passage. The only other occupants of the viewing platform were a group of extravagantly bewhiskered master engineers, peering out through long bronze telescopes before issuing orders for the artillery teams via carrier pigeon.

Karl Franz walked over to the platform's edge and stared out across the windswept vista. His entire field of view was filled with the vast, sluggish movements of men. Whole contingents were advancing into the grinder of combat, trudging through an increasingly ploughed-up mud-pit to get to the bitter edge of the front.

The bulk of the fighting was concentrated in the centre, where the Reikland detachments held firm. Some infantry squares had already buckled under the force of the first charge, but others had moved to support them, sealing any breaches in the defensive line. The Chaos horde beat furiously at a wall of halberdiers, causing carnage but unable to decisively break the formations open.

With the enemy charge restricted to the centre, both Empire flanks had cautiously edged forward. Mecke's gunners continued to launch their barrages, winnowing the reinforcing Norscan infantry before they could reach contact. Karl Franz fancied he could even hear Huss's wild oratory rising over the tumult, urging the fanatics under his command to hold fast. The eastern flank had come under a weaker assault than the centre thus far, but an undisciplined charge by the flagellants so early would undermine the integrity of the whole defensive line.

Karl Franz gripped the rough-hewn edges of the platform's railing, waiting for what he knew was coming. Then he heard the harsh bray of war-trumpets, and saw Helborg's Reiksguard charge out at last.

He caught his breath. As ever, the Imperial knights were magnificent – a surge of pure silver fire amid the bloody slurry of battle. The packed beat of the warhorses' hooves rang out as they powered through the very heart of the battlefield.

Karl Franz leaned out over the edge of the platform railing, peering into the rain to follow their progress. He saw Helborg's winged helm at the forefront, bright and proud, glittering amid a flurry of Reiksguard pennants. His knights hit the enemy at full-tilt, cracking them aside and driving a long wedge into the horde beyond. Lances shattered on their impaled victims. Any who evaded the iron-tipped wave were soon dragged under by the scything hooves of the warhorses.

'Glorious,' murmured Karl Franz.

Shouts of joy rang out from the Empire ranks. The Reiklander infantry squares pushed back, given impetus by the Reiksguard charge. Huss at last relaxed the leash, and his zealots entered the fray from the east, followed more implacably by Talb's state troopers. Mecke's gunnery continued to reap a swathe from the west, now angled further back to avoid hitting the advancing contingents of Empire infantry.

The enemy reeled, struck by the coordinated counter-attacks. From west to east, Empire defenders either held their ground or advanced. The foot soldiers marched steadily through the angled cavalry stakes, held together in tight-packed formations by the hoarse shouts of their captains.

'Not too far,' warned Karl Franz, watching the detachments begin to spread.

Schwarzhelm nodded, and passed on the order. Runners scampered out again, tearing from beneath the stockade and out towards the command positions. An army of this size was like a giant beast – it needed to be constantly reined-in, or it would run away with everything.

Schwarzhelm rested a heavy gauntlet on the wooden parapet. His watchful eyes roved across the scene, probing for weakness. Like Helborg, he would have preferred to be in the thick of it, though his duty as the Emperor's bodyguard prevented him entering the fray – for the moment.

'They're holding,' the huge bodyguard said, cautiously.

Even as the words left his mouth, the sky suddenly darkened. Lightning flickered across the northern horizon, and the jagged spears were green and sickly.

A sigh seemed to pass through the earth, as if giants rolled uneasily underneath. Men lost their feet, and the beleaguered

Norscans found fresh heart. The Reiksguard charge continued unabated, crashing aside swathes of Chaos foot soldiers and crunching them down into the mire.

'Call him back!' cried Karl Franz, watching Helborg's momentum carry him deeper into the gathering shadow.

The storm curdled further, dragging ink-black clouds across a tortured sky and piling them high. More lightning skipped and crackled across the horizon, now a violent emerald hue and boiling with unnatural energies.

Shrieks echoed across the invading army – not mortal shrieks this time, but the fractured, glassy voices of the Other Realm. Karl Franz felt his heart-rate increase. No matter how many times he faced the creatures of the Outer Dark, that raw sense of *wrongness* never dissipated. No other enemy had such power over men's souls. To fight them was not just to fight physical terror, it was to face the innermost horrors of the mortal psyche.

Schwarzhelm tensed as well. 'The damned,' he growled, balling his immense fists.

It was like the very ground vomited them up. They boiled out of the earth, seething and hissing with foul vapours. Tiny malicious sprites swarmed from the mud, clutching and snickering at the legs of mortal men. Stomach-bloated horrors lurched into existence amid gouts of muddy steam, their jaws hanging open and their lone rheumy eyes weeping.

Such apparitions were the least of the denizens of the Other Realm, mere fragments of their gods' diseased and febrile imaginations. *Maggotkin*, they were called, or plaguebearers, or Tallymen of Plagues. As they limped and slinked into battle they murmured unintelligibly, reciting every pox and canker their addled minds could recall.

Beyond them, though, the skies drew together, laced with febrile flame-lattices. A crack of thunder shot out, shaking the earth, and the crows scattered.

Somewhere, far out across the boiling hordes of enemy troops, something far larger had been birthed. Karl Franz could feel it as a cold ache in his bones. The rain itself steamed as it fell, as if infected by the torture of the heavens themselves.

Karl Franz called for his helm-bearer.

'My liege–' began Schwarzhelm.

'Say nothing,' snapped Karl Franz. A servant brought over the Imperial helm – a heavy gold-plated lion-mask with sun-rays radiating out from the rim. 'What did you expect, Ludwig? I fought at Alderfen. I fought at the Bastion. I am Sigmar's heir, and by His Immortal Will I shall fight here.'

Schwarzhelm glowered down at him. Despite the vast gulf in rank, the grizzled bodyguard was physically far bigger than his master. 'That is what they wish for,' he reminded him.

Karl Franz glanced back towards the stockade behind him. He could hear Deathclaw raking against his prison. The creature was desperate to take wing, and instinctive war-lust permeated through the driving squalls.

With difficulty, he turned away. The battlefield sprawled before him again, shrouded in churning clouds and punctuated by the screams of men and the clash of arms. The stink of blood rose above it all, coppery on the rain-drenched wind.

He swallowed down his fury, and remained where he was. Schwarzhelm, satisfied, took the war-helm again.

'For now,' murmured Karl Franz, watching the clouds swirl into grotesque tumours. 'For now.'

The impact of the first lance strike nearly unseated Helborg, but he dug his heels into the stirrups and pushed back, driving the iron point through the heart of a barrel-chested Norscan champion. The force of his steed's momentum carried the creature of Chaos high into the air before the lance broke and the broken halves of its body crashed to earth again. By then, Helborg's warhorse had already carried him onward, treading down more disease-encrusted warriors under its churning hooves.

The charge of the Reiksguard was like a breaking tide, sweeping clean through the very centre of the raging tempest and clearing out the filth before it. Helborg's knights rode close at his side, each one already splattered with bile-tinged gore. Their pennants snapped proudly, their naked swords plunged, the horses' manes rippled. There was no standing up to such a concentrated spearhead of fast-moving, heavily armoured killing power, and the enemy infantry before them either fled or were smashed apart.

Consumed by the power and fury of the charge, Helborg felt the change in the air too late. He did not see the clouds of crows rip apart and fall to the earth, thudding heavily into the mud. As he drew his runefang and sliced it down into the neck of a fleeing warrior, he did not see the columns of marsh-gas spew from the earth itself, coalescing rapidly into the fevered outlines of witchery.

The Reiksguard drove onward, scattering their foes before them. The air stank with blackpowder and blood, flecked with flying mud and storm-rain. By the time Helborg smelled the rank putrescence simmering on the air, his knights were half a mile beyond the Imperial reserve lines and far beyond the advancing ranks of halberdiers. He pulled his steed around, and the vanguard of his cavalry drew up in his wake.

Ahead of them, half-masked by shuddering walls of miasma, the rain was spiralling away from something. Like a glittering curtain of twisting steel, the deluge bulged outwards, veering clear of a scab of shadow at its core. Dimly, Helborg could make out a vast profile beyond – a heaped, piled, bulging mountain of flesh and blubber, crowned with antlers and split near the summit by a thousand-toothed grin. Flabby arms emerged, pushing out from swelling muscle with wet pops, followed by a rust-pocked cleaver that left trails of mucus hanging behind it.

Helborg's mount reared, its eyes rolling, and he had to yank hard on the reins to pull it back into line. The remaining Reiksguard fanned out, forming up into a loose semicircle about their master. On the edges of the formation, cowed enemy troops regrouped and started to creep back into range, emboldened by the gathering diabolical presence in their midst.

Helborg stared at the abomination, and an icy wave of hatred coursed through him. 'Knights of the Empire!' he roared, throwing back his cloak and holding his blade high. 'Break *this*, and we break them *all!* To me! For Sigmar! For Karl Franz!'

Then he kicked his steed back into the charge, and his warriors surged forward with him. Ahead of them, the enormous swell of the greater daemon fully solidified, shuddering into the world of the senses with a snap of aethyr-energies releasing. The ground rippled like a wave, rocked by the arrival of such a glut of foetid, corpulent flesh-mass. Cracks zigzagged through the mud as it *schlicked* open, each one spilling with clumps of scrabbling roaches.

The Reiksguard charged into contact. As they tore along, the ranks of enemy foot soldiers closed on them, narrowing their room for manoeuvre. Some succeeded in waylaying knights on the flanks, and the force of the charge began to waver. The rapidly undulating landscape accounted for several more, causing the horses to crash to the earth and unseat their riders.

Helborg, though, remained undaunted, his eyes fixed resolutely on the hell-creature ahead. He careered through the screaming hordes, his companions struggling to stay on his shoulder, his blade already whirling.

'For Sigmar!' he bellowed.

Ahead of him, still masked by the after-birth tendrils of the aethyr-vortex, the scion of the Plaguefather gurgled a phlegm-choked laugh, and licked a long, black tongue along the killing edge of its cleaver. Its grotesque body shivered with cold laughter.

Beckoning the mortals forwards like some obscene grandfather, it raised a flabby arm to strike, and vomit-coloured aethyr-plasma flickered along the cleaver-blade.

Karl Franz paced to and fro across the platform, never taking his eyes from the unfolding struggle ahead of him. His stockade felt less like a privileged viewing tower and more like a prison, keeping him from where he needed to be. Schwarzhelm remained silently at his side, offering nothing but a grim bulwark for his growing anger to break against.

'Order Mecke to angle the guns higher!' Karl Franz bellowed, sending messengers scampering through the rain. 'And get Talb's reserves further up! They're useless there!'

The situation was dissolving before his eyes. Pitched battles always degraded into messy, confused scrums after the first few hours – formations collapsed and orders were misheard – but the foul conditions north of Heffengen were turning the encounter into a formless crush. He could only watch as Huss's flagellant zealots tore headlong at the enemy Skaelings, losing all shape as their fervour carried them far beyond Talb's supporting infantry. Karl Franz was a powerless spectator as the Reiksguard's spectacular success took them out of reach of the Reiklanders in their wake, and as the daemon-allied northerners finally brought carnage to Mecke's west flank.

The air vibrated with febrile derangement. Clouds of flies had taken the place of the crows, blotting out the thin grey light of the sun and turning the air into a grimy dusk. Artillery strikes had blasted apart some of the more prominent tallymen, but ravening knots of daemon-kind still stalked among the living, bringing terror in their noxious wake. The Norscan bulk of the army had been reinforced by fresh waves of other tribesmen, and already the dull mantra of *Crom, Crom* could be heard over the choir of screams.

Huss still stood firm, as did his protégé Valten. While they still laid about them with their warhammers, hacking through whole companies of Chaos troops, the eastern flank still had a fulcrum about which to turn. For all that, the balance of the battle still hung by a fragile thread. The bulk of the mortals could not stand against daemons – even being in proximity to one was enough to threaten madness – and so the bulk of the state troopers teetered on the brink of collapse.

'They need me,' said Karl Franz, unable to watch the killing unfold.

Schwarzhelm, this time, said nothing. He gazed out across the battlefield, his head lifted, listening. He sniffed, drawing the air in deep. Then a shudder seemed to pass through his great frame. 'They are here again, my liege,' he rumbled, looking utterly disgusted.

For a moment, Karl Franz had no idea what he was talking about. He followed his Champion's stare, screwing his eyes up against the drift of smoke and plague-spoor.

Over in the east, where Talb's troops struggled heroically amid a slew of shifting mud, a chill wind was blowing. The ragged clouds summoned by the daemon-kin blasted back across the wide field, exposing a clear sky. All along the horizon, black figures crested a low rise. Tattered banners hung limp in the drizzle, dozens of them, standing proud above whole companies of infantry. The figures were moving – slowly, to be sure – but with a steady, inexorable progress.

Karl Franz turned to one of the engineers and snatched a telescope from his trembling hands. He clamped the bronze spyglass to one eye and adjusted the dials.

For a moment, all he saw was a blurred mass of winter-sparse foliage. Slowly, his vision clarified, resting on an outcrop beyond the curve of the Revesnecht. As he examined it, he understood why Schwarzhelm had been so appalled.

Again, he thought, bleakly. *But why, and how? And for whom do they fight?*

He moved the telescope's view down the long line of unkempt figures, resting on none of them for long. He swept north, aiming for their leader. Eventually, he found him, and the spyglass halted.

Karl Franz clutched the bronze column tightly. The rumours had swirled since Alderfen, and he had not wanted to believe any of them. It had been *so long ago*. The chroniclers and scholars could have been wrong – it might be an impersonator, a shadow, a lesser demagogue assuming the mantle of an older and more sinister soul.

As he nudged the dials to bring the focus into line, Karl Franz felt a hollow sensation in his guts. There could be no mistake. He saw a long, arrow-straight mane of pure white hair, hanging from a still-noble head. Eyes of purest obsidian were set in a flesh-spare visage, drawn tight across sharp bones. He saw armour the colour of a flaming sunset, blackened with old fires and old blood; a long, ebony cloak lined with finest ermine; fangs jutting from a proud, cruel mouth; a longsword, sheathed in an ancient scabbard.

And, most of all, the ring. Even at such a distance, its garnet-stone glowed like an ember, leaking smoke from its setting.

Karl Franz put the telescope down. 'Then it is true,' he murmured, leaning against the balcony railing heavily. 'Vlad von Carstein.'

Schwarzhelm's face was black with fury. He looked torn between rival hatreds – of the Chaos hordes that hammered at them from the north, and the undead blasphemers that had crept into view in the east. 'There were rumours at Alderfen,' he rasped. 'They say the dead fought with us.'

Karl Franz felt like laughing at that, though not from mirth. 'What surety can we place on that?' He gazed up at the heavens, as if some inspiration might come from there. In days long past, it was said that the comet would appear to men at the times of greatest darkness, such as it had done for Sigmar and for Magnus.

Now, all he could see was the scudding of pestilential clouds.

He reached again for his war-helm, and this time Schwarzhelm made no move to stop him. The undead continued to gather along the ridge. With every passing moment, their numbers grew. Soon there would be thousands. Between them, the armies of Chaos and undeath outnumbered the mustered Imperial forces.

'What do you command, my liege?' asked Schwarzhelm.

'Talb's flank is close to collapse,' said Karl Franz, placing the helm on his head and fastening the leather straps around his neck. 'Take any reserves you can find, join Huss and pull him out of there. Salvage what you can, stage a fighting retreat.'

Schwarzhelm nodded. 'And you?'

Karl Franz smiled dryly, and his hand rested on the hilt of his runefang. As if in recognition of what was about to happen, Deathclaw let fly with a harsh caw from its enclosure.

'We are between abominations,' he said, his voice firm. 'This is my realm. Once again, we must teach them to fear it.'

Then he started moving, ignoring the supplications from his field-staff around him. As he went, his mind fixed on the trial ahead. The whole army would see him take to the air. All eyes would be on him, from the moment Deathclaw cast loose his chains and ascended into the heavens.

'Hold the line for as long as you can,' he ordered, descending from the viewing platform with long, purposeful strides. 'Above all, the daemon is *mine*.'

THREE

Helborg charged straight at the daemon, spurring his steed hard. The vast creature towered over him, a swollen slag-pile of heaving, suppurating muscle. It was now fully instantiated, and its olive-green hide glistened with dribbling excreta.

The stench was incredible – an overwhelming fug of foul, oversweet putrescence that caught in the throat and made the eyes stream. Every movement the thing made was accompanied by a swirl of flies, sweeping around it like a cloak of smog. Under its hunched withers the earth itself boiled and shifted, poisoned by the sulphurous reek and ground down into a plague-infused soup. The daemon wallowed in its own filth, revelling in the slough it had created around it.

Helborg's horse nearly stumbled as it galloped into range, betrayed by the shifting terrain, but its head held true. The daemon saw him approach and drew its cleaver back for a back-breaking swipe. Helborg drove his mount hard towards the target. The cleaver whistled across, spraying bile as it came. Helborg ducked as he veered out of its path, and felt the heavy blade sweep over his arched back; then he was up again, raised up in the saddle and with his sword poised.

Others of the Reiksguard had followed him on the charge, some still bearing their long lances. Two of them plunged the weapons deep into the daemon's flanks, producing fountains of steaming mucus. The daemon let slip a gurgling roar, and swung its bulk around, tearing the knights from their saddles and flinging their bodies headlong across the battlefield.

Helborg's warhorse shied as it tore past the wall of trembling hide, and Helborg plunged his sword into the daemon's flesh while still on the gallop. It was like carving rotten pork – the skin and muscle parted easily, exposing milk-white fat and capillaries of black, boiling blood beneath.

The daemon's cleaver lashed back towards him, propelled by obese and sagging arms, but Helborg was moving too fast. He guided his steed hard-by under the shadow of the other daemonic arm, slashing out with the runefang as he went. More gobbets of flesh slopped free, slapping to the earth in smoking gouts.

The Reiksguard were everywhere by then, riding their steeds under the very shadow of the daemon's claws and hacking with their longswords. The creature throttled out another echoing roar of pain, and flailed around more violently. Its cleaver caught two Reiksguard in a single swipe, dragging them from the saddle. Its balled fist punched out, crushing the helm of another as he angled his lance for the cut.

The clouds of flies buzzed angrily, swarming around the beleaguered daemon and rearing up like snakes' heads. They flew into visors and gorgets, clotting and clogging, forcing knights to pull away from the attack. Maggots as long as a man's forearm wriggled out of the liquidised earth, and clamped needle-teeth to the horses' fetlocks. Swarms of tiny daemon-kin with jaws as big as their pulpy bodies spun out from the greater creature's armpits as it thrashed around, clamping their incisors onto anything they landed on and gnawing deep.

The Reiksguard fought on through the hail of horrors, casting aside the lesser creatures in order to strike at the greater abomination beyond, but the creature before them was no mere tallyman or plaguebearer – it was the greatest of its dread breed, and the swords of mortal men held little terror for it. Its vast cleaver whirled around metronomically, slicing through plate armour like age-rotten parchment. Helborg saw three more of his men carved apart in a single swipe, their priceless battle-plate smashed apart in seconds.

He kicked his steed back into contact, riding hard for the daemon's whirling cleaver-arm. As he went, he pulled his runefang back for the strike, and the sacred blade shimmered in the preternatural gloaming.

The daemon saw him closing in, but too late. It tried to backhand him from his mount with the cleaver's hilt, and Helborg swerved hard, leaning over in the saddle. As the eldritch blade whistled past again, Helborg thrust out with his own sword, ramming the point up and across. The runefang plunged in up to the grip, sliding into the putrid blubber as if into water.

The daemon roared out a gurgled cry of outrage, affronted by the audacity of the attack. Helborg grabbed the hilt of his sword two-handed, fighting to control the movements of his mount, and heaved. The rune-engraved steel sliced through sinews, severing the daemon's arm at the elbow. A thick jet of inky blood slobbered across his helm visor, burning like acid, and he pulled harder.

With a sickening *plop*, the daemon's entire forearm came loose, trailing long strings of muscle and skin behind it. Weighed down by the cleaver, the chopped limb thudded to the earth, sinking into the slurry of saliva and pus underfoot. The daemon *bellowed*, this time in real agony, stretching its wide mouth in a gargantuan howl that made the clouds shake.

The surviving Reiksguard pressed their attack. Noxious fluids slapped and flayed out from the stricken daemon, each lashing tendril studded with clots of biting flies. Helborg pulled his steed around for another pass, his heart kindling with raw battle-joy.

It could be hurt. It could be *killed*.

But then, just as he was about to kick his spurs back into his mount's flanks, he heard it. War horns rang out across the battlefield, cutting through the surge and sway of massed combat.

Helborg had heard those horns before – their desiccated timbre came from the age-bleached trumpets of another era. No Empire herald used such instruments – they were borne by armies that had no right to still be marching in this age.

Helborg twisted in the saddle, trying to scry where the sounds came from. For a moment, all he saw were the grappling profiles of knights and plague-horrors, locked in close combat around the raging mass of the greater daemon. Swirling rain lashed across them all, masking the shape of the hordes beyond.

Then, as if cut through by the harsh notes of the war horns themselves, clouds of milk-white mist split apart, exposing for a moment the whole eastern swathe of the battlefield. Helborg caught a glimpse of huge crowds of mortals and aethyr-spawn, grappling and gouging at one another across the vast sweep on the eastern flank. And then, beyond that, on the far bank of the Revesnecht, he saw the cursed banners of Sylvania hoisted against the squalls, each one marked with the pale death's head of that cursed land. At the head of the revenant host stood a lone lord clad in blood-red armour, his long white hair standing out as starkly as bone in a wound.

A shudder of disbelief ran through him. He knew who had worn that armour. He also knew how long ago that had been. It was *impossible*.

Vlad von Carstein.

The shock of it broke his concentration. As he gazed, spellbound, on the host of undead advancing into the fray, he forgot his mortal peril.

The daemon lumbered towards him, dragging its vast weight forward in a rippling wall of wobbling flesh. Its lone claw scythed down, trailing streamers of smoking poisons. Helborg's horse reared up, panicked by the looming monster bearing down on it.

Helborg fought with the reins, trying to pull his steed away from danger, but the creature had been maddened and no longer heeded him. The daemon's talons slammed into Helborg's helm, ripping the steel from his head and sending it tumbling. Long claws bit deep into his flesh, burning like tongues of flame.

The impact was crushing. The horse buckled under him, screaming in terror, and he was thrown clear. Helborg hit the earth with a bone-jarring crash, and blood splashed across his face. He tried to rise, to drag himself back to his feet, but a wave of sickness and dizziness surged up within him.

He gripped his sword, trying to focus on the pure steel, but the dull ache of his wounds flared up along his flank. He saw the blurred shapes of his brother-knights riding fearlessly at the daemon, and knew that none of them could hope to end it.

He cried out in agony, trying to force his limbs to obey him. A wave of numbness overwhelmed him, racing like frost-spears through his bones. He heard the deathly echo of the war horns as if from underwater. The wound in his split cheek flared, and he smelled the poison in it.

Then his head thudded against the mud, and he knew no more.

Deathclaw soared high above the battlefield. The griffon's huge wings beat powerfully, shredding the black-edged tatters of cloud around it. Its bunched-muscle shoulders worked hard, pulling the heavily built beast into the air.

Karl Franz leaned forward in the saddle, his blade already drawn. The griffon, once released from its shackles by fearful keepers, was a furnace of bestial power. Both of them had saved the life of the other more than once, and the bond that connected them was as strong as steel.

'You have been kept collared for too long,' Karl Franz murmured, running the fingers of his free gauntlet roughly through Deathclaw's feathered nape. 'Let your anger *flow*.'

The war-griffon responded, emitting a metallic caw that cut through the raging airs. Its pinions swept down, propelling it like a loosed bolt over the epicentre of the battlefield.

Karl Franz gazed out at the scenes of slaughter, trying to make sense of the battle's balance amid the confused movements of regiments and warbands. The bulk of his forces were now locked close with the Chaos warriors, gripped by brutal hand-to-hand fighting. The western flank was still largely intact and Mecke had ordered his veteran Greatswords into the fray, where they grappled with ranks of plate-armoured warriors bearing twin-headed axes and skull-chained mauls. The centre remained contested. The bulk of the Reiklanders had no answer to the seething tides of daemonic horrors, though the Reiksguard knights still fought hard amid the raging centre of the field. Over to the east, the Ostermarkers were fighting a desperate rearguard action against utter destruction. Beyond them, the army of the undead was drawing closer to the battlefield, advancing in terrifyingly silent ranks.

Karl Franz's task was clear. Mecke still held position. Schwarzhelm, Huss and Valten would have to salvage something from the wreckage of the eastern flank, whether or not von Carstein came as an ally or an enemy. The malign presence at the core of the Chaos army, though, was beyond any of them, and its baleful aura was spreading like a shroud across the whole army. From his vantage, Karl Franz could see its bloated bulk squatting amid the shattered Reiksguard vanguard, laying about with a gorestreaked fist. Such a monster was capable of ripping through whole contingents of mortal troops, and nothing else on the field was capable of standing against it.

There was no sign of Helborg. No doubt the Reiksmarshal had charged the creature, hoping to bring it down before its full strength was manifest. It was a typically reckless move, but the daemon still lived, despite the gouges in its nacreous flesh and an arm-stump spurting with ink-black blood.

'That is the prey, great one,' urged Karl Franz, pointing the tip of his runefang towards the daemon's blubbery shoulders.

The griffon plunged instantly, locking its huge wings back and hurtling towards the horror below. Karl Franz gripped the reins tightly, feeling the ice-wet air scream past him. The landscape melted into a blur of movement, all save the bloated monstrosity below them, which reared into range like a vast weeping boil on the face of the earth.

Deathclaw screamed out its battle-rage, bringing huge foreclaws up. At the last moment, the daemon's vast head lolled upward, catching sight of the two of them just as their fearsome momentum propelled them into it.

The griffon dragged its talons across the daemon's face, slicing into its eyes. Its rear legs raked across the daemon's slobbering chest, churning the foetid flesh into putrid ribbons. Karl Franz hacked out with his runefang, feeling heat radiate out from the ancient blade – the runes knew the stench of daemon-kind, and they blazed like stars.

Just as the daemon reached for them with its lone arm, Deathclaw pounced clear again, circling as expertly as a hawk. The daemon's talons slashed at it, but the griffon ducked past the attack and surged in close again. Deathclaw's beak tore at the daemon's shoulder, ripping more skin from its savaged hide.

The daemon twisted, pulling its obese haunches clear of the slough below and reaching to pluck the griffon from the sky. Its claw shot out, and clutching fingers nearly closed on Deathclaw's tail.

The griffon shot clear with a sudden burst of speed, and circled in for a renewed strike. As it did so, Karl Franz seized the hilt of his sword two-handed and held it point-down. He knew just what his steed was about to do, and shifted his weight in the saddle in preparation.

The daemon reached out for them again, and Deathclaw plummeted, evading the creature's claws by a finger's width before clamping its own talons into the daemon's back. The griffon scored down the length of the daemon's hunched spine, ripping through sinews and exposing bony growths.

Karl Franz, poised for the manoeuvre, waited until the nape of the daemon's neck loomed before him. It was a foul, stinking hump, studded with glossy spikes and ringed with burst pustules. He aimed carefully.

The daemon twisted, trying to throw Deathclaw loose, but Karl Franz plunged the sword down. The tip bit clean between vertebrae, driving into the bone and muscle beneath. The magic blade exploded with wild light, spiralling out from the impact site and tearing through the drifting filth around it.

The daemon arched its blubbery neck, choking out cries of blood-wet agony. Karl Franz was nearly torn loose, caught between the sway of his prey and the bucking movements of Deathclaw.

He held firm, grinding the blade in deeper. Thick blood raced up the blade, crashing over his gauntlets and fizzing against the metal. Clouds of flies swarmed in close, trying to clog Karl Franz's visor, but he held firm.

Deathclaw roared with bloodlust, steadying itself on the heaving spine of the daemon, and Karl Franz gained the leverage he needed. With a huge heave, he wrenched the sword across, severing the daemon's neck.

With a coiled spring, Deathclaw leapt clear. The huge daemon reeled in a torment of snapping sinew. Weeping from a hundred lesser wounds, it thrashed and jerked, spewing vomit and bile. Rancid coils of greenish smoke spilled from its eyes as the dark magicks required to keep it on the physical plane unwound.

Deathclaw climbed higher. Karl Franz sensed its raucous joy, and shared in it.

'The blood of Sigmar!' he cried, gazing in triumph at the horror he had ended. Its death-throes were ruinous, carving up the earth and mingling it with gouts of acidic blood. The plague-bearers thronging around it held their elongated heads in their hands, and wailed.

Upon such moments did battles turn. Whole hosts could lose heart with the death of their leader, and the momentum of entire campaigns could falter with the removal of a talismanic figure-head. Deathclaw soared above the sea of fighting men, screaming its elation at the heavens.

Karl Franz scoured the ground below, searching for any sign of Helborg. He was about to order the griffon to circle about and swoop lower when a harsher cry echoed out across the battle-field. His head snapped up, and he saw a new terror sweeping in from the north. The Chaos ranks had been sundered by a vanguard of heavily armoured knights on brazen steeds, their pauldrons rimmed with gold and their helms underpinned with iron collars. They thundered towards the surviving Reiksguard, ploughing up the ground on spiked metal hooves. These new-comers rode with greater discipline and verve than most servants of the Fallen Gods, though their livery was as foul as any blood-worshipping fanatic from the frozen north.

Above them all came a truly vast flying creature that bounded through the air with an ungainly lurch. It was the size of a war-dragon, and its colossal wings splayed across the skies like motley sheaves of blades. Unlike a true dragon, no sleek hide of jewelled scales clad its flanks and no flames kindled against its twisting neck. Where tight flesh should have stretched, raw bone glinted from between a lattice of age-blackened sinews. Gaping holes punctured an open ribcage, exposing nothing but coiled shadow within. A heavy skull lolled at the end of a bleached spine, wreathed in wisps of inky smoke, and awk-wardly flapping wings were held together by mere ribbons of atrophied muscle.

The monstrosity's rider was scarcely less extravagant in

grotesquerie – an ivory-white face, elongated to accommodate protruding fangs, jutting from heavy armour plates. Bat-wing motifs vied for prominence on the armour-curves with chain-bound skulls and stretched skins. The rider carried a straight-bladed sword as black as the maw of the underworld, and it rippled with blue-tinged fires.

Karl Franz smelled the foul aroma of death roiling before it, and arrested Deathclaw's swoop. The griffon thrust upward vio-lently, already eager to tear at a new enemy.

Karl Franz hesitated before giving the order. The daemon had been a daunting foe, but it had already been weakened by Hel-borg and the Reiksguard, and Deathclaw was lethal against such earth-shackled prey. The huge creature tearing towards them, carving through the sky with sickening speed, was far larger, and had the advantage of being battle-fresh.

Moreover, something about the rider gave Karl Franz pause. He looked into those dark eyes, still a long way off, and his heart mis-gave him. He looked down at his blade, drenched with the blood of the slain daemon, and saw the fire in the runes flicker out.

With a glimmer of presentiment, a terrible thought stole into his mind.

This foe is beyond me.

Karl Franz knew he could refuse combat. He could do as Schwarzhelm had advised, saving himself for another fight, one that he could win. He was the *Emperor*, not some expendable champion amid his countless thousands of servants. His cap-tains would understand. They would come to see that the Empire came first, and that his preservation, above all, held the promise of survival into the future.

He imagined Altdorf then, its white towers rising proudly above the filth and clamour of its tight-locked streets. He saw the river creeping sluggishly past the docks, teeming with all the burgeon-ing trade and industry of his people.

That place was the fulcrum about which his Empire had always revolved. He had always assumed that if death were to come for him, it would take him there.

Deathclaw screamed at the approaching abomination, straining at the reins. Karl Franz looked out across the battlefield, at the desperate struggle of the faithful against the closing ranks of horror. With every passing moment, more of his subjects met a painful, fear-filled end, locked in terrified combat with a far greater enemy than they had any right to be taking on.

I will not leave them.

'Onward, then,' ordered Karl Franz, shaking the blood from his runefang and angling the tip towards the skeletal dragon, 'and strike it from the skies.'

FOUR

Schwarzhelm strode out into the heart of the battle. As he went, he drew soldiers about him, and the solid knot of swordsmen advanced under the shadow of the racing clouds.

The last of the reserve detachments had been committed to the fighting. Whole infantry squares were being hurled into the maw of the oncoming storm, in the desperate hope that sheer weight of numbers could do something to stop the tide of plague-daemons.

Schwarzhelm advanced immediately towards Talb's eastern flank, roaring out orders to the semi-broken warbands he encountered as the fighting grew fiercer.

'Form up!' he roared, brandishing his longsword and raging at the Empire troops around him. 'You are *men!* Born of Sigmar's holy *blood!* Fight like men! Remember *courage!*'

His words had an instant effect. Schwarzhelm's voice was known to every last halberdier and pikeman in the army, and though he was not loved as Helborg's flamboyance made him loved, no living fighter was more respected. Schwarzhelm was a

CHRIS WRAIGHT

vast bear of a man, clad in plate armour and bearing the fabled Sword of Justice before him, and the mere rumour of his presence on the field kindled hope in men's hearts again.

With his trusted swordsmen beside him, Schwarzhelm cut a channel towards Talb's last known position. The enemy came at them in waves – Skaelings, for the most part, an unruly rabble of fur-clad barbarians carrying the first signs of the sickness and staring wild-eyed from their shaman's ravings. Under Schwarzhelm's direction, the Empire halberdiers managed to restore something like proper defensive lines, and pushed back the hammering cycle of attacks. Ground was regained, and the momentum of the onslaught lessened.

The respite did not last long. Up through the ranks of the enemy came sterner opponents – Kurgan warriors in dark armour and chainmail, bearing axes and long-handled mauls, followed by the scrabbling flotsam of gibbering daemon-kin. Behind them lumbered the obscene bloat of the plaguebearers as they limped and stumbled into battle. Their rancid stench came before them, a weapon in itself, making men retch uncontrollably even before reaching blade-range.

Schwarzhelm laid eyes on the closest of the daemonic plaguebearers, and marked it out with a furious sweep of his blade. 'To *me*, men of the Empire!' he thundered, breaking into a heavy jog towards the scabrous horror. 'They can be killed! *Believe!* Believe in the holy Empire of Sigmar, and *fight!*'

The Empire troops surged after him, smashing into the incoming Kurgans in a flesh-tearing, armour-denting, blade-snapping flurry of limbs and fists. Eyes were gouged, sinews torn, throats cut and throttled, ankles broken. A whole band of halberdiers was ripped apart by a single Kurgan champion; a massive Chaos warlord was dragged down by a dozen sword-wielding state troops, hacking away at their huge opponent like wolves on a bear.

Schwarzhelm drove them onward, kicking aside the scuttling

daemon-kin that raced along the earth to sink fangs into his boots. A Kurgan chieftain squared up to him, hefting a twin-bladed axe in iron-spiked gauntlets. Barely breaking stride, Schwarzhelm slashed his sword crosswise, cutting him across the midriff. Before the Kurgan could bring his axe to bear, Schwarzhelm jabbed the sword back, ripping through addled flesh, then crunching his leading shoulder guard into the reeling Kurgan's face. The warlord staggered, and Schwarzhelm punched him hard with his gauntleted fist, breaking his neck and sending his body crunching to the earth.

The men around him bellowed with renewed bloodlust, and surged after him. All around him, emerald lightning continued to spear down from the heavens. The ground underfoot seethed with a vile mixture of blood and rainwater, pooling in boot prints and gurgling in rivulets.

'Onward!' roared Schwarzhelm, eviscerating another barbarian with a lone thrust of his blade, clearing the last obstacle before the plaguebearer.

The daemon's weeping body pushed past the armoured war-lords around it, stalking eerily on painfully elongated limbs. Its whole torso ran with rivers of pus, dripping onto the mud at its cloven feet in boiling clumps. Its olive-green skin had burst open, exposing loops of entrails. It had no eyes, ears or other features, just a face-encompassing jaw rammed with incisors. As it sensed Schwarzhelm, it let out a phlegmy cry of challenge, and swung a long staff topped with rust-pocked spikes. Every time the spikes were jangled, foul vapours billowed out, creep-ing across the ground like morning mist.

Schwarzhelm charged straight at it, holding his breath as he closed in, whirling his sword around in a blistering arc. The plaguebearer swung its staff to intercept, and the two weap-ons clanked together with a deadening *thunk*. Schwarzhelm lashed out again, feeling vile gases creep up his armour. The daemon lurched towards him, snapping its distended jaws, and

Schwarzhelm ducked to one side as the saliva slapped against his helm.

He shoved out with one fist, catching the daemon in the torso. His hand passed clean into disease-softened tissue, disappearing up to the wrist. He tried to shake it free, but the daemon caught him by the throat with its free claw, and squeezed. Schwarzhelm hacked back with his blade, carving deep into the plaguebearer's raddled body, but the wounds just resulted in more suffocating waves of corpse-gas pouring forth.

Schwarzhelm began to gag, and lashed out furiously, aiming to sever the creature's stringy neck. He missed his aim, hampered by the plaguebearer's cloying embrace, but something else impacted, and the daemon's skull was ripped from its shoulders in a welter of mucus and brown blood-flecks.

The headless body loomed over Schwarzhelm for a moment, held upright by its staff. Then it toppled over, bursting open as it hit the ground. A swell of brackish fluid swilled over his boots.

Schwarzhelm staggered away, momentarily blinded by the spray of thick pus. He wiped his visor and saw the robed form of Luthor Huss standing over the daemon's prone corpse. The warrior priest's warhammer was slick with bodily fluids, and his bald pate was covered in a criss-cross of bloody weals.

Schwarzhelm bowed clumsily. 'My thanks, lord priest,' he muttered gruffly.

Huss nodded curtly. 'And there are more waiting.'

The fighting raged around them unabated. Empire troops grappled with Kurgan, Skaelings and worse. The air no longer stank of blackpowder, for the artillery had long ceased firing. In its place came the rolling stench of long-rotten bodies.

Schwarzhelm's entourage pressed on, sweeping around him and clearing a little space amid the close-packed battlefield. He shook the worst of the bile from his sword, feeling the dull ache of weariness stir in his bones.

'The Emperor sent you?' asked Huss, already searching out

the next fight. From nearby, Schwarzhelm could hear the clear-voice war cries of Valten, the mysterious boy-champion who was wielding Ghal Maraz with a youthful vigour.

'This flank cannot hold,' rasped Schwarzhelm. 'We must fall back.'

'Impossible,' scowled Huss.

'We are outnumbered.'

'By faith we shall pre–'

'Vlad von Carstein is here.'

That stopped Huss dead. He turned his baleful gaze onto Schwarzhelm. 'That cannot be.'

Schwarzhelm snorted impatiently. 'Use your *eyes*. The dead march against the damned, and the living are caught between them. I have my orders – we must fight our way to the Reiks-marshal, rally what we can, then hold the centre until we can fall back in good order.'

Huss looked agonised. Retreat was anathema to him – only surging onward against the foe was sanctified by his austere creed, and he would fight on until the end of the world, unwearied, his warhammer dripping with the gore of the fallen.

But even he was not blind to what was happening. As Schwarzhelm spoke the words, realisation dawned across Huss's face. The stench was not that of disease, but of *death*.

'Where is Helborg?' the priest asked.

Schwarzhelm was about to answer, when a fresh roar of challenge rang out. The voices were different again – not the bestial screams of the Norscans, nor the chill war horns of the Sylvanians, but a bizarre amalgam of aristocratic human and blood-crazed baresark. Both warriors lifted their eyes to the north.

Fresh troops were piling into the fray, their armour arterial red and their steeds towering behemoths of iron and bronze. They were still a long way off, but they were driving all before them. Above the vanguard soared a hideous creature of the darkest myth – a dragon, emaciated and splayed with bone and talon, cawing like a carrion crow and ridden by a lone red-armoured knight. It flapped through the heavens, its vast body held aloft by ancient magic.

In the face of that, even Huss's mighty shoulders sagged a little. Then, with a defiant curl of his mouth, he hefted his warhammer again. 'You will stand beside me, Emperor's Champion?'

'Until the ends of the earth, priest,' snarled Schwarzhelm, brandishing the *Rechtstahl*.

Huss cracked a thin smile then. 'We will smash some more skulls before they drag us down.'

Schwarzhelm nodded grimly. Already the hordes around them were pushing back again, slaughtering as they came.

'That we will,' he growled, striding back into the fight.

Deathclaw surged towards the dragon. The undead creature saw it coming, and reared up in the air, its scythe-like claws extended. Skeletal jaws gaped wide, and a noxious gout of corpse-gas burst from its gaping innards.

Karl Franz brandished his sword. The blade was still inert, bereft of the fire that usually kindled along its runic length, and even amid the rush on oncoming combat, that troubled him. Perhaps the daemon's blood had quashed its ancient soul.

The dragon rider hailed him then, his voice ringing out through the rain like a raptor's shriek.

'You are overmatched, warmblood!' he cried. 'Flee now, while your bird still has feathers!'

Deathclaw screamed in fury, and hurtled straight into close range. Its wings a blur, the griffon swept under the hanging streamers of yellowish gas and plunged straight at the dragon's exposed torso.

The two creatures slammed together, both sets of claws raking furiously. The griffon's fury was the greater, and whole sheets of age-withered flesh were ripped from the dragon's flank. The abomination lashed back, tearing a bloody line down Death-claw's back, nearly dragging Karl Franz clear from the saddle. As the bone-claws scraped past him, Karl Franz cut down sharply with his blade, taking two talons off at the knuckle.

Then the two creatures, powered by momentum, broke apart again, each angling back for a return pass.

'Do you see what is happening here, warmblood?' came the dragon rider's mocking voice. 'Your world is ending. It is ending before your eyes, and still you fail to grasp it.'

Karl Franz had caught a glimpse of his enemy as their steeds had grappled, and what he had seen had been unsettling. The rider wore heavy plate armour of rich blood-red, gilded with fine detailing and bearing the ancient seal of the lost Blood Keep. His jawline was swollen with fangs, and his voice bore the archaic, prideful accent of Empire nobility. Everything about him, from his cursed mount to his imperious bearing, indicated that he was an undead lord, a powerful vampire of the knightly bloodline.

Yet Karl Franz had never faced a vampire like this one. He had never seen tattoos carved into a face like that, nor heavy bronze collars adorning such armour. The rider wore a crude eight-pointed star on his breast, as black as ichor, and his sword-edge flamed as if alive with violent energies.

Can the dead fall to corruption? he wondered as Deathclaw banked hard and sped towards the dragon again. *Can even they succumb?*

The two beasts crashed into one another, writhing and lashing out in a twisting frenzy of mutual loathing. Deathclaw clamped its hooked beak into the dragon's neck and tore through weak-shackled vertebrae. The dragon pushed back with a blast of poison-gas before plunging down at the griffon's powerful shoulders, whipping a barbed tail to try to flay it from the skies.

Deathclaw shook off the dragon's foul breath and thrust back up, all four claws extended. The two riders were propelled close to one another, and for the first time Karl Franz was near enough to strike at his adversary with *Drachenzahn*.

The vampire was fast, as blisteringly fast as all his damned kin, and the two blades clanged together in a glitter of sparks. Despite his heavy armour, the undead lord switched his blade round in a smear of fire and steel, thrusting it point-forward at Karl Franz. The Emperor evaded the strike, but only barely, and the killing edge scraped across his left pauldron.

Deathclaw and the dragon were still locked in a snarling duel of their own, keeping their riders close enough to maintain a flurry of sword-blows. The blades collided again, then again, ringing and shivering from the impacts.

The vampire lord was a consummate swordsman, capable of the refined viciousness of his breed and animated by the unnatural strength that was the inheritance of that fallen bloodline. In addition to that, the marks of ruin emblazoned on his armour made the air shake – they were bleeding corruption, as if leaking dark magic from the Other Realm itself.

'For Sigmar!' Karl Franz roared, standing in the saddle and bracing against Deathclaw's bucking flight. He rammed his blade down two-handed, aiming to crack the vampire from his mount.

The undead lord parried, but the strength of the strike nearly dislodged him. Karl Franz followed up, hacking furiously with a welter of vicious down-strikes. The vampire struggled to fend them all off, and his armour was cut from shoulder to breastplate. The contemptuous smile flickered on his tattooed face, and for a moment he lost his composure.

But his steed was nearly twice the heft of Deathclaw, and even in its deathly state was a far more dangerous foe. The dragon's claws cut deep into the griffon's flesh, tearing muscle and ripping plumage from its copper-coloured back. Karl Franz could feel the fire ebbing in his steed, and knew the end drew near. If he could not kill the rider, the dragon would finish both of them.

'*Why?*' Karl Franz hissed as the swords flew. 'Why do *you* fight for these gods?'

The vampire pressed his attack more savagely, as if the question struck deep at whatever conscience he still possessed. 'Why not, mortal?' he laughed, though the sound was strained. 'Why not take gifts when offered?' His fanged mouth split wide in a grin, and Karl Franz saw the iron studs hammered into his flesh. 'They give generously. How else could I do *this*?'

The vampire's armour suddenly blazed with a gold aura, and the flames on his sword roared in an inferno. Karl Franz recoiled, and the dragon rider pounced after him. Their blades rebounded from one another, ringing out as the steel clashed. A lesser sword than the runefang would have shattered; even so, it was all Karl Franz could do to remain in position. Fragments of his priceless armour cracked free, and he saw gold shards tumbling down to the battlefield far below.

He pressed the attack again, resisting the overwhelming barrage of blows with blade-strikes of his own, when the dragon finally broke Deathclaw's guard and plunged a man-sized talon of bone into the griffon's chest.

Deathclaw screamed, and bucked wildly in the air. Karl Franz was thrown to one side, nearly hurled free of the saddle, and for a fraction of a second his sword-arm was flung out wide, exposing his chest.

The vampire needed no more than that – with a flicker of steel, he thrust his blade into the gap, unerringly hitting the weak point between breastplate-rim and pauldron.

The pain was horrific. Flames coursed down the length of the fell blade, crashing against Karl Franz's broken armour like a breaking wave. His entire world disappeared into a bloody haze of agony, and he felt his back spasm.

He heard roaring, as if from a far distance, and felt the world tumbling around him. Too late, he realised that Deathclaw had been deeply stricken, and was plummeting fast.

Karl Franz looked up, fighting through the pain and fire, to see the rapidly diminishing outline of the vampire gazing down at him.

'You could have had such gifts!' the dragon rider shouted after him, his voice twisted and shrill. '*You* chose the path of cowardice, not I!'

Karl Franz barely heard the words. Deathclaw was trying to gain lift, but the griffon's wings were a ravaged mess of blood-soaked feathers, and the creature's great chest rattled as it strained for breath.

He fought to remain conscious, even as a hot river of blood ran over his own armour. As the two of them whirled and spun earthwards, Karl Franz caught a blurred view of the entire battlefield. He saw the limitless tides of the North hacking their way through what remained of his forces. He saw the deathly advance of the Sylvanians from the east, covering the Revesnecht valley in a veil of darkness. The rain hammered down, shrouding it all in a bleak curtain of silver-grey, drowning the Imperial colours in a sea of plague-infested mud.

He reached out, as if he could grasp it all in his fist and somehow reverse the tide of war.

I have failed, he thought, and the realisation was like poison in his stomach. *There will be no return from this. I have failed.*

Even as the earth raced up towards him, his pain-filled mind recoiled at the very idea. He felt the great presences of the past gazing down at him, lamenting his great negligence. He saw the stern faces of Magnus the Pious, of Mandred, of Sigmar himself, each one filled with accusation.

I was the custodian, he thought, his mind filled with anguish. *The duty passed to me.*

The foul wind whistled past him. Deathclaw was struggling to fly on, to evade the heart of the Chaos horde, but his pinions were broken, and with his last, blurred sight Karl Franz saw that they would not make it.

Karl Franz did not feel himself slip from the saddle, dragged clear by his heavy armour. He never saw Deathclaw try to retrieve him, before the griffon finally collapsed to the earth in a tangle of snapped bones and crushed plumage. He never even felt the hard thud of impact, his face rammed deep into the thick mud even as his helm toppled from his bloodied head.

His last thought, echoing in his mind like an endless mockery, was the one that had tortured him from the first, as soon as the vampire's corrupted blade had pierced his armour and rendered the outcome of the duel inevitable.

I have failed.

From the beleaguered western flank to the shattered east, every Empire soldier saw the Emperor fall. A vast ripple of dismay shuddered through the ranks. They all saw the skeletal dragon tear Deathclaw from the skies, casting the war-griffon down amid a cloud of gore-stained feathers. They all saw the creature valiantly try to drag itself clear of the battlefield, fighting against its horrific wounds. For a moment, they dared to believe that it might reach the precarious safety of the stockade again, and that even if the Emperor was sorely wounded that he might still live. For a moment, all eyes turned skywards, hoping, praying fervently, *demanding* the salvation of their liege-lord.

When the griffon's flight at last dipped to earth, still half a mile short of safety and surrounded by the raging hordes of the North, those hopes died. They all saw Karl Franz fall from the saddle, dragged down into the mire, far from any possible rescue. They saw the war-griffon follow him down, the proud beast dragged to earth as if weighed with chains.

A wild howl erupted from the Chaos armies. Even the undead, now fighting their way west through turbulent formations of Skaelings, paused in their assault. The remaining Empire formations buckled, folding in on themselves as if consumed from within. The weakest soldiers began to run, tripping over bodies half-buried in the mud. The stoutest detachments fought on, though their positions were now exposed by the cowardice of lesser men.

The undead dragon ran rampant, sweeping low over the Empire lines, scooping defenders up in its emaciated claws and hurling their broken bodies far across the plain. The other fallen vampires crashed into contact, borne by monstrous creations whose eyes smouldered with forge-fires and whose hooves were lined with beaten iron. Ranged against them were the last of Huss's zealots, a horrifically diminished band, and what remained of Talb's hollowed-out forces. The Reiksguard still fought on, guarding their fallen captain, but were separated from the rest of the Empire army by a swirling tempest of daemons and fanatical fighters. Even Mecke's western flank now crumbled, its defenders panicking and turning on their tyrannical commander. The army of Heffengen finally subsided, sinking into the morass.

Schwarzhelm fought like a man possessed by the spirit of Sigmar, single-handedly accounting for scores of Kurgan scalps. Huss was scarcely less brutal, shouting out war-hymns as he laid into the enemy with his warhammer. For a time, those two warriors defied the encroaching tides, bolstered by the vital energy of Valten and Ghal Maraz. Amid a sea of seething corruption, the lights of faith endured for a little while.

But even that could not last. Schwarzhelm fought to within a hundred yards of where Helborg had been felled, but as the Empire formations around him melted away, he was forced to turn back at last. Gathering what remnants he could, he hacked his way south, veering east as he reached the curve of the Revesnecht. He, Huss and Valten were harried all the way, though the pursuit faded once the prize of Heffengen itself loomed on the southern horizon.

A few other scraps escaped the carnage – a kernel of the

Reiksguard cut their way free, bearing the sacred Imperial standard and taking control of the army's baggage trains before they could be looted. Many of the wagons were set aflame to prevent the enemy taking on fresh supplies, but a few were driven hastily south. The remnants were joined by the shattered Reiklander companies, plus any outriders from the Ostermarkers and Talabheimers who managed to escape the slaughter.

For those that could not escape, the end was swift and brutal. Champions of Chaos stalked across the war-scorched battlefield, breaking the necks of any who still lived. Spines were ripped out of the corpses and draped over the shoulders of the victorious. Daemonic grotesques capered and belched amid the charnel-debris, sucking the marrow from the bones and spewing it at one another. Though the greater daemon had been slain, its lesser spawn survived in droves, sustained by the crackling magicks animating the air.

The last to quit the field was the spectral Vlad von Carstein, whose presence at the conclusion of the battle remained as enigmatic as his arrival. His undead host had reaped a terrible toll on the Chaos army's eastern extremity, but after the Empire contingents had scattered, they were exposed to the full force of the victors' wrath. Whole regiments of skeletons and zombies were smashed apart by charging warbands of Kurgan, adding to the tangled heaps of bones already protruding from the blood-rich mud.

It did not take long for their dark commander to give the silent order to withdraw. The winds of death were driven east by the stinking fug of decay, and the black-clad host melted back beyond the riverbank just as mysteriously as they had arrived, their purpose still unclear.

Only one duel of significance remained. Few witnessed its outcome, for a strange vortex of shadow swept suddenly across the skies, its edges as ragged and writhing as a witch's cloak-hem. The undead dragon tore into the heart of the vortex, its empty eye sockets burning with an eerie green light. Flashes of sudden colour flared from within, as if a whole clutch of battle wizards had been trapped in its dark heart.

At the end of whatever had taken place in that sphere of magicks, the dragon took flight again, lurching as awkwardly as ever over the bleak plain and following the undead army east. Its rider still wore crimson armour, though not the same as earlier, and he carried a severed, fanged head in one gauntlet.

With that, the legions of the dead quit the field, leaving the plaguebearers to scavenge and plunder what remained. A peal of corpulent thunder cracked across the vista, echoing with faint echoes of laughter. The tallymen trudged through the dead and dying, taking note of the contagions they came across on long rolls of mouldering parchment. Insects of every chitinous variety buzzed and skittered across the rows of corpses, seeking out juicy eyeballs and tongues to feast on.

Across the whole, drab vista, the rain continued to fall, as if the flood could bear away the filth that had infected Heffengen. No natural rain could wash such plagues clean, though, and the sodden earth reeked from it, steaming in the cold as a thousand new virulences incubated in every bloody puddle.

The Bastion was broken. The Empire had been routed across its northern borders, exposing the long flank of the Great Forest to attack. Not since the days of the Great War had the wounds been so deep, so complete. Even in those dark times, there had been an Emperor to rally the free races and contest the Dark Gods.

Now there was nothing, and the winds of magic were already racing. Not for nothing did men say, in what little time of sunlight and happiness remained to them, that the end of all things had truly begun. Not in Praag, nor in Marienburg, but in Heffengen – the dank and rain-swept battlefield where Karl Franz, greatest statesman of the Old World, had fallen at last.

FIVE

Helborg woke into a world of agony.

He reached up with a shaking hand, pressing cautiously against the seared flesh of his raked cheek, and even his old warrior's face winced as the spikes of pain shot through him. He tried to rise, and a thousand other wounds flared up. After two failed attempts, he finally pushed himself up onto his elbows, and looked around him.

He was in a canvas tent, the walls streaked with mud and heavy with rainwater. He had been placed on a low bunk of rotten wooden spars, little better than wallowing on the sodden ground itself. From outside the tent he could hear the low, gruff voices of soldiers.

He reached for his sword, but it was gone. With a jaw-clenched grunt, he sat up fully on the bunk and swung his legs over the edge. His armour was gone, too – he was wearing his gambeson, covered in a mud-stained cloak.

He could not make out what the voices outside the tent were saying – it might have been Reikspiel, it might not. He searched around him for something to use as a weapon.

As he did so, memories of the final combat with the daemon flashed back into his mind. He remembered the *stench* of it, spilling from the wide, grinning mouth that had hung over him at the end.

I should be dead, he mused to himself. *Why am I even breathing?*

Then he remembered the clarion calls of the dead, and a shudder ran through his ravaged body. If *they* had taken him, then the outlook was even bleaker. The servants of the Fallen Gods might torture their prey before death, but at least death would come at last. If he were in the hands of the grave-cheaters then the agony would last forever.

The entrance flaps of the tent stirred, and Helborg searched for something to grasp. The tent was empty, and so he grabbed one of the rotten ends of a bunk-spar and wrenched it free. Brandishing it as a makeshift club, he prepared himself to fight again.

The canvas was pushed aside, and Preceptor Hienrich von Kleistervoll limped inside.

'Awake then, my lord,' he observed, bowing.

Helborg relaxed. As he did so, he felt a trickle of blood down his ribs. His wounds had opened. 'Preceptor,' he said, discarding the spar. 'Where are we?'

Von Kleistervoll looked terrible. His beard was a matted tangle, and his face was purple from bruising. He was still in his armour, but the plate was dented and scored. The Reiksguard emblem still hung from his shoulders on what remained of his tunic, soiled by the wine-dark stains of old blood.

'Ten miles south of Heffengen,' von Kleistervoll said grimly. 'Can you walk? If you can, I will show you.'

Helborg was not sure if he could reliably stand, but he brushed his preceptor's proffered arm away brusquely and limped past him into the open.

The sky was as dark as river mud. A bone-chilling wind skirled out of the north, smelling of ploughed earth and rust. Helborg shivered involuntarily, and pushed up the collar of his gambeson tunic.

Ahead of him, over a bleak field of bare earth, men were moving. They limped and shuffled, many on crutches or carrying the weight of their companions. Some still had their weapons, many did not. All of them had the grey faces of the defeated, staggering away from the carnage with what little breath remained in their cold-torn bodies.

Helborg watched the long column trudge along. So different from the bright-coloured infantry squares that had marched up to Heffengen, their halberds raised in regimented lines. There could not have been more than a thousand in the column, perhaps fewer.

Von Kleistervoll drew alongside him. The preceptor's breathing rattled as he drew it in.

'This is all we retrieved from the Reiklander front,' he said. 'Some of Talb's men, too. Mecke was driven west. No idea where he ended up.'

'Schwarzhelm?'

'He was still fighting at the end. Huss too, and the boy-warrior. They dragged together what they could and headed east.'

Helborg hesitated. 'And the Emperor?'

Von Kleistervoll's stony visage, scabbed with black, did not flicker. 'You did not see it?'

Helborg could not remember. His last hours of awareness were like a fever-dream, jumbled in his mind. He thought he recalled fighting alongside Ludwig, dragging their heavy blades through waves of enemy daemon-kin, but perhaps that was just his damaged imagination.

He dimly remembered a skeletal dragon breaking the clouds, a nightmare of splayed bone and tattered wings. He recalled a rider in crimson armour, surrounded by spears of aethyr-lightning. He saw the grin of the daemon again, bubbling with the froth of madness. All of the images overlapped one another, fusing into a tableau of fractured confusion.

'Could he have survived?' Helborg pressed.

'The day was lost,' said von Kleistervoll. 'If we had stayed a moment longer... I do not know. We could not remain.' The preceptor's voice was strained. 'You were wounded, Huss had been driven east...'

'I understand,' said Helborg. Von Kleistervoll was a seasoned fighter and knew his warcraft – if he had judged that retreat was the only option, no doubt he had been correct. 'What are your plans?'

'You gave the order, lord: Altdorf, with all haste. The enemy tightens its grip on the north, fighting with what remains of the living dead over the ruins. Heffengen is no place for mortal men now – we must save what remains.'

Helborg remembered his final words with Karl Franz.

Altdorf is the key. It always has been.

He pulled the ragged cloak around him. He would have to don armour again, to find a steed strong enough to bear him. The men needed a leader, someone who *looked* like a leader.

'My sword?' he asked.

Von Kleistervoll smiled, and gestured towards a line of heavy wagons struggling through the mud. 'We have it, and your battle-plate. Now that you are restored to health, the runefang will lead the army once more.'

Now that you are restored to health. Helborg felt hollowed-out, his body shriven and his mind tortured. He was sweating even in the cold, and the hot itch of blood under his clothes grew worse. 'I saw him, preceptor,' he murmured, watching as the grim procession of wounded and bereft wound its way past. 'A legend from the past, standing under the world's sun. What times are these, when the princes of the dead walk among us?'

Von Kleistervoll looked at him doubtfully. He did not know to whom Helborg was referring. There was no surprise in that – so many horrors had assailed them over the past few months that it had become hard to choose between them.

'Von Carstein,' explained Helborg, spitting the words out. 'The eldest of the line. It was he that broke us.'

'They say the dead fought the northmen,' replied von Kleister-voll, carefully.

Helborg laughed harshly. 'Do they? Who are *they*? Who still live who witnessed this thing?'

The preceptor had no reply. The bitter wind moaned across the land, cutting through the scant protection of their cloaks. The whole world seemed drained of life and colour, sunk into a rotting mass of corpse-earth.

'He came to feast on the remains,' Helborg said. 'I felt his fell magicks even at the heart of the fighting. These are our darkest enemies, preceptor – the corrupted and the undead. The day has come when they march in tandem.'

Von Kleistervoll looked unconvinced, but said nothing. Helborg's voice was becoming firmer. The pain in his wounds still flared, but he would recover. He would grip the *Klingerach* again. Karl Franz had gone, but there were other powers in the Empire, and there had been other Emperors. A successor would be chosen, and new armies raised. The war was not over.

'My order remains,' Helborg told him. 'We gather what we can, and we march on Altdorf. The other electors will gather now. In the face of this, they will put their rivalries aside. They will have to.'

As he spoke, a banner-bearer walked across the land before them, dragging a limp trailing leg through the mud. His face was a mask of effort – every last scrap of energy was devoted to keeping his rain-heavy standard aloft. The banner itself hung solidly, blackened from mould-spores but still bearing the griffon icon of the Empire on the fabric.

Helborg watched him go. Other marching men looked up at the rumpled griffon, and their glassy eyes fixed on it in recognition.

'We must get that standard cleaned up,' Helborg said. 'Find other regimental flags, and find men to bear them. We will march with the sacred images held before us. We will not enter Reikland like thieves, but rightful owners.' For the first time since awaking, he felt the urge to smile – to let slip with that wolfish grin he wore in combat. '*We* do not matter, Heinrich. *That* matters. When we are long gone in our graves, men will still carry those signs, and they will still fight beneath them. We are but their custodians. There are no End Times, there are only *our* times.'

The pain in his wounds was like a goad, giving him energy again. The road would be long, but the prize at its end was worth fighting for.

'To Altdorf, then,' he ordered, turning on his heel and walking towards the wagon where his armour had been stowed. 'The eternal throne of Sigmar. If there is to be an end to us, we will meet it there.'

Only the living dreamed, he had discovered.

Death was a kind of dream all of itself, so there was no escape there. In truth, he remembered very little about being dead – just vague and horrifying impressions of an absolute, eternal nothingness that extended beyond imagination.

He had once heard it said, a long time ago, that the only thought a mortal was truly unable to entertain was that of his own oblivion. Now he was able to reflect on the deep truth of that. Perhaps it was still true even of him, even after all he had experienced beyond the gates of the living.

There were many levels of oblivion, after all. As far as the faithful of the Empire were concerned, he himself had been dead for a very long time indeed, but that supposition was based on a fearful level of ignorance. There was all the difference in the world between the cold, hard existence of the Curse and the utter, profound oblivion of bodily annihilation.

He was free to dream again, now. His mind had knitted together, and with it had come all the old images, all the old desires and lusts and fears.

Preeminent among them was, of course, *her*. She had come to him in his dreams, dressed in bridal white, her smooth neck exposed, her dark eyes glinting wetly in the light of candles. She still moved in just the way she had done in life. Isabella had never been capable of a clumsy gesture. The sight of her again, after so long, was just as intoxicating as it had ever been. He found himself extending a withered hand into the depths of his own visions, trying to pull her towards him.

Perhaps that was the only preferable aspect to oblivion – the torment of seeing her had been spared him.

Vlad rolled a near-empty goblet in his palm idly, watching the dregs pool in its base. The fingers that cradled the silver bowl were pearl-grey and as dry as dust. Since being restored to existence by Nagash, his body had not entwined together in quite the way he might have wished. Some aspects of his earlier presence had not carried over, others had changed in subtle ways.

He felt... *scoured*. Learning to use muscles again had taken a long time. First, there had been the numbness, which brought on its shameful concomitant clumsiness. Then the pain had come, the raw, burning pain of reincorporation. That had been welcome – it had proved his body was his own again. He had drawn breath, and felt the damp air of the Old World sink into his lungs, and known that it was no illusion, and that he was back again, alive, and with unfinished tasks in the world of the senses.

For a long time, he had wondered whether his heart might beat. He had lain awake during the long nights, expecting to feel the hot rush of blood around his veins, pulsing with the old immutable rhythm he could barely remember.

It never came. He had been restored to the state of semi-life, just as he had been in the last days with Isabella. He still felt the Thirst, and still commanded the same strain of dark magic, and still felt at home in the shadows and the dank hearts of decay. The souls of the living were still translucent to him, burning like torches in the dark, and he still salivated at the sight of a bared vein.

I am an instrument, he ruminated sourly, pondering the time that had passed since his restoration.

In his earlier incarnation, Vlad had been master of his own destiny. Armies had risen and marched at his command. Sylvania, the Empire itself, had trembled before his name.

Much of that old power still remained. The unquiet dead still rose at his bidding, but he knew, in his silent heart, that his will was now a mere proxy for a greater intelligence.

There was no resisting the Master. There never had been. Some souls were so great, so bloated with power, that they transcended the standard order of things, and even a pride-driven aristocrat like Vlad felt little shame in bending the knee to *that*.

Still, it rankled. Deep in his stomach, where the last vestiges of human pride lingered, it rankled.

He lifted his goblet to his grey lips and drained the last of the wine. It was foul. In his former incarnation, even Sylvania had produced better vintages. Truly, the Empire was a shadow even of its earlier, rotten, decadent and miserly self.

Around him, candles burned low, their thick stumps heavy with molten tallow. The stone chamber was dark, and the ever-present north wind moaned through the cracks.

Before him, set on a bronze table, was a severed head. Walach Harkon's eyes had rolled up into his skull. His once elegant features had been defiled by tattoos and scarification, something that made Vlad's lip curl in disgust. Only the fangs gave away his proud bloodline; everything else had changed.

When Vlad had spied Harkon bringing his Blood Dragons into combat during the climax of the battle at Heffengen, he had assumed that the task was near completion – the Chaos forces would be broken between his own and those of the Empire, crushing them utterly. It should have been a great victory, the first step in the long road of bringing the living and the dead together to fight the damned. He had already rehearsed his speech before the mortal Emperor, demonstrating how only an alliance of former enemies could hope to staunch the tide of corruption spilling through the Auric Bastion.

No one, least of all him, could have guessed that Harkon had turned. Somehow, during the Blood Dragon's enforced exile north of the Bastion, his battle-hungry mind had been twisted to the service of the Blood God.

It was shameful. *Embarrassing*. Mortal cattle could have their heads turned by every petty shaman raving under a standing stone, but a lord of undeath, one of those capable of delivering the Kiss, one of the mightiest servants of Death in the entire world...

The thought made him furious. Harkon had driven a wedge between that which should by now be in unity. Far from gaining the trust of the mortal Emperor, he had *slain* him. Such rebellion, propelled by weakness, had earned him the torment of a thousand years. It had given Vlad some little pleasure to crush him, taking control of his draconian mount and using the tortured beast to end its own rider.

By then, though, the damage had been done. The Empire army had been routed, handing the servants of the Ruinous Powers an unbreakable momentum. Vlad himself had been forced to withdraw, an ignominy he had suffered too many times over his many lives.

He placed the goblet on the table next to Harkon's shrivelled head and glowered at the blank-eyed face. 'Glory-hunting *fool*,' he hissed.

The setback was a grave one. Every day saw more corrupted souls flock to the hosts of the North. The Empire was in no condition to offer more than a token resistance – for all Gelt's boasts, the Bastion was entirely breached now, and the hordes would soon pour through it like blood through a sieve. The scattered cities of the northern Empire, over which he had once cast covetous eyes himself, were as good as lost. No doubt the remnants of Karl Franz's army would attempt to make some kind of stand at Talabheim and Middenheim, but if there was to be genuine resistance, a chance to recover something before all was lost, it would have to be mounted further south.

'Altdorf,' he murmured, remembering his last sight of those white towers. He had got close enough to smell the fish being landed on the quays. For a glorious moment, many lifetimes ago, he had stood on the battlements and seen the entire city spread out before him, supine as a lover, tense for the ushering in of a new age of living death.

He did not know how he would feel when he saw it again. Perhaps the old passions would stir, or perhaps that was all behind him now. That was the strange thing about being reborn – he had to learn about himself again.

He sighed, and shoved Harkon's head from the table. It hit the stone floor with a wet thud and rolled away.

There could be no postponing the matter now. He had tarried long enough, uncertain how to break the news. There were few souls in the world that could make Vlad von Carstein hesitate, but the Master was one of them.

He sighed once more, pushed himself from his chair and arranged his cloak about him. The fine ermine settled on the polished crimson war-plate. He ran his fingers through his snow-white locks, ensuring not a strand of hair was misplaced.

From the chambers below, he heard the screams of living sacrifices as the last of the rites was completed. It was a waste to end mortal souls in such a way, and he took no great pleasure in it, but establishing a link with the Master over such distances could not be done without some trivial hardship.

Vlad made his way from the chamber and towards the lower levels of the tower. The disaster at Heffengen had to be recounted, and Nagash was not one to be kept waiting.

It was well, then, that he had something else to tell him – a new path to tread, and an old one to revisit. The future was just another aspect of the past, after all, which was yet another lesson his slumber in the halls of eternity had taught him.

The dead did not dream. Neither, it so happened, did their dreams ever die.

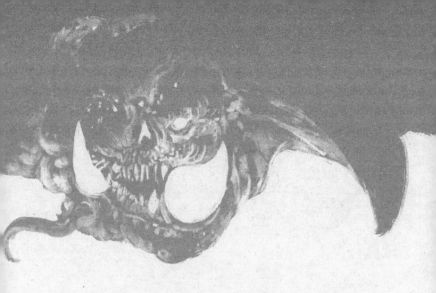

PART TWO

The Road to Altdorf
Spring 2525–Autumn 2525

SIX

Gregor Martak, Supreme Patriarch of the Colleges of Magic, awoke from a fevered dream of ruin and terror.

He had done likewise for the past three weeks, and it made him exhausted and irascible. Previously, he had slept phenomenally well. Wizards of the Amber Order were accustomed to deep slumber – they had little to trouble their unwaking minds, and so they slept like the beasts they emulated: in brief, deep snatches, as dreamless as the empty vistas of the underworld.

Martak yawned and scratched his unruly beard. Then he lifted his coarse robe and scratched the rest of himself. Tufts of hay stuck out from every crevice of his makeshift nightshirt, a result of taking his bed in the Imperial Stables. As one of the three most powerful men in the Empire, he could have occupied the most opulent chambers of the Palace. He could have had a staff of hundreds, a whole series of willing and creative companions, and barrel-loads of fine victuals carted into his personal kitchens every morning.

His predecessor, the avaricious and brilliant Balthasar Gelt, had taken full advantage of such opportunities. Martak had always had a sneaking admiration for Gelt, in the way only a man of such completely antipathetic character could. The two of them had never been rivals, for Martak had spent most of his life in the wilds of Taal's boundless forests, far from the labyrinthine conspiracies of the capital city. Where Gelt had been an accomplished puller of Imperial levers, Martak had been content to remain an uncultured savage, scavenging around the margins while his powers over beast and bower grew steadily stronger.

When news had come in concerning Gelt's fall from grace, Martak had not been one of the many who had secretly rejoiced. Subsequently being named as Supreme Patriarch had come as a complete surprise. He had been stalking through the wildwoods of the northern Reikland when the summons had come. Six messengers had been dispatched to find him; only one made it, and he had been white from primal fear when he had turned up. The deep forest was no place for ordinary men.

Martak was under no illusions why he had been chosen: he was the least offensive candidate to the largest number of people. The Amber College was a filth-ridden backwater compared to the lofty Gold, Light and Bright Colleges, from whose precincts the Supreme Patriarchs were normally drawn, and that made him a non-contentious choice, particularly as the Emperor was not around to oversee a protracted dispute.

The Amber reputation did not worry him. If his colleagues were too preoccupied by their incessant feuding to see just how powerful the Lore of Beasts could be, and just how completely he had mastered it, then that was their fault to remedy. So he had taken the honour when it had been offered, even putting on a largely fresh robe to receive his staff of office. Then he had left the Palace for the stables, bedding down in the straw and breathing in the thick aroma of horseflesh.

For a while, surrounded by thoroughbreds, he had slept well. Then the dreams had come.

Martak ran his calloused hands through his long greasy hair, and belched. Moving stiffly after his troubled night, he staggered over to a water trough and splashed his face. He walked out of the stable doors, yawning again widely. It was the hour just before the dawn. The eastern sky was a deep blue, casting a weak light across the entire cityscape. Mist rose up from the ground, as white as cream and nigh as thick.

The stables were situated on the southern edge of the vast Imperial Palace complex, not far from the upper curtain walls. Martak strolled through courtyard after courtyard, loosening his limbs and rolling his shoulders as he went. By the time he reached the outer parapet, the first rays of the sun were slipping over the distant eastern hills.

He leaned on the stone balustrade, and took in the view.

Below him, a tangle of roofs tumbled away down the steep slope towards the river. Thin columns of dirty smoke spiralled up from the streets, bearing the wet, dirty aroma of Altdorfers' hearths. Ahead of him, a quarter of a mile eastwards, the huge dome of the Temple of Sigmar thrust up from the clutter of houses, its copper skin relatively unscathed by the grime that affected every other building in the city.

Beyond the temple lay the wide curve of the river. The rising sun cast rippling lines of silver across its turgid surface. Barges were already plying the trade-ways, sliding like whales through the muck. Martak could hear the calls of merchants as they unloaded their cargo onto the wharfs.

Altdorf had a kind of rough, unregarded beauty to it. Perhaps Martak was one of the few to appreciate that, for he liked rough, unregarded things. The poet Heine Heinrich had once described Altdorf as having the looks of a toad-dragon combined with the charm of a threepenny harlot. Being strictly chaste, Martak could not attest to the latter, but as for the former, toad-dragons had their own kind of magnificence. They had certainly been around a long time, something that could also be said of the City of Sigmar.

He drew in a long, deep breath. The nightmares were fading. Soon the Palace would begin to stir in earnest. Night-watch soldiers would slope back to their barracks, hoping none had witnessed their snoozing in the shadow of the battlements, to be replaced by bleary-eyed, unshaven day-watch regulars. The great fires would be lit in the hearths, banishing the worst of the night chill, and pigs would be rammed on spits for the evening banquets. The refuse-strewn streets would fill with the harsh, jostling press of unwashed bodies, replacing the cutpurses and petty cultists who had stalked the night shadows.

Until then, Martak's view would be largely untroubled by interruption. The city lay before him peacefully, barely touched by the burnishing rays of the world's sun, as dank and sullen as fungus.

In his dreams, he had seen the city burning. He had seen the cobbled streets erupt in foul growths, and the walls collapse under the weight of rampant vegetation. He had seen monsters stalking through the ruins, their eyes bright green in the flame-lit dark. He had seen the river clogged with strangle-weed and the proud towers of the Imperial Palace cast down in flaming destruction.

He had seen the Emperor, alone, wandering across the lands of the dead, surrounded on all sides by the hosts of the damned. His armies were gone, and the sky had been alive with light of all shades, some hues having no name in the languages of mortal men.

Perhaps, if he had had such dreams a year ago, he would have disregarded them, putting them down to the strange ways of the wizard's mind, but things had changed since then.

The city ran with rumour of imminent invasion. Armies had been sent north months ago under the command of the Emperor, who had taken his finest captains with him and most of the capital's standing army. Since then, the news had been fragmentary and confused. Some reports had it that Kislev had been overrun, just as in the time of Magnus the Pious. Others faithfully recounted tales of carnage across Nordland and the Ostermark, where the dead pulled themselves from the earth to aid the ravening hordes of the Fallen Gods. Those stories had been the most numerous of all – that the necromancers had entered into unholy alliance with the practitioners of Chaotic magic, and that each faction planned to feast on the bodies and souls of mortal men.

None could be sure of the truth of such tales. Those few messengers who claimed to come south from the far north said contradictory things. Some had been driven mad by the journey, and others had always been, so all they brought were fragments – half-truths and whispers, none of which might be true, or all of which might be.

If Martak had not had the nightmares, he might have been inclined to dismiss the refugees as the usual doom-mongering End Times fanatics. He would have left the city and returned to the wilds, leaving the ordering of the Empire to its usual masters, the elector counts. Though they were as squabbling and infuriating as ever, they understood the deep complexities of Imperial government, something that Martak knew he would never comprehend.

In the light of his visions, though, he stayed his hand, and waited in the Imperial Palace, holding on for tidings he could trust. The Emperor would surely return soon, to whom he needed to give his tokens of allegiance as Supreme Patriarch. The latest rumours told of devastation in Marienburg, and the imminent return of the Reiksmarshal to the city. If either of those things were true, then even the most sanguine of the Empire's servants would do well to worry.

Martak coughed up a gobbet of spittle and spewed it over the balustrade. His bodily aroma was strong, mixed in with faint overtones of horse-dung and mouldy straw. That was as it should be. The bestial spirits were strong in his blood, coursing like fine wine. As he drew in the cold, briny air, he felt his wilderness-toughened muscles respond. He would stay, observing, waiting for a signal, doing what he could to live up to the foreign responsibilities placed on his shoulders.

Below him, the city was waking up. He heard the first calls of the stall-holders setting up, the heavy clang of temple doors unlocking, and the clatter of quayside cranes unloading goods.

They were good sounds. They were *human* sounds, in all their inextinguishable variety. Altdorf was home to every vice and cruelty, but it also harboured joy, mirth and generosity. If you wanted to gain a picture of the race in all its messy, fragile and marvellous splendour and folly, there was no better place.

This is the heart of it all, Martak mused, leaning heavily on the stone railing. *This is our soul.*

By then, the sun had risen indeed, casting its thin grey light over the tops of the distant forest and gilding the temple dome. It was a faint, uncertain light, but just enough to lift the murk and fear of the long night.

Martak let it warm his limbs for a little while, before stomping back off to the stables. He had appointments with powerful men later on that day, which meant that he should make at least some effort to scrape the worst of the grime from his hands and face. He did not like the thought of it, but it had to be done.

As he padded back across the stone flags, his bare feet brushing soundlessly like a hunting cat's, he felt the final shreds of terror dissipate from his soul. As the sun strengthened, he knew the memory would fade entirely.

Until the next night, when the visions would come back again.

The lamps were lit in Couronne every night. Teams of armed men patrolled the streets of the stone-walled citadel, keeping the fires going and banishing the shadows.

Bretonnia had become a land of nightmares. Witches were abroad, hideous apparitions crept across the devastated fields, daemons squatted in the ruins of burned-out watchtowers. The new king, the reborn Gilles le Breton, had restored a shell of order to the realm, but he presided over a shattered caste of exhausted knights and half-starved peasantry. Since announcing the start of a new Errantry War, he had been abroad for months at a time, hunting down the dregs of the Chaos armies that had vomited forth from Mousillon.

His regent at Couronne remained Louen Leoncoeur, master of the realm no longer but still a Paladin Champion of the Green Knight. The duke knelt in his private chapel at the summit of his ancestral castle. Tapestries hung in the candlelight, each one depicting great deeds of his ancient House across the generations. A stone altar stood before him, surmounted by a lone marble figurine of the Lady.

Leoncoeur knelt in his full plate armour. He clasped his naked sword, resting it point-down on the stone before him and crossing his gauntlets at the hilt. His long blond hair hung about his armoured shoulders, lank from the battlefield. Like all the knights of the realm, he had been at war near-ceaselessly since the times of strife had descended. On one such sortie, he had nearly met his end under the blade of his own bastard son Mallobaude. For a long time, lost in the far reaches of the Bretonnian wild country, he had walked a fragile path between death and life, teetering on the edge of oblivion.

It had been the Lady who had guided him back – she had spoken to him in the depths of his fever. Her voice, as soft as ermine and yet as firm as the blade he carried, had whispered to him throughout those dark, lost times, refusing him permission to yield. Leoncoeur dimly remembered begging her to let him go, to cast him loose, to let his service die even as the land around him died.

She had never relented. He could recall her stern face looming over him, refusing the command that he yearned for. A lifetime of chivalry and pious devotion had sealed his fate – he could never have refused a boon from her, and so he clung to life, refusing the seductive embrace of the underworld even as it grasped for him. His senses returned in time, and he wandered the lands, near-starved, barely more than a shade himself. When he at last found his way back to Couronne, he was nearly slain for a wraith by a grail knight, and only his mud-splattered emblems saved him.

By then, Mallobaude had been destroyed and Gilles le Breton was the new king, feted by all across the realm as a harbinger of a new dawn for Bretonnia. Leoncoeur had recovered his strength and his wits, recovering under the auspices of the white-robed Sisters of the Lady. It took longer for him to recover his pride. He had ridden out to face Mallobaude as unquestioned monarch of his domain. He had returned to find a legend from the past sitting in the throne-room to accept the acclamation of the masses.

There was no contesting the will of le Breton. The green-eyed king's magisterial presence was unquestionable. A fey light shone in his ageless face, and his countenance bore the raw weight of centuries. All bowed the knee before him, including Leoncoeur himself.

That did not assuage the bitterness. In the long, sleepless nights as his body was restored to health, he found himself gnawing away at the injustice of it. He prayed, over and again, asking to be shown what fault he had committed, what aspect of chivalry he had transgressed that would warrant his kingdom being taken from him and his bloodline disinherited.

If le Breton himself was aware of such anguish, he did not show it. He was one of the Immortals, the avatar of the Green Knight himself, and matters of pride and propriety no longer concerned him. Even his voice was otherworldly, an archaic, haughty speech that belonged to another world. He existed now to take the war to the enemies of the realm: he was a weapon, forged from the myths of the past and given life by the unfathomable will of the Lady. Leoncoeur could not gainsay such commandments; neither, though, in truth, could he understand them.

So he knelt before the altar as the lamps burned, murmuring the words of faith he had known since childhood, seeking the answers that eluded him even in the midst of battle. Every night he did the same, and every night his prayers went unanswered.

As the first stirrings of fatigue ran through his battle-weary frame, his lips finally stopped moving. He opened his frost-blue eyes, and looked up at the image of the Lady.

A chill breeze rattled through the loose stained-glass windows, making the candle-flames shiver. The benign face of his divine mistress gazed down at him, serene and pitiless.

It was as he looked up at her, just as he had done in the dream-lands of his long near-death, that realisation dawned. There would be no answers from Her in this place. It was no longer his. Whether for good or for ill, the realm had been taken from him and given to another. To linger in Couronne like a ghost over its grave was pointless, and only grief could come of it.

Leoncoeur clambered to his feet, bowing again as he addressed the altar. He sheathed his sword.

'Where, then?' he asked, his deep voice soft. 'What path shall I take?'

The figurine of the Lady gave no answer. The flames flared a little, stirred by the wind, but no other sign revealed itself. The faces on the tapestries, picked out by long-dead fingers and faded by time and trial, gazed sightlessly down on him.

Leoncoeur smiled faintly. The ways of the Lady were never easy. That was the point of Her – She was the trial, the anguish, the test. Weakness had no place in Her service, only undying devotion.

'I will discover it, then,' he said. He looked around him. He had prayed in the same chapel since boyhood, and the stones were as familiar to him as his own flesh. 'This is no longer my realm. As you will it, I will find another.'

He bowed again, and turned away. Limping still from his last cavalry charge, the deposed king swept from the chapel, and the great oak doors slammed shut behind him.

In his absence, the candles still burned, and the draughts still swirled around the bases of the pillars. The figurine Lady stood in the flickering dark, her face still serene, her thoughts, behind the sculptor's smooth smile, unknowable.

Marienburg had already fallen, but its torment was not yet over.

The streets that had once bustled with the commerce of a dozen realms were now knee-deep in reeking effluent. The great docks were shattered, their steam-cranes tilting into the brine, the loading chains already rusting into nothingness. The mighty sea-wall built atop the foundations of ancient elven ruins was smashed into lumps of subsiding masonry, and foul slithering creatures with many eyes and splay-webbed feet slapped and slid across its remains.

Bodies lay stretched throughout the ruins as far as the eye could see, and every corpse was swollen with a different strain of pox. Many cadavers had burst open, spilling nests of maggots and black-limbed spiders over what remained of the cobbled thoroughfares. The corpses were piled high at the strategic choke-points, their blood mingling with the dribbling sputum of the Plaguefather's foul gifts. The sea itself was polluted, turned from a choppy grey into a dark-green slurry, as thick as tar and crowned with a crust of yellowish foam. The mixture lapped sluggishly against what remained of the old quay-walls, sucking and wheezing against the disintegrating stone blocks.

Above the fallen city, the clouds hung low, just as they had at Heffengen. The air carried a greenish tinge, and clouds of flies buzzed and droned through the miasma.

Everything was ruined. Every building was a hollow shell, bursting with rotting, preternatural growths. The great guild buildings in the dock-quarter were now temples of decay, draped with putrescent vines like giant entrails pulled from a body. The dull crack of thunder still echoed from the northern horizon, though the spell-summoned storms that had ravaged the city during the worst of the fighting were ebbing at last.

Through the very heart of the devastation, a vast army marched. Just as at Heffengen, they were drawn from the corrupted hosts of the North, and every tribe was represented in their tormented ranks. Norscans strode out, clad in thick furs and bearing ornately crafted axes with runes of ruin carved on the daemon's-head steel. Skaelings and Kurgan came with them, as well as Khazags and Vargs and Kul, a collection of the whole of the Realm of Chaos's sundered peoples, thrown together under a panoply of skull-topped banners.

It took a full day for the huge host to pass from the waterfront, through the dead city and out of the ruined eastern gates. As they marched, daemons flickered and wavered in the mournful half-light, hissing and drooling as they danced. All manner of pestilential beasts, from roaches to rats, scuttled under their feet, welling up like oil from the bubbling sewer-grates.

The host was beyond counting. Every soldier in it bore some mark of the Plaguefather, whether merely a pale pallor scored by throbbing rashes, or an entirely changed body, bloated with pox and bursting with mutations. Thick armour plate buckled outward over tumours, and ragged shirts of chainmail barely concealed festering wounds. Some clearly revelled in their diseases, leering as they crunched the bones of mortal men under their boots. Others limped along in agony, their ribcages protruding as they were consumed from the inside.

For hour after hour, the banners swayed past, each one daubed with a fresh sign of pestilence. The army was larger by far than the one that had broken the Bastion. It had been sent south by Archaon, hurled far out into the trackless ocean before sweeping back towards the Empire coastline. Ship after ship had disgorged its contents into Marienburg's stricken harbour, overwhelming the defenders in a remorseless wave of foul sorcery and dogged blade-work. For many hours the resistance had been heroic, and the fighting had been heavy in the streets.

But the result had never truly been in doubt. Archaon had unleashed his armies on the effete lands of the South in such quantities that even Asavar Kul would have blenched to see them. Two more allied hordes were already grinding their way south, tearing through the Great Forest like blades ripped under the skin. Each one alone was larger than any prior army sent to bring punishment to the unbelieving. Taken together, there could be no stopping them.

The force sent to shatter Marienburg was the mightiest of them all, a tumultuous rabble of pustular, addled, filth-spreading, contagion-fanning glory. As rank after rank trudged east, demolishing the few remaining walls as they went, they were observed by three pairs of eyes.

In the semi-remembered past, those eyes had belonged to mortal triplets, born under the midnight sun of the frozen tundra. Their family name was Glott, though that had meant little at the time and nothing to them now. The eldest, though only by moments, was Otto, who came closest of all of them to being a warrior in the traditional sense – he was a pot-bellied monster with marsh-green flesh and the tripartite marks of the Plaguefather scraped in black ink across his pocked forehead.

Otto stood atop the ruins of the Oesterdock Temple, leaning casually against the broken cupola of the Chapel of Manann. His clammy fingers pressed against the stone, causing mould-spores to spontaneously spider out across it. He laughed throatily, watching his troops lurch and swagger, then reached down for a strip of moss that had sprung up between the bricks of the temple wall. He pressed the wiry fuzz to his slobbering chin in a mockery of an Empire Greatsword's beard, and grinned.

Ethrac, the second triplet, saw him do it, and rolled his rheumy eyes in disgust. Like his brother, he was a wiry, spare figure, emaciated under blotchy robes of coarse wool. He clutched at a gnarled staff of oak heartwood, desecrated with columns of twisting runes, and picked his way through the rubble of the temple's roof. As he moved, bronze bells shackled to the staff-tip clanged dully, and flatulent vapours wafted out from the hem of his torn robes. He kicked aside a few clumps of rubble, and spat at them as they tumbled down to the street below.

'We could have lost this,' Ethrac muttered.

'No, we couldn't,' said Otto casually, picking flecks of plaster from what remained of the cupola.

Their voices were strange, wet rasps, almost like that of beasts, and filtered through mouths of blackened teeth. When they spoke, they overlapped one another constantly, as if each were just a part of one confused mind.

'I did not foresee the dead,' Ethrac said, pausing in his scrabbling search. 'Why did I not foresee the dead?'

Otto picked at his nostril. 'Does it matter?'

'It matters, o my brother. Yes, yes, it *matters*. We are not seeing everything. There are portents withheld. Why? I do not know. I should be seeing the world turn, the minds of men open. I did not see the dead. I did not *see* them.'

Just as at Heffengen, the defenders of Marienburg had been bolstered by the sudden intervention of undead warriors, though, just as at Heffengen, the reinforcements had not proved enough to halt the onward march of Chaos. That bothered Ethrac. He had sent tidings north, hoping to warn Archaon's war council that the Law of Death was proving more mutable than in past ages, and that it posed complications, but he had little hope of any of his messengers arriving alive. The Great Forest was as unforgiving to the damned as it was to the faithful.

'You should learn to calm yourself,' said Otto, scratching at a new and beautiful boil that had emerged under his chin. 'Nothing stands between us and Altdorf now. Nothing of any note, anyway.'

Ethrac shook his bald head impatiently. 'Does not *matter!*

Mortals do not matter. But something has changed.' He screwed his eyes into a frown, and the scabby skin of his forehead broke out in bloody cracks. 'They are rising from the earth like new shoots. Why? Why is the wall between living and dead broken?'

Otto sighed and walked over to his brother. He took Ethrac's cheeks in both hands and squeezed affectionately. 'They are *desperate*, o my brother,' he whispered. 'Every witch-rattler between the Great Gate and the Hot Lands is flailing around for something to call up. You know why? Because *we* are here. They know this is the end. What if a few skeletons are thrown into our path? Do you think they will last longer at the White City than they did here?'

Ethrac nodded reluctantly, some of his agitation subsiding. 'And there is Festus,' he murmured. 'We must not forget him.'

Otto released Ethrac. 'It has been sewn up, tight as a burst stomach. The Leechlord is with us. Brine is with us, the Tally-man is with us. Stop worrying.'

Ethrac started to root around with his staff again, only half placated. 'Festus has been working hard. I can smell it from here. Much joy, to see him again.'

Otto walked back over to the edge of the temple ruins. 'Never forget, my favoured loin-brother, that we are *three*, and that we have not seen the finest of the Father's plague-pots yet.'

As he spoke, a vast, rolling mountain of scabrous flesh lumbered into view. As tall as a guilder's townhouse, the third of the triplets stomped past the teetering shell of the temple. His skin glowed a violent green, as if lit by weird lantern-light. Vast, muscle-thick arms hung, simian-like, from swollen shoulders. One terminated in a long, greasy tentacle that trailed along in the dust behind it. Catching sight of Otto and Ethrac, the monster cracked a wide grin, and a semi-chewed leg dropped from his jaws.

'Good feasting, o my brother?' asked Otto, reaching out to stroke the creature's bald head.

Ghurk, the final triplet, nodded enthusiastically, and more half-chewed body parts slopped from his slack lower jaw. Eating made Ghurk happy, and eating warm human flesh made him even happier. Several hapless victims were still clutched in his clawed hand; some of them still struggling weakly.

Otto took a short run-up, and launched himself from the temple's edge and into mid-air. He landed heavily on Ghurk's shoulders, and shuffled into position. Ghurk gurgled with pleasure, and started chewing again.

'Can anything stand against *this*, o my brother?' called out Otto to Ethrac, proudly surveying the scene from atop his sibling's unnaturally huge bulk. In every direction, the rampant desecration of the Plaguefather ran wild. Soon the last of what had been Marienburg would be overwhelmed entirely, a festering jungle on the western seaboard of the Empire, the first foothold of what would become Father Nurgle's reign of corpulence on earth.

Ethrac gazed at his two brothers with genuine fondness, and his withered face cracked a toothy smile. 'No, my brother,' he admitted, making ready to join Otto on Ghurk's back, from whence the two of them would begin the long march east. 'You are quite correct. *Nothing* can stand against it.'

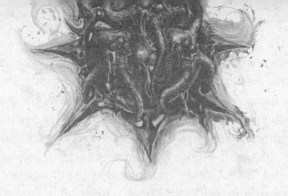

SEVEN

Drakenhof was not how Vlad remembered it. The centuries had not been kind to the ancient structure, and whole wings had fallen into ivy-covered ruin. The ice-cold wind from the Worlds Edge Mountains cut straight through the many gouges and gaps in the walls, skittering around the dusty halls within and shaking the ragged tapestries on their wall-hangings.

Since returning to Sylvania from the far north, he had done what he could to restore something like order to the ruins. He had raised the cadavers of the old castle architects, and they had soundlessly got back to work, ordering work-gangs of living dead to haul stone and saw wood, just as they had years ago.

There was no time to make the necessary repairs though, and so Vlad's throne stood in an empty audience chamber with the chill whistling through open eaves. Sitting in his old iron throne gave him no joy, for his surroundings were scarce better than any common bandit-lord.

He deserved better. He had always deserved better, and now

that he was a mortarch, one of the Chosen of Nagash, his surroundings were little more than a bad joke.

Beyond the castle's crumbling walls, out under the sick light of Morrslieb, the entire countryside was alive with movement. A thousand undead did their dread master's bidding, dragging old sword-blades from graves and fitting them with spell-wound hilts. Armour was pulled from cobwebbed storechambers and dug out from long barrows, all to arm the host that would take Vlad from the margins of the Empire and back into its very heart.

Mortal men worked alongside their dead cousins, swallowing their horror out of fear of the new seigneur of Castle Drakenhof. In truth, it was not just fear that made them work – the old ties of loyalty still had purchase, and there was no doubt in their slow, brutish minds that their true lord had returned.

Vlad did not despise them for that. They were only performing what their station demanded, and he held no contempt for his subjects. When he slew them in order to drink their blood, he did so cleanly, taking libation through the magics of his sword rather than sucking the flesh like an animal. They were *cattle*, as necessary to his kind as meat and water were to the mortal lords of the Empire, and if they served him faithfully then their lives would be no worse than any other of the toiling peasantry across the hardscrabble badlands of the outer Empire.

Some, of course, refused to see that, which required more punitive action to be taken. Thus it was that the witch hunter hung before him, suspended in a writhing aura of black-tinged flame. His arms were locked out wide, his legs clamped together, his head thrown back.

Vlad regarded him coolly from the throne.

'What do you think will happen to you?' he asked.

The witch hunter, his scarred face taut with pain, could only reply through clenched teeth. 'I will... resist,' he gasped. 'While I live, I will resist.'

'I realise that,' Vlad sighed. 'But when your resistance ends, what do you think will happen then?'

'I will be gathered into the light of Sigmar. I will join the Choirs of the Faithful.'

'Ah. I am afraid not,' said Vlad, feeling some genuine sadness. 'Perhaps, in the past, you might have done, but the Laws of Death are not what they were. Perhaps you have not felt the change.' He got up from the throne, and his black robes fell about him as he stepped down from the dais towards his victim. The witch hunter watched him approach, his face showing little fear but plenty of defiance. 'The world is running out of time. My Master has wounded the barrier between realms. The long-departed will soon stir in the earth, and nothing your boy-God can do will have the slightest effect. I admit that, for a time, our kind were troubled by your... faith. Those days, I am happy to say, are coming to an end.'

Vlad walked around the witch hunter, noting with some appreciation how the mortal controlled the trepidation that must have been shivering through him.

'You think of me as your enemy,' Vlad said. 'How far from the truth that is. In reality, I am your only hope. The paths of fate are twofold now: servitude before the ravening Gods of the North, or servitude before the Lord of Death. There is no middle way. I do not expect you to see the truth of it immediately, but you will, in time. All of you will. I merely hope the realisation comes before all is lost.'

The witch hunter struggled against the black flames, but they writhed more tightly, binding him as firmly as chains. Vlad needed to exert the merest flicker of effort to maintain them. Sylvania's soil was now such a fertile breeding ground for magic that his powers were greater than they had ever been.

'Lies,' spat the witch hunter, with some effort. 'My faith is unshakeable.'

'I can see that,' said Vlad. 'And so I am willing to extend a great gift to you. You may join me freely. You may follow me as a mortal man, and learn the ways of my Master. Your life will be extended many times over, and you will accomplish far more against the Dark Gods than you ever would have done while in your current service. The pain can end. You can still fight evil. I have ever been a generous liege-lord – even your annals must tell it so.'

The witch hunter's eyes narrowed, and the muscles on his jaw-line twitched. Vlad could feel the man's willpower eroding – he had been tormented for hours, and every man, no matter how well-prepared, had his breaking point.

'Never,' he said, his voice nearly cracking with effort.

Vlad drew close to him. He extended a finger to the man's throat, tracing the line of a raised vein. 'Your Empire is *over,* mortal. I say that not to crow, for I take no pleasure in seeing the ruin of what I once aspired to rule. It is merely a fact. I saw your Emperor slain at Heffengen. I saw the Bastion break, and I saw what was behind that wall. You are an intelligent man: you can see for yourself what is happening. Plagues run free, wiping out whole villages in a single night. The forest comes alive, churning with unnatural growth. The rivers clog, the crops fail.' He slid his finger alongside the man's ear. 'They say that Marienburg has already fallen. Talabheim will be next. Your house is crumbling around you – I offer a new home for your loyalty.'

The witch hunter's face creased in agony. His fists balled. He was still fighting. Lines of magic-heated sweat ran down his temples and slipped to the floor, fizzing as the drops hit the cold stone.

'*Never,*' he said again, screwing his eyes closed as he struggled to fight on.

Vlad regarded him bleakly. The offer had been magnanimous, but even the patience of lords came to an end. 'One thing, then,' he said. 'Just one scrap. Tell me your name. I will need it.'

The witch hunter's eyes snapped open. He stared up at the open rafters, his expression proud. 'Jan Herrscher,' he said. 'By the grace of our Lord Sigmar, that is the name I have always borne. I never hid it, and may it give honour to Him forever.'

Vlad nodded. 'Herrscher,' he murmured. 'A fine name. And believe me, you have given him honour. Truly, you have.'

Then he withdrew, and snapped his fingers. The black flames flared into a coil, and fastened themselves around Herrscher's neck. The coil contracted, snapping the man's spine. For a moment, his eyes continued to stare upward, then he went limp in his bonds. Vlad gestured again, the fires flickered out, and the witch hunter's body thudded to the stone.

Vlad gazed down at the corpse for a moment. It was a shame. Herrscher was the kind of man that made the Empire worth fighting for.

His thoughts were interrupted by a low cough at the chamber's entrance. He looked up to see one of his white-faced servants hovering anxiously. This one was a living soul, and Vlad felt an involuntary pang as he watched the man's blood vessels throb under his skin.

'You pardon, lord,' the servant stammered, clearly terrified, 'but the first brigades are ready for inspection.'

That was good. It would be a long and arduous task to create the army that Vlad required, even though Nagash had been quite insistent on the need for haste. The hosts of the North were converging on Altdorf already, and Sylvania was far further from Reikland than Marienburg. Even the expedience of raising the fallen to fight again would scarce suffice to meet the need, and so the scouring of Sylvania for living troops had begun in earnest.

'Very good,' said Vlad, pulling his robes about him, preparing to descend the winding stairs to the parade ground below. 'I will attend shortly.' His gaze alighted again on the body of Herrscher. 'And do something with this while I am gone.'

The servant hesitated before complying. Even in death, a witch hunter could inspire terror in a Sylvanian. 'Shall I burn the body, lord?' he asked.

Vlad shook his head. 'Do no such thing,' he said. 'Take it to my chambers and give it every proper burial rite.'

He swept imperiously out of the chamber. As he did so, the last of the black flames guttered out.

'He is too good to waste,' Vlad said. 'We shall have to find ways for him to serve again.'

The Grand Chamber of Magnus Enthroned stood near the summit of the Imperial Palace's main basilica. Vast walls of granite and ashlar stone soared above a wide marble floor. The pillars that held up the high vaulted roof were many-columned and banded with silver. Torches blazed, sending clouds of soot rolling into the heights. Statues of fallen heroes stood in alcoves along the walls, each graven from black veined stone. Magnus himself had been carved from a solid block of dark grey granite, depicted sitting in judgement on a massive throne. His image dominated the far end of the hall, fully twenty feet high, as stern and unbending as he had been in life.

Overlooked by such grandeur, the chamber's few living inhabitants were dwarfed into near-insignificance. They stood in the empty centre in a loose circle, clad in the robes of finest silk and linen and bearing heavy gold artefacts of office – chains, amulets, crowns.

All but one. Martak had not had the time or the will to find something to wear less filthy than the robes he had slept in, and so stood apart from the others. He guessed that he smelled fairly bad to them. That was simply reciprocal – each of the others smelled truly repellent to him, with their thick-wafted perfumes and armour-unguents.

'None have suffered more than I,' said the sturdiest of them, a tall man wearing a fur-lined jerkin and long green cloak. His leonine face was crested with a mane of snow-white, and he wore a goatee beard on his age-lined face. Despite his advanced years, he carried himself with a warrior's bearing, and his flinty eyes gave away no weakness.

Of all of them, Martak liked him the most. This was Theodoric Gausser, Elector Count of Nordland, and there was something attractive about his unflinchingly martial demeanour.

'We have *all* suffered,' replied a woman standing to his right. She was as old as Gausser, and draped in lines of pearls over a fabulously opulent gown of grey and silver. Her face was gaunt, though liberally rouged and slabbed with whitener. She carried herself perfectly erect, as if her spine might snap if she curved it.

This was Emanuelle von Liebwitz, Elector Count of Wissenland, as fabulously wealthy as her subjects were grindingly poor. Like Gausser, she was no one's fool, though her imperious manner even with her peers made her hard to warm to.

'Nordland has borne the brunt of the enemy for centuries,' reiterated Gausser. 'We have fought them longer and harder. I know what it takes to beat them.'

'None of us knows what it takes to beat them,' said a third figure, quietly. He was thinner than the others, as tall as a crane and with a pronounced nose. His attire was less flamboyant – a drab green overcoat and travel-worn boots. That would have come as little surprise to any who knew his province – Stirland was miserably poor, and far from the Imperial centre from which all patronage flowed. This one was Graf Alberich Haupt-Anderssen, a grand name that did little to disguise the poverty of his inheritance. 'If we did, their threat would have been eradicated long before this day. They are unbeatable. All that remains is survival for as long as we can muster it.'

The other two glared at Haupt-Anderssen contemptuously. The first two were warlike electors, and their cousin's blood was too thin for their liking.

Martak said nothing, but took some enjoyment from the incongruity of the situation. None of those assembled could remotely have been described as the finest the Empire had to offer. The greatest names were dead or missing – Gelt, Volkmar, Schwarzhelm, Helborg, the Emperor himself. Other Electors, such as the great Todbringer of Middenheim, were looking to their own defences. What remained in Altdorf were the outriders, those still obsessed enough with the Great Game to seek political advancement even as the wolves scratched at the door.

'Your cowardice damns you, Graf,' spat von Liebwitz.

Haupt-Anderssen shrugged. 'There is no virtue in hiding behind fantasies.'

'You shame this hall,' said Gausser, gesturing to the towering image of Magnus.

Haupt-Anderssen sniffed, and said nothing.

A fourth figure cleared his throat then – Hans Zintler, the Reikscaptain. In Helborg's absence he was the highest ranking military officer, and carried himself suitably formally, with a brass-buttoned jerkin and short riding cloak. His black moustache was neatly trimmed across a broad-jawed face.

'With your pardon, lords,' he interjected. 'Only one task requires our attention this day. The news from Marienburg requires a response.'

'Deserved everything they got,' growled Gausser. 'Dirty secessionists.'

'Maybe so, lord,' said von Liebwitz, 'but the question is what to do about the army that laid them low.'

'Nothing,' said Haupt-Anderssen. 'Look to our walls. That is the only hope.'

'Carroburg stands in their path,' pointed out Zintler. 'If it is not to fall in turn, it must be reinforced.'

'With what?' grunted Martak, his first contribution to the debate. All eyes turned to him, as if the others had only just noticed his presence. Von Liebwitz's elegant nose wrinkled, and she pressed a scented handkerchief to her mouth. 'We can barely man the walls here. Send men to Carroburg and they'll just die a little earlier.'

Gausser bristled. 'We have wizards advising us on military matters now?'

'You invited me,' shrugged Martak. 'I'd have been happier with the horses.'

Zintler coughed nervously. He was a good man, a fine soldier, but he did not like discord amongst his superiors. 'Then, Supreme Patriarch, what would you suggest?'

Martak laughed harshly. 'Gelt was Supreme Patriarch. I'm just a filthy bird-tamer.' He looked at Gausser shrewdly. 'Call the Carroburg garrison back here. Call them all back. Surrender the forest – it can look after itself. You can't weaken this army, not out there. All we have are walls.' He shot a glance at Haupt-Anderssen. 'You're right. We need to use them.'

Von Liebwitz took a short breath, trying not to sniff too deeply. 'It is clear to me, master wizard, that you have little understanding of war. There are *three* armies making their way towards us. Once they reach the Reik valley, we will be without hope of reinforcement. If nothing is done to hamper their progress, the noose will tighten before the solstice falls.'

'They won't hurry,' snorted Martak. 'Do you not see it yet? Geheimnisnacht is the key. They will arrive then, when their powers are at their height and the daemon-moon rides full.' He crossed his arms. 'That is the hour of our doom. We can neither delay nor hasten its coming, so we should just make ready for it.'

Zintler looked uncomfortable. In normal times, Martak's advice would have been balanced by the Grand Theogonist's, but, as with so many others, Volkmar was missing, presumed dead, and the arch-lectors had not answered his summons.

'Superstition,' muttered Gausser, though with no great certainty.

Martak raised a dirty eyebrow. 'You think so? I'll remind you of that when the wind is screaming and the earth beneath our feet begins to move.'

'That is already taking place,' observed Haupt-Anderssen archly. He was right – reports had started coming from across the city.

Panicked residents had begun to flee the poorer quarters after wells had sprouted foul weeds overnight, and gutters had burst open with broods of writhing rats. The nights had been filled with unearthly screams, though the City Watch had never been able to track them down. Some even said that the river itself was changing, thickening up like broth over a stove.

'And that is *your* task, wizard,' accused von Liebwitz. 'Let us look to the defences – your kind should be cleansing the city.'

Martak glared at her darkly. 'We're doing our part. It would help if I weren't summoned to all these damned councils.'

'We need to determine the order of defence,' insisted Gausser, his cheeks reddening.

'So you can master us all,' sniped von Liebwitz.

Haupt-Anderssen laughed at that, and Gausser started to shout something about the noted cowardice of Wissenlanders, to which their elector vigorously responded.

By then, though, Martak was not listening, and neither was Zintler. Heavy crashes could be heard from outside the chamber, echoing up the long corridors. The Reikscaptain drew his blade, and slowly moved towards the double-door entrance. Two guards on either side of the portal did likewise. The commotion drew closer, growing louder on the far side.

Then the twin doors slammed back, and a band of heavily armed men broke in. They were plate-armoured, and bore the marks of a hard road on travel-worn garb.

'Stand down!' shouted Zintler, barring their passage with commendable bravery, seeing as how he was outnumbered eight to three. 'This is a private council – who dares to interrupt?'

The intruders parted, allowing one of their number to stride to the forefront. Unlike the others, he was helm-less, exposing a hawk-like visage barred by a long, carefully lacquered moustache. There could be no mistaking the proud features that adorned coins and devotional lockets from Helmgart to Middenheim, though they had been badly disfigured by claw-marks along one

cheek. The lines were still raw and bloody, making the Reiksmarshal look half daemonic.

'What is this rabble?' rasped Kurt Helborg, striding up to the
electors. 'Where is Todbringer? Where are the Reikland generals? And who is this beggar?'

Martak bowed clumsily. 'The Supreme Patriarch, my lord. Or
so they tell me.'

Helborg stared at him, incredulous, before turning to Gausser.
'My lord elector, tell me this is some foul jest.'

Gausser shot him an apologetic look. 'Times are not what they
were, lord Reiksmarshal.'

Von Liebwitz drew up to Helborg then, a rapt expression on
her aged face. 'You are *alive!* Thank the gods. Now we can plan
our defence in earnest – what of the Emperor? What of Lord
Schwarzhelm?'

Helborg briefly looked lost then, as if the questions confused
him. His gaze ran around the chamber, from Gausser to von Liebwitz to Haupt-Anderssen to Martak. '*This* is the war council?'

Martak sniffed noisily, dislodging a troublesome clot of dried
mucus that had been plaguing him since waking. 'Who were you
expecting? You took every blade worth having north.'

Helborg repeated his incredulous stare, before shaking his
head with resignation. 'Then these are the tools I have. They
must suffice.' He turned to Gausser, the only figure in the room
he seemed to have any rapport with. 'I bring hard truths with me.
The Emperor is slain. Our northern armies are scattered, and the
enemy follows hard on my heels. We do not have much time, and
the city must be secured. What preparations have been made?'

Gausser glanced at von Liebwitz, whose eyes strayed towards
Haupt-Anderssen, who quickly deferred to Zintler.

'We were debating our first moves, my lord,' said the Reikscaptain, haltingly. 'The news from Marienburg is just in, and we
had not yet determined just where to concentrate–'

'Taal's teeth,' swore Helborg. He beckoned to his preceptor.

'Find out what forces are still in the city. Order the gates closed – no man leaves without my order. Secure the armouries. Appoint a quartermaster-general and place all water-sources and food-stores under his protection. See the Imperial standard is flown from the Palace summit, and spread the word that the Emperor has routed the enemy at Heffengen and will soon return. Make sure this is believed.'

His preceptor saluted, and departed to carry out his orders, taking the remaining knights with him. As he left, Martak chuckled softly. This was why Kurt Helborg was Reiksmarshal, and why fighting men worshipped the earth he trod. For the first time since his appointment, Martak wondered whether he actually might survive this war.

'May I say, sir, your return seems timely,' Martak said.

Helborg looked back at him doubtfully.

'We will see,' he muttered. 'We will see.'

Deep in the foundations of the old city, far below the streets and avenues, the vapours never ceased. They curled along the brick-lined sewers, steaming from the surface of the foetid waters. They pooled in the dank, dark recesses of ancient cesspits and long-buried catacombs, curling like hair amid the endless shadows.

No natural light penetrated so far down, and the only illumination was the pale glow of phosphorescent mosses clambering all across the crumbling masonry. The moss had spread quickly since its introduction, racing down the winding shafts and choked tunnels, feeding on the filth that sank to the city's base. It was everywhere now, smothering all other growths and lending the forgotten ways of Altdorf a ghostly sheen.

It got worse the lower one went, until the waterways were a thick soup of throbbing spore-clumps and the luminous tendrils hung from the low ceiling like stalactites. At the very bottom, in the deepest shafts of the undercity, the infestation was so complete that it felt like the entire structure was built from nothing more than fronds of softly iridescent lichen.

Down there, behind a locked door under a low stone archway, the noise of bubbling and hissing never ceased. The vapours poured out from the cracks in the door, seething out from between planks of long-rotten wood before drifting off down the myriad tunnels of the labyrinth beyond.

Within the chamber lay a bizarre panoply of instruments – copper kettles, alembics, condensers, cauldrons and mixing-pots. Concoctions bubbled in a dozen bronze jars, sending lurid coloured steam twisting up to the low chamber roof. Further in, the contents became more grisly – corpses, as thin and wasted as rabbits, hung from iron hooks on the wall, each one bearing the signs of horrific illness. Some had burst torsos, their entrails hanging from the rupture and dripping steadily onto the filth-strewn floor below. Others had no eyes, or obscene growths suspended from their agonised flesh. All bore expressions of unbearable horror on their drawn faces, the marks of their final struggles against the poxes that had killed them.

Further down, moving along narrow passageways, the sounds of bubbling and gurgling grew louder. Gouts of steam hissed from tangled iron piping, and an immense pendulum ticked back and forth as if counting time towards the end of the world. More jars and phials cluttered every surface, each one fizzing and boiling with an endless variety of lurid liquids.

Right at the far end of those chambers, deep down in the basement, a hunched figure worked steadily over a long, low bench. He was grotesquely fat, and the jowls of his under-chin wobbled as he moved. A thick-lipped mouth murmured and drooled, sending lines of yellowish sputum coursing over a boil-encrusted face. Perhaps once he had been a mortal man, for he still wore the remnants of Imperial garb amid the folds and sags of his overspilling corpulence. Now, though, he was changed, given unnatural bulk beyond the dreams of even the most assiduous glutton. Tiny creatures, no more than jaws and eyes attached to slug-like sacs of blubber, crawled all over him, wriggling between the grease-stained fabric of his clothes.

He hummed to himself as he worked, transferring frothing potions from vial to vial, mixing them, testing them, observing the results on a long, ink-stained ledger before stacking the glassware back amid the racks on the walls and starting again.

Behind him, huger than any of the others, a black iron cauldron stood, squat as a gravid sow and thick with the patina of ages. A daemon's face had been hammered onto the swollen curve of the bowl, spewing excreta from a fanged mouth. Within that cauldron bubbled the strongest broth of all – a noxious brew that made the air above it tremble. The fat-slick surface broke, and a desperate hand burst out, clutching at the side of the cauldron and gripping tight.

The grotesque alchemist saw the fingers scrabbling for purchase and chuckled wetly.

'Oh, no,' he chided, reaching over and prising the hand from the cauldron's edge. 'Not again. Stay down, and drink it up. It will be over quicker that way.'

He shoved the arm back under and held it there. A flurry of bubbles plopped up, accompanied by what sounded like desperate gagging. After a while the bubbles ran out, and the alchemist withdrew his hand. He brought it up to his mouth, and licked the liquids from it with a long, prehensile tongue.

'Almost there,' he murmured, savouring the taste.

From further along, past the cauldron and into the shadows beyond, came the sound of desperate, furious weeping. The alchemist frowned, and looked up.

'What is this?'

He shuffled past the cauldron, squeezing his heft past the cluttered work surfaces, wobbling over towards a series of iron cages bolted to the walls. Living men and women huddled inside them, their faces stark with terror. Most already showed signs of sickness. All were famished.

'No more of this!' the alchemist warned, brandishing a huge ladle like a weapon. 'You are the *lucky* ones. You have been chosen. Show some respect.'

The captive mortals stared back at him, some with disbelief, some with rank fear, a few with some residual defiance.

They had seen what had happened to the others. They knew what was coming for them.

'We are *nearly there* now,' said the alchemist, his phlegmy voice almost tender. 'Nearly there.'

He shuffled back to the cauldron, and started to stir. As he did so, the surface steamed and bubbled, filling the air with a hot, sweet, overpowering aroma of putrescence. Translucent slops hit the floor as the ladle stirred. Some of those slops were moving.

The alchemist leaned over the cauldron's edge and took a long, deep sniff. As he did so, something stirred under the surface – a shadow moved, as if a creature of the deep had made its home amid the greasy soup of flesh and fat.

'Quicken, now, great one,' cooed the alchemist. 'Festus calls you. The Leechlord smoothes the way between the worlds.' His grin broadened, exposing flattened, butter-yellow teeth. 'Altdorf awaits. It has no idea of the delights in store.'

He stirred faster, making the broth ripple.

'But it will soon,' he slurred, growing sweatily excited. 'Oh, yes. It will very soon.'

EIGHT

Leoncoeur rode out, feeling the harsh wind brush against his face. His sword was already slick with the blood of the slain – no excursion into the countryside around Couronne passed without encountering the dregs of Mallobaude's corruption. The land still crawled with sorcery, as dark as oil and stained deep into the soil.

Ahead of him, barren fields marched away to the north. To his right stood a scraggy mass of forest, choked with briars and bearing the dank smell of decay. The land fell away sharply as the trees clustered, tumbling towards the river Gironne as it wound its uncertain way towards the distant coast.

Leoncoeur leaned forward in the saddle, scouring the landscape ahead. His quarry could not be far off.

Then he saw it – a ragged bundle of robes, scampering madly, haring for the cover of the trees. Leoncoeur recognised the long pointed hat, the trailing wisps of a ruddy overgrown beard.

He kicked his steed into a gallop, hoping to run the hedge-witch down before he vanished into the shadow of the trees. Such wizards were petty necromancers and curse-pedlars, but in such straitened times even their trivial malice was cause for concern.

The hedge-witch sprinted hard, knowing his danger, nearly stumbling as he careered down the slope towards the woodland. He was already close to safety.

Leoncoeur spurred his mount on, kicking up mud as he went, tearing towards the rapidly approaching line of trees. He pulled his blade back, readying for the lean and swipe that would take the witch's head off.

Just at the last moment, the man swerved aside, darting as if alerted by premonition, and scampered under the protection of the first gnarled branches.

Leoncoeur did not hesitate. Crouching low, he crashed through the forest's edge after his prey, ignoring the whiplash branches across his face and arms.

'Yield yourself!' he commanded, made angry by the missed chance.

He could still see the hedge-witch ahead of him, swerving desperately between black-barked tree-trunks and slipping on the greasy leaf-litter. Soon the forest would grow too dense for the pursuit, and Leoncoeur's charger would become useless.

With a savage kick of his spurs, Leoncoeur goaded his steed into a final burst of speed, sending it thundering across the rapidly closing terrain. Just as the hedge-witch made for a screen of wickedly thorned brambles, Leoncoeur's sword lashed down, raking across the man's cloaked back and cutting down to the bone beneath.

The witch screamed, dropping to the ground and writhing. Leoncoeur pulled his steed around tightly and spurred it back towards the stricken wretch. The wizard tried to rise, to drag himself to his feet and somehow stagger out of danger, but it was too late. Leoncoeur rode him down, crushing his bloodied frame into the mire and silencing the shrill screams. Then he drew his horse to a halt, working hard to calm the enraged steed, before dismounting and striding over towards the remains.

He gazed down with disgust. The man was just another impoverished village trickster with delusions of power. It would have been better to have made an example of him, to have drawn his guts slowly out in front of a crowd of appreciative peasants. Out here in the wilds, the lesson was wasted.

Leoncoeur plunged his sword into the twitching corpse, just to be sure, then pulled the blade free, noting with distaste the stains along the steel.

He felt soiled. Running down such filth was a task barely worthy of his station. He needed something better, something *grander*, befitting the station he had once enjoyed.

Ahead of him, the Gironne churned at the base of a deep creek, its banks thickly cloaked with trees and creeping vines. The leaves had an unhealthy sheen to them, as if rot had penetrated down to the sap.

Leoncoeur tied his horse up and trudged down to the water's edge. He slithered down the muddy bank and knelt down, dipping his sword into the murky water. Grabbing tufts of grass, he wiped the gore from the blade, working slowly and patiently. His sword was his life, and had been ever since he had been a raw novice with more bravery than sense.

He had always done things diligently. He had always served, and yet the reward had been snatched away.

His blade now a little cleaner, he replaced it in the scabbard. Then he knelt over the water's edge, thirst kindling in his throat. He stared at the scummy surface, and changed his mind. Something foul was getting into the rivers – they were beginning to smell like sewers.

Just as he was about to pull away, he caught sight of his reflection gazing up at him. He looked haggard, his noble bearing thinned out by Mallobaude's treachery and le Breton's acquisition of his birthright.

Then, looking closer, he saw that it was not his reflection at all – he had not lost *that* much weight. The golden locks were too long, the face too slender. A face clarified below the filmy surface, one he remembered from the distant past.

'My Lady,' he breathed, falling to both knees.

The waters stirred, bubbling into a froth, then broke. A figure rose from the river, lithe and translucent. She wore a gown of purest emerald, and it flowed across her like cataracts. Her face was hard to look at for long – it had a fey, dangerous quality, as if touched by elven magic. She remained standing in the river, the weeds draped around her ankles, gazing benevolently down at the kneeling knight before her. The sunlight became a little less grey, and the leaves were touched with a golden sheen.

Leoncoeur felt his heart-rate pick up, and his face went hot.

'Lion-heart,' the Lady murmured, her voice as ephemeral as the wind in the reeds. 'You were ever my favourite. My *champion*.'

Leoncoeur looked up at her, and the sight of her unfiltered beauty pierced his heart. 'Then *why*, lady?' he asked.

She knew what he meant. Her face did not give away pity – it would never do that – but understanding shone in her emerald eyes.

'All things are changing,' she said softly. 'The world turns faster, and the old gods are passing. This realm is only one of many, lion-heart – you could not be contained by it forever.'

Leoncoeur struggled to hear her. When they had spoken before, so long ago that it seemed like a dream of infancy, she had been proud and imperious, a queen in her invincible realm. Now, she whispered as if sick, her otherworldly voice as faint as an invalid's.

'My *soul* is Bretonnia,' Leoncoeur said, not understanding what she was telling him.

'It was. The Green Knight has come to claim his kingdom. It has always been his. Your destiny is different. You will die alone, my champion, far from home. You will never take the throne again.'

The words were harsh, and they cut him deeply. Deep down, Leoncoeur had never quite lost the half-hope that le Breton was an apparition sent by the fell gods, some terrible shade who would be exposed in due time, leaving the throne free for him again.

'Once, you told me different,' he said, unable to keep the ghost of reproach from his voice.

'I never tell false,' she said. 'I told you that you would lead your people into glory. That remains your destiny, should you be strong enough to seize it. Are you strong enough, lion-heart? Or has this bitterness quenched your fire?'

'Never. Command me.'

A chill breeze made the river ripple, stirring the trees around them. The Lady shivered, and her impeccable features creased. 'Great powers are moving. They converge on Sigmar's city. The Fallen covet it, as do the Dead. Those who remain will not stand unaided. That is where the hammer will fall, and that is where the world will change.'

'But my realm–'

'It is no longer your realm.'

'My people are hard-pressed.'

'The Green Knight is their guardian now,' the Lady said, almost sorrowfully, as if that alone presaged the end of her hopes for something better. 'I tell you the truth. Is that not what you have been praying for?'

Leoncoeur looked at her intently. The beauty was still there, as was the ethereal power, but both were diminished. She was fighting against something. This apparition was costing her, and the price would be steep. 'All lands are dying,' he said, realising what made her sick. 'They have poisoned the rivers.'

'You asked for a way to serve,' she said. 'I have given it to you.' She gave him a fond, faint smile. 'If you spurn the offer, you might yet live. There might be some kind of service for you in safer places, of a meagre sort.'

Then it was Leoncoeur's turn to smile. When their faces cast off the most oppressive lines of care, they looked so alike. 'I never craved meagre service. I was a king.'

'You still can be.' The Lady began to sink, sliding down into the brackish waters. 'The City of Sigmar, my champion. Already its foundations tremble. That is the anvil upon which the fate of man will be tempered.'

'Then will you live, Lady?' asked Leoncoeur, watching with concern as she slipped towards the Gironne's tainted waters. 'Can you be saved?'

'Ask only of mortal fates,' she whispered, her tresses sliding under the surface. 'Look for me in pure waters, but the games of gods do not concern you.'

But they did. They always had. As Leoncoeur watched her subside into nothingness again, as the golden edges faded from the leaves and the air sunk once more into mud-stinking foulness, he felt as if his heart had been ripped out. He remained immobile for a long time, his knees sinking steadily into the mire, his hands limp by his sides.

'The City of Sigmar,' he murmured.

No force of the Empire had stirred itself when Bretonnia had been riven by war. Very rarely had the great and the good of Karl Franz's realm given much thought to their chivalrous cousins over the Grey Mountains. Then again, it was foolish to assume that they had not been hard-pressed themselves. Leoncoeur had heard the rumours running through court – that disaster had overtaken Marienburg, that the north was aflame, that even the greenskins were terrified of something and remained hidden in their forest lairs.

He felt icy water creep under the skin of his armour plate, rousing him from his lethargy. He stood cumbersomely, hauling on looped creepers. No remnant of the Lady's presence remained, and the Gironne looked as turgid and weed-choked as before.

Leoncoeur trudged back to his mount, slipping on the mud-slick riverbank as he went.

'Altdorf,' he said, musingly, already gauging the distances. 'If that is where the fates are to be written, we must not be missing.'

He thought of the hot blood of his countrymen, and their desire to exchange the grim hunts after petty quarry for the blood-and-thunder of a real war. Many still looked to him; if he ordered them, they would ride with him still.

He reached his horse, and untied it.

'So be it,' he said to himself, smiling dryly as he prepared to mount again. 'I asked for a path. I have been given one.'

He vaulted into the saddle. He turned one last time, gazing back to where ripples still radiated, and saluted.

'Thank you,' he said.

Then he kicked his mount up the slope, and was soon gone.

In his absence, the riverbank sunk into silence once more, broken only by the faint slap of the river-current against the shore, and the mournful wind in the twisted branches.

The deathmoon rode in the eastern sky, glowing with a sick greenish sheen. Its wholesome companion was nowhere to be seen.

Such as was foretold, Vlad thought, looking up into heavens.

The land around him was limned with a ghostly light, tainted as stomach-bile. Morrslieb had ever cast a corrupted illumination, but now its noxious effluence seemed worse than ever. Its scarred face was bloated, presaging the onset of Geheimnisnacht.

That should have made him glad. In the old days, when the deathmoon rode high on bitter, cloudless nights he had gloried in the visions it had brought him. He had raised scores of unliving to march under his black banners, and their bones had shone under the glow of the tainted heaven-spoor.

He stood before Castle Drakenhof's ruined gates, his long cloak snapping in the night wind, and gazed out over the host he had summoned. As yet it did not compare to the vast armies he had once marched west with, but it was grand enough for now. Crowds of Sylvanian troopers, shivering in the cold, stood in decent approximations of Imperial infantry squares. They were dwarfed by the clattering ranks of skeletons and zombies, some pulled from the dark soil just hours ago by Vlad's necromancers. Skinless horses walked silently along avenues between ghostly regiments, their skull-faced riders showing no emotion as they surveyed the lines of the undead host. Black banners flew, their tattered edges pulled by roving winds.

'Will it be enough?' Vlad asked.

No one answered. He stood alone. On his first such crusade, Isabella had been by his side, counselling him, encouraging him. Her absence made his heart ache – to the extent he had a heart, at any rate. The grief was real enough.

In the far distance, thunder cracked along the eastern horizon. The sawtooth edge of the mountains briefly became visible, black against the outer dark. Carrion crows cawed as they flocked above in huge swarms, ready to fly west ahead of the main host.

Vlad watched them mob and swirl. There were many hours left before the dawn, and they could make good time under cover of night. Though he planned to drive the army onwards even during the daylight hours, he knew they would struggle under the sun's harsh glare. The mortals would need to be fed and rested, and even the dead would require constant supervision from his covens of spell-winders.

They would make for the Stir, taking any towns and villages on the way and turning their impoverished inhabitants to the cause. Since the Law of Death had been loosened, the many graveyards of his cursed province would readily yield up more fell troops for the host, and so the numbers of both mortal and unliving would swell with every league they marched. Once at the river, they would take barges downstream, riding the flood as the dark waters foamed and rushed west.

He did not expect any serious resistance before reaching the borders of Reikland. The Empire was like a rotten fruit – still intact on the outside, but eaten hollow within. The fortified city of Wurtbad might prove a temporary delay, but he had already taken steps to ease that potential barrier.

Behind him, he heard the howls of vargheists as they loped and swooped amid the ruins. He sensed the shuddering movements of ghouls, and saw the shimmer-pattern of unquiet spirits. Those spectral presences would soon send the entire realm into paroxysms of fear, just as they had done so long ago. And yet, this time he was not marching to bring the Empire to its knees. Far from it.

He looked down at the roll of parchment in his left hand, sealed with a great wax glob and marked with the signet-device of the von Carsteins. He remembered how difficult it had been to find the words to use.

> I am aware that the mutual enmity between our peoples will make this proposal a hard one to entertain fairly. I have no doubt, though, given the circumstances, you will see past ancient prejudices and buried grievances. You will have seen the same auguries as we have, and you will know what is at stake. And, after all, do I not have some prior claim to this title? Or does right of conquest count for nothing in these debased times?

Vlad was not sure about those lines, but he had left them in. The detail of the law could be hammered out in person – the important thing was to make the approach now, before the city was cut off by the hosts of the North.

He looked up, just in time to see an enormous bat flutter down from the castle rafters. Its body was as big as a wolf's, and its leathery wings had a downdraft like a hunting eagle's. More bats followed their leader down, hovering in pack formation, until nine pairs of red eyes glowed before him in the night.

Vlad wrapped the parchment tightly in oilskin and tied the bundle with twine. He held it up, and the hovering bat took it in its powerful jaws.

'Go swift, go safe,' whispered Vlad, reaching up to caress the animal.

Then the whole flock of fell creatures shot upward into the night, spiralling high over the assembled army and heading west.

'Their pride will be the greatest obstacle,' he mused aloud. 'Can the Empire humble itself enough to see sense? That is yet to be decided.' Then he smiled coldly to himself, feeling his long fangs snick on his lower lip. 'All men can change, and every mortal has a turning-point. We just have to find where that is. Would you not agree, Herrscher?'

The witch hunter stepped from the shadow of the gates, flanked by ashen-faced guards. His own skin was as white as bone, shrivelled dry onto his prominent skeleton. The clothes he had worn when fully alive now hung from him loosely, and his pistol-belt had slipped almost comically about his thighs.

Herrscher stared out at the host before them. Then he looked down at his hands. He was trembling.

'The shock will pass,' said Vlad, not unkindly. 'You forget the worst of the pain, in time.'

Herrscher looked at him, a mix of horror and hatred on his face. For all that, he did not reach for his weapon. 'How is it... *possible?*' he rasped, and his once-powerful voice was as thin as corpse-linen.

Vlad sighed. He would have to get used to many such initiations into the half-life of undead servitude. 'You do not need to know that. All you need to know now is that my will gives you breath. You will accept that. You will come to cherish it. The power of resistance you once commanded has gone, and you are my lieutenant now.'

Vlad regarded Herrscher with something approaching fondness. The witch hunter would never truly know it, but his position was one of the highest honour – other captains would be appointed, but he was the very first.

Herrscher looked like he wanted to scream, to dash his own brains out, to launch himself at Vlad and wring his neck, but of course none of those things were possible now. The witch hunter might be screaming on the inside, but he would do the bidding of the one who had raised him, just as Vlad did the bidding of Nagash who had raised *him*.

'Now come,' said Vlad, placing a gauntlet on Herrscher's shoulder and leading him out from the gate's shadow. 'We march within the hour. Let me show you your new servants.'

Helborg woke with a jolt. He was still on his feet, propped up against a wall. He did not remember falling asleep. He had hardly been able to close his eyes for the three days since he had been back in Altdorf, and when he did his mind swiftly filled with nightmares. He saw, over and over, the Emperor felled above Heffengen, plummeting to the earth in a deathly spiral before disappearing from view.

The grief was still raw. Karl Franz had been the undisputed master of the sprawling Empire, the only man with the patience, the guile and the sheer presence to hold the fractious provinces together. Only Karl Franz could have faced down Volkmar in one of his tirades, or kept Gelt from flying off into another half-considered magical endeavour, or resisted the grim implacability of Schwarzhelm in his worst moods. Karl Franz had kept them all in line.

If Helborg was honest, only in the past few days had he truly understood what a titanic achievement that had been. The demands of electors, courtiers, wizards, engineers and generals were endless. Every hour brought new demands to his door, burdening him with both the vital and the trivial. For the moment, he had cowed the three electors into submission and ensured his mastery over the city defences, but it would only be a matter of time before they started scheming again. Both Gausser and von Liebwitz saw the present crisis as an opportunity for advancement, and even Haupt-Anderssen sniffed the chance to profit from the flux. Only the wizard Martak seemed to understand the Empire's desperate straits, and he was little better than a pedlar, looked down on by his more elevated kin in the colleges and disregarded by the Palace staff who served him.

Helborg pushed himself from the wall he had been leaning against, cursing himself for losing consciousness. He was still in full ceremonial armour. He wore his Reiksguard symbols at all times to remind the populace – and, in truth, himself – that he was the last remaining link to the past. Out of all the great heroes of the Empire – Gelt, Volkmar, Schwarzhelm, Huss – only he remained, isolated and cut off from what remained of the northern armies. There was no knowing if any of them still lived, and to even contemplate mounting a significant defence without them felt alien and uncomfortable.

Helborg blinked heavily, hoping none had seen his lapse. The corridor around him was empty, a stone shell lined with torches. Through narrow slit-windows he could see that it was nearly dark outside, and the night's chill was creeping through the granite. For a moment he could not remember why he had come this way, then it all came back – inspection of the northern gate with Zintler. He had made it as far as the fortified citadel above the gatehouse. He must have just paused for a moment.

He shook himself down, still feeling groggy from lack of rest, and went quickly up towards the parapet level. He climbed two spiral staircases, strode down a long archer's gallery, then finally emerged into the open air again.

Zintler was waiting for him on the open summit of the gatehouse, a wide courtyard ringed with shoulder-height battlements. A huge flagpole stood in the centre of the space, hung with an Imperial standard. As he passed it, Helborg could smell the mould-spores on the fabric.

Even here, he thought grimly.

Zintler saluted as Helborg approached, not giving any indication that he had been kept waiting.

'How stands it?' asked Helborg, joining him on the northern edge of the courtyard.

'Plague has reached the city,' said Zintler. 'Barely two-thirds of the men capable of carrying a sword can still lift one. It will only get worse.'

Helborg nodded grimly. Similar reports were coming in from all across Altdorf. Despite guarding the water supplies tightly, something was infecting the poorer quarters and spreading out to the garrisons. The air itself was foul, and carried an edge of bitterness when the wind blew.

'The walls?' Helborg asked, peering over the edge to look at them for himself.

The northern gate had been built up and augmented over hundreds of years, and was now a vast pile of age-darkened stone, crested with gunnery emplacements and the snarling golden gargoyles of griffons and lions. Bulwarks and kill-points jostled with one another in a cunning series of funnelling formations. By the time an enemy got anywhere close to the gates themselves, they would have been pummelled by artillery and ranged magic, doused in boiling oil and pelted with building rubble, then finally overwhelmed by sorties streaming out from hidden posterns all along the ingress way.

At least, that was how it had been in the past, when the Empire's armies were more numerous than the sands on the grey Nordland shore. Now Helborg doubted whether he had enough able bodies to occupy more than half the defensive positions available to him.

'The walls are crumbling,' said Zintler flatly. He reached over to the top of the battlements and prised a section of mortar from the joints. It disintegrated between his finger and thumb. Once again, Helborg smelled the stench of rot.

'It can't be crumbling,' Helborg muttered. 'This is granite from the Worlds Edge peaks.'

'The Rot,' said Zintler, as if that explained everything.

They were already referring to the Rot in the streets – the malaise that seemed to spread through everything, spoiling milk, fouling foodstuffs, infecting living flesh.

'Enough of that,' snapped Helborg. 'Summon the master engineer and get him to shore up the foundations. The gates must hold.'

'Master Ironblood is already engaged–'

'Summon him!' Helborg snapped. 'I don't care what he's tinkering with – the gates must hold.'

Zintler bowed, admonished. The Reikscaptain had the grey lines of fatigue around his eyes, just as they all did. Helborg wondered if he had had any sleep either.

'What reports from the west?' Helborg asked, running a weary hand over his cropped scalp.

'The enemy draws close to Carroburg.'

'Have the Greatswords been pulled back?'

'The messages were sent.'

'That is not what I asked.'

Zintler looked rattled. 'I do not know, lord. We send messengers out along the river, and never hear from them again. We send fortified contingents in barges, and they disappear. I do not have enough men to chase them all down. We do what we can, but–'

'So be it,' growled Helborg, not wanting to hear any more excuses. Zintler was doing his best, but the inexorable tide of work was getting to them all. Carroburg housed some of the finest regiments in the Reikland – if they could be salvaged, then the city's defences would look a lot more secure. If they decided to make a doomed stand at the western city, then things looked even bleaker. 'There is nothing more to be done.'

Helborg's cheek flared with pain. The daemon's claws had bitten deep, and though the wound had closed over, it had never truly healed. He was aware how it made him look. He could feel poisons at work under the scabby skin, and knew that no apothecary would be able to salve them.

It is my penance, he mused bleakly. *For failing my liege.*

Zintler's face flushed. 'I can try again,' he said.

'Too late now,' growled Helborg, cursing the luck that seemed ever against them. 'If they come, they come. Until then, look to the walls. Organise details to begin work on the gatehouse this night, and bring me reports from the watch. We need clean water from somewhere, and I cannot believe *all* the shafts are tainted.'

Zintler saluted smartly, and walked across the courtyard to the stairwell. Helborg watched him go, noting the stooped line of his shoulders.

Karl Franz would have handled him better, he thought to himself. *He would have handled all of them better.*

Helborg limped over to the very edge of the parapet, and gazed moodily north. Out under the cover of the encroaching dark, the tree line brooded like a vast slick of tar. The foliage had been allowed to creep closer to the walls than it should have done. Everything seemed to be growing at a burgeoning rate, blooming in a mire of foulness far more quickly than it could be cut down again.

Above the jagged lines of the firs, Morrslieb rode low, its virulent orb glowing yellow-green. As Helborg's eyes strayed towards it, the wound in his cheek throbbed harder.

Behind him, the soft light of lanterns flickered into life, one by one, as the citizens began the nightly chore of warding against the night-terrors. Bonfires would be lit at every street intersection, and patrols doubled up. That did not stop the regular disappearance of citizens, nor the growing spread of the pox, nor the uncontrollable nightmares that made children and adults alike scream in their sweat-sodden cots.

Out there, somewhere, the hordes of the End Times were coming, burning and hacking, and with only one goal in mind.

'I will *resist* you,' murmured Helborg, fighting against exhaustion, knowing how much labour still lay ahead of him. 'We will not retreat. We will meet you with our blades and our hearts intact, for we are *men*, and you have never extinguished us, not after three thousand years of trying.'

As he spoke, his gauntlets curled into fists. He stood atop the pinnacle of the northern gate, with the entire city at his back, and cursed the darkness.

Out in the gathering night, nothing changed. The trees rustled in the distance, rubbing branches against one another as if they were greedy hands clutching weapons. The eerie calls of night-birds shrieked into the gloom, and the uncaring stars came out, just as they had done since the world was made.

Slowly, his body shot through with the gathering weight of exhaustion, Helborg turned from the vista, and limped back into the gatehouse. His tasks for the night were only just beginning.

NINE

The river Reik had once flown strongly west of Carroburg. It had plunged into a narrow gorge, foaming and hissing, before reaching the cataracts that sent it tumbling down forty feet of rock-strewn white water. The cliffs on either side of the valley soared up precipitously, clad in dark firs and dripping with a constant mist of spray. The famed citadel itself had been raised on the northern shore – a spur of black rock, wound about with tight circles of inner walls and close-packed towers. Carroburg perched above the drop like a crow poised for scavenging. The banners of Middenland hung from its sheer-angled tower roofs, bearing the device of the white wolf atop a blue ground.

Dominating the city was its fortress, built for defence, with soaring outer walls jutting from sheer cliffs of rain-slick rock. Only two gates broke the circle of the citadel's lower walls, one looking east towards Altdorf, the other west towards Marien-burg. In normal times both were kept open during the daylight hours, though for many weeks they had been barred and locked tight. A meagre force of Greatswords had issued out along the great western road to relieve Marienburg once news of its siege had come in, but no news had returned regarding their fate, and the city's burgomeisters had feared the worst. After that, no living soul passed the cordon of the walls, and the populace huddled within their protection even as the nights were filled with lurid screaming and the waters around them seemed to thicken and spoil.

Travelling at the head of their vast host, Otto and Ethrac paused at the point the Reik curved steeply north towards the Carroburg gorge. They were both riding Ghurk, and had to yank his ears hard to get him to stop lumbering.

'What do you make of it, o my brother?' asked Otto, licking his lips.

'Satisfactory,' replied Ethrac, running a wizened finger around the lip of his plague-bells. 'Better than I hoped for.'

In years past, they would have been staring up at a daunting defensive position, a natural funnel-point overlooked by formidable gunnery and backed up by the feared garrison of Greatswords. Now, the Reik was clogged with great mats of grey-fronded moss. In defiance of the strong current, the mats had floated upriver, lodging against the bank and blocking the flow. As the flood around them ebbed, more clots of foliage bumped and twisted upstream, further silting up the power of the waters.

Even as the river had choked on the thick layers of unnatural vegetation, the forest on either bank had burgeoned and burst its bounds, sending meandering tendrils snaking out into what had once been open ground. Tree-trunks had burst, exposing thick smears of throbbing mucus within. Briars had shot from the boiling earth, tangling and throttling anything they came across. The naked cliffs below Carroburg were now writhing with tentacles, spikes and suckers. The cataract itself was gone, replaced by a slithering slop of viscous algal slime.

Otto gazed up at the fortress. The base of its still-mighty walls was a hundred feet away. He reached for a copper spyglass at his belt, and placed it against his bloodshot eye. As he did so, the lens blinked.

'They are locked up within it, o my brother,' Otto observed, moving the spyglass across the battlements. He could see spear-tips moving across the parapets. There were still artillery pieces on the high battlements, and some of them might do a little damage. 'They are not getting out now. Ghurk will feast on hot flesh this night.'

Ghurk chortled, making his rolling shoulders shudder. Ethrac stood up, shaking his bell-staff. 'The foundations will moulder,' he muttered, invoking the dark magic that welled up all around him so easily now. 'The stone will break. The bones will snap.'

Otto joined his brother's chuckling. He had not slain in earnest since Marienburg, and the blood on his scythe was almost dry. 'It will be a *mercy* for them,' he said. 'Your medicines! They will splutter on them.'

Ghurk started to lumber onwards, his cloven hooves sinking deep into the muddy mulch below. He waded across the channel where the river had been, and sank barely up to his shins. All around him, the vanguard of the pestilential host advanced in turn, surging across what should have been a raging torrent. Norscan warriors strode out, swinging their cleavers in armoured fists, followed by the long ranks of disease-addled plague-zombies.

The trees around them shivered, and strange beasts crept out from the shadows – wolves with swollen bellies and sore-thick jowls, bears with split torsos and glistening ribcages, goat-like horrors with eyeless faces and dribbling withers. The whole of nature had been perverted, and the coming of the Glottkin roused them all from whatever dank pit of misery they had curled into.

Otto felt a savage joy kindle in his rotten heart. Ethrac's magicks would do their work soon, and the citadel's foundations would begin to crack. He could already see the results – poison-vines prising the block apart and freezing it into powder. The air stank with glorious virulence, ushering the numberless hordes up the gorge mouth and towards the high gates.

'Faster, Ghurk-my-brother,' Otto urged, slapping his brother on his shoulder. 'We are dallying. Show some speed!'

Ghurk issued a joyous bark, and started to pick up the pace. His hooves splashed deep as he rolled up the choked river-bed. In his wake, the entire horde did likewise, shambling and surging like some colossal tide of incoming filth. A thousand parched throats croaked out battle-cries, and sonorous war horns boomed a hoarse, echoing dirge.

Far ahead, from atop the tallest tower, the trumpets of the Empire issued their counter-challenge. Puffs of white smoke rippled along the parapets, presaging the blackpowder volleys that would soon be cracking and spitting among them.

Otto cared nothing for that. The seamy air coursed through his lank hair as he held tight onto Ghurk's yawing body. Soon they would be up among them, breaking skulls.

There were times when the resistance of mortals genuinely puzzled him. What could be better than indulging in the glorious foulness of the Plaguefather? What could be better than to be blessed with such noxious, bountiful gifts?

Still, for whatever reason, they failed to grasp the possibilities and held on to their dreary, grey lives surrounded by fear and privation. He could not be too miserable about that – it meant that there were wars to be fought, and so his scythe would always run with glutinous fluids, melting from the body and ready to be slurped down quick.

He grinned, seeing how quickly Ghurk ate up the ground and brought the doom of Carroburg closer. Ethrac continued to mutter, and inky clouds roiled across the beleaguered fortress, spinning out of the lead-grey sky like bile dropped into spoiled cream.

'Onward, my creatures!' Otto croaked, waving his scythe wildly and straining to catch the first sight of a terror-whitened mortal face. 'Climb fast! Drag them down! Suck their marrows and squeeze their eyes!'

The host answered him with a chorus of eager roars. Like some enormous, unnatural flood breaking in reverse, the host of the Plaguefather surged up the gorge mouth, clambered up the rocky cliffs and swarmed up towards the walls, its eyes already alight with slaughter.

Leoncoeur stood on the balcony of the old stone tower south of Couronne and gazed out across the assembled throng. The rain hammered down, just as it seemed to do all the time these days, turning the turf below into a quagmire. The eastern horizon grumbled and snapped with thunder, heralding the latest storm to blight the eastern marches. It was just as the Lady had told him – the world was coming apart at the edges, torn like a worn saddlebag.

He had chosen to make his appeal outside the boundaries of the city. Gilles le Breton had given him leave to make the case for Errantry, but it would have been discourteous to do so within the confines of Couronne. So the tidings had gone out to every keep and knightly hold between the coast and the mountains. Despite the weariness of the long and grinding war, those tidings had been answered handsomely, and knights had ridden through the wild nights to answer the summons.

That alone gave Leoncoeur some respite from the doubts that had plagued him. He may not have been king any longer, but they still responded to the House of Couronne when it called.

'My brothers!' he called out, shouting hard to make his voice carry across the crowds. Several hundred faces, many wearing open helms, others with their long hair lank from the rain, looked up at him expectantly. A riot of colours was visible on the collected tabards and tunics – a chequerboard of knightly houses in azure, sable, argent and crimson. Beyond the crowd, squires stood with the horses, enduring the ice-cold rain with grim fortitude.

'Much has changed since I last addressed you,' said Leoncoeur. 'The traitor Mallobaude is dead, and the kingdom rests again with its founder. We have seen signs and wonders in the night sky, and the curse of foul magic creeps across our realm. You know in your hearts that this is no ordinary war, such as we have endured for time immemorial. For once, the prophecies of End Times strike at the heart of it. My brothers, the final test is coming.'

As he spoke, he studied their reactions carefully. Bretonnian knights were hard-bitten warriors, some of the finest and most dangerous cavalry troops in the entire Old World. They were not given to flights of fancy, and took tales of woe and prophecy in their stride.

'Daemons are abroad again, and the servants of the foul gods march south with the storm at their backs. But as the winds of magic stir, other powers rise to contest it. I have seen the Lady, my brothers. She came to me from the waters and told me of the trials to come. This is why I call you here, so that her summons may be answered. I call Errantry, a crusade to strike at the heart of the new darkness.'

The knights watched him intently. From any other mouth, they might have scoffed at claims to have spoken with the Lady, but they knew Leoncoeur's past and none raised so much as a sceptical smile. As Leoncoeur spoke, he thought he even detected something like longing in their steady expressions. They had endured so much over the past months, and the prospect of something turning the tide of long, slow defeat spoke to their martial hearts.

'The axe will fall, not here, but on the City of Sigmar,' Leoncoeur told them. 'Even now, the enemy burns its way south, turning forests into haunts of ruin. We do not have long. If we muster as quickly as we may, even an unbroken ride across the mountains will scarce bring us there in time.'

Some scepticism showed on their faces now. The Empire was far away, and far removed from the concerns of Bretonnia. Relations between the two foremost kingdoms of men had ever been distant, riven as they were by both tongue and custom.

'I know what you feel!' Leoncoeur urged, forcing a smile. 'You say to yourselves that Altdorf is distant, and has armies of its own, and that the Emperor did not send his own troops to aid us when we were staring devastation in the face. All these things are true. If you refused this summons then no Bretonnian would blame you. None of your ladies would scorn you, and your people would not whisper of your honour in the shadows of their hovels.'

Leoncoeur leaned out, clutching the railing of the stone balcony.

'But consider this! The fire is coming. The war that will end all wars is breaking around us, and no realm on earth will be free of it. The anvil, the *heart* of it, is Altdorf. Here will the fates of men be decided, and here will the trials of the gods play out. Would you miss that contest? Would you wish to tell your children, if any future generation still lives in years to come, that the flower of Bretonnia was given the chance to intervene, and turned aside?'

The crowd began to murmur. Leoncoeur knew what stirred their hearts, and what kindled their ever-present sense of honour.

'There is *glory* to be had here!' he thundered, striking the railing with his gauntlet. 'When we swore our vows, we swore to guard the weak and cast down the tyrant. We swore to ride out against any creature of darkness that threatened our hearth and home, and to take the vengeance of the Lady to every last one of them.'

Shouts of agreement now, and a low murmur of assent. Their spirits were roused.

'In these times, every realm stands as our hearth, and the whole *world* is our home!' roared Leoncoeur. 'The corrupted will make no distinction between them and us. If Altdorf falls, who can doubt that Couronne will be next? When we shed blood on the Reik, we shed it for Bretonnia; when we shield the Empire from the storm, we shield the vales and towers of Quenelles and Bordeleaux!'

'Leoncoeur!' someone cried out, and the chant was taken up. *Leoncoeur! Leoncoeur!*

'I can promise you nothing but hardship!' Leoncoeur went on. 'We may not return from this adventure, for I have seen the hosts of the north, and they are vast beyond imagination. But which of us has ever shied from the fear of death? Which of us has ever shown cowardice in battle, or refused a duel against the mightiest of foes? If we are to die, then let it be where the storm breaks! If our souls are forfeit, then let it be fighting in the last battle of the Old World, where our sacrifice shall echo down the ages! And when the tally of years is complete and the reckoning made for all nations, let no man say that when the call came, Bretonnia failed to answer!'

They were roaring now, drawing swords and crying out for vengeance. Leoncoeur felt savage joy rise up within his gorge.

They are still my people, he thought. *And I am still their master.*

'For the Lady!' he cried, raising both arms high in defiance of the tempest that raged about the tower.

The knights before him replied without hesitation, shouting out their fealty in a single massed roar.

The Lady!

Leoncoeur relaxed at last then, knowing the first task was over. Errantry had been called, and the heavy cavalry that made Bretonnia feared throughout the world had been unleashed. The road ahead would be dark, but at least the path was set.

The Lady had spoken. Her crusade had begun.

The vampire army travelled fastest by night. Only the weakest of Vlad's servants suffered under the glare of the sun, but as the skies were relentlessly overcast and dark with rain even they were able to make some progress. In any case, the forest around them had burst into incredible growth, and the trees snaked and throttled one another in an orgy of tumescence.

Vlad rode at the head of his skeletal vanguard, looking about with distaste at the corruption of his land. Creepers twisted across the road, all bearing virulent fruits that burst with acid when trodden down. The soil itself seethed with fungi and clinging mosses, all striving with perverted fecundity to assert themselves against the foul growths around them.

This was *life* in all its disgusting, liquid excess. Even as a mortal man he would have found such violent displays of fertility alarming. As a lord of undeath, committed to the austere night-world of his Master, it was almost more than he could bear to endure it.

If he chose, he could have halted the army and summoned his necromancers and lesser vampire lords. They could have shrivelled the growths and bleached the fruits white. If they committed themselves for long enough, they could have parched the land from the Stir to the mountains, draining it of the noxious mucus that leaked from every suppurating pore and returning it to the barren waste it deserved to be.

But there was no time, and his energies needed to be husbanded for the trials ahead, so he grudgingly suffered his homeland to be overrun.

Not forever, he thought darkly, running his ancient eyes over the tangle of vines. *The cold fire will come, once all is accomplished.*

Herrscher rode beside him. Both their steeds were skeletons, their bones knitted together by dark magic and held in place by Vlad's will. The undead witch hunter looked a little less miserable than he had done, though he still slumped in the saddle.

'How do you find your gifts?' asked Vlad, trying to take his mind off the filth around him.

Herrscher shot him an incredulous look. 'Gifts?' He shook his emaciated head. 'You have poisoned me.'

'Learn to appreciate what you have been given. You are stronger than you were. You hear better, see better, and you will endure against all magic. Scorn this, and you remain a greater fool than when you lived.'

'This is what you wish for,' muttered Herrscher. 'Slaves, all of us.'

'Not quite. I wish for *order*. I wish for the weak to know their place, guarded over by their betters. Do sheep resent their shepherds? Or would they rather take their chances with the wolves?'

'I would have done,' retorted Herrscher, his face a picture of resentment.

'And that would be a terrible waste,' said Vlad. 'You are better at my side, where your talents can flourish. Do not resent the past – soon you will have trouble even remembering it.'

'So the past does not trouble you?' asked Herrscher, his lips curling sardonically. 'That is not what I heard.'

Vlad's anger rose, and he made to turn on Herrscher, when he suddenly noticed a flash of white in the road ahead. In an instant, he saw Isabella riding to greet him, alone under the trees, a look of admonishment on her perfect alabaster face, and he froze.

The illusion faded. More than one figure emerged from the arboreal gloom – eight shades, each as thin and drawn as dried fruit, carrying between them a palanquin of shimmering glass. Silently, they set the carriage down, and three women emerged, all of them wearing lace-edged gowns of purest white. They seemed to glow like moonlight, and their footfalls left no tracks in the sodden earth. They curtsied archaically, and shuffled closer.

Vlad mastered himself. He knew the names of the ladies well enough, and which master they served, though he had not expected to encounter them so soon.

'My lord von Carstein,' said the foremost of the pale creatures, her voice as dry and hollow as a coffin-echo. 'We had begun to worry. This land has become an abomination.'

'All lands have,' said Vlad, offering his hand for the lady to kiss. 'Why are you here, Liliet? I did not seek to find you for days hence.'

The white lady gave him a dry smile. 'Your servant Mundvard failed. Marienburg is a nest of writhing horrors, and the Empire has been driven back like whipped curs to Carroburg.'

'They are moving fast, then. What strength do they have?'

'They are led by three siblings – foul triplets, each blessed with grotesque gifts. One is the size of a house, and chews his way through fortifications like a fat child through sweetmeats. Their host is swollen beyond counting. Your servant did his best – I can vouch for that – but they will not be halted.' She shuddered distastefully. 'Such numbers. I would not have believed it, had I not seen it.'

Vlad pursed his fleshless lips together. 'And where is Mundvard now?'

'Gathering what forces he can. He sent us to you, and begs leave to join his army with yours north of Altdorf. He says that no action further west can delay the enemy now, and only a combined stand at the city holds the hope of resistance.'

'Oh, he said that, did he?' Vlad was irritated. Mundvard was a supreme fighter, but a poor general. More than that, it was not his place to dictate tactics to his betters – he should have delayed the Chaos forces for longer at the coast, giving time for Vlad to gather the greatest host he could. Now the need for haste, already pressing, had become overwhelming.

'He fought skilfully, lord,' said Liliet, a little coquettishly, given her cadaverous appearance.

'Not skilfully enough,' snarled Vlad. 'You do not need to return to him. Remain with me, and together we will cut a faster path. I will send messages via other means, and if he still commands more than a rabble of zombies, he can meet us in the Reikland.'

Liliet bowed, then looked sidelong at Herrscher. 'And who is this, my lord? Surely you have not been doling out the Kiss to mortals without the consent of the Master?'

Herrscher was looking at the three women with a mix of horror and fascination on his face. That was good – in the past, it would merely have been horror.

'My new lieutenant,' said Vlad kicking his horse into motion again and forcing the ladies to give way. 'Ride with us awhile, and tell us tales of old Marienburg. We make all haste to Wurtbad, and I am sure he can learn much from you on the way.'

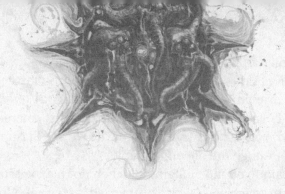

TEN

Captain Hans Blucher felt the stone crack before he heard it, and it made his blood freeze. The flags beneath his feet sprouted paper-thin fractures, which then widened to a blade's width.

'Maintain fire!' he bellowed, striding along the ranks of gunnery pieces. 'Let no man leave his station, or by Taal's beard I shall break his head apart with my own hands!'

The walls of Carroburg had been under sustained attack for over an hour. In his worst nightmares, Blucher could not have imagined such an assault. The earth itself seemed to have been roused against them, and the forest in every direction now rang with the tramp of hooves and iron-shod boots.

The rain had started to fall soon after the enemy had arrived. At first it had been like any other deluge, though soon the drops became heavier and heavier, until it was like trying to fight under a hail of mud splatters. Every exposed surface became greasy and treacherous, fouling the cannon wheels as they were rolled out and making men slip and stagger.

Blucher was stationed on the south wall, in command of many

of the bigger artillery pieces. Helblasters jostled on the narrow parapet alongside the bigger Great Guns, each one christened by their foundries in Nuln – *Grosse Bertha, Todslingeren, Trollsbane.* They had been firing without pause since the first emergence of the enemy, hurling their shot out at the horde and blasting great channels through the oncoming ranks.

'Ulric damn you all!' hollered Blucher, not paying too much attention to which god's wrath he invoked, so long as it inspired a faster work-rate from his men. 'Reload! They are pouring into the outer curtain!'

The blackpowder guns had reaped a terrible swathe, but it had merely sliced a tithe from the oncoming masses. They showed no fear, clambering over the twitching corpses of the felled, whooping and gurgling with glee. The driving mud-rain should have slowed them, washing them back down the steep cliff edges and into the grimy channel that had once been the Reik, but they seemed to thrive on it, slithering up through the deluge with the effluent streaming down their calloused faces.

Blucher's guns were arranged on the inner wall, high up above the first ring of courtyards. From their vantage they had been able to rain mortars and cannonballs with impunity, but now it felt as if the fortress's very foundations were shaking under them.

Blucher ran to the edge, skirting carefully around the red-hot maw of *Grosse Bertha* and taking care not to touch the metal. He reached the lip of the parapet and peered down.

What he saw took his breath away. The curtain wall was gone – overwhelmed, lost under a simmering carpet of limbs and tentacles. Shocked to his core, Blucher nearly lost his footing, and grabbed hold of the battlement's edge to steady himself.

Mere moments ago, the outer perimeter had been held by companies of archers and handgunners, bolstered by the few Greatswords Aldred had left behind before marching out on his doomed attempt to relieve Marienburg. It had been a diminished company, to be sure, but it should have held out for longer than that. Now the walls' summits were crawling with all manner of mutants and dae-mon-spawned horrors. Even as he watched, he saw the remaining defenders caught up in a rolling wave of tortured flesh, hacked apart and absorbed by the racing riptide of green and brown.

The enemy ranks were a bizarre assortment – some mortal men in plate armour and matted furs, some grotesque plague-victims carrying hooks and spike flails, some forest-beasts swollen to obscene proportions and slavering with unnatural hungers. Amid them all shimmered the faint outlines of daemons, screaming and shrieking amid the downpour.

There was no fighting against those numbers. They swarmed like rats, scrabbling up the sheer walls along living briars and thorn-tendrils. The stone underfoot gave way, crushed by their weight, but still they came on, chortling as they trod on the tum-bling bodies of their own kind.

They would be across the inner courtyard in moments, and after that the great doors to the keep would not hold them for long, not if the outer walls had been demolished and surged over so ruthlessly.

'Belay that!' Blucher cried, unholstering his pistol and cocking the hammer. As he did so, he noticed his hands were trembling. He had been a captain for twenty years and a trooper for ten more, and was used to the sights and sounds of battle, and they had never shaken before. 'Fall back to the towers!'

There is no resisting this, he found himself thinking even as he retreated across the parapet towards the tower beyond. *This will be over within the hour.*

All around him, men deserted their stations and fled for the last bastions of defence. As they did so, more stone flags cracked and splintered, sending shattered masonry flying high. The rain intensified, splattering green gobbets across the tortured citadel.

Blucher resisted the urge to run. The main gate to the tower was less than twenty yards away, and already clogged with gun-nery crews trying to cram their way in.

'In good order!' he cried, trying to give his orders a clarity that his mind lacked. 'Up to the top level, form up in the Great Hall!'

He was almost there – he could see the safety of the archway before him. Then, just as the last of the artillery crews slipped inside, the ground beneath him erupted.

He was thrown back, landing on his back several yards away. Dazed, he looked up, trying to make out what had felled him.

The parapet's stone floor had burst open, and a fountain of mud and earth was jetting from the breach. Something huge was clawing its way to the surface, flinging aside stone flags as if they were children's toys.

The entire wall-section groaned and tilted, listing out over the courtyard below. Blucher grabbed hold of a stone railing and hauled himself to his feet, bracing unsteadily as the world swayed and cracked around him.

The beast flailed its way into the open, tunnelling up from where the gunnery level had just been. It was vast, a leviathan of earth and rubble, surging up with the bulk and weight of a river-barge and slewing debris from its massive shoulders.

For a moment, Blucher did not have anything to aim at, just a shower of loose soil and broken stone pieces, but then the beast itself shook loose and turned on him.

He had never seen a monster so big. It was the size of the officer's mess at his old parade ground, a nightmare of bulging veins and fat-slick limbs. Its pocked flesh was the green of rotten fruit. A tiny head protruded from absurdly muscled shoulders, drooling with butter-yellow saliva and grinning inanely. A low *hhurr, hhurr* rattled out from its vast lungs, and an overpowering stench of un-sluiced night-pans wafted out from its sweat-moist haunches.

Blucher raised the pistol, holding it two-handed to quell the shakes, then fired. The shot spun out, perfectly aimed, and hit the creature square in the forehead.

The monster stopped dead. For a moment, Blucher dared to

believe that he had felled it, as a line of thin blood ran down the monster's face. He saw it begin to topple, swaying amid the ruin of its ascent, before it blinked heavily, shook its head, and grinned again.

Blucher tried to reload. He scrambled for another shot, pulling it from the wallet at his belt and tipping it into the palm of his hand.

The monster lumbered towards him, shattering what remained of the stone floor under its tread. With a lurch of pure horror, Blucher saw that there was no stopping it. He could fire again and again, and still make no impression on that thick hide.

He pushed himself back towards the edge of the tilting parapet, and glanced down over his shoulder. Below him, a drop of over thirty feet, the courtyard filled with enemy troops. He could see Carroburgers being pulled limb from limb amid the cackling laughter of daemons. Others were being dragged before cauldrons of boiling liquid and forced to drink, gagging and screaming as the corrosive poisons boiled their innards away. Huge booms rang out as the enemy got into the blackpowder storerooms, sending cracks racing up the flanks of the tortured fortress.

It was already over. In the space of just a few hours, one of the oldest and proudest garrisons in the Empire had been overrun. Blucher's fear was replaced by a deadening sense of shame. They should have done better. They should have fought *harder*.

By then, the behemoth was nearly upon him. Blucher cast his pistol aside and reached for a short sword, staring up at the monster as it loomed over him. As he did so, he saw two twisted figures crouching on the beast's shoulders, one in dirty robes and carrying a bell-bearing staff, the other wielding a scythe. Neither of them seemed to have noticed him – they were both absorbed in the carnage bursting out all across the reeling citadel.

'This is *not* the end!' cried Blucher, holding his blade as firmly as he could. 'The Emperor will have his vengeance! Sigmar protects the faithful! The fate of the fallen is–'

His tirade was cut off by a single down-stomp of the monster's hoof. His body was smashed into the stone, crushed into a bloody pulp as the earth beneath was shivered into scree.

Atop Ghurk's shoulder, Ethrac paused and turned to his brother. 'Did you hear something?' he asked.

Otto was in a frenzy of war-lust, barely sensible to anything outside his own world of slaughter. His red-rimmed eyes sparkled with delight as he surveyed the volume of destruction around him. 'Hear what, o my brother?' he asked, absently.

'Never mind it,' muttered Ethrac, preparing the next phase of the noxious deluge that would rip the roofs from the towers and expose the last of the cowering defenders within. 'Press on, Ghurk. Break and shatter, snap and wither.'

Ghurk barked with enthusiasm, too enraptured with the joy of destruction even to scrape the remains of his last kill up to his mouth. Turning cumbersomely, he swayed drunkenly towards the pinnacles of Carroburg.

The sky above them lanced with flashes of green, exposing the shimmer-pattern of daemons in the air. All around them, a symphony of screams, flesh-*schlicks*, ribcage snaps and eyeball-pops swelled in the storm.

The battle was won. Now the true carnage could begin.

Another day dawned over Altdorf, as dank and rotten as all the others. The Reik's flow had slowed to a grimy halt, and the stagnant waters now lapped at the edges of the streets above the quaysides. Insects multiplied on the filmy surface, and their massed buzzing drowned out even the cries of the merchants on the loading wharfs.

Martak strode down the winding streets through the poor quarter, trying not to slip on the grime-soaked streets. Altdorf's thoroughfares were filthy places at the best of times, but the endless rain and damp and plague and misery had turned them into little more than rivers of mud. The drenched and half-starved populace shuffled around in the margins, hugging the dripping eaves of the wattle-and-daub townhouses and shivering in the cold.

For Martak, used to the wilds of the Great Forest, the confinement and the stink were especially trying. He had long since given up trying to get used to it, and had actively turned his finely honed sense of smell towards the task of detection. The plagues were being borne by foul winds from the north, that was certain, but there had to be a source within the city as well. Every chaplain of Sigmar was chanting nightly to banish the contagions, and the fact that they had failed suggested either that the power of faith was waning, or a greater power was at work, or both.

There was no shortage of places to look for the plague's root – the City of Sigmar was built upon a warren of alleys, cesspits, warehouses and thieves' dens, all of which were suitable nesting places for the Rot. There might be just one source or hundreds – it was impossible to know, not without tearing the entire poor quarter apart, brick by rotting brick.

Ahead of him stood the Temple of Shallya. It had been deliberately placed in the darkest and most impoverished district of the old city, and stood like a shaft of sunlight amid piled-high tenements. Very few inhabitants of Altdorf were free of the fear of being assaulted or pick-pocketed while abroad in that district, but the Sisters of the Goddess lived their lives unmolested in the very heart of the lawless slum-city. Every day they would receive long lines of supplicants, desperate for relief from the panoply of maladies that afflicted them. Since the full onset of the Rot those lines had grown fourfold, and the temple was now permanently besieged by a throng of blistered and scarlet-faced sufferers.

As he neared the temple precincts, Martak pushed them aside, using his staff to drive them from his path.

Sister Margrit, the head of the order in Altdorf, watched him struggle. Her stern, matronly face showed some disapproval as she waited for him at the top of a wide flight of stone stairs. By the time Martak had reached her, he was sweating like a hog in midsummer.

'Tell me, sister,' he panted, wiping his greasy forehead, 'how do you stand it?'

'Stand what?' Margrit asked.

'The smell.'

'You are not that clean yourself.'

Martak ran his fingers through his clotted beard. 'True enough. But you know why I'm here.'

Margrit nodded. 'Come.'

The two of them passed from the crowded courtyard and walked under an open colonnade. Beyond the pillars lay a shaded cloister, free from the worst of the clamour outside. A fountain played amid a knot garden of carefully tended herbal plants. Martak felt like he had stepped into another world, and took a deep breath. The faint tang of corruption still laced the air, but it was less overpowering than outside.

'It is rare, for one of your kind to come here,' said Margrit, walking slowly along the cloister paths. 'Wizards and priests – we have not always seen the world the same way.'

'Times are changing,' said Martak. 'And I'm not a very grand sort of wizard.'

'You are the Supreme Patriarch.'

Martak winced. 'Come, you know that means nothing. The Reiksmarshal has more than a dozen better battle wizards on his roster.'

Margrit stopped walking, and regarded him carefully. 'But they are not here.'

'No, they are not.'

Margrit considered that. Then she swept a pudgy hand around her, demonstrating what she presided over. 'We dwell in an island now – a drop of clear water amid a sea of pain. We guard it, and we tend it, but it cannot last forever. Mark it well, my lord. All gardens wither.'

'Where is the sickness coming from?' asked Martak. 'Helborg has his eyes on the walls, on the Great Guns and the Knightly Orders. He looks out from the ramparts, searching for the coming storm, but he is blind to what is happening *here*. What is the source?'

Margrit smiled sadly. 'Our masters are military men. What do you expect?' The smile faded. 'I cannot tell you where the Rot wells up from. We have made enquiries. The people tell us things, as long as we bandage their sores and listen to their sorrows.'

'You have nothing?'

'It comes from the sewers, but that will not help you. There are miles of them down there, and the City Watch does not send its men under the streets.'

'They might need to.'

'None would come back.' Margrit looked at him sympathetically. 'You don't spend much time in the city, do you, wild-man? There are things under Altdorf that have lain undisturbed since the time of the old Emperors. Only a fool would venture far down there.'

Martak shrugged, scratching his neck. 'Wise men have not got us very far. Perhaps fools are needed.'

'Then take armed men,' said Margrit, seriously. 'Take whole bands of them. Flush the tunnels with fire – if you have a Bright magister or two, all the better. I would not venture down beneath the streets with less than a hundred troops at my back.'

'A hundred,' said Martak, amused by the thought of this stout, severe-jowled woman leading an expedition into Altdorf's hidden underbelly. 'I think you'd need less.'

'This is just the beginning,' Margrit warned, starting to walk again. As she went, she trailed a hand along the tops of severely-harvested medicinal herbs. There were not many fresh leaves left. 'We can feel it growing. Shallya, may She be blessed forever, does not answer us. We have a gifted sister, a young woman from Wurtbad whose power for prophecy and healing is the most powerful I have ever known, and even she hears nothing now.'

'Why not?'

'She hears nothing because she dashed her head against the fountain you see over there. Before we got to her, she had polluted the sacred spring with her own blood. She had been sent mad, they tell me. She had seen what was coming, and it turned her mind.' Margrit looked close to angry tears. 'She would have been so *powerful*. She would have done much good.'

Martak halted her, placing his burly hand on her arm. 'Listen, I have to speak to the Reiksmarshal,' he said, his gruff voice as soft as he could make it. 'I will tell him what you told me. He has men. I will tell him we need to purge the sewers, and I will tell him to send no less than a hundred men in each party. Plus a couple of Bright mages, which I can handle.'

Margrit nodded, looking grateful. 'If you can do that, it would help. We need our health back. If the enemy comes on us now, we will be too weak to man the walls.'

Martak knew the truth of that. As much as Helborg struggled manfully with the thousand tasks at hand, he was blind to the fundamental truth. Altdorf was not like a Reiksguard regiment, full of superbly trained men in the prime of condition – it was home to the weak, the ragged and needy. They were being given nothing, and in the final test that would cost them.

'Lord Patriarch, tell me one thing,' said Margrit, glancing up at him with an odd expression in her eyes. 'We were told the Emperor will return. If he were here, I could believe that the storm will pass, but the days go by and we hear nothing. Have you any news to give me?'

Martak looked at her for a long time. They were all under strict instructions to maintain the fiction that Karl Franz was on his way south, riding at the head of his armies with Schwarzhelm at his side. Helborg had been insistent on it, fearing uncontrollable panic if the truth of his loss got out.

Martak understood the strategy. He saw the need for it. Still, the falsehood stuck in his craw.

'You want the truth?' he asked, hoping to evade giving an answer.

Margrit's gaze never wavered. 'Tell me,' she said. 'I need to know.'

Martak thought of his dreams. They had grown more vivid with every night, and he had seen the Emperor in them all, alone and cast adrift in the benighted north.

Then he thought of the young sister, smashing her skull against the stone fountain, all through despair. He thought of the deathly faces in the streets outside, all desperate for something to believe in. If the gods had deserted them, then all they had was each other. In the end, perhaps the stories now told by the city's generals were as good as those once told by its priests.

'He will return, sister,' Martak told her, doing his best to smile. 'He *is* the Empire. In the hour of greatest need, how could he not be here?'

All across the north, the campfires still burned.

A frigid gale howled over the blasted lands, tearing straight from conquered Kislev across the shattered provinces of Ostland and the Ostermark. The settlements of men in those places were now no more than smouldering mazes of half-walls and gaping lintels, their inhabitants slain or enslaved. Nightmare creatures limped across the far horizon, some as tall as watchtowers and carrying heavy crowns of antlers on their bulbous, swaggering necks. Thunder cracked across an uneasy horizon, echoing with the half-heard laughter of glowering gods.

The realm of dreams was expanding. Spreading like a cancer in the wake of its victorious armies, the warping misrule of the Realm of Chaos was gradually twisting and carving through the

Realm of Nature. Rivers dried up, or turned to blood, or boiled into poisonous smog. Birds fell from the sky to roll blindly in the muck, and creatures of the earth sprouted wings and flapped around in pathetic confusion.

In the wake of the great victory, Heffengen had been plundered down to the bone. The armies of Chaos, freed from the attentions of the undead and with the Empire forces destroyed, had been given free rein to sack the city, and had applied themselves with gusto. Very little now remained, save the long rows of gibbets and wheels that lined the road south, each bearing the broken, twitching corpse of a hapless defender. The Revesnecht still ran red, though the cloying mats of greymoss and throttle-vine had already started to knit together from its silty banks, choking what flow remained.

It had been that thirst for plunder that had saved him. For a long time he had lain insensible at the base of a pile of rotting bodies. The course of battle, as confused and blind as it ever was, had raged about him, driving south and fixing on the walled prize of living flesh. If fate had been otherwise, he would have been trampled by cloven hooves, his neck broken and his spine crushed into the mud.

But the fates had not abandoned him entirely. A huge, bloat-bellied champion had seen him come down and had charged over to finish him off. A massed volley of musket-shot had felled the champion before he could swing his cleaver, just as the barrages mowed down a whole warband of marauders on the charge. Their bodies *thunked* into the mire, overlapping one another in a bloody carpet of limp flesh.

The champion had been the one to preserve him, masking his prone body with a heavy, rotten corpse. The sweep and ebb of battle had passed over them both, tearing south with all its grinding momentum, leaving behind the corpse-gardens of the dead and dying.

He awoke much later, while the broken walls of Heffengen still rang with the screams of the captured and the battlefield itself had not yet been plundered of its riches. He pushed the still-warm cadaver from him, grunting from the pain as his cracked ribs creaked. He dragged himself out from under its shadow, feeling the sharp pang of a broken arm. His helm had gone, lost on the dreadful plummet earthwards. For an awful moment he thought *Drachenzahn* had gone as well, then he saw the hilt protruding from beneath the doubled-back arms of a slain Norscan.

Hobbling to his feet, he took up the blade again. If the weapon's spirit recognised him, it gave no sign – the rune-etched steel remained blank and lifeless.

After that he trudged north, knowing the danger, grateful for the night's cold shadows as they stole across the fields of slaughter. He found a ditch to shelter in, part-masked by brambles and with a sliver of blood-foul water at its base. He shivered there for the rest of the night, plagued by the howls and shrieks of raucous joy, parched and yet unable to drink.

Karl Franz, Sigmar's Heir, lay shuddering in the filth, listening to the sounds of Heffengen's agony. Only as the eastern sky brightened to a death-grey dawn did he creep forth again, trusting that the aftermath of the night's debaucheries would give him some cover. He limped north again, then west, skirting the city and hugging the sparse patches of undergrowth that still remained.

In the days that followed, he brushed against death a dozen more times. He was almost discovered twice by armoured patrols. His wounds festered in the dank air, and he passed out from hunger and thirst more than once. He was forced to drink brackish water that made him vomit, and gorge on spoiled grain from plundered storehouses.

Only the amulet kept him alive – the silver seal at his neck that had been imbued with sustaining magic by the magister Tarnus. In the dark of the frigid night, he could feel its aethyric energies warming his chest, staving off the worst of the injuries that threatened to overwhelm him.

A few times, when the sickness raged and despair mounted, he was tempted to cast it aside. As fever raged thickly through his mind, tormenting him with visions of the laughing vampire lord, he listened to the voices that echoed within.

You do not deserve to live. You were slain, and now only prolong the agony. Let it go! Give it up!

He grasped the chain with sweaty hands, intending to rip it clear. Only weakness prevented him – he could barely lift his arms, let alone break the links.

So he lived. He kept walking, each day a fog of pain and confusion, somehow avoiding the enemy columns as they marched south around him. The enemy's own contagions helped him, for the rampant vegetation that erupted across the conquered land soon gave ample cover.

Slowly, painfully, he recovered himself. The amulet worked its subtle power, and his body dragged itself back from the edge of death. He was still wracked with pain, and as weak as any of his sickly peasant subjects, but the worst was past.

He no longer entertained thoughts of giving in – that had been the fevers polluting his mind. He no longer considered heading away from the danger. In fragments, his memory came back, and with it his certainty.

Nothing substantial had changed. He was the Emperor. He was alive. His duty was to fight.

With that, and for the first time, Karl Franz's thoughts turned from survival, to revenge.

ELEVEN

Otto lashed out with his scythe, ripping through the chest of the state trooper and ending his challenge. It had always been an unequal contest – Carroburg had been reduced to little more than rubble, and the only sport remained hunting the last holed-up defenders and rooting them out.

The man tottered for a moment, his legs not getting the message immediately that his heart had been ripped out, before he crashed face-first onto the stone floor. As soon as he did so, a dozen tiny daemon-kin leapt onto the corpse, tearing at it with their teeth and squeaking like excitable kittens.

Otto watched them indulgently. Twenty more corpses lay prone around the basement of the old brewery, all of them leaking guts onto the stone flags where the scythe had whirled. Their bodies would be dragged off at some point and added to the vast cauldrons simmering in Carroburg's old town square. The army had to eat.

As he gathered his breath, Otto reflected coolly on the futility of opposing powers such as his. The fall of Carroburg had been achieved with almost embarrassing ease. Marienburg, a city over three times the size, had not been much more arduous. Perhaps the Empire had finally lost its spine. Perhaps there were no more mortals truly capable of standing against the destiny that, in truth, had always been theirs.

A frog-like daemon the size of Otto's fist pounced onto the state trooper's face and started to suck the eyes from their sockets.

'Greedy, o little one!' laughed Otto, feeling a wave of affection for it.

He watched it feed for a while, before turning from the scene of slaughter and retracing his steps up a long, winding stair. The brewery building he was in was a towering edifice of many levels, and the resistance there had been stouter than almost anywhere else in Carroburg.

The men of the Empire value their beer, Otto mused, as he clambered methodically towards the top level, his scythe-blade dripping over his shoulder as he went.

From outside the thick brewery walls, he heard the ongoing crash and thud of Ghurk's rampage through the town's shabbier regions. There were still morsels of living flesh to be found in some of the hidden pockets, and his corpulent brother's hunger knew no limits.

He would have made his mother proud.

After a long haul, Otto reached the summit and entered a large vaulted chamber. Once it had been lit by rows of tall mullioned windows under a high ceiling, though now the windows were all smashed and the roof sagged. Great copper kettles stood on the tiled floor, each one capable of holding hundreds of gallons. A thick slime of grease and bloody lumps churned and bumped in them now, boiling amid a soup of altogether nastier fluids.

Otto sniffed deeply, appreciating the complex fug of aromas. He could have spent whole days in that place, revelling in the creations his brother had painstakingly piped and funnelled together, if only time allowed. Already, though, the appeal of

Carroburg was beginning to wane, and the need to keep moving was making him impatient.

'Where are you, o my brother?' Otto called out, unable to see the far end of the chamber through the clouds of steam.

'Here, o my sibling!' Ethrac replied from the far side of the largest of the kettles, his voice muffled from chewing.

Otto sauntered over to him, noting the elaborate array of tubes that had been strung between the old brewery's impressive range of glass vials. 'What keeps you busy here?' he asked. 'Must be on the move soon.'

'Come,' said Ethrac, beckoning Otto over to where he stirred a thick slop of acrid matter. 'This was worth the effort. We are far from home now, and need all the help we can get.'

Otto joined him at the cauldron's edge. Ethrac mumbled a few incantations, and shook his bell-staff over the liquid. The cauldron's contents popped and seethed, sending a lumpy lip of froth over the edge. At the very centre, shapes began to shimmer into life.

'Observe our cousins,' said Ethrac eagerly. 'We are not alone.'

For a few moments, Otto struggled to see what he was being shown. The cauldron's contents morphed into bubbling shapes, like wedges of the moss that had brought the Reik to a standstill. Then he understood – he saw the wriggling path of rivers, and the crumpled mounds of mountains. He was looking at a map, albeit one that fizzed like molten metal on the forge.

At the centre lay the object of their march – the city of Altdorf, clustered in a wobbling series of towers by the shore of a trembling Reik. Otto peered closer, leaning low over the cauldron.

'Do not break the water!' snapped Ethrac. 'Ignore the city. It is the others I will show you.'

He extended his clawed fingers over the vista, and it began to zoom out. Forests and mountains swept into view, all of them picked out by the foaming bubbles of Ethrac's sorcery.

'We were three, when we set off,' said Ethrac, pulling the portal expertly. 'Autus Brine, Lord of Tentacles, hacks his way through the Drakwald, slaying the greenskin as he comes.'

As Ethrac spoke, Otto made out a long wound in the vast face of the forest. It might have been his imagination, but he thought he even saw tiny figures crashing their way through the thick foliage.

'Is that–?' he began, but Ethrac shushed him impatiently.

'He has been slowed, but he picks up his pace now. He brings the Harbinger with him. You know of this?'

'Who is it?'

'A shaman. Beast-kind.'

Otto wrinkled his nose in distaste. 'Reduced to such. Brine will be angry.'

Ethrac chuckled. 'Allies are allies. They make a good pace now. The Drakwald is emptied, and they tear south with haste.' The scope of the cauldron's roving eye switched east, passing over more overabundant tracts of deep forest. 'And the third of all – the Tallyman himself.'

Otto sniffed again. It was not good to be reminded of their rivals for the Urfather's affections. If Archaon had not been so insistent on the need for an overwhelming, three-pronged attack, he would have preferred to have had no supporting armies at all. 'Epidemius is foundering, it must be so,' he said, grudgingly.

'Wish it not, o my brother,' chided Ethrac, shifting the cauldron's eye over a vast crater set within the forest. 'We will need his daemon-horde. Dharek rides with him, and they tear apart Taal's city even as we linger here.'

Once again, Otto fancied he could make out infinitesimally small figures struggling across the face of the conjured mapface. It looked like driving rain was hammering against the walls of the rock-bound city. A great swathe of glimmering daemons was assaulting a beleaguered force of mortals. Otto screwed his eyes up, trying to gain a better view. 'They are winning,' he murmured.

'That they are,' said Ethrac, with some satisfaction. 'Old allies fade, new allies arrive. Dharek will be at the walls of Altdorf in good time to meet us.'

Otto scratched a pustule on his cheek absently. 'So many,' he muttered. 'Who will take the prize?'

'Prizes for all,' said Ethrac. 'We should shackle Ghurk again – if he spends his strength on gluttony, we shall be late.'

Otto nodded. 'I shall loop the chains around his neck. He will not be happy.'

Ethrac snapped his fingers, and the map zoomed out again, exposing the whole vast panorama of the Empire. In that instant, it was clear what was happening – the three great arms of the northern host were converging with inexorable, steady progress on the Reikland, smashing aside every obstacle in their path. It was unfolding just as the Everchosen had ordered, and the heart of the Empire was being slowly torn inside out.

'And the dead?' asked Otto, remembering Ethrac's concern at Marienburg.

'No skeletons here,' said the sorcerer, sending the boiling visions slopping back into the cauldron. 'Perhaps they have been seen off.' He grinned at his brother. 'Or maybe they turn on the living. What matter? What could stand against the three of us?'

Otto grinned back. Ethrac was right. It helped to be shown the full majesty of the plan. It helped with the nagging doubts that, every so often, snagged in his feverish mind. 'That is good to see, o my brother,' he said, clapping Ethrac on the shoulder. 'So we should be off now.'

'That we should,' said Ethrac, gazing around himself wistfully, no doubt speculating what sport he could have had in such a place. 'Festus will be waiting for us.'

Otto blurted a throaty laugh. He always forgot about Festus, but, in truth, the Leechlord was the pin around which the whole scheme revolved.

'Then all hastens towards the purpose,' he said, satisfied.

'It does,' said Ethrac. 'Now fetch our brother, and feed the armies until their stomachs swell.' He shot Otto a smile of pure, lascivious darkness. 'Just one more march. That is all. One more.'

The knights of Bretonnia on the march was a sight unequalled in the Old World. Each warrior took with him three or four warhorses, all draped in fine caparisons and marked with the heraldic signs of a hundred different bloodlines. Squires and grooms came with them, and reeves, cooks, heralds, priests and a hundred other officials and servants. A vast train of baggage followed them all, carrying all the supplies and weaponry for a long campaign in the saddle. The whole cavalcade coursed through the countryside in a single, vast column, winding its way east from the fens of Couronne and into the highlands north of the Pale Sisters range.

Leoncoeur rode at the head of the column, pushing the pace hard. He had studied the maps long in the vaults of Couronne while the army had mustered, debating with his counsellors which path to take. Throughout, the mysterious Gilles le Breton had held his silence, offering neither blessing nor condemnation of the Errantry. Towards the end, exasperated, Leoncoeur had asked him outright what his counsel was.

'The Lady ordained you,' le Breton had told him, his green eyes as unfathomable as the sea. 'I have no part in this.'

Le Breton spoke to him as if he were already dead – a walking ghost, just like so many that had been loosed across the realm.

So Leoncoeur had plotted his own course – south-east, across the highlands of Gisoreux, before descending into the border-lands of Montfort. They would cross the Grey Mountains at Axebite Pass, heading swiftly north and emerging into Reikland south of Altdorf.

That path was not the swiftest, but the news from the waste-land was now unequivocal – Marienburg had been destroyed and daemons loosed across the marshes. There was no profit in getting bogged down in fighting with such creatures when speed was of the essence. Since his vision of the Lady, Leoncoeur's dreams had become ever more vivid, and he needed no scouts to tell him the scale of the host that was grinding its way east across the lower Empire.

Still, if the Bretonnians could maintain the blistering pace that he had set, the prospect still survived of reaching Sigmar's city before the enemy had it completely surrounded and beyond hope of rescue. Once clear of the Grey Mountains, the race would truly begin.

For now, they picked their way up from the plains and into the granite highlands. Huge outcrops jutted into the sky on either side of them, pocked and striated from the racing winds. Lush pastures gave way to thinner grassland, littered with chalky boulders.

It was a relief to get away from the low country. The air became fresher as they climbed, rippling the pennants and making the colours flow across the flanks of the steeds. The skies above them never cleared of the oppressive grey mantle they had worn since the coming of Mallobaude, but the rains held, and the worst of the thunder growled away in the far north.

As he rode, Leoncoeur was joined by his lieutenant, Yves Jhared of Couronne, who had fought alongside him on many previous engagements and was as trusted a companion as the king had ever had. Jhared had the flaming red hair and ice-pale skin of a native of Albion, though no one had ever dared to suggest such ancestry to his face.

'Hail, lord,' said Jhared, pulling his horse level with Leoncoeur's. 'We make good progress.'

'Needs to be faster,' Leoncoeur replied, still preoccupied with the pace. With every passing day, the prospect of missing out on the battle loomed a little larger.

Jhared laughed easily. 'We are the best of the realm. Command greater speed, and we will answer.'

'I have no doubt of it,' said Leoncoeur, scouring the skies ahead. The clouds remained blank and unmoving, which troubled him. He had not chosen the route across the Pale Ladies idly, but his hopes had not yet come to fruition.

'Do you search for spies?' asked Jhared, half-seriously. 'Have the Dark Gods turned even the birds of the air?'

Leoncoeur snorted a bitter laugh. 'Do not jest.' He inclined his head a little, sniffing the air carefully. 'But do you not sense them? You disappoint me.'

Jhared looked amused, then uncertain, and peered up into the skies in turn. 'Pray, what am I looking for?' he asked, just as the question became superfluous.

Ahead of them, where the land rose steeply towards a forked granite peak, the clouds suddenly swirled, like cream stirred in a pail. Leoncoeur held up his gauntlet, and the column clanked to a halt. He drew himself up in his saddle, turning to address the long train of knights behind him.

'Stand fast, brothers!' he cried. 'You are not the only warriors to answer my summons.'

As the words left his mouth, the clouds were pierced by a dozen winged horses, swooping earthwards with the poise and grace of swans in flight. Their outstretched pinions gleamed like pristine ivory, and their proud heads tossed and bucked. More pegasi emerged in their wake, flying in formation. They wheeled around in a wide arc, galloping through the high airs just as their earth-bound cousins did on the charge.

Jhared whooped with joy, as all Bretonnians did at the sight of such rare and prized steeds. 'Never so many!' he exclaimed, eyes shining. 'In the name of the Lady, how did you achieve this?'

Leoncoeur could not stifle a laugh himself. It felt good, after so many months of brooding. The sky-host circled above them, four-score of the semi-wild pegasi of the mountains, each of them answering the call he had sent out, trusting to the Lady's influence that the summons would be answered. 'I was lord of this realm, once,' he said, watching them soar. 'That still counts for something.'

Jhared looked at him wonderingly. 'So it does. But how did you give them the summons? These are wild creatures.'

Leoncoeur smiled. 'I have one loyal servant who never lost faith.'

As the last of the pegasi emerged from the cloudbanks, they were followed by a far huger creature, a bizarre amalgam of raptor and horse, with a greater wingspan and a bulkier, more powerful body. Where the pegasi soared across the skies with an acrobat's grace, this creature plunged through the air like a galleon crashing through breakers. It dropped rapidly, folding its huge wings as it extended four huge clawed legs beneath it.

Leoncoeur's mount reared up, panicked by the plummet of the monstrous beast. 'Fear not!' Leoncoeur commanded, yanking hard on the reins. 'This is your cousin, and it would no more eat horseflesh than I would.'

The huge hippogryph landed heavily before them, flexing its shaggy limbs and cawing harshly. Leoncoeur dismounted and raced over to it. The beast lowered its beaked head and nuzzled against its master's embrace. Leoncoeur breathed in the familiar aroma again, and it instantly reminded him of past wars and past victories.

'Beaquis,' he murmured, feeling the plumage brush past. 'Now I am complete.'

Then he turned to the assembled knights, and laughed again. It was a pure laugh, a warrior's laugh, free of the care that had trammelled it for so long.

'Can any doubt the favour of the Lady now?' he cried. 'With weapons such as these, what enemy will dare stand against us?'

The knights roared back their approval, hammering on their shields with the hilts of their blades. At the head of the column, Jhared saluted his liege.

'Smartly done, my lord,' he said, bowing as the pegasi circled above them all protectively.

Leoncoeur gave Beaquis a final affectionate thump on the thickly muscled neck, then strode back to his stamping, wide-eyed mount. 'They will fly before us over the mountains. They will take saddle and halter when Altdorf is in sight, and not before. I will not have them wearied before time.'

Then he mounted once more, and kicked his horse back into motion. 'Until then, the march continues. Ride on.'

The sun slanted weakly through the high windows of the Imperial Chamber of War, striking the veined marble floor in thin grey streaks. Columns soared up around the chamber's circular perimeter, enclosing a vast auditorium of concentric seats. The hall's capacity was considerable, for it had been designed to hold representatives from every elector's staff, every senior ranking magister from the Colleges, the Grand Theogonist and representatives of the sanctioned Imperial Cults, the Engineering Colleges, the Knightly Orders and the standing regiments of the Empire, plus trading guild observers and members of the various diplomatic corps from all over the known world.

Looking up from his throne at the very centre of the chamber, Helborg noted how sparsely it was filled. Fewer than two hundred seats were occupied, and most of those by deputies and functionaries. The three resident elector counts sat in the inner circle, along with their official staff and some minor Imperial courtiers. The Colleges of Magic had sent four delegates, including the peasant-stock charlatan Gregor Martak, whose presence in the Imperial Palace continued to baffle Helborg. Zintler was there, as well as von Kleistervoll and a few dozen high-ranking generals. The Knightly Orders were headed by the brute figure of Gerhard von Sleivor, Grand Master of the Knights Panther, who sat brooding with eight of his peers in full plate armour. Several other delegates were unknown to Helborg, which in itself was an eloquent statement of how far the defenders' numbers had been thinned.

'Very well,' he said thickly, feeling the weight of his eyelids as he looked down the long agenda. 'What is next?'

'The forest draws close to the walls,' said Magister Anne-Louisa Trinckel of the Jade College, her grey hair falling messily around a droopy face. 'It must be culled, for the growths are not natural.'

'It is scheduled to be done, Herrin Magister,' said Helborg, wondering how on earth such a woman came to be the head of her Order. 'We are short of men, and the rebuilding of the outer walls takes priority.'

'That is a mistake,' said Trinckel, looking around her for support. 'The enemy will use the trees. There is *power* in the trees. We have long counselled that the felling of the forest has been neglected – now the consequences have come to haunt us.'

Helborg shot a dark glance at Zintler. 'Do we have any work details that can be spared?'

Zintler raised an eyebrow. 'Spared?'

Helborg nodded, understanding his frustration. Every able-bodied man and woman in the entire city was being worked to exhaustion just to keep on top of the landslide of tasks. The state troopers were being drilled relentlessly, the engineers spent hours atop rickety scaffolds working on the fortifications, the gunnery crews ceaselessly practised running out the great cannons and re-arming the mortar launchers.

'I am sorry, magister,' Helborg said, remembering the courtesies with some difficulty. 'At this time, we just do not have the hands for the task.'

Trinckel was about to protest, when she was overruled by Arek Fleischer, the acting Arch-Lector of the Church of Sigmar. 'Forget the trees!' he blurted impatiently. 'The temples are falling into ruin. We are nothing without *faith*. My priests have been pressed into the service of the army, even those who do not carry the warhammer. This is unacceptable – they are not trained for war.'

Von Sleivor slammed his armoured fist on the table before him. 'Where is Volkmar?' he hissed. 'He would have had you drawn and quartered for less – priests must do their part.'

'The temples will be restored, arch-lector,' explained Helborg, as patiently as he could. 'Now, though, is not the time. All must take their turn on the walls. Surely you can see our weakness is in numbers?' Fleischer did not look convinced. Helborg attempted to smile, knowing that it was more likely to emerge as a grimace. The arts of persuasion, rather than brute force, did not come easily. 'I myself fought with Luthor Huss, your brother-in-arms. There is no finer warrior in the Empire. Surely *he* is the example we should be following here.'

At the mention of Huss, Fleischer's face reddened, and he started to shout something unintelligible about heresies even in the bosom of Sigmar's congregation. This was angrily contested by Magister Willibald de Champney, the ludicrously coiffured magister of the Celestial College, appointed following the departure to war of his superior Raphael Julevno. His fellow wizards soon piled in on his behalf, following by Haupt-Anderssen's chief of staff and the Grand Master of the Knights of the Sable Chalice.

'Silence!' roared Helborg, standing up and smashing his gavel on the lectern before him. His voice rang around the chamber, quelling the restive quarrels before they became unstoppable. Looking down, he realised he had snapped the small hammer with the force of his strike.

A broken hammer. Oddly appropriate.

'This is a council of *war*, my lords,' said Helborg, his darkening visage sweeping the rows of occupied chairs before him. Not for the first time, he wondered just how Karl Franz had kept such a disparate and dysfunctional body politic operational for so long. 'With every passing day, the enemy comes closer. Marienburg has already fallen. We have no word from Talabheim or Middenheim. The river-passages are closed to us, and our attempts to contact Nuln and Couronne have yielded nothing. If we are to survive this, we will have to start worrying less about *trees* and *temples* and more about *blades* and *blackpowder*.'

For the first time, Helborg let a little of the parade-ground earthiness into his speech, and his voice assumed the rasping quality it took on when ordering his knights into the charge. Some of the assembled worthies, like von Kleistervoll and Sleivor, appreciated that. Others, the electors among them, murmured unhappily among themselves.

'Now,' said Helborg, deliberately inflecting his words with as much calm, clear authority as he could, 'let us take stock of what we have determined here. The remaining grain supplies will be removed to the main barracks, as will the surviving quantities of ale and unspoiled water. We will carry out the levy in the poor quarters, drafting any man who can stand into the reserve battalions under General von Hildenshaft. There will be *no exemptions* from the watch rotations. When the enemy gets here, I wish to see every able hand clutching a sword.'

Then he fixed his eyes on each of the delegates in turn, daring them to question the scant resolutions that had been painstakingly agreed. 'Is there anything else?' he asked.

Only one man had the gall to stand. With a sinking feeling in the pit of his stomach, Helborg recognised Martak.

'I come to speak of the Rot,' said the Supreme Patriarch, speaking haltingly in his strangely accented Reikspiel. 'It does not matter how strong we make the walls – the plague spreads from within. We must purge the undercity.'

Martak's voice fell flat in the huge echoing spaces of the chamber. As soon as he mentioned the Rot, irritated muttering started up again.

'There is no such thing,' said von Liebwitz confidently. 'If the peasants only bathed more and ceased their rutting, all this sickness would cease.'

'It is carried by the air,' opined de Champney, to much nodding from his fellow magisters. 'It cannot be eradicated while the foul winds blow.'

'It comes from the river,' said Fleischer. 'And we will not dam that.'

Helborg felt a vice of weariness settle like a yoke on his shoulders. Was there *nothing* they could agree on? 'And just what do you suggest, my lord Patriarch?' he asked. 'As you can clearly see, every ready hand already has a task to perform.'

'I need teams of armed soldiers,' said Martak. 'A hundred strong each, all to be led by a magister of my colleges. The Rot rises from the sewers. Only by purging them all can we reach the source.'

'Purge them all?' blurted Elector Gausser. 'You are mad, Supreme Patriarch.'

'It cannot be done,' added one of the master engineers, a bearded man with a bronze-rimmed monocle and gold braids on his epaulettes. 'The undercity runs for dozens of miles.'

Martak remained calm in the face of the scorn. Throughout the uproar, his steady gaze never left Helborg. 'Something is working against us down there,' he insisted. 'Something that grows stronger. It must be rooted out.'

Helborg struggled to control his irritation. Martak had not bothered to pull out the straggles in his filthy beard. Helborg could smell the man from twenty paces away, and his robes, such as they were, were streaked with dirt. 'I do not doubt you,' Helborg said, trying not to let his jaw clench. 'But there is no question of those numbers. They are needed on the walls.'

'Just one company, then,' said Martak, stubbornly. 'I will lead it myself.'

'Out of the question.'

Martak bristled. 'You're... *banning* me?'

The insolence was intolerable. For a moment, fatigue made Helborg think he was addressing some dishevelled soldier out on the fields of war, and he nearly drew his blade. 'This is not a priority,' he growled.

'Have you been down to the poor quarter?'

'Of course not. Do not deflect this to some–'

'They are dying down there. Dying like dogs.'

'I cannot be concerned about that now.'

'Your whole city is dying, Reiksmarshal.'

'Silence. You have had your–'

'The city is dying before your eyes and you cannot see it.'

'I said, silence!'

'If the Emperor were here–'

'*Enough!*' Helborg's raw shout echoed from the high vaults, shocking even the hardened warriors into startled looks. 'Who *are* you? What pit of filth were you drawn up from, to be thrust into my face like some mockery of your ancient office?'

The words poured like water from Helborg's mouth. The anger made him feel *alive*, after so many hours, so many days, biting his tongue and abasing himself before men he would have slain on the battlefield without a second thought. Once he started, he could not stop – it was cathartic, to vent his spleen again, to pour out all his pent-up fury and frustration at a single source.

'You come here dressed like some peddler from the back-woods of Stirland's foulest shit-hole and dare to address the Reiksmarshal of the Empire? You *dare*? I walked these streets for decades while you rolled in the muck of the Reikswood and sniffed the spoor-trails of beasts. This is *my* city! It is *my city!* If you wish to challenge that, then Sigmar damn you and you may leave it!'

The echoes lingered for a while after the spittle-laced tirade had ceased. No one spoke. A few mouths hung open.

Martak himself remained icily calm. His brown eyes never left Helborg's, who stood, trembling with rage, his chin jutting defiantly.

Then, very slowly, Martak drew in a long breath. 'So we under-stand one another,' he said, his gruff, uncultured voice heavy with contempt.

He shuffled from his place, and clumped heavily down to the chamber floor. As he left, his shoulders held stiffly, his clogs clanked noisily against the marble. It took a long time for him to leave, and the clanks rang out uncomfortably until at last he had been ushered into the corridors outside.

Gradually, Helborg recovered his composure. Almost immediately, the loss of control shocked him. Part of him wanted to rush after Martak, to apologise, to explain that he had not slept for days and that the burden of wresting an entire city from its indolence and dragging it into a war that every instinct told him could not be won was more than any man could bear.

But he could not, not with the eyes of the entire council on him. He was still the Reiksmarshal, and a display of weakness now, any weakness, would see the electors onto him like wolves on a lamb.

There were always disagreements. They could be overcome later. For now, what mattered was *control* – keeping Altdorf together just long enough to give it a chance.

Moving stiffly, he sat down again. The silence in the chamber was total.

Clearing his throat, Helborg turned a leaf of parchment over, moving to the next item on the long agenda.

'Now then,' he said, forcing his voice once more into calmness, as if nothing untoward had just happened. 'Where were we?'

TWELVE

It look Karl Franz a long time to find his quarry. Something had changed since his fall, and a kind of prescience seemed to have lodged in his mind. The world around him seemed a little more vivid than it had done, as if the colours and smells had somehow cranked up. He saw more, he felt more, and his dreams were as startlingly immediate as anything that happened when awake.

Chief among those dreams was the figure of the great antlered god, reeling under the influence of a thousand cuts. Like some stricken stag, the god stumbled in a fog of darkness, assailed from every side by hidden foes. When Karl Franz saw the wounds in the god's flanks and limbs, he wanted to weep.

He saw other things, too. Every night he had the same vision – a bearded man in dirty robes pacing on the battlements of a far city. In the depths of his slumber, he would call out to that man, not knowing why. He never answered, lost in struggles of his own.

In his waking hours, Karl Franz nursed himself back to something like strength. The wilds of the north were vast beyond imagining, and even with the hordes of Chaos marching through them, there were still blank tracts where he could hide and gather strength. There was even food to be found for those with sharp eyes and a searching mind, and since his rebirth Karl Franz had never had sharper eyes.

He knew he needed to head south, tracing the path of whatever remained of his once-mighty armies. He had no idea how many of his generals had survived. Helborg, surely, was dead, since the greater daemon at Heffengen had been a foe beyond him. He could not quite believe that Schwarzhelm was also gone, nor Huss, but there were no clues as to where they had been driven by fate and the currents of war. His thoughts turned to Valten often. That youth had been the great hope for so many – an image of Sigmar for troubled times. Perhaps he still would be, though it was hard to see what he could accomplish now.

For the time being, though, Karl Franz did not hurry to quit the wasteland. He followed the trails of warbands, creeping close to the bonfires at night and doing what he could to divine the movements of the fractured hosts. He understood some of what they said to one another, picking up meaning from the guttural speech of the north in a way he had never been able to do before. One word was repeated over and over again – Glottkin – though he had no idea what it meant.

He heard other words he did recognise – Talabheim, Drakwald, Altdorf. The plan of attack was simple – striking towards the Empire's heart, just as he had told Helborg.

He would never make it to the city, though, not alone and on foot. The leaguer had been broken, and he was already a long way north of the rolling battlefront. He was isolated, cut off in a desolate land of refugees and broken corpses.

As the sun set on another lonely day of foraging, Karl Franz crouched low amid a thicket of briars. With a twinge of wry amusement, he wondered how he must have looked – the Emperor of the greatest realm of men on earth, crouching like a beggar amid thorns, his beard ragged and his clothes torn.

Ahead of him, blood-red in the gathering dusk, burned another campfire. Armed men sat around it, grunting and slurping. Something turned on a spit above the coals, too big to be a hog, though with a similar stench to burning pork. There must have been over twenty warriors there, hulking tribesmen from the far reaches of the Chaos Wastes with bones hammered through their cheeks and god-marks inked on nearly every inch of exposed flesh.

They were careless, marching through a land they had scoured of enemies, and the watch was lax. Karl Franz saw a ramshackle corral on the far side of the camp, and noted the lack of guards. Just one sentry, half-asleep and resentful at being banished from the fireside, huddled against the driving wind, wrapped in a thick, fur-lined cloak.

Going silently, keeping low, Karl Franz crept away from the flickering light-circle and skirted around the edge of the campsite. Hugging the scant cover of the thorn-bushes, he edged closer to the lone sentry. Once within strike-range, he crouched down again, his hand on the hilt of his blade, and waited for the moment.

The sentry was a balding, bearded man with boiled leather armour and an iron ring through his nose. His head slid forward, his eyes half-closed.

Karl Franz moved. Padding softly, he sprinted over to the half-aware guard. Before he had had time to look up, *Drachenzahn* had slipped silently into his neck, killing him instantly. Karl Franz lowered the body to the ground, casting a wary eye over at the campfire.

The tribesmen were still eating, tearing chunks of meat from the spit and ripping it with their teeth. Karl Franz propped the sentry back up, making it look as if he was simply slumped against the cold earth, then moved towards the stockade.

It was a clumsy, makeshift thing, no more than shafts of wood nailed loosely together and crowned with a crude fence of twisted thorn-vines. By rights it should not have held its prisoner for more than a few moments. Karl Franz could already smell the familiar musk, though there was something else there too – the over-sweet tang of muscle rot.

He prised the planks of the stockade apart, and squeezed inside. Deathclaw immediately hissed, and tried to rise, but long leather bindings held the creature down. Karl Franz hurried over to the griffon, sheathing his blade.

'*Calm*, great one,' he whispered. 'You know your master.'

The huge creature immediately relaxed, and the hissing turned to a low rumble within its cavernous chest.

The creature had been sorely abused. Both wings looked broken, and dozens of arrow-shafts protruded from its flanks. Clumps of plumage had been ripped from its haunches, leaving bloody weals glistening wetly in the faint light. It had been tied to stakes hammered into the ground, its limbs compressed into a permanent crouch.

As soon as Karl Franz had severed the last of the leather bindings, the griffon nearly collapsed, issuing a strangled caw of pain as its tormented muscles gave way.

Karl Franz hurried over to its head, cradling the thick neck in his arms. He reached for the amulet and pressed it against the creature's rapidly beating heart.

Gradually, the griffon's yellow eye regained focus. Its heartbeat slowed to normal, and something like firmness returned to its stance.

'This will be painful,' said Karl Franz, hearing the first noises of alarm from the campfire. 'But it is better to be alive and in pain, yes?'

Deathclaw hissed an angry response. From outside the stockade, Karl Franz heard the tramp of boots running and the cries of the blasphemous northern tongue.

'You have the strength for this?' he asked, brandishing his runefang.

By way of answer, Deathclaw dragged itself to its haunches, staggered over to the corral's wall and hurled itself into it. Freed from its bonds, it smashed through the wooden staves, ripping them up and tossing them aside with an imperious flash of copper-gold plumage. The Norscans halted in their charge, suddenly faced with a freed griffon, one whose anger they had stoked over long nights of torment and who now faced them with the flash of bestial fury in its eyes.

'The vengeance of Sigmar!' roared Karl Franz, charging into battle alongside the enraged Deathclaw. Even wounded, the unshackled creature was more than a match for its captors, and *Drachenzahn* knew it would drink deep before the night was done.

The Norscans charged straight back at them, bellowing their strange war-curses with flamboyant bravery. As Karl Franz scythed his blade around for the first strike, cracking heavily against a blunted axe-face, he felt a strange euphoria thrill through his ravaged body.

I am fighting again, he thought, as the runefang danced and the shrieks of the enraged war-griffon split the night. *May it never cease.*

The town of Wurtbad clung to the southern shore of the Reik, a sprawling conurbation built by the trading guilds who plied the great river barges down to Altdorf and the coast beyond. It was not distinguished by grand buildings or fine fortifications – it was a functional place, built by practical men for practical purposes. A thick stone wall ringed a motley collection of townhouses, inns, warehouses and loading derricks. Even by the standards of the provinces, it had always had a shady reputation, the kind of place a cunning man would make a fortune and a simple one would lose it. Taverns and bawdy-houses crowded the streets, jostling alongside temples, barracks and customs stations.

Since the start of the troubles, Wurtbad had been hit hard. First the barges had stopped coming down from the north. No explanation for the stop in traffic had ever been forthcoming, so the burgomeister sent members of the City Watch upriver to investigate. They came back on a single, empty vessel, hanging from meat-hooks amid piles of rotting pig carcasses.

Then news of the war in the north had come in, carried by draggled refugees from Stirland and the Ostermark. As the Empire's creaking war-machine responded, some of the cannier Wurtbad merchants made a quick profit hawking supplies to desperate generals at inflated prices. For a time, the passage of arms wending its way up the river from Nuln and Altdorf kept the taverns and brothels in roaring business, and, also for a time, a steady flow of regiments kept coming to replace those ordered onwards.

Then the flow dried up. Every company due to be sent to the distant front was deployed, hollowing out the defences along the Reik and the Stir. The streets fell quiet and the warehouses were locked. Barges stood empty at their berths, waiting for trade to resume, just as it always had when the worst was over.

Except that, this time, no soldiers returned from the north. No proclamations came out of Altdorf celebrating deliverance in Sigmar's name. The temples began to fill, as a previously ambivalent populace suddenly remembered its piety.

The plagues came next. No one knew from where – perhaps the thick miasmas churning in from the east, or the lines of impoverished peasants fleeing the blight in the fields, or the curdling waters themselves as they lapped the empty wharfs. Soon the bodies were piling up, and every dawn a new cart left the town gates, heaped high with cloth-covered lumps. After a while even those stopped – no one dared venture out to where the forest sprouted unnaturally under the endless sheets of rain, and so the dead lay festering in the rubbish pits where they had been dragged.

By the time the watchmen on the southern wall caught sight

of black banners on the far horizon, few believed the newcomers brought salvation with them. A few zealots started chanting, taking a kind of perverse, vicious pleasure in the vindication of their endless prophecies of the End Times. The rest of the city's survivors grimly took up arms. The gates remained locked and barred, and every surviving militia member was called to the armouries to equip. Then they waited, watching the sable-clad host creep closer through the cloying mists.

The new arrivals did not advance further while the sun shone. They waited south of the river, issuing no challenge and making no demands. Inside the town, a vociferous and terrified faction argued that the burgomeister should sue for peace, since the garrison was in no condition to resist a siege and the Empire, such as it still was, had clearly abandoned them. By nightfall, as the true nature of the attackers became horrifyingly clear, those voices subsided, and a gnawing, crawling fog of despair took over.

Ghouls flickered through the frigid air, screaming at a gravid Morrslieb above. Flocks of bats raced across the sky, their blood-red eyes glowing in the velvet dark. Rank upon rank of bone-white warriors advanced under death's-head banners, never issuing a sound. Some warriors stalked by their own will; others glowed luminously from within with the flickering light of corposant, impelled by the necromancers who cried out in grave-scraped voices and whirled staffs hung with clattering human skulls.

Black-armoured knights nudged bony steeds through the undead throng, and wights wearing ancient tomb-garb limped and shuffled in their wake. Most horrifying of all were the vargheists, which loped into battle with huge, ungainly strides, half-flying, half-running, their animalistic faces twisted with bloodlust and their claws already extended.

At the sight of that onslaught, many of Wurtbad's mortal defenders lost heart and fled, wailing that the gods had abandoned them, trying to find somewhere in the shadowy maze of the narrow streets to hide. Others stood firmer. The burgomeister, Jens Bohr, was a veteran of the state levy and had faced down larger armies of greenskins in his time. His warrior priest, a fervent Sigmarite by the name of Kalvin Wolff, whipped the remaining troopers into a frenzy of pious defiance. Huge fires were kindled across the walls, flooding the land beyond in a writhing aura of crimson. Every captain on the walls was given a flaming brand, and teams of runners kept the stores of wood replenished. Desperate battle-hymns rose up from the battlements, competing with the shrieks of the living dead.

That did not stop the vice closing. Gradually, the undead host spread out, moving up the southern bank of the Stir and crossing the flood on either side of the town. The still-living troops traversed using barges looted from further upstream, while the truly dead simply waded across the river bed, emerging on the far bank covered in a thick layer of slime and weeds.

Then, once Wurtbad had been fully surrounded, the assault began.

The night's cacophony was broken by the snap and rattle of trebuchets. The warped machines, looking more like giant ribcages than engines of war, hurled clusters of human skulls high over the walls, and where they impacted, they exploded in gouts of greenish gas. Any defenders too close to the impacts immediately succumbed to the blooms, their skin falling in shreds from their bones. They died in agony, clawing at their own sinews as their bodies fell apart around them.

Next came the bats. Some were taken down by hurried volleys of arrows, but most got through, grabbing men from the parapet and sending them tumbling, their chests torn out. Ghouls and grave-shades followed, floating eerily over the defensive perimeter in shimmering clusters and latching their cold magic around any who dared face them.

As the walls were ringed with horrors, the greater mass of skeletons and zombies reached the base and started to raise siege ladders. Dozens were cast down by the defenders, but more were immediately hoisted up. Whenever a weakness was isolated, deathly warriors surged up into the breach, falling into soundless combat with the troopers who rushed to repel them.

For all the ferocity of the initial assault, however, the main ring of defence held firm. The roaring fires did their job, daunting the undead horde and preventing them from advancing recklessly. Wolff kept up his furious defiance, showing the way by smashing swathes of skeletons apart with his warhammer. Bohr used his limited corps of gunners well, picking out champions with as much accuracy as the fire-flared night would allow.

Ladders were cast down, smashing amongst the seething masses below. The zombies moved too slowly to evade the blades of determined defenders, who fought with the ferocity of men who knew their lives were forfeit if they faltered. Some of those who had fled at the first sign of the undead recovered their spirits and returned, shamefaced, to the fray, shuddering with fear but still able to clutch a weapon in their clammy hands.

Combat raged on the wall-tops for over two hours, with neither side able to land the killer strike. The fires continued to crackle, the hymns rang out, but the undead could not be shaken from their grip, and just kept on coming.

If any Imperial chronicler had been present on that night to witness the battle of Wurtbad, he would have noted, perhaps with some grim pride, that the end did not come from outside. Freed from the need to guard their backs, the defenders of Wurtbad might have held out through the darkness, perhaps using the dawn to clear their besieged walls and restore a solid line of defence. But just as the undead attack began to lose momentum, a fell prince in blood-red armour rose up in his saddle, standing high above the town on a rise north of the river. He raised a lone, clawed hand, holding it palm-upward, and cried out words in a language of the distant hot sands. Those words somehow cut through the clamour of fighting, piercing the soul of every mortal and sending the undead advancing with renewed energy. A ring blazed from his withered finger, sending coils of smoke churning out into the night.

For a few moments, nothing else happened. The deadly struggle continued, and the battle-cries kept coming. Wolff even managed to clear the enemy from the summit of the southern gatehouse, felling a vargheist with a savage blow from his hammer before launching himself at the lesser troops.

But then the earth began to boil. Sodden soils shifted, churning like molten oil. A wild snap rang out across the city, and the air buckled with actinic lightning.

The first hand shot up from the ground, withered and pale. Then another, then a dozen more. Corpses pulled themselves free from their graves, hauling their etiolated bodies out of the mire. The tottering cadavers swayed for a moment, then set off, shuffling blearily towards the noise of combat.

The people of Wurtbad had not been foolish – they had always buried their dead outside the city walls, facing down and with the marks of Morr set over their graves. But now the Law of Death had been breached, and those many hundreds who had died on the site of the town before Wurtbad had been established as an outpost of Sigmar's Empire suddenly shifted in their cold slumber. With a shiver and a sigh, they came scratching and scrabbling back into animation. Arcane armour of lost ages and blades long-rusted into stabbing stumps cracked up through the topsoil, followed by creaking bodies slaved to a new master.

It took a while for the new arrivals to be noticed. Intent on keeping the walls free of attackers, the troops of Wurtbad resolutely devoted their attentions to the host at their gates. By the time the screaming from the heart of the town could no longer be ignored, it was too late.

Hundreds of living dead had been wrenched from their ancient graves, and they thronged in Wurtbad's alleys and backstreets, twittering and hissing. With blank, rotting faces, they dragged themselves towards the living, their only desire now to drink the hot, dark liquor of mortal blood. They crept out of the town's central courtyards and fanned out through the crooked streets, feasting on any unfortunates they were able to overwhelm. Even the river-rats, which had clustered in Wurtbad's river-front, ran before them, streaming out towards the outer walls in a rippling wave of panicked grey.

Wolff was the first to notice the tumult. Dispatching a final skeleton into a clattering pile of bones, he plunged down from his position over the gates, leading a charge against the growing crowds of living dead within the town's perimeter. Others joined him, and the fragile bodies of the newly-raised were soon being cracked and smashed apart.

That left the walls depleted, though, just as the shot for the gunners began to run low and the fires lost their vigour. The hordes outside sensed the presence of their kin on the inside, and the assault redoubled in ferocity. The real killers among the skeletal army took their chance, and armour-clad warriors wearing tattered cloaks and ornate liveries of forgotten, cruel ages pushed up the siege ladders and on to the parapets.

Dark magic raced across the night, reaching a crescendo in tandem with the greater mass of human screaming. The fires began to die one by one, doused and chilled by the advancing dead, and shadows welled and pooled more thickly, plunging Wurtbad into a slick of oily darkness.

The battle-hymns rang out right until the end, growing fainter as more and more defenders were cut down. Those mortals who were slain did not rest easily, but soon got up again, this time taking the fight to their erstwhile comrades, and so the advance of the undead grew ever stronger as the will of men was eroded.

Bohr was eventually killed after his position at the northern gate was overrun by ghouls. He died shouting in outraged defiance even as icy fingers were plunged into his thick chest and his heart was ripped out. With the death of the burgomeister, the last organised defence of the northern walls collapsed, and those who could ran for whatever temporary refuge they could find.

Knowing the futility of flight, and knowing too that hope had gone, Wolff was the last one standing. He cut his way back to his temple, gathering a few dozen of the stoutest defenders around him as he went. They made a stand before the dome of the Sigmarite chapel, overlooked by granite statues of griffons and with the final bonfires guttering about them.

Waves of undead swept towards them, chattering excitedly as they sensed the prospect of drinking the blood of the valiant, but all were repelled. Wolff's band held the outer precinct against them all, hacking and smashing with desperate strokes until the ground at their feet was knee-deep in broken bones and parchment-dry flesh.

One by one, though, fatigue and ill-chance took their toll. The relentless numbers could not be defied forever, and in the end Wolff stood alone, his throat raw from war cries and his hammer as heavy as lead in his bloodied fists.

Just as the vanguard of the undead host was poised to launch a final push, though, a chill voice rang out. The undead fell back instantly, shuffling into the shadows and clearing a space before the temple gates.

Wolff stood under the lintel, his forehead sheened with sweat, breathing heavily. Between the parted crowds of lesser warriors, the Master of the Host strode out, his black robes rustling in the wind. Ice-white hair rippled about his shoulders, part-obscuring the scarred and cracked mask of his skin. The ring he had used to raise Wurtbad's dead still smouldered on his finger.

The warrior priest did not flinch. His eyes fixed on the vampire lord's, and never moved. He murmured battle-curses in an endless litany, and prepared to lift his hammer once more. He knew he was overmatched, but he could at least die on his feet, taking the fight to the enemy just as his immortal patron demanded.

Then Vlad von Carstein spoke.

'You, too may serve,' said the vampire, coming to a halt before the priest and folding his arms. He made no attempt to defend himself, even though he was in range of the warhammer's strike. 'This is why we do this. You are too good to be sacrificed to gods who appreciate nothing but mania.'

Wolff's lip pulled back in contempt. 'Your kind has come this way before,' he snarled. 'You were always turned back. You will be again.'

'By whom?' Vlad sighed. 'There is nothing left. Look around you – you can see what ruins remain.'

'From ruins come glory. From the darkness comes light.'

Vlad smiled thinly. 'Come, you have fought enough. I always offer the valiant a place at my side – take the offer, priest. You can still fight against the greater darkness.'

'At your side?' Wolff laughed. 'You know so little that you would even ask?' He spat at the vampire, and the spittle landed on the crimson armour, sliding across its lacquered surface. 'You have come amongst *men*, abomination. You may crush us for a time, you may tread across our broken bodies and burn our temples and strong places, but we will always come back at you. If I were given a thousand lifetimes, I would choose the same path every time – to *smite* you with the holy fire of my calling.' He smiled with contempt. 'And you came too close.'

He swung his warhammer. It was a fine strike, one that Huss himself would have been proud of – fast, hard, well-aimed. The hammer-head flew out, angled at the vampire's neck.

At the same time, a single shot pierced the night, just as well-aimed. It struck Wolff clean in the forehead, penetrating the bone and punching a clean, round hole through his skull. The warhammer clanged to the ground, and the warrior priest tumbled backward, collapsing under the lintel of his own temple before coming to rest amid the shattered bones of his victims.

Vlad looked down at the corpse thoughtfully. The man's zeal had been striking. Had he himself been capable of such fervour, once? Of course he had, but it was hard to remember just how it felt.

Herrscher emerged into the light, his pistol still smoking. The witch hunter had a tortured look on his face.

'There,' said Vlad, turning away from Wolff to look at him. 'That was not so hard.'

'I could not let you be harmed,' said Herrscher, his voice shaking. 'I killed... my own.'

'He is not your own,' said Vlad, impatiently. 'Look around you. *We* are yours, you are ours. You have killed for us, and we will kill for you.'

Herrscher looked like he wanted to vomit, though his body was no longer capable of it. Before he could reply, the sound of overlapping laughter wafted across the temple courtyard.

Liliet and her sisters had climbed on to the dome of the temple. Their gowns were streaked with blood, and it dripped from their long fingernails like tears.

'Rejoice!' they chorused. 'A thousand new blades for the army of the night-born! A thousand more to come before dawn-fall!'

All across Wurtbad, those of Vlad's army with the self-command to respond lifted their parched voices in victory-cries.

Vlad laid a gauntlet on Herrscher's shoulder. 'The Empire trains its hunters well – that was a good shot.' Then he turned on his heels, his cloak swirling about him, and strode away from the temple, back towards the river-front where the empty barges had been tethered, ready for the passage of the Reik. 'Do not dwell on it. The night is still dark, and we have work to do. By the dawn, our new servants must be on the move.'

Martak's fury took a long time to ebb. He had stormed up to his barely used chambers in the Imperial Palace and smashed a few things up in there. He gave a glimmering simulacrum of

Helborg's gaunt face to every item he hurled across the room before it smashed into the wall.

No one dared interrupt him. By then, every servant in the Palace had all heard tales of the half-feral Supreme Patriarch, and kept their distance. Gelt had been capable of rages, but at least he was vaguely understandable. Martak, deprived of even that measure of respect, took a grim satisfaction in causing fear instead.

Let them fear me, he snarled to himself. *They deserve what is to come.*

He did not mean that. No one deserved the horrors that lay ahead, not even the stiff-necked Reiksmarshal, and certainly not the flunkeys who struggled to do his impossible bidding.

By the time he had calmed down, his personal chamber was a mass of ripped parchment and broken crockery, and he was a sweaty, panting mess.

Martak cracked his knuckles, stomped over to the chamber's narrow window and pushed the lead catch open. The window faced east, giving a view out over the great mass of the city.

He took a deep breath. The stench was becoming unbearable, even at such a height. He thought again of Margrit – sensible, dutiful Margrit. He had promised her that something would be done. Every hour that the Rot was allowed to swell and grow was another hour for the temple's supplies to run down and the energies of the sisters to ebb a little further.

He propped his elbows on the sill and rested his chin gloomily on locked hands. Far below, the Reik was the colour of spoiled spinach and barely flowed at all. He could make out the sullen blooms of algae lurking just under the surface, and could smell the acrid stink of its steady fermentation.

He had made a mess of his short time as Patriarch. Helborg was making a mess of the city defences, and the electors were making a mess of assisting him. They were like children caught by the glare of a predator, frozen and witless, unable to do more than bicker in the face of oncoming disaster.

It is the city.

The realisation came to him so suddenly and so easily that he immediately wondered how he had not seen it before.

It is the poison.

Martak was a creature of the wilds, of the windswept tracts of unbroken forest. He had been known to spend months in the wilderness, kept alive by his arts and native cunning, eschewing all comforts and embracing the idiosyncratic path of his college's disciplines.

I have allowed them to cage me. This is their world, not mine, and they have made me useless in it.

He was a sham Patriarch in a sham Empire, playing out his role in dumb-show as the world unravelled around them. He could not command men, and had no desire to. Helborg had been right about one thing: this was *his* city, not Martak's.

He stood up again, and shuffled over to the writing desk he had just half-smashed. After a few moments scrabbling around, he found a scrap of intact parchment and a near-empty jar of ink. He pulled a quill from under a disarranged collection of broken-spined tomes, and started to write. Once he had finished, he folded the parchment and sealed it, stowing the letter in his grimy robes.

Then he moved over to Gelt's old Globe of Transmigratory Vocalisation within a Localised Aethyric Vicinity – a bronze-bound sphere set atop an iron web of intricately-woven threads. It was a meagre device for one of such talents, but it had its uses.

Picking it up and setting it before him on the floor, Martak placed both palms on the cool surface of the sphere. Something like clockwork clicked inside it, and he felt the tremble of moving parts. Previously hidden runes glowed into life on the bronze, welling softly with a sudden heat.

Martak concentrated. This was Gelt's toy, and he still was not sure he had mastered it properly.

'Search her out,' he whispered gruffly, imposing his will on the machine's. 'The soul of Sister Margrit.'

It resisted him. The device knew its gold-masked master, and resented being used roughly by a stranger. In the end, though, Martak's presence prevailed, and the Globe performed its function. The air above it trembled, warmed, then parted, revealing a blurred and translucent image of Margrit's garden. The priestess herself was standing with her back to the Globe's view. As soon as Martak laid eyes on her, she stiffened, turned, and made a warding gesture.

'Be at ease, sister,' said Martak, knowing that he would appear to her as nothing more than a ghost, hanging above the herb-garden like a puff of steam in summer.

'Patriarch,' said Margrit, her voice muffled and distorted. She looked at him through the Globe's portal, peering as if into murky water. 'Could you not come in person?'

'I am leaving the city,' said Martak. A soon as he saw her face fall, he regretted his clumsy way with words.

'All is lost, then,' she said.

'No, you were right – the Emperor is master. While he remains lost, we cannot stand. I go to find him.'

Margrit's expression brightened into an almost childlike hope. 'You know where he is?'

'He is coming, sister. The stars foretell it, and the elements gather to witness it.' Martak had no idea whether this was true. All he had to go on were his dreams, which had been getting more vivid with every sleepless night. He had dismissed them for too long, and knew now that he should have listened to the whispered voices much earlier. 'It will not be easy, but yours will be the harder road. I can give you no promise the Reiksmarshal will act. I would stay, if I could, but...' He struggled for the words. 'This is not my place.'

Margrit nodded, accepting what he told her. 'Then you can give me no sign.'

Martak racked his mind for something that would appeal to her. 'When the hour is darkest,' he said, hoping he sounded vaguely plausible, 'look to the heavens above the Imperial Palace. Look for the sign of Sigmar reborn.' It was poor stuff, this deception and fakery, but it was all he had. 'In advance of that, *endure*, sister. Endure for as long as you are able.'

Margrit looked satisfied, and Martak found himself marvelling once again at her quiet resolve. Given the tiniest sliver of hope, she would hold fast to her station until the very ending of the world. If the Empire deserved any kind of salvation, it was for the ones like her – the faithful, the decent, the selfless.

'Do not be long gone, Patriarch,' Margrit said. 'I liked the colleges better with a wolf at the helm.'

Martak laughed, and bowed at the compliment. He would have been happy betting that Gelt had never walked the streets in the shadow of the temple. 'Go with Shallya, sister,' he said, and lifted his hands from the Globe. Margrit's image rippled into nothing, and the runes on the sphere faded back to blank bronze.

Back in the realm of the senses, Martak looked about him. His chamber looked as if an animal had got in and destroyed everything in its frantic efforts to escape again. Perhaps that was not so far from the truth.

He walked over to the heavy oak door and pulled it open. The corridor outside was empty, and he had to walk through two more antechambers before he found an official. The servant, wearing a crimson tunic marked with the sign of the griffon, looked startled to see the Supreme Patriarch back on the prowl.

'My lord?' he asked, shrinking from Martak's malodorous presence.

'Send this to the Reiksmarshal's office immediately,' said Martak, handing over the ink-stained letter. 'Ensure that it is placed before him at the first occasion – he will want to read it.'

The servant handled the letter nervously, as if it might be a mortar primed to go off in his hands. 'Very well, my lord. Where shall I tell him he may find you?'

Martak snorted. 'Find me? He'll have trouble.' He looked

around him. The corridors and chambers of the Palace were still mostly a mystery to him, a vast web of tunnels and spirals and shafts and towers. 'But you can help me with one small thing.'

The servant looked up expectantly. Martak smiled darkly, already enjoying the thought of what he was going to do.

'Tell me,' he said, 'what is the quickest path to the Imperial Menagerie?'

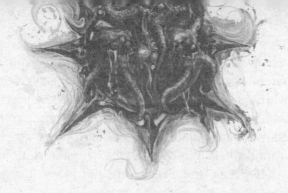

THIRTEEN

The wind was bitter and never-ending, driving down from the high peaks with the shrieks of fell voices echoing in its wake. The skies had turned from a screen of blank grey into a churned mass of violent thunderheads, surging and boiling as if some immeasurably vast pair of hands was tearing the heavens apart.

As Leoncoeur rode up to the head of the pass, wrapped in his cloak, the deluge drummed on the rocks around him. Rivulets poured down from the rising land ahead, slushing and bubbling as the torrent picked up pace, and the stony track up to the entrance to Axebite Pass was now little more than a stream of gushing water.

Ahead of the Bretonnian column reared the mighty peaks of the Grey Mountains, piled up into the tortured sky in ranked visions of granite-headed immensity. To Leoncoeur's left soared the double-headed summit of Talareaux, called Graugeleitet by the Imperials. To his right was the colossal bulk of Findumonde, which the Empire dwellers called Iceheart. Both summits were lost in the haze of storms.

Gales were always strong in the passes, but those during this passage had been unreasonably ferocious. Baggage wains and valuable warhorses had been washed away on the precipitous pathways, and at times every footfall had been treacherous. Progress had slowed to a grim crawl. Each night, Leoncoeur had sat sullenly around the campfires with his lieutenants, noting the growing gap between where they were and where they wanted to be.

Still, they had persevered. The highlands had slowly fallen behind, replaced by the jagged, hard country of the mountains proper. The last of the pasture disappeared, replaced by a stoneland of sheer, hard-edged severity. The rain stung like ice, and the wind whipped it into wicked eddies, creeping into every fold of fabric and armour-joint.

The raw enthusiasm of the crusade was hard to sustain in such conditions. Battered by the ferocity of the elements, the knights kept their dripping heads low, saying little. The hundreds of peasant workers in the baggage train suffered worse, their coarse woollen garments offering little protection, and many succumbed during the frozen nights, left behind in scratched, shallow graves by the roadside.

As the head of the pass loomed before them at last, Leoncoeur called a halt. He peered ahead towards the high entrance. Slushy snow lay in grey-white drifts higher up, draped across the striated shoulders of the mountains. The winding road ahead was overlooked by near-vertical cliffs of broken-edged stone, narrowing near the summit to a gap of less than thirty feet across.

His eyes narrowed. He sniffed. It was near-impossible to sense much in the shifting gales, but *something* registered. Something he felt he ought to recognise.

Jhared drew alongside him. Of all of them, the flame-haired knight had retained his humours the best, but even he looked windswept and rain-soaked. 'Why are we halting, lord?' he asked, shivering as the driving sleet bounced from him.

'Can you hear it?' asked Leoncoeur, inclining his head a little.

Jhared listened, then shook his head.

Leoncoeur was about to speak again, when a hard, massed roar suddenly broke out from up ahead.

Every knight in the entourage knew that sound – it had been engraved on their minds from their earliest days. The ancestral enemies of the Bretonnians could be purged, burned and driven back a thousand times, but they would always come back.

'To arms!' cried Leoncoeur, drawing his sword in a spray of rain.

The column's vanguard formed up immediately, kicking their horses into a line and drawing weapons. Each knight carried a heavy-bladed broadsword, and they threw back their cloaks to expose moisture-slick breastplates marked with the livery of their houses.

Before the knights could charge, the gorge before them filled with what looked like a rolling tide of earth and rubble. It was accompanied by throaty bellows of challenge, rising quickly to a deafening crescendo that ripped through the scything curtains of sleet.

'Charge!' roared Leoncoeur, digging his spurs into his steed's flanks.

With a hoarse battle-cry, the Bretonnian vanguard surged along the throat of the gorge, picking up speed rapidly despite the treacherous footing. Accelerating to the gallop, ten horses abreast, they thundered towards the landslide hurtling towards them.

Except that it was no landslide. A host of green-skinned monsters had burst from cover, their red eyes blazing with fury. The rubble that came with them was flung from their backs as they emerged from the ambush, and stones the size of fists *thunked* and rolled about them. There must have been hundreds of orcs before them, all jostling and tearing down the funnel of the gorge, sliding on the slippery rock and trampling their own kind like cattle on a stampede.

When the two forces collided, it was with a sick, hard smash that sent the bodies of both orc and human flying. Bretonnian warhorses were huge, powerful beasts, and their whirling hooves were quite capable of cracking skulls and snapping ribcages. The greenskins were battle-hardened monsters, each of them far larger than a man and with corded, muscled limbs that hurled axes and mauls around with plate-denting force.

Leoncoeur crashed through the hard glut of the toughest of the orcs, laying about him in flamboyant sweeps of his blade. He rode his mount with imperious perfection, compensating for every buck and rear. As the greenskins clawed for him, he laid waste to them, hammering with all the pent-up strength of the long ride.

Jhared remained close by, working his own blade furiously. 'For the dead of Quenelles!' he thundered, his lank hair thrashing around his un-helmed head. 'For the dead of Lyonesse!'

Every knight of the company fought in the same way – with a cold anger generated by the many humiliations suffered by their realm. They were devastating on the charge, as pure and violent as the cascades around them. The orcs died in droves, and soon the rivulets at their feet ran black with blood.

Leoncoeur wheeled his steed around and thrust his sword point-first into the open maw of a slavering greenskin. He ripped the blade free in time to meet the swiped challenge of another, and a dull clang of metal on metal rang out. Two swift parries, and he had dispatched the next challenger.

The impetus of the orc attack was already failing. They began to retreat back up the gorge, desperate now to escape the close-serried Bretonnian onslaught. There was no escape for them that way, though, for the pegasi plummeted from the clouds, drawn by the scents and sounds of battle. Even without riders they were deadly, swooping low to lash out at the stumbling herd of greenskins.

'Let none escape!' shouted Leoncoeur, riding down a stumbling orc and spurring his mount towards the next. The Bretonnians loosened their formation as they gained momentum. Gilles de Lyonesse, a rider with a love of the chase that exceeded even his hunt-obsessed brethren, broke clear with a small band of like-minded brother-knights and galloped up the gorge's flanks, aiming to cut off the rearmost greenskins. Leoncoeur and the main body of warriors advanced up the centre, cutting into the heart of the orc herd. The pegasi continued to dive and swoop, bludgeoning the slow-moving greenskins with impunity, and so the orcs were soon assailed from all sides.

The remainder of the fighting was little better than a slaughter, with the last of the creatures surrounded by a ring of stamping horses. Leoncoeur killed the last orc himself, as was his right, and lifted its severed head high in triumph. Gore slopped in a torrent from its serrated neck-stump, mingling with the deluge of crimson foam below.

'First blood of the crusade!' he shouted, and his knights returned the cry with genuine gusto. After so long suffering from the grinding cold, it was good to indulge in their proper calling again.

De Lyonesse soon returned, and the slower-moving infantry of the baggage train caught up, hauling their wagons over the broken ground.

In normal times the peasants would have been employed to drag the bodies of the slain for burning, for allowing the corpse of a greenskin to moulder in the open air was asking for trouble. On this occasion, though, Leoncoeur suffered none of them to waste time. The way was cleared for the passage of the largest wains, and the bodies of fallen knights were retrieved and buried with all honour, but no funeral pyres were lit.

Less than two hours later, the cavalry column was on the move again, snaking higher up into the mouth of Axebite Pass. The clouds above did not relent, but poured out their violence ever more intensely, washing the blood from the rocks and sending it tumbling down the throat of the killing ground.

Leoncoeur let his knights pass first, led by de Lyonesse, who had started singing hymns of praise to the Lady for deliverance. The old king remained at the site where he had slain the last of the greenskins, lost in thought.

'You were right,' said Jhared, nudging his mount past Leoncoeur's and preparing for the final push towards the summit. 'First blood. A good omen.'

For a moment, Leoncoeur did not reply. The severed head of his victim lay on the near-frozen earth, gazing blankly up at the heavens. 'I do not recognise them,' he said at last.

Jhared looked down at the piles of corpses, then back at Leoncoeur, then shrugged. 'They look much the same as any I've killed.'

Leoncoeur leaned down in the saddle, poring over the piled heaps of the slain. Jhared's confidence was misplaced – the orcs' wargear was like nothing a greenskin south of the mountains would have worn. Leoncoeur had travelled far across the Old World and had fought in a dozen different lands. The different tribes of greenskin fought amongst themselves even more than they warred with other races. Each strain had their own territory, which was only breached on the rare occasion when an exceptional warlord would unite them into the rare explosions of aggression that gouged trails of carnage across the civilised lands.

This was not one of those occasions. The slain orcs' wargear was in poor shape, and their armour – to the extent it could be called that – hung from their bodies in tatters. It was clear that many of them had been wounded before the fighting had even begun, and their bulk was far less than it should have been.

'They did not come here to attack us,' said Leoncoeur.

Jhared laughed. 'Then why were they here?'

'They are from north of the mountains. The Drakwald, I'd warrant. They have been driven south.' Leoncoeur looked steadily at Jhared, letting him be in no doubt what had happened. 'They were fleeing. Whatever waits for us, it has cleansed the forest of orcs.'

Jhared started to laugh again, but the sound trailed off. He forced a smile. 'The forest can never be cleansed.'

Now that the fervour of battle had faded, Leoncoeur could reflect on how poorly the greenskins had resisted. He had never seen them give up, not so completely, not so quickly.

'They were hunted,' he said, finding himself strangely appalled by the thought. 'They were scared.'

'Of us.'

Leoncoeur smiled wryly. 'Believe that if you wish.' He kicked his horse's flanks, and it began to move again. 'I do not.'

He looked up, to where his knights wound their way ever northwards, passing under the night-dark shadow of Talareaux. It looked like they were snaking their way into the underworld.

Perhaps that is so, he mused. *In which case, the Lady willing, we will soon set it alight.*

The sun had only just risen, and its light was grey and diffuse, barred by the heavy layer of cloud that had hung over Altdorf for weeks. The parade ground was sunk into a kind of foggy twilight, part-masking the movements of the men out on the sand.

Helborg barely remembered the last time he had seen a clear sky. Ever since the first stirrings of the hosts in the north, the heavens had been masked by a grimy curtain, washing all the colour out of the world and plunging it into a dreary fog. Everything was dank, wet, sopping and grime-encrusted. Under such a constant weight of oppression, it was easy enough to believe that the gods had deserted the world of mortals at last, and that the little remaining light and heat was draining out of reality one sodden day at a time.

It got under the skin after a while, the lack of blue in the sky and freshness on the breeze. When the air tasted foul for day after day, and the nights were clammy and the days were humid, and the rain kept coming in a fine drizzle that made everything mouldy and turned the earth underfoot into a spore-infested mire, it crushed the spirit. Even if the tensions of the impending battle had not been there, the city's people would have suffered badly under such unrelenting misery – their sleep would have been as fitful, and their nightmares just as vivid.

Reports were coming in of rioting in all quarters. Brawls started up over the most trivial of disputes, triggered by hunger, or despair, or the kind of futile anger that came simply from waiting for the axe to fall. Food shortages made the situation worse – unspoiled grain supplies were running low, despite the heavy guard placed on the remaining stores, and water was little better. Most of the populace avoided water in any case, preferring the strong beers brewed by the alemasters and the few dwarf refugees still lingering in the taverns. They said that beer warded against the Rot. Perhaps they were right.

Helborg had not had a decent drink in days, and it made his nerves brittle. The wounds across his face still had not healed, and the pain was getting worse. Whenever he found a scrap of sleep, the lacerations would flare up, waking him in sudden pain. His apothecaries could not do anything – their old remedies, never reliable, had long since ceased to work at all, and the best they could offer was to bandage the lacerations and apply a soothing salve.

Helborg refused. He would not walk around the Palace with linen strapped to his face, and nor would he seek to dampen the raw pain of the daemon's wound with potions. The pain was a reminder to him of the price of weakness. Moreover, it kept him awake, which with his chronic lack of proper rest was becoming essential.

'Make them do it again,' he rasped, running his hands through days-old stubble and resisting the urge to scratch the itching weals.

Von Kleistervoll, standing by his side, barked out the orders, and together, he, Helborg and Zintler watched the drills unfold.

They were standing on a narrow balcony overlooking the parade ground. The sandy surface had begun to go black from rot, despite the incessant raking from the groundskeepers and near-endless prayers from the arch-lectors.

Down below, formations of men began to move. Sergeants yelled out the drill orders, and troopers formed up into squares and detachments. The orders kept coming, just in the same sequence as they had been for the past two hours, rehearsing the various defensive tactics set down in Robert de Guilliam's great compendium of martial lore, the *Codex Imperialis*, that had provided the cornerstone of Imperial defence since the time of Mandred.

Helborg watched the detachments wheel around one another. He watched the halberdiers shuffle together, keeping tight in the first rank and holding their blades stiffly. He watched them perform the feints, the fall-backs, the rallies, all under the hoarse expletives of their taskmasters. Five hundred men moved across the parade ground, their every movement orchestrated like a masque in one of the old grand balls.

Except that there were no grand balls anymore, for the gowns had rotted away and the ladies' rouge and face-paints had mouldered in their tins, and the glittering halls where they would once have been worn were carpeted with dust.

'They are holding up,' remarked von Kleistervoll, looking for the positives.

The Reiksguard preceptor had taken a personal interest in improving the readiness of the standard Altdorfer garrisons since the defeat at Heffengen. Cohesion was everything to an Empire army – in any conflict, an individual human trooper was likely to be weaker and less well equipped than his enemy, but coordination with the warriors on either side of him made up for this deficiency. A Chaos horde charged into battle in ragged bands of berserk ill-discipline, against which the only defence was tight-ordered rows of steel. If the enemy managed to breach Altdorf's outer walls, as it surely would before the end, then such disciplined ranks would be needed to hold them up for as long as possible.

Zintler looked less sure. 'They grow weary,' he said, watching one squadron of pikemen fall out of step, and stumble as they tried to make it good.

'We're all weary,' snapped Helborg, observing the proceedings with a critical eye. 'Keep them at it.'

Then he turned away from the balcony's edge and stalked back inside, followed by Zintler. Von Kleistervoll remained where he was, scrutinising his charges like a kestrel hovering over its prey.

Helborg strode down the long corridor leading away from the balcony and into the Palace interior, and Zintler hurried to keep pace.

'How stands the gate repair?' Helborg demanded.

'The work was complete,' said Zintler. 'As soon as they finished, more defects were found. The engineers are working through the night. The West Gate will be complete by the end of this day; the others, a little longer.'

Helborg grunted. It was like trying to build with gravel – as soon as one wall was shored-up, another opened with cracks. 'Did the Gold magisters answer the summons?'

'They are working on the problem,' said Zintler. 'But in Gelt's absence–'

'Do not talk to me of Gelt. I do not want to hear his name.'

'Understood. His deputy is Gerhard Mulleringen. I will speak to him again.'

Helborg felt light-headed as he walked. Chambers passed him by, one by one, their edges blurred and their doors gaping. He was vaguely aware of functionaries and knights bowing, and the muffled sound of orders echoing from other corridors, and the clatter of running feet. It might as well have been a dream – all

VLAD VON CARSTEIN

Nearly five hundred years ago, Vlad von Carstein, first and greatest of his vampiric line, brought the Empire to its knees. He stood before the walls of Altdorf with an army of the dead at his command and his wife Isabella by his side. Only the heroic sacrifice of the Grand Theogonist of the time prevented Vlad from taking the Imperial throne for himself. Now he has returned to the world of the living, resurrected by Nagash to act as one of the Great Necromancer's mortarchs. Vlad commands the forces of the undead in the north, helping to protect the Empire – *his* Empire – from the hordes of Chaos. Though bound to his immortal master's will, Vlad has his own agendas as well – he wants to be recognised as Elector Count of Sylvania, with the rights and power that entails, and most of all he wants to discover what happened to his beloved Isabella after his demise.

THE FALL OF ALTDORF

The Monstrous Horde

RIVER REIK

The Tattooed Tribes

The Tattooed Tribes

Road to Marienburg

Altdorf
Undead

Altdorf
Undead

Altdor
Undea

Altdorf
Undead

Hammerplad

South Road

Altdorf
Undead

Leon
Sk

The Crusades of
Bretonnia

Road to Montfort

REIKWALD
FOREST

DRAKWALD
FOREST

Drakwald
Beasts

Dragon
Ogres

Reiksguard
Assault

Knightly
Orders
and State
Troops

Road to Middenheim

Golden Plaza

RIVER TALABEC

Road to Talabheim

Fischemarkt

The Empire's
Blades

Sigmarsen Street

Dampfplatz

Steam
Tanks

The
Tallyman's
Host

Fleischmark

Altdorf
Undead

RIVER REIK

Road to Nuln

DRAKWALD
FOREST

THE EMPEROR
KARL FRANZ

For twenty years, Karl Franz has held his crumbling Empire together by sheer force of will. He is a great statesman, respected by all, and a fierce warrior whose very presence is a herald of victory. Whether in his throne room moderating the petty squabbles of the elector counts, or leading troops from atop his loyal griffon, Deathclaw, Karl Franz embodies the spirit of Sigmar's realm, a spirit that has been shaken in recent years by the loss of some of his most trusted servants, the escalation of war in the north and the appearance of Valten, a young man who seems to be the herald of Sigmar's return. Ever mindful of the power of faith, Karl Franz has encouraged Valten's rise, gifting him Ghal Maraz, the legendary Hammer of Sigmar, as a symbol of his belief in the god's return. But as the hordes of Chaos advance into his Empire, Karl Franz wonders what his role will be in the tumultuous times to come.

that mattered was the army, the walls, the supplies and the defence plans. He had to remain *focused*.

Suddenly, he realised that one of the vague shadows flitting about him was not moving. He blinked, to see one of the Palace servants standing directly in his path. The man looked terrified, but remained where he was.

'Your pardon, lord!' he stammered, bowing low. 'I was charged to deliver these as soon as I could, but you have been... hard to find.'

Helborg glared at him. The servant held two rolls of parchment, one in each hand. 'What are they?' he demanded, wondering whether he could face more ledgers and dockets to sign.

'Letters, lord. One is marked with the seal of the Supreme Patriarch. The other was delivered from the Grey College.'

Helborg shot Zintler a dry look. 'The shadow-mages. What have they laid hands on now?' He grabbed both rolls, and broke Martak's seal first. As he read, his reaction moved from curiosity, to disbelief, to fury.

'He's gone,' Helborg said flatly.

'What do you mean?' asked Zintler.

'He's left the city. The *damned traitor*. I'll have his eyes. I'll rip his throat out and hang it from the Imperial standard. I'll punch his–'

'I can send a search party. We'll bring him back.'

Helborg rolled his eyes. 'He's an Amber battle wizard, Zintler. Your men would limp back as green-eyed hares, if they came back at all. It's too late – he broke into the Menagerie and worked some trickery on a war-griffon. They're both long gone.' He leaned heavily against the nearest wall, putting out a hand to support himself. Martak had been a pestilential fool, a peasant of the worst and most scabrous order, but he had been gifted, and his staff was needed. His loss was just one more blow amid a thousand other lesser cuts.

Zintler looked shocked, and for a moment did not say anything. When he did, his voice was weak. 'Why?'

Helborg laughed harshly. 'He thinks the Emperor lives. He's gone to *find him.*' His voice dripped with sarcasm. 'The pressure's got to him. I knew he was weak. Damn it all, what were they *thinking*, appointing a man like that?'

Zintler shook his head sympathetically. 'Anything else?'

'He advises me to perform a purge of the sewers – still on that old saw.' Helborg snorted another bitter laugh. 'Even now, he still presumes to advise me.' He screwed the parchment up and hurled it away. 'We do not need him. We still have magisters, and we still have priests, and I will not waste men on a fruitless trawl of the undercity.'

Even as he said the words, he realised how he sounded.

Desperate. I am clutching at any morsel of hope now.

He unravelled the second roll of parchment, finding himself yearning for some better news.

'From the Grey College, you say?' he asked, breaking the seal.

The servant nodded. 'They told me it was found on the roof, surrounded by blood. They do not know how long it was there.'

Helborg raised a weary eyebrow – just one more portent of doom. The tidings had been so relentlessly horrific over the past few days – Carroburg lost, Talabheim silent, Nuln cut off. In the deep of the night, when he struggled for just an hour of sleep, he feared that even his iron-hard defiance was beginning to crack at the edges.

Let it be news of reinforcements – from somewhere. Anywhere!

He started to read.

To the most sublime and majestic Karl Franz, Prince of Altdorf, Count of the Reikland, Emperor of the Eleven Provinces and Heir of Sigmar (Or his deputy, given the uncertain times that have overtaken us.)

I have no doubt you will not wish to read a letter

such as this, and from one such as me. You will be
tempted to throw it into the fire as soon as you see
the signature. I urge you to resist — I do not make
this communication lightly, nor do I wage this war
without urgent cause.

Your scryers will by now be telling you what all
men of reason can see for themselves — the order
of the world is changing. The Law of Death has
been broken, and the remaining Seven Laws are
straining at the edges. Powers that have stood firm
for millennia are fading, while others are growing
with unseemly haste.

Can any now doubt that the Gods of Ruin have
put aside their ancient quarrels, and are now
acting in concert? And, if that is so, can there be
any further doubt that they must be victorious?
The great heroes of the past are with us no more, for
we dwell in a time of lesser souls.

And yet, not all is foregone. There is another
way. Only one soul stands a chance of enduring
the storm of Chaos: my Master, who even now
strives to return from the banishment of ages.
Already he has struck down enemies older than
the stones you stand on, and soon he will turn his
gaze northwards.

Your great ancestor once ended him in a duel
that still echoes through the ages. And yet, if you
wish to see the forces of Order prevail in this time,
you will need to welcome him now. I am but an
emissary, a forerunner of this greater soul, and I
offer my services to you. My armies have already
marched at the side of yours, though you may not
have known it then. They will march alongside

you again, should you consent to my offer, freely
given and motivated by nothing more than
mutual need.

The living and the dead have ever been at odds,
but we are more alike to one another than to
the corruptions of the Outer Dark. Where they
would turn the world into a howling maelstrom
of perpetual flux, we understand the principles of
order, of command, of endurance. There is a future
taking shape, one in which the foundations of
reality are made firm again, where the weak
are protected and the strong given dominion. It is
not the future your priests were wont to pray for,
but it is one in which humanity is preserved, and
that, let me assure you, is the very best that can
be hoped for now.

Make no mistake, my lord, this is the choice:
alliance, or oblivion. Just as your ancestor
Magnus swallowed his pride to make common
cause with the elves of Ulthuan when they were
denounced as witches by the ignorant, so must
hard choices be made in our own time.

I demand nothing but that which has always
been my birthright: Electorship of Sylvania,
a province which has unfairly been denied its
existence for too long. The rights and privileges
of this station shall be the same as the others of
that rank: a runefang, a place at the Imperial
Council, the old exemptions from the common law
and the freedom to raise and keep men-at-arms.
I only ask one more boon of you: the chance to
search the Reikland for the resting place of one
who was dear to me. If the world is to be remade,

then I must discover her before all is cast anew.

I am aware that the mutual enmity between our peoples will make this proposal a hard one to entertain fairly. I have no doubt, though, given the circumstances, you will see past ancient prejudices and buried grievances. You will have seen the same auguries as we have, and you will know what is at stake. And, after all, do I not have some prior claim to this title? Or does right of conquest count for nothing in these debased times?

I trust that this missive will reach you, despite all the turmoil that even now seeks to overwhelm us. By the time you read it, I will be on the march, heading along the path of the Stir towards Altdorf. By the time I arrive, I will command a host larger than the last time I camped outside your walls. I earnestly hope that I do not arrive too late, and that you will at least have the opportunity to make your judgement under clear skies and with a free heart.

Until then, I remain, as I ever have been, your loyal and ever-obedient servant,

Vlad von Carstein

Helborg took a long time over the words. When he had reached the end, he read it again, hardly able to believe what was before his eyes.

If he had not been at Heffengen, he might have assumed the letter was some malicious forgery, despite the authentic-looking seal and appropriately archaic hand. But he had been at Heffengen, and so could believe only too well that the provenance was genuine.

He remembered von Kleistervoll's words after the battle.

They say the dead fought the northmen.

Helborg had not believed that then. He had seen von Carstein emerge, just as the battle remained in the balance. He had seen the skeletal dragon, and the onrush of the fanged knights in blood-red armour. Until *he* had arrived, the day had not been altogether lost.

Zintler hovered at his side, clearly itching to know what had been written. Helborg let him wait. His mind was racing.

Could he be trusted? Could I have been wrong?

As soon as the treacherous words entered his mind, he cursed himself for even thinking them.

He lives for nothing more than destruction! All of his kind do! They sense weakness, and circle for the kill.

Zintler could not restrain himself, and coughed delicately. 'My lord?'

Helborg did just as he had done with Martak's letter, and crumpled the parchment into a tight ball. He stuffed it into a pocket sewn on the inside of his half-cloak, and shoved it down deep. It would not do to have any but him aware of its contents. Just as with so many other things, he would have to bear the burden alone. Even the electors could not be told.

'It is nothing, Zintler,' he said, pushing himself clear of the wall. He dismissed the servant with a curt wave and started walking. 'Nothing worth a damn.'

Zintler trotted to keep up. 'And Martak? Can we do nothing?'

Helborg whirled on the Reikscaptain, fixing him with his hawk-dark eyes. As he did so, the wounds on his cheek spiked with fresh pain.

'We do what we have to do,' he snarled. 'We prepare. We train. We fight the darkness. We never give in. And we do so *alone*. There is no salvation from outside these walls, Zintler – you understand that? We have everything we are going to be given, and it must suffice.'

He felt the thrill of mania begin to run away from him then, and he tripped over his words. When these dark moods came on him, he felt almost like laughing.

Zintler shrank back, anxiety written on his dutiful features. 'Just so, my lord. But – forgive me – we are all mortals. There is also need for rest. When did you last take any?'

Helborg's eyes flared at the impudence. 'Rest?' he blurted. '*Rest?* Did Mandred take rest? Did Magnus? Would Schwarz-helm, or Karl Franz?'

He started walking again. He could feel his joints ache, his ribs creak, his wounds leak blood in a thin trickle down his neck.

'To the walls,' he croaked, keeping his shoulders back, his neck stiffly upright. 'Our labours are not yet done, and neither are the stonemasons'. I will see the works for myself, and if they have slackened from the task I will gut them with their own trowels.'

The cauldron overflowed, sending frothy, fatty matter splatting on the stone floor.

Festus stirred more vigorously, knowing the delicate juncture he had reached. He had been working for so long now, so patiently and so carefully that even a minute error now would be more than he could bear. As his flabby body sweated from the fires, the alembics and glassware funnels bubbled violently.

From one of the cages he could hear a woman weeping. Those cages were almost empty now – he would have to find a way to step up procurement before the final stage, which would not be easy. The City Watch was getting vigilant, and he had seen evidence of those damned Shallyans poking their noses around the margins of his domain.

The Shallyans were the only thing Festus truly had anything like fear for. A normal mortal could be so easily corrupted, since their appetites were so typically gross and their fear of sickness so habitually complete. The inhabitants of Altdorf were just like the inhabitants of any other Imperial city – petty, spiteful, grasping and timorous. Being turned into vessels of a greater sickness was the best thing they could possibly have aspired to, not that they ever evinced much gratitude for it.

But the sisters – they were tricky. They did not fear illness. How could they, since they spent their whole lives immersed in it? They did not suffer from gluttony, and they had no crippling fears. They accepted the world for what it was, and felt no need to change it, other than to ease the suffering of those stricken by its more painful aspects.

That, frankly, was perverse, and was just what made the Leechlord shudder. When his work was done here and the Tribulation was complete, Festus knew exactly where he was going and exactly what he was going to do. He could already hear the screams of the sisters as they writhed on the tip of his scythe. He would take his time killing them, one by one, letting them experience the full strength of what they had always denied.

It did not matter how strong or stoical they were – when confronted with the utter inevitability of defeat, they would all crack. They would be lapping up his potions sooner or later, and they would be *thankful* for it.

He sniffed a slug of mucus up and swallowed. Tiny daemonkin scurried around at his hooves, licking the drops of yellowish sweat that coursed from his bulging muscles. They were excitable now. They could sense what was in the cauldron, and they knew what it meant.

All along the walls of the subterranean chamber, vials and jars rattled and shivered. The drones of tumour-sized blowflies hummed through every vaulted cavity and undercroft. His realm had spread quickly, and now occupied hundreds of forgotten shafts and pits beneath Altdorf's foetid ground-level streets.

This was his kingdom, a foretaste of the greater kingdom of contagion to come, but it was still fragile. If he were discovered, if the mortals chose to look beneath their blocked noses and seriously try to track down the source of what ailed them, he might yet be vulnerable.

He stirred harder. Beneath the cauldron's surface, the dark shape grew ever more solid. A misshapen antler-prong briefly broke the brackish water, before sinking again. A gurgling sigh echoed from underwater, potent enough to make Festus shiver with anticipation.

They were all looking to him. The Glotts, the Tallyman, the Lord of Tentacles, the beasts, the damned and the god-marked – they were all looking to *him* to unlock the Great Tribulation.

He sweated harder. He was no longer chortling as he worked, and he no longer took any pleasure in his allotted task.

Time was running out. The deathmoon was riding low, and would be full soon. The massed hosts of the Urfather were crashing through a tangled, twisted forest of nightmares, and would be hammering at the gates uncomfortably quickly.

If he failed... if any of them failed...

Festus wiped his forehead. A diminutive toad-creature nipped his foot, and he kicked it irritably away. From the cauldron, a bubbling fountain briefly erupted, but did not sustain.

'Come on,' Festus muttered, putting more energy into the endless stirring. 'Come *on*...'

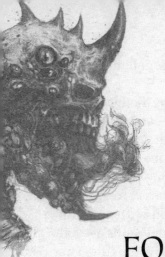

FOURTEEN

Martak hung onto the griffon's neck and gritted his teeth. A range of terrors coursed through him.

This is the realm of birds, he thought grimly. *I have no place in it.*

It had been easy enough to break into the Menagerie. With the attention of the city locked on the walls and the impending arrival of the enemy, the internal watch had grown slack and undermanned. Martak had slipped into the vast array of pens and cages during the night, using every ounce of his art to placate the creatures that slavered at him from behind iron bars.

Initially he had hoped a Bretonnian pegasus might have been held there – he knew how to ride a horse, and guessed it would be much the same to control one of their winged brethren – but the only creatures capable of flight were the colossal Imperial dragon and the select herd of Karl Franz's war-griffons. He had not even got close to the dragon before gouts of sulphurous smoke had forced him back, and even he was not boastful enough to think he could master that living furnace of scale and talon – the world would have to be ending around his ears for him to contemplate rousing *that*.

The griffons were scarce less fearsome, though, rising to over twice the height of a man at the shoulder and with flesh-ripping beaks that curved like scimitars. They all growled and hissed at him as he passed their pens, pawing at the straw beneath them and watching him with beady, unblinking yellow eyes.

In the end, he had selected a russet beast, marginally leaner than the others and with bands of crimson and gold on hawk-like wings. He had held its gaze and whispered words of control and reassurance. It had taken a long time before the griffon was calm enough for him to break the locks and dare enter, and then it still reared up, cawing furiously, and Martak was forced to delve deep into the Lore of Beasts to prevent it clawing his eyes out.

Eventually the creature suffered him to lead it by the halter, and the two of them walked out of the Menagerie's main cage-chambers and into the dung-strewn exercise yards beyond. It took him three attempts to mount, during which the noble beast glared at him coldly with a mix of irritation and contempt. Eventually the commotion, punctuated with earthy swear-words of dubious origin, roused the less soporific members of the watch, and the thud of footfalls echoed down from the watch towers around the yard.

Cursing, Martak hauled on the reins. 'Fly, then, damn you,' he hissed, having no idea how such a creature was ridden. Griffon riders were vanishingly rare in the Empire's armies, and they trained for years before mastering the tempestuous natures of their wild mounts. Very quickly Martak felt the spirit of the beast defying him – it was perfectly aware what he wanted, and perfectly aware that he had no power to compel it.

Faint lights blinked into life from the summit of the watch towers as torches were lit. A bell began to clang somewhere in the depths of the Menagerie's guardhouse, and doors slammed.

Still the griffon remained on the ground, its wings unfurled, but resolutely unmoving. Martak cried out every word of command in his lexicon, racking his mind for the correct cantrip or word-form. Perhaps there was not one – griffons were not like the dumb beasts of the deep wood that could be charmed with a gesture, they were ancient and proud scions of the mountains, with souls as fiery and untamed as the peaks they circled.

'Fly!' he growled again, brandishing his staff over the creature's neck as if the splinter of gnarled wood would intimidate such a colossal mount. The griffon hissed back at him, and strutted around the yard aimlessly. More shouts came from the surrounding buildings, at ground level this time, and the red glare of firelight spread from the barred windows. Men burst out of the doors leading back to the beast-chambers, each carrying a long spear and clutching nets between them.

A huge, burly figure, bald-headed and with an iron stud in his nose, roared up at them, his face puce with anger. 'Get back in there, you flea-ridden fly-hog!' he bawled, gesturing frantically at the other men to fan out and surround the griffon. 'Sigmar damn you, you will suffer for this!'

At the sight of that man, the griffon immediately reared again, nearly throwing Martak from its back. Its forelegs scythed, and it let rip with a piercing shriek of fury.

The first net, weighted with iron balls, was thrown. With a coiled pounce, the griffon leapt into the air, flapping powerfully to gain loft.

More nets were thrown, then spears, but none reached the target. The griffon powered upward rapidly, climbing higher with every powerful down-beat of its huge wings.

Martak hung on, his heart racing, clutching to the beast's plumage with fear-whitened knuckles.

'Taal's teeth,' he swore, realising belatedly what he had taken on.

Altdorf fell away below him, a patchwork of faint lamplight amid the overcast gloom of the night sky. The griffon banked, and Martak saw the baroque sprawl of the Imperial Palace stretched out, glistening faintly from the light of a thousand lanterns. Even in the midst of his blind terror, it was hard not to be awed by the spectacle.

'*North*, damn you,' he hissed, trying again to impose his will.

The griffon did not listen, but headed east, instinctively heading for the mountains where it had been hatched. Martak persevered, reaching out to the beast's mind and trying to quell its wilfulness.

Slowly, painfully, it began to respond. Martak whispered every scrap of the Lore of Beasts into its ears, piling on the words of command.

Eventually, with a frustrated caw of defeat, it began to listen. It toppled to one side and angled north, heading over the seas of dark-limbed trees and flying steadily.

Ever since that moment, Martak had battled with it, forcing it to obey him through sheer bloody-mindedness. There was no beautiful meeting of souls and no mutual respect between them – every wing-beat was a struggle, a draining battle of psyches. The griffon toiled through the air as if mired in it. Just staying mounted was a challenge in itself, and Martak nearly slipped from his perch more than once.

Somehow, though, they flew on until the sunrise, by which time they were far out over the forest and the Reik valley was a long way behind them. Both of them were exhausted, bad-tempered and stinking with sweat.

Martak gazed out over the vast expanse of land below. Although he had often tramped far and wide into the Great Forest, it was only from the air that one could appreciate just how immeasurably immense the Empire was. During the long flight they had barely passed any settlements, and yet the forest still stretched off towards the four empty horizons in an unbroken, daunting mass. Night-mists curled and boiled atop the crowns of the trees, spiralling into eerie columns that twisted up to meet the weak light of the sun. The eastern horizon was a weak strip of pale gold, glistering faintly under heavy bands of iron-grey.

The griffon cawed harshly. Ahead of them reared several out-crops of dark rock, thrusting clear of the canopy like leviathans breaking the ocean surface. Martak sensed the beast's desire to set down, drawn perhaps by a landscape that reminded it of its mountainous home.

Martak allowed it to lose height, and soon they were circling down towards the nearest column of stone, angling with surprising dexterity through the chill dawn air. The griffon crouched as it touched down.

Martak gripped it tightly by the nape of the neck, and hissed into its ear. 'You are mine, now. I do not release you. One way or another, we are bound to one another, so do not get any ideas.'

The griffon hissed back at him, and scraped its talons along the rock, but did not make any further protest. They understood one another, and a bond, however tenuous and irascible, had been established.

Martak dismounted stiffly and hobbled to the edge of the stone island. He stood fifty feet above the tallest of the trees, and could see nothing but a landscape of leaves in every direction – no rivers, no castles, no cultivated land. The forest reeked of slowly mouldering fruit. The more he looked, the more he felt the marks of slow corruption. The Great Forest had always been a perilous and dank place, but now it was truly festering.

Martak slumped to his haunches. He would have to make a fire soon. Somehow, he would have to find something to eat – if anything that still lived in the forest was worth eating.

He gazed out to the north, and at the sight of the endless ranks of trees, his heart faltered.

Is this a mistake? he ruminated. *Should I have stayed? My absence will make Helborg spit blood.*

He smiled grimly. That, on its own, probably made it worth the labour.

Behind him, the griffon began to preen itself, pulling at its tangled feathers with its hooked beak. Martak shuffled away from the precipice, and started to look for dry tinder. The fire would do more than keep them warm – it was the precursor to a spell, one that would allow his sight to roam far beyond the confines of his mortal vision.

It would not be easy to summon up the requisite power – scrying was not his strength, and the dreary tang of mutation hung in the air, thicker and more durable than the rolling mist.

'But I *will* find you,' Martak said aloud, startling the griffon. 'By the Eight Winds, this journey will not be wasted.'

He hobbled across the bare stone, limping from muscle-ache and the cold, muttering to himself. Out in the wilds, the clouds hung heavily, and the plague-wind moaned.

It would be a long, cold day.

'Consider it, o my brother,' said Otto, softly.

'I do so, o my brother,' replied Ethrac, his voice hushed in awe.

Neither of them spoke for a little while after that. The two of them sat on Ghurk's shoulders, lost in thought. Below them, their army waited for orders. They waited for a long time.

Ghurk stood at the summit of a bald, windswept hill on the north bank of the Reik. The close press of thorn and briar had given way a little there, exposing the vista to the east in all its untrammelled glory. Ahead of them, at last, lay their goal.

Just below Ghurk's hooves, the terrain fell away sharply in terraces of foliage-clogged undulation. The Reik valley had widened since Carroburg, and was now a broad, shallow bowl. The land had once been cultivated across the flat floodplain, but now the crops rotted in their drills, reeking with a subtle aroma that Otto found immensely pleasing. Everywhere he looked, the forest had crept past its ancient bounds, smothering everything. The new growths had taken on a wild variety of hues – pus-yellow, olive-green, the pulsing crimson of blood-blisters. Above it all, the clouds still churned, making the air as thick and humid as half-warmed tallow.

A mile away, Altdorf lay, rising from the tormented plain like a colossus, straddling the wide river and thrusting its towers up towards the uncaring heavens. Far bigger than Marienburg, far bigger than Talabheim, it was the greatest of prizes, the jewel of the southern Empire.

It had never been a beautiful place, even before the Rot. It had none of the soaring grandeur of Lothern, nor the stark geometry of the Lustrian megalopolises. What it had was *solidity* – the huge, heavy weight of history, piled atop layer after layer of construction until the final ramshackle, glorious heap of disparate architectural and strategic visions reached up to scrape at the lowering rainclouds themselves. Mighty buttresses reinforced vast retaining walls, straining amid the lattice of bridges and causeways and spiral stairs and gatehouses and watchtowers, all surmounted by slender tiled roofs that poked upward like fire-blackened fingers. A thousand hearths sent sooty trails snaking over the tiles, casting a pall of smog that hung like pox over the entire gaudy display. Copper domes glistened dully amid the tangle of dark stone and grimy daub, and the noise of forges and manufactories could be made out even from so far away, grinding away somewhere deep in the bowels of the vast, vast city.

Its walls were intact. Otto permitted himself some surprise at that – he had been told to expect the masonry to have crumbled away. Perhaps the defenders were more capable than he had expected. They had certainly worked hard.

It mattered not. Walls of stone were of little impediment to the hosts he commanded. Altdorf was just a microcosm of the Empire itself – the true rot came from *within*. There was no point in reinforcing borders and bastions and parapets if the flesh contained beyond them was withering away with every passing hour. They were weak, now. Terribly weak. How many of them could still lift their weapons? How many even had the desire to?

A low crack and growl of thunder played across the eastern horizon. Great pillars of cloud were gathering, driven west by gales from the Worlds Edge Mountains. Stray flickers of lightning briefly flashed out across the grey, drab air, glinting on the Reik's dreary surface.

The river had almost entirely turned into a glutinous slurry, and it barely lapped its own banks any more. Huge vines had slithered out of the encroaching tree-cover and extended into the water, making what remained even more viscous.

Otto smirked as he saw the transformation. The god he served was a mighty god indeed. The very earth had been poisoned, the waters thickened, the growing things perverted and sent thrusting into feral parodies of themselves. There was no resisting this – it was the wearing weight of entropy, the corruption of all purity, the glorious potential of the sick, the foul, the decaying.

'We march now,' Otto breathed, knowing how little time it would take. The army would sweep east, filling the valley before them from side to side, surrounding the city as the ocean surrounded its islands.

'Not yet,' warned Ethrac. 'We wait for the others.'

Otto felt like snapping at him. Ethrac could be tediously particular. He loved his brother – he loved *both* his brothers – but Ghurk's pleasing enthusiasms never ceased to be endearing, whereas Ethrac could, on occasion, be harder to like.

'We may crush it *now*, o my brother,' said Otto, forcing a smile. 'Crush it like Carroburg.'

'No, no.' Ethrac waved his staff to and fro, and the bells clanged. 'Not long to wait. The others grow closer. We will need all three – the Lord of Tentacles, the Tallyman, the beasts of the dark wood, the hosts of the far north.'

Otto rolled his eyes. 'They are *starved*, o my brother! They are timorous.'

Ethrac shot him a crooked smile. 'Not as starved as they will be, o my sibling. Not as timorous as they *will* be. While they still have a little of their native strength left, we must creep with caution. How many battles have been lost to impetuosity? Hmm? You can count them all?'

Otto was about to retort, knowing the argument was futile, when the clouds parted overhead. The fine drizzle that had accompanied them since making landfall at Marienburg guttered and trembled. A new light flooded across the valley, weaker than the shrouded sun, like a pale flame.

The hosts of ruin looked up. Otto did likewise.

He saw the flames of the comet flicker, masked by the shifting airs and made weak by the filth in the skies, but there nevertheless. Tongues of fire glimmered in the heavens, just as they had done in the half-forgotten days only recorded in forbidden books.

Otto made the sign of ruination. 'The twin-tailed star,' he muttered.

Ethrac chuckled. 'It surprises you, o my brother? You have not listened to me. The comet was there to witness the birth of Sigmar's realm, and it will be there to see it out. Such signs and portents were written into fate's tapestry since before you or I were woven into it.'

Otto continued to stare at the comet uneasily. He could barely catch sight of it, and its light was washed out by the gloom of midday, but the brief snatches he did perceive made his stomach turn.

'It presages nothing,' he muttered, to convince himself as much as anything else.

'That is right,' said Ethrac, satisfied.

'The full deathmoon is due.'

'That it is.'

Otto drew in a phlegmy breath. He could sense the tension from the thousands of warriors waiting behind him. All they needed was an order.

'Then we wait for it,' said Otto. 'We wait for the Night of Souls.'

'We do.'

Otto grinned. His mood was oddly changeable. Why was that? Nerves? Surely not – he had been shown the future, and it was gloriously, infinitely putrid.

'Not long now, then,' he said, drumming his fingers on Ghurk's leather-hard flesh.

Ethrac smiled contentedly, and looked up at the heavens.

'Not long at all, o my brother.'

The wait was over. The scouts had returned from the forward stations, and the reports had been sent down from the Celestial College's scrying towers.

In a way, it was a relief. The sham-war was over, the real one could begin. Whatever Helborg might have done better, it mattered not now. All that remained was the fight itself, the clash of steel against iron, and in that at least the Reiksmarshal had never been found wanting.

At the first sound of a warning clarion, he had donned his full battle-garb. Three menials were required to help him into it, and when they were finished he was encased from neck to knee in plate armour. They had polished it furiously hard over the past week, and the steel gleamed like silver. The scabbard of his rune-fang had been lovingly restored, and the icons of the griffon and the insignia of Karl Franz looked as pristine as they ever had done. The menials draped a new cloak over his shoulders, and it brushed against the stone floor with a sigh of fine fabric.

He banished them once all was done, and remained for a moment in his private rooms, donned for war.

From outside, he could hear the growing clamour of the city readying itself. Bells rang out from every temple tower, sounding the alarm and rousing the sick and the exhausted from their beds. Great arcs of lightning crackled across the rooftops as the magisters of the colleges readied their arcane war machines. Trumpets sounded in every garrison, calling the thousands of troops still in the employ of the Palace to their stations. Scaffolds cracked and groaned as huge cannons were winched into position and rolled forward on their parapet mounts.

Helborg smiled. They were the sounds he lived to hear. The troops were responding as he had drilled them to. They might have learned to curse him since he returned from the north, they might have spat his name with hatred when he had forced them into another exercise or commandeered another water-supply or made the engineers work through the night to keep the battlements intact and the foundations strong, but they were *ready*. The standards still flew from the turrets, and the cancer of fear had not undone them just yet.

He walked over to the door. As he did so, he caught sight of his reflection in a grimy window-pane, and paused.

He looked much the same as he had done in the past – the lean, aquiline face with its hook nose and flamboyant moustache. When he turned to one side, though, he saw the long rakes along his cheek, still flecked with scab-tissue. As if aware of the attention, the wounds flared again, hot as forge-irons.

'Keep it up,' Helborg snarled. 'Keep the pain coming. It'll only make me angrier.'

He swept out of the chamber and into the corridor outside. He walked swiftly, banishing the fatigue that had dogged him for so long. He still had not managed to sleep, but the adrenaline of the coming combat sustained him, flooding his muscles and making him itch to draw his blade.

As he went, commotion built around him. Palace officials ran to and fro, carrying orders and last-minute requisitions. Knights in full armour stomped from the armouries up to their stations, saluting smartly as they caught sight of the Reiksmarshal. Helborg saw the sigils of the Sable Chalice, the Hospitallers, the Knights Panther, the Order of the Golden Wolf, and there were no doubt more already stationed across the city.

And, of course, there were the surviving Reiksguard, restored to combat readiness following von Kleistervoll's punishing regimen. Nine hundred were ready to deploy, counting those that had remained in Altdorf prior to Heffengen – a formidable force, and one that he would personally command when the time came.

He neared the high doors of his destination. When they saw him coming, the door-guards hurriedly pushed them open, bowing as he strode through.

On the far side, the circular Chamber of Ghal Maraz opened up in all its many-arched splendour. In times of peace, the priceless warhammer itself was hung on chains of gold from the domed roof, guarded by four warrior priests and ringed with wards from the Light College. Only the mightiest or the most faithful were ever permitted access to the chamber while the weapon hung suspended over its iron war-altar. That altar had been forged from the guns used in the defence of the city against the vampire lords of legend, and was as black and sullen as pitch.

Now the chains swung emptily, for Ghal Maraz, like so much else, was lost, borne by the boy-warrior Valten somewhere out in the wilds of the north. The city's defenders still mustered before the altar nevertheless, as if some lingering aura of power still hung over the empty hooks.

They were all there: von Kleistervoll in his full preceptor's regalia, Zintler looking very different in his ceremonial Reikscaptain's war-plate, the grand masters of the Knightly Orders, the masters of the Colleges of Magic, the arch-lectors and the master engineers and the Imperial generals with their captains and lieutenants in tow. Von Liebwitz, Haupt-Anderssen and Gausser were present, all in their own ancestral battle-gear. They might have been quarrelsome, power-hungry schemers, but they each carried a runefang and had been tutored since infancy on how to use it.

The display of collected power was comforting. It would have looked better with Schwarzhelm there, or Huss, or Volkmar or

Gelt, but it was still a daunting panoply. As the doors slammed closed behind Helborg, all head were lowered in deference.

'So, the enemy has been sighted,' said Helborg, standing before them and fixing each in turn with his gaze. 'We know now that they are three: an army to the north that still marches; an army to the east that is almost upon us, and the largest host of all, fresh from the sack of Marienburg and within sight of the walls. They will wait until Morrslieb is full, or so the arch-lectors tell me.'

Fleischer bowed. The head of the Celestial College nodded in agreement – they all knew the power of the witching-night.

'They outnumber us many times over,' Helborg went on, his harsh voice echoing strangely in the huge chamber. 'They bring foul creatures from the wilds on the edge of the world, and think to break us as easily as they broke Marienburg and – so we fear – Talabheim.' He smiled wolfishly. 'But they have not reckoned on the soul of this place. It is Sigmar's city. It is *our* city.'

Gausser grunted approvingly. All the true fighters – the grand masters, the Reiksguard – appreciated words like this. They had spent their lives going into battle, often against horrific odds, and only needed to know that their liege was with them; that he suffered alongside them, and that, in the final test, he would stand in the mud and blood with blade in hand.

'This is the heart of the Empire,' growled Helborg, gesturing to the golden pilasters and columns surrounding the empty altar. 'This is where the seat of power has always been, where the Emperors rule, where the Law was set down and where the source of our greatness was first delved. While Altdorf lives, the Empire lives. As fortune's wheel turns, it is we who have been charged with the sacred task of keeping it secure for the next thousand years.'

As he spoke, Helborg could see doubt in the eyes of those he addressed. If even half the scouts' reports were accurate, than the enemy was almost ludicrously vast – a host greater even than the swollen armies of Kul.

Let them doubt. What mattered was whether they stood up or fell to their knees, and there had never been a day of Helborg's life when he had not faced his enemy on his feet.

'Even as I speak, our troops are reaching their stations,' he said. 'They will remain firm so long as *we* remain firm. They will look to us, the masters of men, to lead the defence and show just what stuff the Empire is made of. They will not be afraid if we do not feel fear. They will not retreat if we hold fast, and they will not contemplate defeat if we do not let it enter our minds. So I say to you all this day: stand firm in Sigmar's image! As night falls and the terror grows, stand firm in Sigmar's image. As they bring fire from the firmament and summon horror from beyond the grave, stand firm in Sigmar's image. He has not abandoned us, for He is a god of *battle*. Wish not for a world in which there is no strife or bloodshed, for that would be a pale reflection of the world of glory we have been given to dwell in.'

He grinned, feeling the seductive mania return, and his wounds broke open on his cheek. 'And this will be the most *glorious* of days! Men will sing in after-ages of the heroes of Altdorf, and will curse their fortune not to have witnessed the deeds that will be done here. They will look up at the white towers of this city, standing prouder than they do today, and marvel at their eternal strength, just as they curse the darkness that thought to bring them low.'

Helborg drew his sword. 'You know what this is!' he said, brandishing the blade before them. 'This is the Sword of Vengeance, the *Klingerach*, and it has drunk the blood of the faithless across every province in the realm. I have driven you hard, and I know the burden has been heavy, but now the Sword of Vengeance marches to war, and you will march with it.'

He lifted the sacred runefang towards the empty altar. Ghal Maraz may have been missing, but his own weapon was ancient enough to honour the sacred space.

'And so, on this day, when the fates converge on Altdorf and we become the fulcrum of the war to end all wars, I pledge this,' he swore, feeling the lines of blood trickle down his neck. 'I will take no backward step. I will not retreat, I will not cower, I will not relent. I will *fight*. I will fight for this place with every breath and with every drop of blood in my body. And if the world is to end and if all is to be cast in the fire, then I will die in the service of the Empire as I have lived, as a *warrior*.'

He raised the sword high.

'For the Empire!' he roared.

As one, the assembled warriors raised their own weapons towards the altar.

The Empire! they cried in unison, and the massed voices soared into the dome above, echoing in fractured harmony. *The Empire! For Karl Franz!*

Helborg looked at them all, his blood pumping. They were as ready as they would ever be, each of them filled with the zeal of combat. This was what made the Empire great – that, for all its folly and corruption, when the storm broke they had never refused the challenge.

'Now then,' he snarled, feeling the dark swell of battle-lust throbbing through him. 'The time for words and prayers is over. Take your positions, and may Sigmar guide your blades.'

FIFTEEN

More orcs came over the mountains after the first gang, jogging in loose bands, their maws drooling and their eyes rimmed with madness and fatigue. Every time they were dispatched, another herd would follow, not in huge numbers, but enough to slow the Bretonnians further.

The knights rode in full battle-gear all the time, keeping lances to hand and changing horses often. Snow began to fall, dusting the bare rock with a grey slush that made the horses' hooves skid and slip, and they lost more precious steeds and men during the vicious, short-lived brawls.

'They just run onto our blades,' Jhared remarked. 'It is as if...'

They no longer wish to live. Leoncoeur could have finished the sentence for him. That, beyond all he had seen since the rise of Mallobaude, filled his heart with foreboding. An orc was a crucible of nature's wrath, a furious avatar of martial excess. They lived to fight, to scrap, to roar out their feral abandon into the world as they tore it apart. An orc feared nothing.

And yet now they were broken. Just as Jhared said, they

stumbled blindly into combat, going through the motions in a kind of dumb rehearsal of their old terrible glory. For the first time in his life, Leoncoeur took no pleasure in slaying them. It began to seem... cruel.

The series of skirmishes slowed their passage through Axebite Pass, but did not halt it. Leoncoeur gave the column no respite, and they trudged on through the swirling, snow-laced squalls. Peasants who succumbed to the grinding cold were left where they fell, and the baggage train became steadily more and more undermanned. Soon they would have scarce enough hands to keep the carts rolling and the teams of warhorses guarded, but the pace never slackened.

Eventually, they cleared the worst of the bitter high path, and the road began to snake downhill again. The vast peaks of the Grey Mountains still rose impossibly high above them, their distant heads blocked by thick cloud, but the hardest portion of the traverse was over. The knights began to pick their way down the gravelly paths of scree and boulders, going carefully lest more horses go lame.

The purity of the high airs soon collapsed once more into the thick filth they had breathed in Bretonnia, except it was far, far worse on the northern side of the range. On the second day of the descent, the vanguard rounded a tight bend in a narrow gorge, and beheld for the first time the land beyond the mountains.

Barring their path a few dozen yards away was a thick snarl of tangled briars. Beyond that lay a seething glut of vines and throttle-weeds, all gently moving as if propelled by intelligences of their own. Trees studded the congested road, looking like they had sprouted from the living rock just moments ago, their gnarled roots frozen onto the cracked stone and their crowns gasping for air and light.

From his vantage at the head of the column, Leoncoeur could see that the thick undergrowth extended for miles. It ran away from them, close-bound and endless. To their right reared the old fortress of Helmgart, once a mighty citadel, but now abandoned to the clutching vines, its walls crumbled and its keep hollow. It looked like it had been empty for weeks.

Leoncoeur sensed the dismay from the warriors around him. The way was blocked, and it would take days to hack through just a tithe of it. The pegasi would soar above it all, of course, but they were merely the spear-tip of his force.

Leoncoeur whispered an order and his horse walked on, approaching the first clumps of moss that marred the stony path. As the rank wall of growths neared, he smelled the over-sweet stench of fermenting fruit.

This is the spawn of corruption, he mused, watching the polyps flex and swell under his mount's hooves. *If it comes from magic, it can be dispelled with magic.*

To the left of the path, an ice-white cataract plunged down the mountainside, swollen from the storms in the peaks above. It remained pure when all around it was foetid. Leoncoeur halted before it, remembering the words of the Lady.

Look for me in pure waters.

The white river ran on ahead of him, foaming in its narrow course and throwing up a fine spray. Far ahead, it plunged under the shadows of the trees, hissing as if angered by the contagions around it.

Leoncoeur drew his blade, stained from greenskin blood, and held it high.

'By the Lady we march!' he cried. 'And by Her grace will all taint be cleansed from the world!'

His warriors remained at a distance, unsure. They had been sorely tested by the passage of the pass, and Leoncoeur was not so deaf that he had not heard the mutterings of discontent. They had been promised glorious battle, not an endless slog through poison-vines.

They would need to be reminded just who they served.

Leoncoeur pointed his sword towards the river, holding the

tip just above the gurgling surface. 'They have not removed you from the waters just yet, my queen,' he murmured. 'I can sense your power here, just as it was in Couronne. Their faith wavers. I beseech you, humbly, restore it.'

Nothing happened. The rain started up again, drizzling down from the grey sky and making the standards heavy. The thick filigree of branches and vines seemed to tighten, drawing across the path ahead in a heavy wall of interlocking boughs.

Leoncoeur held his weapon in place, and closed his eyes. *What do you demand of me, Lady? I have already pledged everything. What is there left?*

He saw her then, in his mind, just as she had been in Bretonnia. If anything, her slender face seemed even more careworn.

Everything, my champion? she whispered back. *You have barely been tested.*

That hurt. He had lost a kingdom, and forfeited any chance of taking it back by following her command. He had already lost more than most men would ever have to give away.

The way is barred, he said.

All ways are barred, she breathed, her voice little louder than a child's whisper. *Are you sure you wish me to unlock it? If this road is made straight, you will never return along it.*

Leoncoeur stiffened. She had already warned him of this. What did she expect – that he would forget his vow?

Do you wish me to live?

That startled her. She looked at him, a sudden desire playing in her immortal eyes. *Of course, beloved*, she insisted. *I desire that of all things. Turn aside, and I will preserve you for as long as my power lasts. When you die, my heart will break.*

Leoncoeur nearly opened his eyes. For a moment, he saw a future unravelling before him – the two of them, mortal man and wife, riding out across a wide grassland, the sun rising swiftly in a dew-fresh dawn. He saw her face turn to his and smile, the care wiped from it. She reached out, and their hands touched.

The vision made his heart ache. It had been forbidden even to countenance such a thing, and here she was, *showing* it to him.

He looked down, still locked in the dream-image. His steed's hooves trod in the damp earth. In the marks of the hooves, tiny worms wriggled. They were white and blind, and their mouths were ringed with fangs.

There would be no escape, he told her, letting go of her hand. *It would pursue us to the ends of the earth. You know this.*

The Lady nodded, smiling sadly. *And now you do, too. So ask me again, my champion. You wish me to give you a path to Altdorf?*

He did not. He wished for nothing but the vision, even in its falsity and its deception. He wished only for a scrap of time alone with her, just as he had always dreamed of, even if it meant an eternity of damnation thereafter.

But wishes were for peasants, and he was a knight of the realm.

If it lies within your power, Lady, he breathed, *make the road straight*.

She bowed, her expression a mix of sorrow and satisfaction, and the vision ebbed away. Leoncoeur opened his eyes again.

Nothing had changed. His warriors gave no sign of impatience – however long the exchange had seemed to him, it had clearly been no time for them.

He straightened in his saddle, and turned to the foul morass ahead.

'Your reach does not yet compass the world,' he announced, gazing out at it with his fierce, blue-eyed glare. 'While we may yet contest you, we will.'

His words rang out, echoing strangely on the air. The vines shivered, and straggling roots withdrew. The entire forest seemed to falter, as if stirred by a sudden gust of wind.

Leoncoeur smiled coldly. He could feel the divine power now, warm against his flesh like summer sun. She was weakened, to be sure, but not yet destroyed.

'Rise,' he commanded, raising his blade and pointing it ahead.

The waters began to surge, let loose like a dam breaking. The river burst its banks, welling up and flooding the path ahead. Leoncoeur backed up, never letting his blade waver, as the road ahead dissolved into foaming silt.

The trees immediately shrank back, and a thin hissing broke out from among the branches. The waters kept on rising, boiling up out of the ground in defiance of all natural law. Fresh springs burst through the open rock, gushing in plumes of white before crashing to the ground again and sluicing down the slope.

Leoncoeur backed up further, watching with some satisfaction as the river's banks crumbled away, unable to accommodate the roaring torrent that now coursed through it. Boulders were dislodged, rolling along with the flow and crashing into the twisted trunks ahead. The roar of the waters mingled with the snap and crack of wood breaking.

Where the Lady's water-magic hit the sorcerous forest, great gouts of smoke leapt into the sky, fizzing and spitting with emerald aethyr-energies. The raging river seemed to carve straight through whatever it touched, burning the foul woods away as if acid had been poured onto them. A stench like burning flesh rose up, harsh and acrid.

'Stand firm!' commanded Leoncoeur, working to keep his steed from panicking. The waters frothed and swirled around its hooves, causing no more harm to it than a non-magical river. Ahead of them, the torrent gouged deeper, cutting a path through the woodland and leaving ragged wound-edges on either side. The up-swell of water kept on rising, roiling and churning out from the fractured earth. The forest was ripped open, its roots torn up and its tight-wound growths carried away. As the waters smashed onwards, tearing ever deeper into the country beyond, the sound of a woman's laughter could be heard over the thunder, faint but unmistakable.

Soon the sounds faded away, heading north as the magically roused river cut its way onward. An empty road stood in its wake, dripping and sodden, overlooked on either side by the surviving trees. The path was like a tunnel, overhung and hemmed in on all sides. The Lady's power had only been sufficient to rid the river's path of its filth, and the clear route extended no further than the road's edge.

Leoncoeur looked into the shadows, his heart thumping. Witnessing the extreme release of such magic had been a mixed experience for him. On the one hand, being in close proximity to the divine strength of his lifelong queen was what gave him the reason for living. On the other, he was under no illusions that this march would be his last. The brief, snatched vision of another life had made the choice even crueller, though he knew the purpose of it.

She had to be sure. Even the slenderest chance that he would turn aside had to be discounted. He did not resent her testing him, for his whole life had been a test, and the knowledge that he had passed it made up for some of the grief.

Not all of it, though. It would take him a long time to forget the vision.

'You have been shown the way,' he announced, lowering his blade at last and sheathing it. His horse stamped in the waters. Ahead of them, the river level gradually subsided as the tide-face worked its way further north. 'Now we begin the final march. Ride on, for Bretonnia and the Lady.'

The warriors about him saluted piously, and began to move. One by one, trooping in file, the knights of Bretonnia passed under the shadow of the plague-wood, and trod the last road to Altdorf.

The host of the undead grew ever larger, feeding from the slain of the battles and pulling corpses out of the ground every passing hour.

It was all so familiar. Vlad remembered doing the same thing just the previous year – gathering the lost souls to himself, giving them purpose, making them far greater than they ever had been in their first life.

Then he smiled to himself, embarrassed by the false recollection. It had not been last year – it had been over a thousand years ago, and everything in the world had changed. It was so easy to forget how long he had been away. His old enemies – Kruger of the Order of the White Wolf, Wilhelm the Theogonist – had been dead so long that no mortals outside the dusty archives still remembered their names. And yet, to him, it felt like mere months ago. He could still see the walls of Altdorf reeling before him, ripe for destruction. He could taste the blackpowder on the air, and feel the pressure of Isabella's hand in his as they jointly planned the final assault.

She had been his strength, back then. Everything he had done had been through her, driven onwards by the raw passion that had so surprised him. To be alone, truly alone, never lost its bitter aftertaste. He could summon as many courtesans to his side as he liked, taking his pick from the cadavers of a thousand years of ossified beauty, and it would make no difference.

Perhaps, he had thought to himself in the lonely hours of the night, that was why the Master had been able to pull him back. In true death, Vlad must have been an unquiet soul, ripped untimely from the world and still hungering to return for the love he had left behind.

'Now I am a *mortarch*,' he said to himself dryly. 'The titles he has given us, to usher in the reign of eternal order. I would have preferred *Emperor*, but such is fate. Perhaps I shall still be *elector*, which will be a decent consolation.'

He had not heard from Altdorf since sending his letter. He had not expected to, though to have no response at all, not even a denunciation, wore at his pride a little. As far as he was concerned, the offer remained open. He might have to wait until the walls were broken and the mortal armies were reeling, but waiting was something he had always been good at.

'My lord,' said Herrscher, sounding concerned. 'Regard the river.'

Vlad snapped out of his thoughts, and looked up.

He sat on a throne mounted atop the high quarterdeck of a shallow-hulled river cruiser. Ranks of oars dipped and hauled into the murky waters around, dragging the ship south and west along the course of the Reik. Behind him, in a long procession of bleak ugliness, trade barges followed on, each one stuffed with the bodies of his servants. Every barge carried several hundred soldiers, and there were dozens upon dozens of them now, plundered from the destroyed Imperial settlements along the Stir and the upper Reik. The sable banners of Sylvania hung from every one, held aloft by cold hands. No sound came from those barges, save for the slap of oars in the water and the thump of reed-clumps hitting the solid bows.

Since taking to the river, progress west had been rapid. With the need to negotiate the clogged and treacherous forest paths negated, the entire army had slipped towards their goal without obstruction, travelling just as well by day as by night, pausing only to sack any of the riverside towns they came across. Kemperbad had been the last big one, a walled fortress to rival Wurtbad, and the fight to subdue it had been just as vicious. The outcome had been much the same, in the end – a cohort of newly dead and newly cowed to bolster the truly huge host now under his thrall.

Vlad had begun to relax then, safe in the knowledge that they would be there in time. He should have known better – the forces of Ruin were not led by fools, and they had formidable powers of their own.

'I have never seen the like,' said Herrscher.

Ahead of Vlad's position, in the bows, the Pale Ladies stood on the very edge of the deck railing, peering into the gloom and exchanging exclamations of outrage. Even the reanimated Wolff, still sullen and moody, looked out at the approaching vista.

Half a mile downstream, where the broad flow of the river expanded into a wide, slate-grey expanse of choppy, wind-whipped froth, the forest had crept from its bounds. It had started a mile or so back – heavy clods of moss floating in mid-channel, fouling the oars and bumping against the hulls. As they had made headway, the clots and mats had grown more numerous, breaking free of the tree-lined banks even as he had watched them.

The barrier before them, though, was something else. The trees themselves had burst open, throwing obscene spears of rotten wood into the water. More had followed, building on those sent before. Vines had snaked into the splintered bulwark, binding it all tightly. More mosses had latched on to that frame, swelling and pulsing under the perpetual twilight.

Somehow, the forest had managed to block the entire river, throwing out tentacles and sinking deep into the main flow. Backed up by the obstruction, the Reik had burst its banks, filtering into the woods on either side and welling up in pools of fly-encrusted muck.

Vlad stood up. The blockage was not a temporary thing. It looked like the unnatural outgrowths continued far beyond the first barrier, breaking the flow of the Reik entirely. Leeches wriggled across the top of the arboreal dam, pale-skinned and red-eyed. The stink was even worse than it had been higher up the river, magnified by the standing water that now mingled with rotten roots.

'We cannot break that, lord,' said Herrscher.

The witch hunter at least had the grace to sound concerned. Herrscher had long since given up the pretence of anger at his predicament, and was now a loyal member of Vlad's entourage. They all gave up caring, sooner or later, and settled into their new life. It was hard to sustain the old angers when one owed one's existence to one's enemy.

'Of course we can,' said Vlad, irritably, watching the twisted dam drift closer.

'We should order the barges to halt.'

'They will keep going.'

Herrscher looked exasperated. 'We will run aground!'

From the bows, the Pale Ladies had started to laugh. Their chins were all glossy with blood. They had drunk too deeply the night before, and it made them giddy.

'Who do you think you are with, Herrscher?' asked Vlad, pushing his cloak back and raising a clawed hand. 'I was mighty when I lived before, and I am mightier now. Nagash does not just give life, he also gives *power*.'

Vlad extended his arm before him. Knowing what was coming, the Pale Ladies giggled and scrambled for cover. Wolff and Herrscher looked on, one sourly, the other with interest.

The clouds above the forest-dam began to curdle. Thick slabs of stone-grey shifted, and flickers of silver lightning rippled across the horizon. The wind picked up, whipping the tips of the waves and making them froth.

Vlad began to recite words in a language he had never understood in his previous life. Now, though, they came easily, tripping from his dry tongue as if he had been chanting them since childhood.

The air shuddered, and the colour slopped out of it. Virulently green leaves crackled and shrivelled, turning black as if burned by fire. There were no flames – just a cold, cold gust as if from the maw of the underworld. The water turned slate-dark, and the trees beyond snarled and curled up. The wood dried and cracked, ageing lifetimes in mere moments. Vines unravelled from their clutch-holds and sprang back, their sap hardening and making them brittle.

With an echoing snap, the first of the bulwarks broke. Mighty tree-trunks, turning grey-white as if made of embers, dissolved away, splashing into the river below. Massive shivers ran through the entire structure. It began to give way, breaking back up into desiccated chunks. The leeches scurried for the safety of the banks, or plopped messily into the water below, screaming blindly.

Vlad smiled coldly. The unlocked Wind of Shyish surged through him, as chill as pack-ice. In the face of its limitless power, the perverted corruptions of life had no choice but to wither and collapse. In the end, that was the fate that awaited all mortal creation. The vagaries of life were impressive in their variety, but ultimately nothing compared to the bleak majesty of eternal death. Vlad had always guessed at the power of the Shyish Unlocked, but it had taken Nagash to truly reveal its potency to him. When victory came, as it surely would, *this* would be all that remained – empty lands, bled dry of filth and squalor, populated by the meek, whispering armies of the mortarchs. Even the sun and the moon would obey the new Law, bound into new circles and following regulated paths. There would be no more rebellion, no more misery, no more *fecundity*.

Herrscher shook his head in disbelief, watching the river-path open up once again. The waters rushed to fill the void, sweeping away the tinder-dry wreckage, and the river cruiser's deck trembled as the current picked up once more.

The Pale Ladies laughed uproariously, pointing out to one another where the leeches thrashed in the waves, slowly drowning.

Vlad maintained the pressure. There were miles of matted effluent to clear, and the closer they got to Altdorf the worse it would become. 'They are scared of us,' he told Herrscher, as his ring boiled and coughed with magic. 'They did not expect this on their eastern flank – all their prophecies were bound up with mortal men.'

Herrscher nodded slowly. 'They know we are coming, then.'

'Of course they do. They will rouse every pestilence against us, just as they always have done, and they will fail, for the dead do not sicken.' He smiled at the witch hunter. Then he gazed across the deck of his commandeered vessel and smiled at all of his servants. They were so lucky. 'Nothing will stop us, my friend. We will sweep towards Sigmar's city like the cold wind over graves, and when we arrive they will see just how badly they have miscalculated by ignoring the scions of Sylvania.'

'Who, lord?' asked Herrscher. 'The corrupted, or the mortal?'

'In time, both,' said Vlad evenly, resuming his place on the throne and keeping his claw extended before him. 'But if the Emperor has the sense to take my offer, then all things are possible.'

He settled into position, watching the forest crumple and deteriorate before the waves of grave-magic. The display pleased him, just as it did the Pale Ladies, who still cackled like urchins.

'Send orders to the barge commanders to row faster,' he said. 'I smell the first whiff of rotten fish on the air – the city must be close.'

The greater part of the enemy hosts had already moved south, but that did not make the north safe.

Deathclaw had partially recovered from its wounds, but not yet enough to take wing, and so Karl Franz and the griffon remained earthbound and vulnerable. They travelled by night, trusting to the overcast darkness to hide them against the iron-dark earth. The unlocking of ancient Law had freed all manner of foul spirits from their long-established shackles. Ghosts floated across the lurid skies, shrieking in long-forgotten tongues. Cadavers pulled themselves from the ground without the aid of necromancers, and limped off in search of living flesh to gnaw. Splinter warbands from the main Chaos armies roamed the ruined lands, hunting down what little mortal prey remained for food and torture.

Every village Karl Franz passed through was abandoned, its houses empty and its fields standing fallow. Even the fauna had fled, excepting those bloated, dull-eyed mutations that flapped and limped in place of birds and beasts. Deathclaw would kill them, but not eat them. All they had for sustenance were the rotting remains in grain-stores or the trodden-down remnants of bread and pastries in looted taverns.

Karl Franz had long since stopped hoping to meet any survivors. At first, soon after he had rescued the war-griffon, he had entertained dreams of coming across resistance fighters. He would rally them, day by day, and the news would spread. Soon he would find a way to link up with Helborg and Schwarzhelm, who surely still fought on somewhere, and jointly they would take the fight to the invader again. The enemy may have been mighty, but this was *his* land, and they were *his* people.

It had become slowly apparent, though, that there were no fighters left. The invaders had driven every one of them away, or killed them all, or had dragged them all into slavery. Every hovel was empty, and every townhouse echoed with silence. Karl Franz trudged through them all, rooting through the remains under the yellow light of Morrslieb, now a mere whisker from fullness.

It was the little things that struck at his heart – the broken looms, the cold anvils, the tin plates half-buried in the straw. He soon realised that he could not have faced any of his subjects, had they still lingered by their cold hearths. He would not have known how to meet their gaze. He was their protector, and he had failed more completely than any Emperor in the annals ever had.

During the day, when he fitfully slept, he would see them come up to him in his dreams, their plague-ravaged faces accusatory.

'We toiled for you,' they would say. 'We cut land from the forest, and scraped crops from it. We built chapels, and armed ourselves, and served in your armies. We looked to you when the winter storms came, or the beasts tore up our fields, or the greenskins broke from the deep wood with blood in their eyes. We would say your name as we reached for our swords. That gave us all the hope we ever had. We would say your name.'

He would wake then, his breathing shallow and his heart pounding. He would lie in the twilight of the cloud-bound day, shivering as his body lay against the cold ground, wishing he had not seen those faces.

We would say your name.

Deathclaw was able to travel for miles without tiring, though his wings still hung broken by his harrowed flanks. Every night, they would break from whatever cover they had found the morning before, and set off. If they found stragglers from the Norscan hordes, they would kill them, and for a few moments the grief would be forgotten in the sudden heart-rush of combat. Karl Franz's runefang would flash in the dark, wielded by angry hands, and the blood of the Fallen would spill on lands that still hated them.

He knew it could not last. Sooner or later, word of a lone griffon and its rider abroad in the wastes would filter back to whatever dark mind controlled the conquest of the north, and more serious forces would be sent to hunt them down.

Karl Franz found himself hoping for that day to come quickly. Better to die fighting than wither away from starvation, lost and unmourned amid an Empire he had allowed to pass into the hands of its ancient foes. Until then, though, he never stopped searching. He never stopped praying, even though the petitions became steadily bitterer. At the end of each fruitless day, he would kneel against the sickened soil, pressing his knees and fists into the earth, and offer his soul to Sigmar.

'Anything,' he would whisper. 'Any suffering, any pain, just to be *worthwhile*. To serve again. The runes on my blade remain dark, the sun does not shine. What power remains in your people? Is Ghal Maraz still carried? I would know, surely, if it had passed into darkness.'

Silence. Always silence. He would fall into exhausted sleep with no answers being given, just the skirl of the wind and the stink of the foul woods.

He had lost track of how long it had been since Heffengen. On one particularly cold night, the clouds underlit with yellow-green and distant thunder crackling away in the far south, the two of them crawled along a choked river bed, hugging the shadow of the rising banks. Above them, strange lights played across the heavens, dancing like flames poured from an alchemist's vial.

Deathclaw suddenly froze, crouching low against the ground. Karl Franz tensed, recognising his steed's threat-posture, and gripped the hilt of his sword tight.

He sniffed. Experience had taught him it was easier to smell the enemy than see them in the dark. All he could detect was the filmy muck trickling at the bottom of the riverbed.

'What is it?' he whispered, reaching up to rub Deathclaw's neck. 'What do you sense?'

The griffon's head rose. Its golden eyes glittered, and it opened its hooked beak. One wing extended, but the broken pinions did not unfurl. With a muffled cry of agony, the creature started to shuffle up the broken riverbank.

Karl Franz cursed. The land above the dry gulch was open, offering precious little cover, and a griffon was a big creature to hide, even at night. 'Wait!' he urged, struggling up after it.

They broke into higher ground, and the earth ran away from them in all directions, empty and featureless. The strange lights in the sky were more visible up there – they were like ripples of ink across the heavens, and it made him nauseous to look at them.

There were no troops marching across the ink-black wasteland, only the wind, as frigid and merciless as ever.

Deathclaw, however, remained agitated. It tried to flap its wings again, only to give up in agony. By then, Karl Franz could hear something for himself – a rhythmic beating on the air, followed by a faint tang of foulness.

He advanced warily, peering up into the unquiet skies, seeking out the source. He saw nothing, but the beating became stronger. The air shifted, stirred by some powerful force above him.

He gripped his sword-hilt two-handed.

So it comes at last, he thought, knowing that whatever approached would be far more powerful than the scattered warbands he had previously encountered. The word must have got out – he had a sudden mental flash of the zombie dragon tearing towards him, its empty eye sockets flaming.

Then something huge and dark burst from the clouds, plummeting fast. Deathclaw hissed, and rose up, its claws extended. Karl Franz crouched, his sword held point-up, coiling for the spring.

'My liege, put your weapon down, if it please you!' cried a gruff, part-panicked voice from above.

A second later, and the huge profile of a war-griffon emerged above them, holding position awkwardly less than twenty feet from the ground.

Karl Franz straightened. He knew that beast. He knew all the griffons stabled in the Imperial Menagerie. It was young, barely broken-in, hellish to control. It should have been unrideable.

With a sudden flare of joy, he realised what that meant – loyal men still lived. Even if all else had failed, even if his northern armies had been utterly destroyed, something still remained.

'Declare yourself,' Karl Franz ordered, keeping his blade raised. Deathclaw remained at his side, hissing angrily.

'Gregor Martak, Amber College,' came the voice from above, as harsh as rotten tree-bark. And then, as if he were strangely embarrassed by the addition, 'Supreme Patriarch.'

Karl Franz remained wary. There had been too many deceptions for him to take him at his word, and he did not even recognise the name. 'Supreme Patriarch, you say. Who authorised this?'

'My fellows, as is the way of the colleges,' came the defensive reply. 'De Champney, Reichart, Theiss.'

Karl Franz frowned. 'Those are deputies.' The true Heads of the Colleges had accompanied him to the war at the Bastion, including Gormann, Starke and Kant. If they were no longer involved in decision-making, then that hardly boded well.

'These are confused times, my liege,' said Martak. 'We do what we can. May I land?'

Karl Franz almost laughed at that. The wizard was a comically bad griffon rider, and his mount was quick to display its contempt, nearly throwing him from his seat as it laboured in position. 'If you can manage it,' he said, sheathing his sword and reaching out a calming hand to Deathclaw.

Martak's mount crashed to earth, and the wizard slipped awkwardly from between its wings, losing footing as he landed and sprawling onto the ground. He picked himself up, swearing under his breath as he brushed himself down.

Karl Franz observed the man coolly. He was dishevelled, even for one of his wild Order. A matted beard hung from a grimy face, and his loose robes were streaked with mud. He hardly bore himself with the demeanour of a magister. Gelt would have descended from the heavens wreathed with coronets of fire and accompanied by a glittering staff of gold.

This is what we have been reduced to, Karl Franz thought grimly.

'My pardon, lord, for taking so long,' muttered Martak, retrieving his own knotted mage-staff from amid his griffon's ruffled plumage. 'The Winds are disarranged, and searching for a single soul, even one as mighty as yours, is no longer as easy as it was.'

Karl Franz folded his arms. 'You come from Altdorf. It still stands?'

'When I left it, it did. I don't know for how long, what with an idiot of a Reiksmarshal in charge.'

'So Helborg lives.' The relief almost made his voice shake.

'He does, aye.'

'And Schwarzhelm? Huss?'

'They were not there.' Martak fixed him with a half-guilty, half-anxious look. 'To be frank, it matters little – the city will fall. I have seen it, and I have seen the state of the defences. I could have stayed and died, but I chose to find you. While you live, something can be salvaged. There may be armies still intact somewhere. Middenheim, or Nuln, perhaps.'

Karl Franz lost his smile. 'You are not speaking seriously.'

Martak sighed. 'I knew this would be your response, but please, *believe* me. There is nothing to be done for Altdorf.' His brown eyes stared out at the Emperor from the dark. 'I have witnessed your death there, lord. Night after night, and the visions do not lie.'

'Then why come to find me at all?'

'Because fate can be cheated,' said Martak, almost desperately. 'You were never destined to die out here, alone. Nor do you need to die in the city. There will be other ways.'

Karl Franz smiled thinly. It was interesting how other men regarded their fate within the world. Some, he knew, cared greatly for their own preservation, or for glory, or for evasion of duty. He had never so much disapproved of those men as found them baffling. Not to be governed by duty – the iron vice of obedience to a higher power – was so far removed from his philosophy as to be almost unintelligible.

'I thank you for searching me out, wizard,' said Karl Franz, sincerely enough. 'You have done what none of your fellows managed, and that alone earns you your rank. But if you have come here to persuade me to abandon the city, you are more a fool than you look. It is my place. I instructed Helborg to hold it, and if there is any chance I can join him in its defence, I must take it.'

The wizard stared back at him, looking like he was earnestly thinking of a way to change his mind. Then he shook his shaggy head. 'You will not be persuaded.'

'Persuasion is for debutantes and diplomats, wizard, and I am neither.'

That seemed to remind Martak of just who he was talking to. The wizard nodded wearily. 'Don't think I was running away,' he muttered. 'I'd have stood and fought, if I thought I couldn't find you. There are... good people there, ones who don't deserve to be abandoned.'

'Good or not, none deserve that.' Karl Franz turned to look at Deathclaw. The griffon was wheezing in pain, just as it had done since its rescue. It looked barely able to remain on its feet, let alone take to the skies. 'But I fear your quest has damned one of us to remain in the north. My steed will not fly.'

Martak limped up to the griffon, studying it hard. He reached out with a calloused hand, and Deathclaw bucked.

'Steady,' whispered Karl Franz.

'I can heal your creature, if it will let me,' said Martak, running his hand down Deathclaw's snapped pinion.

Karl Franz raised an eyebrow. 'Really?'

'I am a magister of the Lore of Ghur. I may be a weak scryer and a poor judge of visions, but I know beasts.'

'You do not know how to fly them.'

Martak grimaced ruefully. 'My feet were never meant to leave the earth.' Then he looked more serious. 'Come to that, I should never have been elected. If Gormann or Starke had been in Altdorf when the news of Gelt's fall had come in, I would not have received so much as a vote. But consider this: as fate has it, you were found by an Amber wizard. None of them would have been able to make this creature whole again, but I can.'

Karl Franz considered that. Good fortune had been thin on the ground since his reawakening. For a long time, it had felt as if his immortal patron had vanished, withdrawing His presence from the world just as it was overcome by darkness.

And yet, the filthy wizard standing before him, scratching his cheek and running his thick fingers through Deathclaw's flight-feathers, had a point.

Do I dare believe again?

He drew in a long breath. Above him, the vile lights danced in the skies, proof of the deep corruption of the world. Much of the situation had not changed – his Empire was overrun, his armies were shattered, he was far from refuge, and even if he were to make it to some safe city, it was not clear how the tide of war could possibly be turned back.

Still, it was a start.

'Heal him, then,' Karl Franz said, walking over to the other griffon and taking it by the halter. 'Where we are going, we will need both.'

PART THREE

The City of Sigmar
Geheimnisnacht 2525

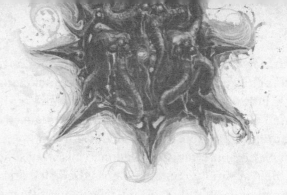

SIXTEEN

Festus cracked a wide grin as he sensed the elements come together at last. Somewhere up above street level, the last of the paltry sunlight was fading and the stars were beginning to come out. The clouds would be splitting open, ready to usher in the sick light of the deathmoon, bathing the land below in the yellow glare of putrescence.

He had stopped stirring, staggering back in exhaustion from the cauldron's edge. The last of the mortal sacrifices had been added to the infernal stew, dragged from their cages by drooling daemon-kin. Smoke poured out from the bubbling surface, as green as bile and thick like rendered fat. The flames reared up, licking the sides of the vast kettle and making the liquids inside seethe.

Festus wiped a sweaty hand across his forehead, wincing as pustules on his skin burst. After toiling for so long, he hardly knew what to do. Should he just watch? Or was there some other rite to perform, now that the power had been unleashed?

A child-sized daemon with webbed feet and a head entirely

taken up by jaws capered in front of him, laughing uncontrollably. Festus chuckled himself, finding the laughter contagious.

'I know it, little one!' he agreed, reaching out with a burly hand.
The daemon clasped it tight, and together they danced a lumbering jig around the laboratory. 'I share your joy!'

All through his subterranean kingdom, vials were shattering,
spewing their steaming contents across the brick floors. The
glassware ran with bubbles, and the valves burst their sleeves
in puffs of skin-curling heat.

Festus cast off the attentions of the little daemon, and wobbled
over to the next chamber along. The cages stood empty where
he had left them, their doors swinging open and the soiled straw
within buzzing with flies. Beyond the final set of arches, a wide
shaft ran upwards, lined with mouldering brickwork and heavy
with moss.

Festus entered the shaft, standing at the base and looking
upward. The circular vent soared straight above him, unclogged
and ready to vent his fumes into the world beyond.

'Are you ready?' he cried, his throaty, phlegm-laced voice echoing up the circular space. 'Do you know the bliss that awaits
you? Are you *prepared?*'

Of course they were not. They would be retreating to their tiny
hovel-rooms now, ready for the night terror to begin. They should
be out on the streets, ready to witness the coming storm. They
should be *revelling* in it.

From the cauldron chamber, huge booms were now going
off. The reactions had started, bringing to fruition months of
work. Every carefully placed jar of toxins was now exploding in
sequence, kindling the baleful smoke that even now surged and
blundered its way along the interconnecting tunnels.

Festus pressed himself to the shaft's edge, breathing heavily.
His jowls shivered as he began to get the shakes, and a mix of
terror and pleasure shuddered through his flabby body.

'You are coming!' he cried. 'At last, you are coming!'

The sound of metal snapping resounded down the tunnels, followed by the hard clang of the fragments bouncing from the keystones of the arches. A vast, earth-shaking roar boiled up from the depths of Festus's realm, making the water in the sewer-depths bounce and fizz.

Festus spread his arms wide, pressing his fingers into the mortar, and closed his eyes. Steam rushed past him, coiling and snaking up the shaft. He felt the heat of it blistering his skin, and relished every pop and split of his facial boils.

'It begins,' he breathed.

The bells tolled across the poor quarter, puncturing the increasingly fervid air. The Bright College had sent menials to light pyres at every street corner in the hope of rallying the populace in the face of the mounting terror, but all that did was send more smoke pluming up into an already polluted dusk.

Margrit dragged herself up to the balcony overlooking the Rathstrasse, feeling the age in her bones begin to tell. She had been working non-stop for weeks, coping with the gradually mounting toll of sick and dying. After so long resisting the contagion in the air, the endless filth had begun to overwhelm her at last. She wheezed as she leaned against the railing.

Below her, the city was burning. Bonfires blazed in every platz and strasse, throwing thick orange light up against the grime-streaked daub of the townhouses. She watched as a regiment of Reikland state troopers marched through the street immediately below the temple's east gate, clearing the lame from their path with a brutal military efficiency.

She hardly had the energy to be outraged anymore. They were just doing their job – strutting off to wherever they were destined to die – and the sick were everywhere, blocking the doorways, the drains and the marketplaces.

She breathed deeply, feeling her heart pulse. She felt light-headed, and the charnel stink in the air made it worse. Something was coming to a head. Whenever the clouds briefly split, the sickening illumination of Morrslieb flooded the rooftops, making Altdorf look like a forest of spikes set against an ocean of yellow-green.

Where are you? she found herself wondering. *For a moment, I believed you were different. You came down here, at least. Perhaps that told you all you needed to know.*

The image of the bearded wizard still hung in her mind. There was something about him – a rawness, a lack of cultivation – that she had found appealing.

Too late, now. This thing, whatever it is, is beginning.

Her head started to ache. The air was like it was before a summer thunderstorm, close and clammy. The smoke of the fires made it worse. She looked down at her hands, and saw that they were trembling.

Then she sniffed. There was something else in the air. Something... alchemical. She looked up, screwing her eyes against the drifting smog. Over to the north-east, across the Unterwald Bridge and towards the slaughterhouse district, a column of smoke was rising. Unlike all the others, it glowed green from within, glimmering in the night like phosphor. While the fires of the Bright magisters burned fiercely, this column rose into the sky like oil poured in reverse, slinking and sliding upward in violation of nature's order.

'There you are,' she said out loud, vindicated, though far too late. The column continued to grow, piling on more and more girth until it loomed over the entire district. Flashes of light flared up inside it, flickering and spinning, before guttering out. The hunchbacked roofs of the abattoirs were silhouetted, flashing and swinging amid the riot of colour. 'It was under us the whole time,' she murmured. 'Just one regiment would have sufficed.'

A dull boom rang out, making the earth shake, and plumes of

emerald lightning lanced upward, shooting like geysers in the gathering dark.

Margrit swallowed, trying to remember the words of the Litany Against the Corruption of the Body. She knew, perhaps better than anyone else in the city, just what strain of magic had been unleashed in the depths of the city. It had been there for months, cradling slowly, growing like an obscene child in the dripping sewers, and now it had been birthed under the light of Morrslieb and with the hosts of Ruin camped outside the walls.

'Blessed Mother,' Margrit whispered, watching the column lash and unfurl, 'preserve us all.'

Ethrac was the first to see it.

'There it is!' he shrieked, jumping up from his long-held crouch and nearly losing his position on Ghurk's back. 'He has done it!'

Otto roused from a half-sleep, in which dreams of sucking the marrow from living victims had been making him salivate, and looked blearily at his brother. 'Who has done what?'

Ethrac cracked him over the head with his staff, making the bells chime. 'Festus! His spell breaks!'

Otto clambered to his feet, rubbing his forehead absently, trying to see what the fuss was about.

Then he did. Altdorf lay under the night's thick cover, lit up along its walls by a thousand grimy lanterns. The towers soared darkly into the void, black on black, each crowned by a slender tiled roof. Just as before, he was struck by the sheer vastness of it, like a mound of rotting fruit ready for gnawing on.

The roofs were overhung by lines of smoke, just as always, except that one of them was glowing green and curling like burning parchment edges. It towered over the city, rearing up like a vast and vengeful giant, swelling and bloating into flickering excess. Its green light, as gloriously lurid as anything Otto had witnessed, sent shadows leaping across the landscape. Half-defined faces rose and sank in the smoke, each one contorted into mutating expressions of agony and misery.

'It is beautiful,' he murmured, absently letting his hand fall to his scythe-stave.

A low rumble from below told him that Ghurk agreed. The triplets stood, lost in admiration, as the first mark of Festus's Great Tribulation began.

'I can feel the aethyr bending,' said Ethrac appreciatively. 'He has been working on this for a long time.'

Otto chuckled darkly. 'He enjoys his labours.'

'As do we all.'

The column continued to grow. The clouds above the city responded, sending down tendrils like stalactites, and soon a vortex began to churn over the battlements, glowing and flickering like embers. The growl of thunder rocked the valley, though this time it was not the world's elements that stirred. Lightning snapped down from tormented clouds, flooding more emerald light over the sacrificial city.

'It is fitting, is it not?' mused Ethrac. 'That the first strike should be self-inflicted? The City of Sigmar will gnaw its own innards out, and all before the first standard is lifted.'

Otto was barely paying attention. The column of smoke was twisting like a tornado, only far vaster and slower, rotating ominously as it gathered girth and momentum. The rain started up again, as if triggered by the pillar of aethyr-energy churning up out of the city's innards. Droplets pinged and tumbled down Ghurk's vast bulk.

A rumble drummed across the land, lower than the thunder, like the unsteady foundations of the world grating together. The rain picked up in intensity, sheeting down in thick, viscous gobbets of slime.

Otto lifted his head and grinned, feeling cool mucus run down his cracked features.

'And do you see them?' asked Ethrac, his bony face twisted into a look of ecstasy. 'The others? Look out, o my brother, and observe what the beacon has summoned.'

Otto blinked the slime from his eyes and peered out into the gloom. The sun was nothing more than a red glow in the far west, but all across the northern horizon, crimson pinpricks were emerging from the forest. First a few dozen, then hundreds, then thousands. 'I see it, o my brother,' he said. 'That is the Lord of Tentacles, and the scions of the beast-forest. So many! So, so many.'

'And, though you do not see it yet, Epidemius is closing from the east. The river will be blocked from both compass points.' Ethrac reached down to playfully tug at Ghurk's lone eyebrow. 'You will be feasting on live flesh again soon, great one!'

Ghurk chortled eagerly, and his shoulders rolled with mirth.

Over Altdorf, the column of green fire burst into ever more violent life, revealing a twisting helix of luminescent power coursing at its heart. The heavens responded, and the storm overhead rotated faster in sympathy, a vast movement that spread out over the entire forest.

Altdorf was now the fulcrum on which the heavens themselves turned. As the thunder ramped up and the slime-rain fell ever more heavily, a delicious air of terror lodged firmly over the Reik, seeping up from the slime of the earth and bleeding into the churn of the ruptured skies. The column of green fire punched a hole through the heart of the swirling vortex, fully exposing the damaged face of Morrslieb, hanging at the very heart of the heavens like a severed tumour set among the stars.

'My people!' Otto cried out, turning from his vantage to face the colossal army that had waited for so long within sight of the prize, held in place by the triplets' peerless command. Ranks of grizzled Norscans, wild Skaelings, gurning lesser daemons, plague-afflicted mortals and corrupted beast-mutants lifted up their sore-pocked faces and waited for the order. A thousand banners were hoisted into the dribbling rain, each one marked with a different aspect of the Urfather. Cleavers were pulled from leather slip-cases, mauls unhooked from chains, blunt-bladed swords from human-hide sheaths. 'The sign has been given!'

Otto raised one arm, holding his scythe aloft in triumph. The heavens responded with a violent crack, and green lightning exposed him in sudden vividness, his mutated face broken by a manic grin of pure battle-lust. 'You have waited long enough! The deathmoon swells full, the Tribulation has begun. Now for the final neck to snap!'

A guttural snarling broke out from the limitless hordes, and they began to shuffle forward, impatient for the command.

Otto laughed out loud, and lowered his scythe towards the epicentre of the maelstrom.

'To the gates!' he commanded.

Helborg stood with Zintler on the towering summit of the North Gate, overlooking the walls below. The two of them were sur-rounded by a twenty-strong detachment of Reiksguard, as well as the usual panoply of senior engineers, battle-mages and war-rior priests. Below then, the parapets were stuffed with men. Every soldier on the walls held a bow or long-gun, and all eyes were fixed to the north, where the plague-forest had crept ever closer. They felt the tramp of massed boots long before they saw the vast array of torches creep towards the perimeter. They heard the brazen blare of war horns, and the low chanting of dirges to the god of decay.

When the rain began, Helborg had initially ignored it. The drop-lets felt heavier than normal, and splatted wetly on his helm's visor before trickling down the steel edges. His gaze remained fixed outward, ready to give the command to open fire.

The great cannons had been wheeled into position. Many were

manned by the infirm and the elderly, for the plague had thinned out the gun-crews terribly. He would never have tolerated such a state of affairs in the normal run of things, but this was not, as had long been evident, in any way normal.

'Ready for the order,' he said, watching the enemy emerge from the tree-cover, barely three hundred yards from the outer walls.

Zintler passed on the command, which was relayed to the master engineer, which was sent down to the gunnery captain in the firing vaults, which was dispatched by the wall-sergeants, which was finally picked up by the dozens of crews standing ready by the piles of shot and blackpowder kegs.

Helborg's mind briefly ran over the order of defence for the final time. He and half of the Reiksguard had been stationed in the north, where the assault from the Drakwald was expected. Von Kleistervoll had taken the West Gate with most of the remaining Reiksguard force, bolstered by the sternest of the Altdorfer regiments. The East Gate defence was dominated by the Engineer's School, which stood just inside the walls to the north of the gate itself. The engineers had somehow coaxed four steam tanks into operation, which stood ready inside the gate itself, surrounded by companies of handgunners and artillery pieces. Magisters had been deployed in every formation, mostly drawn from the Bright College where possible, as well as warriors of the Church of Sigmar and priests of Ulric. The Knightly Orders had been mostly stationed in the north, though, as in all things, Helborg had been obliged to spread them thinly.

The vast majority of the state troop defenders were arranged on the walls, and given any ranged weapons that could be drummed up. The scant reserve forces stood further back, ready to be thrown into the fray whenever a section looked in danger of being lost. Scattered bands of pistoliers stood ready at all the main platzen, operating as a fast-reaction force.

It was as well-organised as it could have been, given the time and circumstances. Most regiments stood at no more than two-thirds strength, but every man who could stand on his own feet had answered the summons. Even those that could not had dragged themselves into the streets, clutching a sword and preparing, with feverish minds and sweaty hands, to do what they could to staunch the onslaught. They knew that there would be no prisoners taken, and nowhere to flee to if they failed.

'My lord,' said Zintler, hesitantly.

'Not now,' growled Helborg, scrutinising the growing horde ahead as it crawled into position. He saw trebuchets being hauled into position, and heavier war engines grinding through the forest, dragged by teams of obscenely huge creatures with slobbering jaws. There were so many of them, more than he had ever seen in all his years of battle.

'My lord, you should see this,' insisted Zintler.

Helborg whirled on him, ready to tell him to stand down and attend to his own station, when he caught sight of the green light flooding the parapet.

He turned slowly, dreading what he was about to see.

A massive tornado had erupted from the heart of the poor quarter, over in the cramped south-eastern sector of the city. The rain whipped and danced around it, seeming to fuel the accelerating movement of the immense aethyr-walls. Already it had snaked high up into the skies, glowing like corpse-light and casting a foul sheen to every surface under it.

'What, in the name of...' Helborg began, lost for words.

Lightning scampered down the flanks of the enormous pillar. It boiled and massed and thrust ever upwards, making the rainfall heavier, driven by ever-faster winds that howled with the voices of daemons. The dense cloud cover above it broke, exposing the sickening light of the deathmoon. As the two lurid lights mingled, a booming crack rang out across the entire city, shaking it to its foundations. The war horns of the enemy rose up in answer, and a deafening wall of noise broke out from every quarter. Drums began to roll wildly, and the rain started to slam down with ever greater intensity.

'Where are the magisters?' roared Helborg. 'Order them to shut it down!'

He had a sudden, terrible recollection of Martak then, but there was no time to dwell on it – the column exploded into light, thundering into the heavens with the roar and crash of aethyr-tides breaking. Huge streamers of blistering coruscation shot down in answer from the skies, laced with white-edged flame, and he had to avert his eyes.

The rain now thudded around them in thick eddies, pooling and sliding on the stone. It was not water but a kind of milky slime that loosened footing and seemed to dissolve the surfaces it slopped over.

A vast, rolling laugh broke out across the city, resounding from one end to the other. No mortal being laughed like that, nor even the daemon-servants that stalked among the enemy armies – it was the laugh of a horrific, eternal and infinitely malevolent presence of the divine plane.

The twisting column broke open, bursting like a lanced boil, spilling multi-hued luminescence into the night and banishing the last of the natural shadows. The entire city swung and lurched with crazed illumination, dazzling the eyes of any who looked directly into it.

The battle-mages were already sending counter-spells spinning up at the raging tempest, but their hastily contrived wards had little effect on the gathering inferno.

The laughter picked up in volume, but this time it spilled from more than one mouth. Within the writhing pillar of steam and fire, dark clots emerged, galloping into reality with terrifying speed. They burst from their aethyr-womb and were flung out over the city, their limbs cartwheeling and their mouths wide with mirth. Every contorted, wizened and twisted denizen of the Other Realm vomited forth – horned-faced, bulbous-bellied, wart-encrusted, boil-bursting, cloven-hoofed and rheumy-eyed, the daemons had come. They spilled out of the gap in reality like a swarm of insects dislodged from the darkest corner of the deepest dungeon, snickering and dribbling as they came.

There was no time to respond. Before Helborg had a chance to rally his forces to resist the horrors capering among his own streets, the charge was sounded from outside the walls. The war horns reached an ear-ripping crescendo, and tens of thousands of hoarse voices lifted in lust and expectation. The trebuchets opened up, hurling strangely glowing projectiles into the walls, where they shattered in foul gouts of marsh gas. The enemy hosts to the west, north and east charged simultaneously, crashing towards the perimeter in a sweeping tide that soon joined up into a seamless scrum of jostling, hard-running, weapon-brandishing hatred.

The numbers were overwhelming, both inside and outside the walls. It was as if the world had split open and thrown every monstrous servant of the plague-god into the same place, replete with daemons and half-breed terrors and mutated grotesques. It was unstoppable. It was never-ending. They would just keep on coming, smashing aside any resistance, fuelled by the unclean magicks that played and burst above them in vortices of pure destruction.

Zintler froze. The gunnery captains looked to him, lost in shock. Even the warrior priests seemed uncertain how to react to such sudden, shattering force.

Helborg, his heart beating hard, his armour running with slime-rain, thrust himself to the very edge of the parapet where he knew he would be seen by the greatest number of his troops.

'Open fire!' he roared, bawling into the inferno with every ounce of strength. 'By Sigmar's blood, *open fire!*'

That seemed to galvanise the others. Zintler shouted out orders to the captains, most of whom were now moving again, relaying instructions to the firing vaults. The first of the great cannons detonated, sending its shot whistling out into the seething press beyond the walls. The crack of pistol and long-gun fire rippled down the walls, followed by the hiss of arrows leaving bows.

The magisters responded to the sea of sorcery with spells of their own, and soon the raging skies were riven with the arcs and flares of unleashed magic. More cannons boomed out, shaking the walls with their recoil and hurling lines of iron balls deep into the heart of the onrushing enemy. Whole sections of the walls disappeared behind rolling curtains of blackpowder discharge, further adding to the cacophony.

The heavens were broken. The laws of reality were shattered. Men and daemons fought on the streets, while the engines of war blazed at one another across a battlefield already choked by death and madness. The rain scythed down, drenching everything in curtains of sickness, and the deathmoon presided over a lightning-flecked, smoke-barred picture of devastation.

At the heart of the storm, Helborg stood proudly, his fist raised in defiance of the arrows that already clattered and rebounded from the stone around him.

'Stand fast!' he bellowed, knowing he would need to stay visible. This was the hammer-blow, the hardest strike. If they faltered now, it could be over in hours – they needed to fight back harder than they ever had, and keep fighting harder. They were all that remained, the final redoubt, and that knowledge had to keep them on their feet. 'Men of the Empire, *stand fast!*'

SEVENTEEN

The Bretonnians rode clear of the worst of the plague-forest as the sun was setting. They had been moving without pause the whole time, unwilling to make camp under the eaves of such diseased trees. The knights had remained in full armour, ever watchful for attacks from the shadows. In the event, none came. It was as Leoncoeur had surmised – even the greenskins had been driven from the woodland, something he would have thought impossible had he not witnessed it himself.

The harsh pace had taken its toll, but they were now in range of the city. The pass was behind them, as was the worst of the Reikwald. Each knight could call on no more than two horses each, and some now rode the mount they planned to take into battle. They would arrive weary from the road and scarred from repeated encounters with the orcs. It was not ideal preparation for the battle to come, but the need for haste had always been the overriding concern.

As Leoncoeur rode out from under the plague-forest's northern fringe, he whispered a silent prayer of thanksgiving. The last of the river waters had dissipated, sinking back into the earth in gently steaming wells, leaving the original watercourse just as it should have been. At least this stream still ran clear – so many were now little more than polluted creeks, black with drifting spores and mutated, blind inhabitants.

The standards of Couronne and the other principalities were raised under the twilight, unfurled to the full once more as the trees gave way. A bleak land of scrub and heath undulated away from them, looking more grey than green under the failing light. Behind them rose the now-distant crags of the Grey Mountains.

One by one, the Bretonnians emerged to join him. The knights removed their helms and ran tired hands through sweat-slick hair. The peasantry did as they always did – hauled on their loads, shouldering the brute burden of the now much-diminished supplies.

Leoncoeur watched his fighters assemble, and let himself feel a glow of pride. They were intact, and still ready to fight. Their losses had been regrettable, but containable. Several thousand knights of the realm still marched with him, enough to count against any conceivable foe. When displayed in such concentrations, it was easy to forget the Lady's warnings.

These are my brothers, Leoncoeur thought. *There is no certainty in any fate. We will fight, and, who can tell? We may prevail.*

Above them, the pegasi still flew, shepherded by Beaquis. They had remained in close contact through the long trek, swooping low so as to remain visible through the filigree of clutching briars. They circled lazily now, saving their strength for what was to come. Beaquis snarled and snapped at the winged horses, as much their master as Leoncoeur was master of his men.

Jhared was one of the last to emerge, having ridden to the rear of the column to guard the vulnerable supplies. He greeted his liege with a rakish grin.

'A place to sleep, at last,' he said, saluting. 'I had begun to forget what that felt like.'

Leoncoeur smiled tolerantly. Resting his head against moss and grass rather than dozing in the saddle would be a welcome change.

'We must ride a little longer yet,' he said, casting a wary glance back towards the brooding forest-edge. 'I will not rest this close to those woods.'

'And you will have no argument from me.'

The last of the big wains trundled into the open, hauled by lines of peasants. The carthorses that should have pulled them had been lost in the passes.

Leoncoeur and Jhared rode on. The air smelled... foreign. It was not just the taint of corruption on the wind – this was a land as alien to them as any other, populated by strangers with strange ways. Many of those who rode with him would never have strayed across the border before. Their lust for adventure would be enough to fuel them over the last leg of the trek. Whether it was strong enough to make them fight as they would for their homeland, that had yet to be tested.

'All this way, for visions,' he murmured.

Jhared looked at him, surprised. 'Doubts, my lord?'

Leoncoeur smiled. 'No, not doubts. Never doubts.' That was not quite true. He had had plenty. 'And you saw Her power for yourself. Can any doubt that we were meant to be here?' He lost his smile. 'But still, the sacrifice. I do not remember the Empire being so swift to come to our aid.'

Jhared shrugged. 'This war would have come to us, in the end. So you said, at any rate, back home.'

Leoncoeur was about to reply, to agree, when the north-eastern sky was suddenly illuminated by a flash of pale green.

Every warrior immediately went for their weapon, and the horses whinnied in alarm. A cold gust of wind rustled across the brush, making the gorse shiver.

'In the name of the Lady...' began Leoncoeur, spurring his horse onward.

In the distance, to the north-east, a slender line of emerald was snaking up into the heavens. More flashes of pale light burst out, accompanied by the sporadic dart of lightning.

'What *is* that?' asked Jhared gazing up into the sky with uncharacteristic trepidation. Even as he did so, the earth shuddered underfoot, causing the warhorses to stumble. The bloom of unearthly green grew stronger, streaming heavenwards in a slender column.

'The city,' breathed Leoncoeur, feeling a terrible fear strike at him. 'We are come too late.'

Though far away, the luminescence kept growing, spreading across the fast-moving cloud cover in vile shades of pale jade. It must have been massive. It must have been more than massive.

'Hold firm!' ordered Leoncoeur, unable to resist looking at the baleful flame. As he did so, it seemed as if the storm above it coalesced into a vast, misshapen face, leering earthwards with lust in its blurred and fractured features. If it was a storm, then it was no storm of the earth.

Some of the peasants threw themselves onto the ground then, burying their heads under their arms and whispering hurried prayers. Even the seasoned warriors were unsettled by the vision, and struggled to control their steeds.

For a moment, Leoncoeur himself was unsure what to do. He had planned to make camp for the night, giving the chargers and their riders precious rest before leading them into battle. That was no longer possible – if they waited even an hour more, they would arrive at Altdorf to see nothing more than charred stone.

As he vacillated, Beaquis swooped down from its position, cawing furiously. There was no uncertainty in its feral eyes, just a rapidly kindled battle-lust. The hippogryph was under no illusions about what had just taken place, or what to do about it.

Leoncoeur reached up to grasp the beast's reins, which hung below its feathered jowls. The hippogryph flapped down lower, coming level with Leoncoeur's mount, and he leapt across the gap and hauled himself into position. Once righted, he drew his blade.

'We are *not* too late!' he cried as Beaquis gained loft. 'Had it not been for the Lady's grace, we would still be hacking through the forest, but we have been given a *chance.*'

Every warrior in his entourage looked up at him as he circled higher. The pegasi, following their master's lead, remained in close formation. None of them yet had a rider, but that would quickly change.

'You are weary,' Leoncoeur told them. 'You have already ridden hard. If you were any other people, I would not dare to ask more of you now.' He shot them a savage smile. 'But you are not *any other people* – you are the finest knights in the world, and you have been given one final chance to prove your mettle.'

By now every rider had controlled his steed, and the column was already forming up into battle order. The sky continued to glow with an ever more intense shade of sickness, but the first shock was already wearing off.

'We ride *together!*' Leoncoeur roared. 'The winged and the earthbound, united unto the walls of Sigmar's city!'

It would be brutal riding. The ground between them and the city walls was unknown and no doubt crawling with the enemy. By the time they arrived, they would have to move straight into battle, with no rest and no chance to prepare. It would be a desperate race.

'You have followed me this far,' Leoncoeur thundered, climbing into the tortured heavens. 'If we stumble now, then all is for naught, so ride now, with me at your head, and we shall yet break the darkness with our valour!'

Vlad sensed the build-up of sorcery before he saw the tempest erupt over Altdorf. For over an hour, as the river had slipped past, he had felt the gathering of an almighty conflagration. It was like the beating of some immense heart, just beneath the surface of the world, but gathering strength with every pulse.

When the towers of smoke poured up at last from the western horizon, accompanied by the distant sound of war-drums, his fears were confirmed in full.

They have worked some great spell, he thought to himself grimly. *Well then, what did I expect? That they would walk up to the gates and beg for entry?*

Herrscher still had the presence of mind to be shocked. It was a difficult time for him – still caught between his old residual ties to the Empire and his new allegiance to Nagash. Vlad remained confident he would fall on the right side of the argument when the test came, but his transition had taken place in such a short period, and he had had much to absorb.

'What *is* that?' the witch hunter asked, appalled.

Vlad sat back in his throne, drumming his fingers on the armrest. 'Your first sight of the enemy. Mark them well – if we fail here, you will be seeing a lot more of this.'

The smoke curled and writhed over the tops of the trees, burning its way into the sky. Vlad's army was still many miles away, hampered by the Reik's sluggish pace. As fast as his magic had cleared the river-path, more creepers and moss-mats had reached out to drag them back again.

Even the Pale Ladies looked impressed by the fires ahead. They gazed up at the gently turning storm, mouths open, watching as the heavens burned.

'We must go faster,' hissed Herrscher, his voice tight with impatience.

'Calm yourself, witch hunter,' said Vlad. 'Look at what else approaches.'

The cavalcade of barges was still in convoy, a huge train of heavily-laden troop carriers, following like cattle in the wake of Vlad's flagship. The entire convoy was passing around a wide bend in the river, curving from right to left as the watercourse opened up for the long straight passage towards Altdorf's eastern wharfs.

As they neared the curve's outside bank, a grey strand appeared, pale under the dusk shadow of the trees beyond. It widened rapidly, exposing a marshy beach on the northern shore, dotted with mottled reeds and studded with plague-webs.

The plain was not empty. Ranks of soldiers stood waiting, organised into disciplined infantry squares and carrying flaming torches. Black banners fluttered in the contrary winds, exposing old devices of Marienburg and silver death's-head emblems against a sable ground.

One lord stood apart from the others. Even for one of his lineage, he carried himself with a studied arrogance, his cloak flung back over one shoulder and his pale chin raised.

Vlad sighed, and motioned for his ghoulish steersmen to ground the cruiser on the shoals ahead. The vessel ground to a halt, and undead menials immediately splashed into the knee-deep water and locked their hands together. Vlad rose from his throne and descended a wooden stairway hastily lowered over the side, then used the interlocking arms of his servants to avoid getting his boots wet. He alighted at the far end of the silent processional, stepping lightly onto dry sand. Behind him came Herrscher and the Pale Ladies, who were already cooing with delight.

'My dear Mundvard,' said Vlad, extending his ring-finger.

The vampire lord before him looked at the garnet jewel with distaste, before stiffly bowing and kissing it. 'We are in danger of missing the party,' he said.

Mundvard the Cruel was one of the most powerful vampires outside Sylvania. For years uncounted he had plied his grisly trade in Marienburg, only leaving once the doom of that city had become assured. He bore the marks of the degenerate aristocracy he had once been a member of – an excessively thin frame, sharp bone-structure, decayed attire harking back to a forgotten age of elegance. His lean fingers were studded with golden jewellery, and he wore a velvet frock-coat.

'I had expected you to bring more guests,' said Vlad, casting his eye over the forces Mundvard brought with him. Some were the dead of Marienburg, still arrayed in tattered remnants of their old uniforms. Others must have been raised on his march east, and others still were creatures of Mundvard's old hidden retinue. At the rear of the throng, hissing under the leaves, lurked a greater beast, one that had once terrorised the Suiddock, and now slithered abroad again under new magical commandments.

Mundvard affected a look of disinterest. 'We do what we can. Times are not what they were.'

Vlad shot his deputy a dark look. Mundvard was a skilled killer, one of the finest exponents of the dagger-in-the-dark school of murder, but his long sojourn in Marienburg had made him flighty and high-strung. If there had been time, Vlad might have been tempted to give him a lesson in command, a painful one, but Morrslieb was now full and the gaps between the worlds had already been punctured.

He withdrew his claw.

'Tell me what you know.'

'Three hosts assail the city,' said Mundvard. 'They have already started the assault. Some hex has been enacted, and daemons are falling from the sky.' He wrinkled his slender nose in distaste. 'Altdorf is a rotten corpse. It will not last the night.'

'And that is why we are here,' said Vlad, patiently. 'Is your army ready to march?'

'Whenever I give the word.'

'Then give it.'

Mundvard looked at the barges, which were coming in, one by one, to ground on the beach. 'Should we not take the river?'

Vlad shot him a contemptuous look. 'I will enter the city when I am invited.' He drew closer to Mundvard, pleased to find that he was a half-head taller than his lieutenant. 'Let me instruct you in how this thing is to be done. I will not sneak into Altdorf like some beggar, fighting up from the quays and the sewage-bilges. I will demand my electorship before I raise so much as a sword to aid them. When their desperation finally forces them to crack, I will ride through the gates atop a war-steed, my head held high, and I will take the salute of the Emperor himself. They will *invite* me in. Do you see this? Nothing less will suffice.'

Mundvard looked at him doubtfully. Vlad could read the thoughts flickering across his elegant face. *Is this what Nagash intended? Can it be worth the risk?*

Eventually, though, the vampire nodded in acquiescence. 'So be it,' Mundvard said, as if he cared not either way. 'The North Gate is the quickest route from here. The forest is crawling with daemons, mind.'

Vlad raised an eyebrow, and gestured to where his troops were making landfall. Shades fluttered overhead, their long faces breaking into piercing moans. Ghouls slipped between the shadows of the trees, and hulking undead champions trudged through the lapping surf, uncaring if the brackish waters slopped over the tops of their age-crusted boots. Greater beasts were waiting on the barges in iron cages – skeletal leviathans, raving vargheists, crypt horrors wearing bronze collars marked with runes of control. Thousands had already landed, and thousands more would come.

'Daemons are but the dreams of mortals,' Vlad said, witheringly. 'Just wait until they clap eyes on *us*.'

The underworld kingdom was breaking apart. Sewer arches collapsed under the strain, showering broken bricks into the steaming channels. The air burned, throbbing with released magic that bounced and swerved through the honeycomb of chambers.

Festus went as quickly as his sagging muscles would carry him, sloshing through the turbulent slurry and making his way back to the cauldron chamber. It had been a magnificent thing to witness – his Great Tribulation, soaring up the shaft and breaking into the city above, rupturing the skin of the heavens and ushering in the deluge of daemon-kind. He could feel unreality flex and buckle around him, warping the very fabric of the undercity.

Such complete success did not come without risks. He had unleashed forces that now ran far beyond his capability to control. If he did not get out soon, he would be buried by the destruction he had caused. All he had been charged to do was start the process, and like fermentation in a barrel, it would now bubble away without his further involvement, taken over by an intelligence far greater and subtler than his own.

He stumbled along the sewer-path, kicking past a gurgling gaggle of half-drowned daemon-kin. More of the masonry around him collapsed, sending dust spiralling through the echoing tunnels. Ahead of him stood the cauldron chamber, still lined with popping vials.

This was the crowning achievement of his long art. Most of the petty daemons summoned by the Tribulation would be ripped from the tortured skies by the plague-tempest, but that would not suffice for the greatest of the breed. For such titans of contagion, a more direct route was required.

Festus hurried over to the cauldron, wincing as more glassware exploded above him. The liquids within still bubbled as violently as ever, even though the fire at the cauldron's base had long gone out. Truly gorgeous aromas spilled from the lip, exuding freely as globular slush dribbled down the obese flanks.

A vast hand thrust up from the boiling broth. That hand alone should have been far too large to fit inside the vessel – it was a scaly, clawed and mottled hand, steaming gouts from its immersion and still wrinkled from the moisture.

Festus clapped his palms together in joy, watching as another claw shot out from the far side of the cauldron. Two enormous fists clamped onto the edges of the vessel, and flexed.

The broth spilled over, cascading to an already swimming floor, and a pair of antlers burst into view. Two enormous yellow eyes, slit-pupilled like a cat's, blinked at Festus.

'Plaguefather!' cried Festus, taking a hesitant step towards the emerging monster.

Like all its kind, the daemon had many names in many realms, all of which were but a distant mockery of its true title, which was unpronounceable by all but the most studious of mortal tongues. In Naggaroth it was cursed as Jharihn, in Lustria feared as Xochi-tataliav, in destroyed Tilea hated as Kisveraldo the Foul-breathed, in distant Cathay reviled as Cha-Zin-Fa the Ever-pustulent. In the Empire it had earned the moniker Ku'gath the Plaguefather, and its ministrations had ever been most virulent in those lands.

Festus cared little for true names, for he was no scholar of the dark arts, just a meddler in potions and the delicious fluids of sickness. He *did* recognise the enormous power erupting before him, though – an unstoppable mountain of gently mouldering hides, crowned with a grin-sliced face of such exquisite ugliness that it made him want to reach up and chew it.

Ku'gath looked around, seemingly a little bewildered. It hauled itself up higher, and a truly colossal bulk began to emerge, flopping over the side of the now absurdly tiny cauldron. The daemon's bulk was far greater than the mortal vessel could possibly have contained, a conceit that Festus found particularly amusing.

'Where... is this?' growled the daemon, its slurred, inhuman voice resonating throughout the gradually disintegrating kingdom.

'Altdorf, my prince,' said Festus, wobbling for cover as a whole rack of vials crashed to the floor, scattering the glass in twinkling fragments. 'The Tribulation. You remember?'

That seemed to clarify Ku'gath's mind. The giant mouth curled as it snorted up remnants of the broth, before it vomited a pale stream of lumpy effluent straight at Festus. The Leechlord revelled in the slops hitting him, sucking up as many as his purple tongue would reach.

Then Ku'gath dragged its quivering flanks clear of the cauldron. A vast foot extended, terminating in a cloven hoof and trailing long streamers of pickled gore. Laboriously, puffing and drooling, the enormous creature extracted itself from its tiny birth-chamber, standing tall before its summoner.

Unfurled to its full extent, the greater daemon was immense. Its antlers scraped the high arched vault, and its withers slobbered over broken potion-racks. When it turned around, whole shelves of priceless liquors were crushed against its sloping flanks, streaking down the steaming flesh like thrown dyes.

'We have to leave,' said Festus, shuffling out of the daemon's path and knocking over an empty prey-cage as he did so. 'This place is no longer... commodious.'

Ku'gath grunted, and started to shuffle through the chambers, smashing and crushing as it went. 'I can smell the fear,' it slurred, spitting through the flecks of vomit still clinging to its lower lip. 'They are... *above*.'

'Yes, yes!' agreed Festus, doing what he could to usher the beast towards the only exit large enough to accommodate it. 'Follow the stink! They are lucky to have lived to witness you.'

Ku'gath spat a gobbet of mucus the size of a man's fist, and it splattered stickily against the wall. 'I *hunger*,' it gurgled.

Festus smiled lasciviously. 'As do I, bringer of ruin, but it is just a little way now.' He thought ahead, wondering how he would direct such a leviathan to its true target. 'Plenty of souls to suck up, plenty of guts to slip down your gullet. They are lining up, one by one.'

'I *hunger*,' the daemon drawled, as if it were incapable of saying anything else.

'I know you do,' said Festus, rubbing its lower spine

affectionately. 'Your ache shall be sated.' His smile broadened as his plans crystallised. 'To the temple, great one. To the Temple of Shallya.'

EIGHTEEN

The army of the Urfather tore across the final stretch of open land, charging en masse towards the reeling walls. Altdorf was directly ahead, just a few hundred yards away, looming up into the madness of the Tribulation. The Glottkin's hordes spread out into an immense swarm of churning bodies, bearing torches as they ran and screaming the death-curses of the uttermost north.

Ghurk was at the forefront, leaping and blundering towards the vast West Gate. His breathing was already frantic and wheezing, his lust for flesh overtaking everything. His distorted right arm flailed around, and in his other hand he clutched an enormous maul that was still viscous with blood from older battles.

The city reared up before them, a soaring black silhouette amid the sheeting plague-rain. The towers starkly framed a cracked sky beyond, shrieking with daemon cries and the swirling power of the aethyr unlocked. Banked ramparts flashed and smoked with blackpowder weapons, and the hard *snap* of cannon-fire, followed by the boom of the report, briefly punctured the background roar of the winds and the flames and the screaming. Petty mortal magic flared in the night, shimmering with every colour of the spectrum, something that made Ethrac snort with derision.

The first ranks were already at the walls. Teams of plate-armoured Norscans strode up to the foundations bearing siege ladders. Wooden poles were hoisted up, swaying in the gales, before being shoved back by desperate hands on the high battlements. Boiling pitch was hurled down at the first rank of attackers, sending huge columns of steam spiralling up as the liquid burst over its targets.

The fighting quickly spread all along the western walls, before joining up with Autus Brine's assault from the north. Soon the outer perimeter, extending for miles in both directions, was completely besieged. The Chaos host surged up to it, bearing yet more siege ladders, crashing against the thick stone base like the tide.

War horns rang out, one after the other, overlapping in a maddening, glorious assault on the senses. The horns were soon matched by the bellows of the fell beasts that had been driven out of the forest – scaled and tusked monsters with flame-red eyes that ground their hooves into the mud and blundered in their madness towards the looming behemoth ahead of them.

In all directions, across the churning fields of war, battle-standards swung and swayed, crowned with skulls and lined red by the fires that had already kindled in defiance of the hammering squalls. Massive war engines were dragged out of cover and into range – trebuchets with thirty-foot throwing arms, lashed by chains to the ground and daubed with runes of destruction; bronze-wheeled cannons shaped with snarling wolf's-head barrels; siege towers pulled by teams of massive, six-horned oxen that lowed and thundered from shaggy throats even as they inched their immense burdens towards the distant target.

Otto gazed out across the measureless horde, and raised his scythe in salute. His heart was full to bursting, his whole body animated by a raw war-lust that made him want to scream aloud to the lightning-scored heavens. His forces compassed the earth in every direction, mile upon mile of battle-maddened warriors, each with only one purpose – to maim, to slay, to choke, to break bones.

Aethyric thunder snarled across the skies, making the tormented earth shake further.

'Death to them!' Otto bawled, waving his scythe around him wildly as Ghurk galloped towards the beleaguered gates. 'Death! *Death!*'

The cry began to spread through the army, and the myriad different tribal chants and curses moulded into one, repeated, terrible word.

Death! Death! Death!

The drums matched the beat, thudding like hammers on anvils, driving the hordes on and making their eyes roll and their mouths froth with drool.

Death! Death!

Further north, where the Reik's broad flow poured westward under the shadow of the great watchtowers, the Chaos forces leapt into the sludge and started wading towards the gap between the walls. The defenders had blocked the way with slung chains, each the width of a man's waist, and had lined up ships, hull-to-hull, to deny passage across the unnaturally viscous Reik. Otto saw the first warriors reach their target, braving showers of arrows and blackpowder shot to clamber across the chains. They died in waves, but the tide of corpses crept closer with every surge, clogging the river further and turning it into a semi-land of trodden cadavers.

Death! Death!

The first of the big hellcannons opened up, ripping the night apart and sending flaming streamers arcing high above the toiling masses. Enormous iron-spiked balls crashed into the walls, smashing the parapets apart and showering the ground below with powdered masonry.

Death! Death!

A siege tower reached the walls, the first to do so, and drawbridges slammed down onto the battlements. A team of wild-eyed Skaelings tore across the narrow span, charging straight into the defenders on the high parapet. They were repulsed, and the siege tower was stricken with flame-bearing arrows, going up like a torch in the fervid night. Otto laughed as he watched his slaves leap from the burning tower, smashing into the ground thirty feet below before being crushed by the iron-shod boots of the advancing thousands.

Death! Death!

The West Gate drew closer, and Ghurk began to wade through the screaming bodies of his own forces, shoving them aside to get closer. Two mighty towers thrust out from either side of the massive gatehouse, each one flying the Imperial standard from iron poles. The rounded battlements were ringed with furiously firing cannons, causing angry weals of smoke to tumble and drift across the raised portcullis.

Death! Death!

Beyond the blackened walls, already charred from the sorcerous fires flung against them, Festus's aethyric column was now glowing bright green, leering maleficently like some eerie phosphorescence thrust into the night. Otto could hear the knife-thin screams of the daemons as they tumbled from the rift, slapping and thudding onto the streets beneath and causing terror.

He could smell that terror most of all – more than the blood, the blackpowder, the stink of the corrupted river and the Rot that ran through the city's arteries. The mortals were gripped by it now, frozen by it, and with every second the vice twisted tighter.

Death!

For the first time, Otto saw torches on the far eastern side of the valley. That meant Epidemius the Tallyman had thrown his forces into the fray. Altdorf was surrounded on all sides, brought low like a stag being dragged down by hounds.

Death!

He looked up, sweeping his joyous gaze to the summit of the gatehouse tower. A huge Imperial standard flapped wildly in the preternatural gales, half-tearing free from its pole. Men clustered beneath it, firing pistols and letting fly with arrows. There must have been dozens on the battlements, given heart by the image of the griffon that rippled above them.

'O my brother,' said Otto, turning to Ethrac.

The sorcerer nodded, seeing what was intended. He raised his scrawny arms, lifting his staff above his head. The bells clanged, spilling dirty smoke from their insides as the hammers hit. Ethrac mumbled words of power, the first that he had uttered since the assault had begun, then shook the staff a second time.

The standard, over two hundred yards away and separated by howling gusts of plague-rain, burst into green flames. It flared brightly, dropping fragments of its disintegrating fabric over the defenders at its base. Every scrap seemed to kindle where it landed, and the battlements were soon in confusion as men ran from the fires or tried to stamp them out.

Otto grinned. Few had died, but the mortals attached great importance to their little flags. One by one, they would all be turned into crisped piles of ash, and each loss would be like a dagger-strike to their weak hearts.

'Very good, o my brother,' Otto murmured, running a finger along the edge of his scythe. The gate was now close, and Ghurk was pushing his way towards it with ever greater zeal. 'Now for the doors.'

Ethrac was already preparing. Battering rams were being brought up, dragged by blind and diseased river-trolls. The portal itself, twenty feet high and barred with crossed iron over age-seasoned oak, waited for them. It might resist force for a while, or even magic, but not both, and not in such strength.

It had stood for so long, that gate. Otto could sniff out the age in the timbers, in the granite foundations, in the ancient ironwork that clad and bound it. He could sense the waning power of faith stained deep in its fabric, and could feel the spells of binding laid across it by Empire magisters. The mortals still manned every battlement and pinnacle above it, furiously determined to hold on to it.

The very idea made him smirk.

'Break it,' he ordered.

The North Gate had been hit as hard as the rest. The army raging against it was a mix of Chaos warriors and beastmen dragged out of the Drakwald's deepest pits, and the infernal alliance poured out of the storm-lashed gloom in an endless torrent.

Helborg paced the battlements, his fist clenched tight on his undrawn sword-hilt, his cheek almost unbearably painful, his mood black. The foul slime-rain continued to lance down from the churning skies, swilling across every stone surface and making footing treacherous. Archers slipped when they loosed their darts, gunners lost their footing with every recoil. The deluge got into eyes, wormed its way under collars and beneath breastplates. When it touched bare skin, it burned like acid, and several troopers had fallen to their deaths while frantically trying to rip the armour from their bodies.

'Tell the master gunner to angle his great cannons by two points,' ordered Helborg, furious at the delays.

The cannon crews were struggling just like everyone else. Aside from the plague-rain and the almost unbearable howl of the vortex above them, they could all hear the agonised screams of men being torn apart by daemons within the city. Helborg had dispatched every wizard and warrior priest he could to try to buy some time against them, but it was a desperate gambit, and it weakened the wall defences further.

Out in the dark, the enemy started to chant a single word, over and over again.

Shyish! Shyish! Shyish!

He knew what it meant, and needed no Amethyst magister to tell him.

Huge creatures were now stalking to the forefront of the host, barging aside or treading down any that barred their path – hulking, misshapen beasts with lone eyes and twisted horn-crowns, bellowing in cattle-harsh voices. They were followed by grotesque amalgams of dragon and ogre, which were so horrific that even the Chaos warriors around them gave them a wide berth. The stench of rotting meat washed over the whole army, sending those defenders still able to fire a pistol gagging and retching.

Helborg screwed his eyes up, leaning against the battlements, and peered into the tempest. Out in the murk, past the first detachments of infantry, colossal engines were being pulled into position. He recognised a gate-breaking ram in the centre of the cluster, hauled by centaurs.

He turned to Zintler. 'If that gets close...'

Zintler had seen the same thing, and nodded, wiping a patch of plague-mucus from his helm's visor. 'We're losing the battlements around the gate,' he noted grimly.

On either side of the vast gatehouse, men were struggling under the relentless onslaught of the slime-rain and thick clouds of projectiles from the trebuchets and war engines. Some sections already looked close to being abandoned. If the enemy managed to get siege towers closer, then the remaining defence would be hard-pressed to hold out.

Helborg drew in a deep breath. They were assailed on all sides, and any hope he had of maintaining a tight grip on the outer walls was fast dissolving. 'It had to come,' he said grimly. 'Just sooner than I'd have liked. The Reiksguard are ready?'

Even amid the carnage, Zintler could still smile at that. Of course they were.

'General, you will oversee the defence of the gatehouse,' shouted Helborg to Graf Lukas von Mettengrin, the grizzled Altdorfer assigned to the wall defence once, as they had always planned, Helborg was called to take the fight directly to the enemy. 'May Sigmar be with you.'

The general saluted, as did his staff and the other members of the field command still on the parapet. De Champney was one of the few magisters still present on the outer walls, though he was far too busy summoning up pyrotechnics to respond.

Helborg and Zintler hurried down from the parapet, jogging down winding stairways into the heart of the gatehouse. Once away from the edge, the sounds of battle became muffled by the thick stone, but there was no dousing the lingering screams and cries from within Altdorf itself.

'This must be swift, and it must count for all,' said Helborg, testing the straps under his helm and pulling the leather tight.

'The Knights Panther and of Morr are assembled,' reported Zintler, rolling his lance-shoulder in readiness for the sortie.

'Good,' said Helborg, noting, almost for the first time, how quietly efficient Zintler had been throughout. He was unassuming in the flesh, but once in his Reikscaptain's armour and given an order, he was the model of quiet resolve. 'Well done.'

Zintler looked at him, startled. He did not seem to know how to reply.

He did not need to. The two men broke out at ground level on the inside of the gatehouse, into a wide marshalling yard. The full strength of the North Gate's inner defence waited for them: nine full companies of Imperial knights, all saddled up and bearing lances. The white of the Reiksguard mingled with the black of the Knights of Morr and the blue and gold of the Knights Panther. Their war-horses were arrayed in full barding, each one adorned with the gilt emblems of their order. Every rider saluted as the Reiksmarshal and his captain emerged, and two chargers were led towards them.

Beyond the Knightly companies stood the reserve regiments of state troopers – some of the best men still at Helborg's command, several thousand of them, drilled mercilessly in repulsion manoeuvres, almost all armed with halberds and pikes.

Helborg mounted, adjusted his battle-plate, flicked down his visor, and took his lance. His heart was hammering hard, driving blood around his battered body. For the first time ever, he felt a spasm of guilt at leaving the command station to take the charge. In the past, there had never been any conflict – he had been there to fight, to break the enemy's will, to drive them from the field. Now his duties were many. The city needed him. They all looked to him, and he could not be in all places at once.

He remembered his last words with Karl Franz, back in the cold morn at Heffengen.

We may fall in battle, you may not. You are the Empire.

Would he be as indispensable? Surely not. Once again, Helborg felt the burden of measuring up to the real Emperor.

'Open the gates,' he growled, turning his horse around to face the coming tempest.

As he did so, every knight in every company readied himself. Lances were lowered, visors were closed. Final prayers were whispered, and the sign of the comet was made across breast-plates and leather jerkins.

A huge *clang* broke out as chains were hauled over iron wheels. The mighty gears of the gate-doors shunted into position, and steam vented from the brass valves. The doors ground open, running on their iron rails across stone flags. The heavy portcullis was released, and fell open with a dull thud against the earth.

On the far side was a vision of pure madness. The sky danced with fell energies, and the earth boiled with countless bodies. The front ranks of the enemy saw the gate opening, and surged towards it, weapons in hand. They looked infinite.

Helborg picked his target, lowered his lance, and tensed.

'For the honour of the Empire,' he roared, '*charge!*'

'Seal the gates!' shouted Margrit, hurrying from the garden and towards the temple's entrance. 'For the love of the Lady, seal the gates!'

The order wrenched her heart – there were thousands still trying to push their way into the temple enclosure, praying that the building could give them some kind of respite from the hells unravelling outside the walls. When the plague-rain had started, the sisters had done what they always did – ushered as many wounded and infirm into the healing gardens, assessing the grades of sickness, binding wounds and whispering prayers of restoration.

But then the daemons had come, gibbering and slobbering, dropping out of the sky like hailstones. They were flung from the shrieking walls of the vortex, crashing into the sides of houses and smashing straight through mould-weakened walls. Shards of green-edged lightning danced amid the tempest, skewering men even as they ran for cover, and the sound of maniacal voices rang down every reeling alleyway.

The defenders had been caught wanting. With the emphasis on the walls, whole areas of the city had been stripped of watch-patrols and state troopers. Margrit had been forced to watch from the safety of the temple as swell-bellied grotesques had chased down and slain those who were left behind – the old, the children, the weak. Her every instinct had been to storm out onto the streets, raging, doing what she could to banish the stalking nightmares that were literally falling out of the sky.

She resisted. The powers of Shallya ran deep, but they were not martial powers. Her duty was clear – to endure, to resist, to remain pure. Once the storm hit in full, Margrit ordered the shutters to be locked, the doorways to be sealed, the precincts to be purified. The last of the temple's priceless blessed water was handed out to the remaining sisters, carried in earthenware vials to be sprinkled around the temple's perimeter. That might halt them for a while – as painfully insignificant as it looked, such gestures had proved their worth in the past.

All was at risk, though, as the panicked crowds outside surged towards the temple walls, ripping down the tents in which they had been tended to and wailing for sanctuary. The outer doors had been forced open, and the mob now beat at the gates to the inner courtyard, which were only lightly barred.

Margrit rushed along the walls, crying out more orders. From her vantage on the top of the battlements she could see down into the inner courtyard, where the temple guards were struggling to barricade the gates with whatever they could find – wooden planks, heavy metalware from the sacred chapels. She could also see outside, across the heads of the milling crowds and over the roofs of the houses beyond. The volume of screaming was terrific, and the stench of human fear nearly masked the ever-present musk of the Rot.

As she neared the main gatehouse, the air was ripped apart once again by the stink of magic. Bright magisters, three of them, had appeared on the far side of the grand platz before the temple, and were unleashing withering bursts of flame against the daemons that ran amok. At the same time, finally, a troop of soldiers charged into the square from the north, where the streets ran towards the river's-edge. They bore the white and red of Altdorf's own, and looked disciplined and prepared. Defying the slime-deluge, they barged their way through the crowd towards the clots and gluts of daemonic creatures, crying out prayers to Sigmar and Ulric as they came.

The new arrivals broke the momentum of the crowd. Caught between the battle wizards and the aethyr-creatures, many of the sick broke for easier cover, limping into the shadows of the burning townhouses. Those that remained were easier to repel, and the pressure on the inner gates lessened.

Margrit reached the gatehouse, where Gerhard, her guard captain, and many of her priestesses were gathered. All of them had pale faces.

'Will they hold?' asked Margrit, panting heavily.

'For now,' said Gerhard, watching the battles breaking out across the square with some trepidation. 'But if they rush us again...'

CHRIS WRAIGHT

Margrit turned to one of the sisters, a dark-skinned woman named Elia from the distant south whose Reikspiel had never been perfected. 'And the well?'

Elia shook her head. 'Some waters remains. We did not wish to make all dry now.'

'Draw the rest. All of it. Take every last drop and make a seal around the inner sanctum. They will not cross the line, not if the ring is unbroken.'

Elia bowed, and was about to rush off down to the sacred wellsprings, when a fresh bellowing broke out from the far side of the square. All faces on the gatehouse snapped around, ready to witness whatever fresh terror had been unleashed.

Something was emerging from the eastern end of the platz, pouring out of the narrow, overlooked streets and into the rain-drenched open. Margrit saw petty daemons spill from the shadowed openings of burned-out houses, their jaws streaked with blood and their claws dragging clumps of entrails.

The Bright wizards, who had by now taken the fight to the centre of the square, rushed to staunch the new invasion. Flares of crimson flame shot out into the gloom, making the daemons squeal and pop as they were caught. The Altdorf state troopers rushed to support them, forming a ring of halberds around the three magisters.

'My place is there, sister,' said Gerhard, strapping his helm tight and making ready to descend to ground level.

'Your place is *here*, captain,' said Margrit, her voice hard. She could sense something coming, something far greater than the squalid daemons that had so far shown themselves.

'They are fighting back,' protested Gerhard, gesturing to where the Bright wizards were going on the offensive, backed up by their company of bodyguards.

'Stay in the temple,' Margrit ordered. She turned to the other assembled sisters. 'No one leaves. We have done what we can – now we tend to the wards and keep the gates locked.'

282

As she finished speaking, a great crack rang out from the square's eastern end. With a boom, one of the massive wooden-framed houses disintegrated, its beams snapping and its brickwork dissolving into a cloud of reddened dust. Something was thrusting up *through* it, tearing it apart from the foundations. The wizards retreated, launching bolts of fire at the house's carcass. As the smoke and dust cleared, something enormous waddled into view.

Its girth was phenomenal, far greater than any mortal creature had any right to possess. Slabbed flanks of grey-green, pocked with warts and sores, overflowed in a pyramid of scarce-contained blubber. The monster crashed through the remains of house, crushing the rubble under two stump-like legs. An obese belly dragged in its wake, mottled with sticky residues. A flat, grinning head emerged from the ruins, topped with a heavy coronet of slime-slicked antlers. In one claw the creature carried a thick-bladed cleaver; the other was free to clutch, rip and maim.

Gerhard's mouth fell open. The wizards immediately launched all they had at the greater daemon, bombarding it with flurries of starburst-pattern flames. It roared at them, flooding the entire square in yellow spittle. The flames would not catch on its hide, and the wizards retreated steadily, loosing more bolts as they fell back.

The monster lumbered after them, accompanied by the last remnants of the house it had crashed through. Despite its phenomenal size, it moved with unnerving speed, seeming to flicker and shift out of reality, suddenly lurching closer before rearing up high again.

It lunged, managing to catch one of the magisters as he fled. The daemon picked up the struggling wizard effortlessly, breaking his spine with a squeeze of his massive claw.

The remaining two redoubled their efforts, dousing the creature in a rain of rippling liquid fire, causing clots of ink-black smoke to curl from its hide. That seemed to hurt it, and it wobbled backward, hurling aside the broken body of the slain wizard and roaring angrily. The halberdiers rushed in close, displaying insane bravery, poised to thrust their long staves into the daemon's flesh.

They never made it. Before they had got within twelve feet of the monster, their torsos burst open, spraying entrails across the rain-drenched flagstones. Screaming, they fell to the ground, rolling and clutching at their shredded skin.

A second figure emerged from the shadow of the fire-bound daemon. This one was still massive, more than twice the height of a normal man, though barely a quarter the size of the greater beast beside him. He was dressed in a parody of normal garb, though torn apart by his flabby belly and wobbling jowls. A similarly crooked grin disfigured a bloated face, stuffed with yellowing and rotten teeth. Pots hung from straps over his sloped shoulders, each one boiling with noxious fluids or stuffed with bloody clumps of human flesh.

The newcomer gestured to the two remaining wizards, and their bodies were instantly consumed with fronds of clutching vines. The strands burst from the ground below them, grasping and clutching at their throats. The wizards fought back furiously, crying out counter-spells and tearing at the tendrils.

By then, it was too late. Freed from the wizards' fiery attentions, the daemon surged back towards them. It did not even use its claw this time – it simply rolled into them, crushing them both under thick skirts of suppurating flesh. Even then, half-wrapped in clutch-vines and crushed under the oncoming avalanche of stinking daemon-hide, they fought back, but only for a few, futile moments. With a sickening snap of bones breaking, they were both sucked under the daemon's foul bulk.

The creature sat atop them for a moment, grinding itself over their pulverised bodies, gurgling with what looked like vile pleasure.

Margrit looked on, her jaw set defiantly. The surviving mortals in the square below, whether soldiers or supplicants, scattered.

Lesser daemons scampered and scuttled after them, licking cracked lips in anticipation of the feasting to come.

The two larger horrors remained where they were. The lesser creature gazed up at Margrit, catching her directly with his rheumy gaze. His grin never went away, and a thin line of excited drool spilled from his lower lip.

'Hide while you can!' the creature screamed. 'Walls will not aid you!'

Then the two of them started lumbering towards the gate, crunching bodies underfoot as they came, a leering light of conquest in their addled faces.

Margrit could sense Gerhard's fear. She could sense the terror in her sisters. She thought of the rows of bunks inside the temple, each one occupied by at least two sick charges. She thought of the gardens, and the young acolytes fresh from the villages, all of whom she had trained herself.

It was all so, so fragile.

She made the sign of Shallya across her chest, then clutched the battlements with both hands. 'Faith is always to be tested,' she said. 'We fight for every last chamber.'

That seemed to rouse the others. Gerhard barked orders to his men, and the other sisters hurried down the stairwells to draw more sacred water from the wells.

Margrit barely noticed them go. Her temple was now a lone bulwark against a miasma of degradation. In every direction, the creatures of Chaos had free rein, burning, stabbing, infecting. Flames licked ever higher, reaching up like questing fingers to the pus-thick storm above. The vortex continued to twist and curl, bringing more destruction in its wake.

The two daemonic horrors began to move again, dragging corpulent bodies ever closer. The jowly creature with the jangling collection of plague-pots was laughing uncontrollably. He looked deranged by hatred, and drew a wickedly spiked meathook from a loop around his straining waist.

'In all things,' Margrit murmured, working hard to control her fear, trusting even then, against the face of pure loathing, that something would intervene to save them, 'Shallya be praised.'

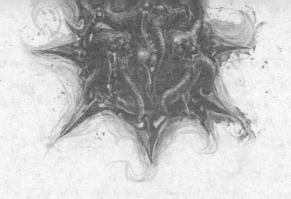

NINETEEN

Martak lurched awake, panting like a terrified animal, his skin clammy. Shadow lay heavily on him, and he could smell burning. He scrabbled for his staff, and his hands clutched at nothing.

Then, finally, his fingers closed over the reassuring weight of the wood, and he clutched it tight. The smell of burning came from the night's fire, which they had let smoulder down as they slept. He was lying on the floor of a cave, little more than a scratch in the side of a moss-overhung cliff.

The dream-visions remained vivid. He saw Altdorf burning, and knew that all he was being shown was reality. More than that, he saw the antler-crowned god again, writhing in agony, his body covered in lesions. He saw vistas of pure devastation, mile after mile of land tortured and twisted into sickening pools of endless decay.

And, as always just before waking, he saw Karl Franz dying, his agonised face lit by the light of the deathmoon. That was the worst of all. It was all futile – such dreams did not lie.

Martak hacked up the night's phlegm, and dragged himself

up onto his haunches. When he looked up to the cave-mouth, he saw the huddled silhouette of the Emperor, staring out over the forest below their vantage. Did he ever sleep? Had he taken any rest since Martak had rescued him?

Martak shuffled up to join him, hawking and spitting to clear his throat.

'Bad dreams?' asked Karl Franz.

Martak reached for the gourd of water they shared. It was almost empty, and neither of them had dared refill it from the polluted forest streams they had passed. He poured a dribble of it down his parched gullet, and felt the temporary pleasure of the liquid against his cracked lips.

'No change,' he said, settling down on the rock and rubbing his hands against his face.

They were high up above the forest. Since Deathclaw's recovery they had made use of every exposed patch of stone and earth amid the mind-bending vastness of the forest. The outcrops were like tiny islands, ringed by impenetrable overgrowth and sundered from one another by almost unimaginable distance. If they had not had the two griffons to bear them, they would be far to the north still, trudging through the brambled mire, hopelessly distant from their destination. As it was, Martak reckoned they were less than a day away.

'Even a wizard may dream without it coming true,' said the Emperor.

'I never dreamed before,' grumbled Martak. 'Perhaps it comes with the position.'

Karl Franz looked at him carefully. 'You are a strange Supreme Patriarch. I ask myself, would I have let them choose you?'

'It would not be your choice – the colleges decide.'

'What a quaint idea.' Karl Franz stretched out. His face was still gaunt from the long sojourn in the wilds, but he had gained in strength during the flight south. There was a steely light in his eyes, something that both impressed and worried Martak.

He knows he won't survive this. Does he look forward to death? Is that what this is about?

'I will not ask you again, lord,' said Martak, gathering himself for a final effort. 'For all we know, Middenheim still stands. Schwarzhelm may have made for it. Of all your cities, it has the greatest defensive potential.'

'Defensive potential? You sound like an engineer.' Karl Franz shook his head. 'We have been over this. I will not skulk around the margins. It is my city, and I will be there.'

Martak considered asking again, but decided against it. Once the Emperor's mind was made up, he had no doubt it was impossible to shift.

He watched the sun struggle to rise, its wan light filtering slowly through the grimy soup of the night's cloud cover. Palls of mist boiled clear of spiny conifer tops, tinged with yellow from the poisons now gnawing the roots. The stench was getting worse, like fungus unearthed from dank cellars.

The southern horizon had glowed throughout the night, a sick green that flickered and pulsed without rest. The clouds were being pulled towards the source like a gigantic blanket, rippling and furrowed in a vast, gradual rotation. At least there was no doubt over where they were headed.

'And here they come,' remarked Karl Franz, who had studiously avoided looking south. The two griffons were on the wing, returning from whatever hunting they had been able to find in such ravaged country.

Martak watched them approach. He took a little pride in seeing Deathclaw restored to something like its full prowess. The Emperor's beast was far larger than his own, with a raw power to its movements that betrayed an enormous aptitude for killing. If it was still in pain from his earlier ministrations, it gave no sign of it, and now flew as strongly as an eagle.

With a whirl of claws and feathers, the two creatures landed on the ledge just below the cave-mouth, cawing at them both in what Martak guessed passed for a greeting. The Emperor acknowledged his mount's arrival gracefully. Martak scowled at his, already dreading the prospect of riding it again.

'You have seen the light, I take it?' asked Karl Franz, almost casually.

Martak grimaced. 'How could I miss it?'

'Not the burning. The other light.'

Martak looked up. The skies were just as they always were – a sea of dirty, dingy grey, tinged with an unhealthy bruise pallor. Not knowing if he were being made fun of, he searched for something more. When he failed, he shot Karl Franz a suspicious look. 'You mock me?'

Karl Franz shook his head, looking quite serious. 'The twin-tailed star scores the heavens. I see it even when my eyes are closed. They can mask its light for a while, but it will burn through eventually.' He smiled wryly. 'What do you suppose that means? A sign of hope?'

Martak snorted. 'What you propose is not hope but folly.'

Karl Franz looked at him tolerantly. Perhaps, in the past, wizards would have been put to the rack for such impertinence, but there were no henchmen out in the wilds, and the Emperor had proved surprisingly indulgent of Martak's irritable ways.

'It would not be here if our course were not sanctioned. I would perceive that.' Karl Franz nodded towards his sword, propped up in its scabbard against the cave wall. 'The runefang no longer answers, my armies are scattered, the sun's light is quenched, but Sigmar's star still burns. That is something to be cherished, I think.'

Martak did not say exactly what he thought of that. His empty stomach growled, souring his mood. They would have to be gone soon, straddling their half-feral mounts and heading towards deaths that were as certain as the rising of the moons. His counsel to head to Middenheim had been scorned, and the only consolation was that he stood a chance of fulfilling his vows to Margrit, which was very little to cling onto, since the chance of her being alive when they returned was slim indeed.

'I am sure you are right, lord,' he muttered, pulling his dirty cloak around him, thinking of what lay ahead, and shivering.

The knights of Bretonnia crested the last rise to the south of the city, and beheld the end of the world.

The vortex unlocked by the Leechlord was now a raging tornado, twisting its way through the lower city, ripping up roofs and throwing the tiles around in hailstorms of shattering clay. Flames roared around the walls, leaping up against the towering stone like sails in a gale, fuelled and spread by racing winds. Blooms of rot and canker flourished in spite of the inferno, glowing eerily in the fervid night and matching the unclean glare of the deathmoon, which presided over the carnage like some obscene god peering through the torn curtain of the skies.

Dawn was close, but the nearing sun made no impression on the mottled patchwork of magicks and sorcery. Altdorf was a lone rock amid a raging furnace of unrestrained madness. The Realm of Chaos had come to earth, and to witness it was to witness the birth of a new and horrific order.

The first rank of warhorses lined up on the ridge, marshalled by Jhared, de Lyonesse and the other knight commanders. The fleur-de-lys standard was unfurled, and it snapped madly in the tearing winds.

Leoncoeur himself flew above the vanguard, mounted on Beaquis. The remaining pegasi all now carried riders, each one hand-chosen to command the powerful beasts. The last of the lances had been distributed, and the clerics had cried out their benedictions. Every horse was already lathered with sweat from the desperate ride, and now yet more trials awaited them. The foremost were already stamping impatiently, tossing their manes and itching for the charge.

Leoncoeur urged Beaquis to climb, surveying the battle. The West Gate was closest, and was already tightly surrounded. An army of such immensity that it defied the senses stretched all around the walls, hammering at the perimeter amid a storm of projectiles and flashing spell-discharge. Trolls lumbered through the swarms of lesser warriors, crazed by mushrooms and waving flaming brands, only matched in ferocity by the towering, one-eyed beastmen from the deep forest. The noise was incredible – a wild chant of *Shyish!* bellowed out to the roll and slam of endless drums.

Already the defences were reeling. Leoncoeur could see the gates begin to buckle, the first siege ladders hitting their mark, the great engines crawling closer to unload their lethal contents. The topmost towers rose precariously above the tumult, looking impossibly fragile set against the hurricane that had enveloped them.

There would be no returning from this. To enter that maelstrom was to give up hope, to strike a single blow before the tide crushed them.

Leoncoeur looked down at his army, forged in haste and driven mercilessly across the mountains. Knight after knight took his place on the ridge, resplendent in plate armour and bearing the sigils of his heritage. It was a devastating force, one that Leoncoeur would have trusted to match any foe of the known world – until this day.

Now all had changed. The old rules had been ripped up and discarded, lain waste before the all-consuming hunger of the Ruinous Powers.

'Jhared, lead your blades west!' he cried. 'Cut to the gate, and slay all before you! Teach them the fear of Bretonnia!'

The flame-haired knight saluted, still grinning as he slammed his visor down.

'De Lyonesse, ride east, cutting off the assault on the southern walls! Hold them as long as you can, then break for Jhared's position. Hit them hard! Hit them *fast!* They shall die choking on their laughter!'

The last of the vanguard drew up, over a thousand fully armoured warriors, each bearing a heavy lance. More waves readied themselves behind, forming a devastating series of thundering charges.

Leoncoeur surveyed the lines one last time, feeling pride mingle with raw grief.

They were beautiful – brave, vital and vivid, a flash of flamboyant bravado amid a world of gathering decay.

You will die alone, my champion, far from home.

Leoncoeur pulled Beaquis's head north, facing the burning city head-on, and flourished his blade.

'Now, the final test!' he roared. 'Unto death! Unto the end! Ride, my brothers! *Ride!*'

The charge took them clear of the gate, hurtling northwards under the first pale rays of the shrouded sun. Helborg lead the vanguard, driving his steed hard and balancing the long lance against the buck of the gallop. The Reiksguard came with him, just as they had in the north, an ivory wedge of steel-tipped murder carving its way through the heart of the mustered enemy.

For a few moments, it looked as if the beastmen did not see the danger. They lumbered towards the walls as before, roaring and bellowing in a stinking fug of battle-madness, but then even they seemed to see their fate unravelling, and sudden fear kindled in their feral eyes. By the time they recognised their peril, the lances were among them.

'Sigmar!' Helborg cried out, taking a raw pleasure from the surging pace of the charge.

Behind him, a thousand knights spread out across the battlefield, sweeping in an all-consuming line across the fire-flecked plain. Every rider lowered his lance, selecting a target and guiding his steed with unerring precision.

The two forces collided with a crack and whirl and thud of limbs breaking, shafts splintering and bones shivering. The Reiksguard vanguard hit as one, smashing into the ragged lines of beastmen and northmen, driving a long wound through the body of the horde.

Helborg speared a raging gor in the heart, and felt the impact radiate along his arm as he lifted the monster bodily from the earth. The shaft plunged deep, eviscerating it cleanly, before breaking mid-length under its weight. He discarded the remnants and drew his runefang, circling it into position before plunging it into the neck of another war-gor.

The Reiksguard were followed out by more Knightly Orders, each sweeping after the Reiksmarshal's spear-tip in successive waves. Most rode mighty warhorses, but some lumbered into battle astride the ferocious demigryphs, land-bound scions of the larger griffons, with all their cousins' furious temper and scything claws.

The main charge thundered on, plunging further into the rotten depths of the limitless hosts. The momentum was savage, carrying the horsemen in a wild hunt of speed, flair and unshackled bloodlust. Having had to watch powerlessly for days as their city was slowly consumed by Rot and sorcery, the pride of Altdorf's mighty armies was now cut loose.

Helborg pressed northwards, slashing out with his blade to slice down two fleeing beastmen, before his steed trod three more into the slurry underfoot. Ahead of him, he could see greater concentrations of heavily armed warriors trudging into battle, each company bearing a skull-topped standard bearing sigils of the plague-gods. The truly vast creatures of Chaos – shaggoths, ogres, cygors – bellowed as they swayed towards the interlopers who dared to take the fight to the open.

Then the direction of the charge veered westwards, bludgeoning its way out towards the straggling fringes of the forest. Helborg guided them away from the core of the enemy host, leading his squadrons of knights among the rumbling war engines.

As they galloped through the towering constructions, each rider sheathed his sword and reached for a gift from the College of Engineers – a small spiked ball, stuffed with blackpowder and crowned with a small brass lever. The warhorses weaved between the trundling battle-towers, evading the flame-tipped arrows that shot down from the topmost platforms.

Helborg waited until the last of his cavalry warriors was under the shadows of the siege machinery before giving the order.

'Let fly!' he roared, hurling his own device at the skin-wrapped flanks of a battering ram.

As one, the knights loosed their tiny spheres. Where they hit the edges of the war machines, tiny clamps locked them fast, and the faint tick of clockwork started to whirr down.

Helborg maintained the ferocious pace, drawing the vanguard ever further west and breaking clear of the main enemy advance. Out on the flanks, the killing became easier, as the bulk of the heavy warriors remained north of the main gates.

With a flurry of sharp bangs, the grenades thrown by the horsemen went off, cracking into multi-hued explosions. Those devices were the final creations of the colleges – an ingenious fusion of engineer's art and wizard's cunning. An unholy concoction of blackpowder mechanics and Bright magic resulted in violent explosions far out of proportion to the devices' size, and the hulking battle-engines rocked under the assault. Chain reactions kicked off, crippling heavy artillery pieces and sending trebuchets folding in on themselves, hurling smoke up into the lightening skies.

Helborg hauled on the reins then, bringing the long charge to a halt. He was joined by the vanguard of Reiksguard, and quickly followed by the other Knightly Orders. Their numbers had been thinned during the perilous ride, but they still remained cohesive.

The charge had punched through the enemy vanguard and taken them a long way west of the horde's core advance, a fact which had not been lost on the heavy concentrations of Chaos infantry and warbands of Drakwald beastmen. Assuming the knights were breaking for safety, they had continued to advance south, leaving their siege towers to burn and opting to press the assault on the city. The gates, now undefended, lay before them, too far away for the Imperial knights to give defensive cover to before the infantry got within blade-range.

With a lustful roar, the bulk of the northern host's infantry broke into a shambling charge, heading towards the undefended gates. Isolated out on the western flank, Helborg could only watch them go. Zintler rode up to him, flicking his bloodstained visor open as his exhausted mount whinnied and stamped. 'They could not resist,' he observed.

Helborg nodded. The northmen were brutal foes, but they could never leave easy bait alone. 'Give the signal.'

Zintler drew a long-barrelled pistol and aimed it above his head. He fired, sending a blazing flare spiralling into the twilit murk above.

The signal was received. The infantry held in readiness inside the walls now advanced en masse, pouring through the open gates and out onto the battlefield beyond. Whole sections of artillery, concealed until that moment, suddenly opened up from the parapets, sending cannonballs and rockets ploughing into the onrushing hordes. The defence that had looked so shaky now presented its true shape – ruthlessly drilled, impeccably disciplined, and marching in the knowledge that only the most desperate fighting would stave off their encroaching fate.

The Chaos vanguard had advanced too readily, trusting in the flightiness of the mortals and deceived by the knights' sham bolt for freedom. Despite their huge numbers, they were now poorly positioned – caught between a stern defence at the walls and a powerful cavalry force on their right flank already mustering for the return strike.

'Now we take them,' said Helborg.

Zintler shouted out the orders, and the knights quickly formed up again. As soon as they were marshalled, the counter-charge began, driving back towards the exposed flank of the enemy.

Helborg did not lead the charge this time, opting to survey the battlefield more fully before following the Reiksguard back into the fray. He rode a short way towards higher ground, accompanied by his immediate bodyguard of Reiksguard, then pulled a spyglass from his saddlebag and placed it against his eye, sweeping across the expanse of the field.

As he did so, a sick feeling grew in his stomach. The manoeuvre had been executed impeccably, and he watched thousands of enemy troops being ripped apart by the combination of high-density artillery fire from the walls and the returning cavalry attacks. The pressure on the gates had been relieved for the moment, allowing the entire northern battle line to recover and restore a semblance of order.

But even as he watched the carnage unfold, he knew it would not be enough. He could see the west gates burning, and the enemy pouring in through the gap. He could see evidence, from the far side of the city, that the east gates had gone the same way. Pillars of smoke from all over the interior of Altdorf betrayed the desperate fighting taking place in every street and every courtyard. The Palace itself was wreathed with the greatest plumes of oily smoke. With the first shafts of sunlight angling through the murk, the whole edifice seemed to be covered in a film of grasping vegetation.

Helborg felt his heart sink. He might have saved the North Gate, but he could not be everywhere. The Reiksguard were spread too thin, the magisters were overwhelmed by the daemons in their midst, and the fragile protection of the outer walls was breaking apart.

'Lord, what are your orders?' asked Zintler.

The Reikscaptain was anxious to be riding again. They were

exposed, and if they did not return to the battle soon then they risked being cut-off entirely. Already, enemy reinforcements were massing on the forest's edge, creeping out from the shadows and lining up along the northern horizon. Their numbers seemed to be limitless – for every warband that was destroyed, three more took its place.

Helborg slammed his spyglass closed and stowed it away. He took up the reins and prepared to give the order to fall back to the gates. If death awaited him, he would meet it inside the walls, fighting alongside those he had worked so hard with to avert the inevitable. Perhaps they could still salvage something, a last-ditch defence of the Palace, retreating in the face of the hordes but preserving just a fragment of defiance until some relief force – he had no idea where from – could somehow reach them.

It was then, just before he spoke, that he noticed the strange devices on the armour of the reinforcements steadily bleeding out of the forest. Unlike the first wave of attackers, their banners were pure black, with none of the sigils of contagion. Their troops were neither bloated nor mutated, but looked painfully thin in ill-fitting armour. They came on silently, with none of the feral roars of the wild tribes of the Chaos Wastes.

And then, finally, he realised the truth. Just as at Heffengen, he was staring straight at the armies of the undead. With a cold twinge of horror, he recognised the fell prince at their head, wearing crimson armour and riding a skeletal steed. Helborg froze, compelled to witness the same forces that had brought down Karl Franz, and the same monster that had broken the Empire armies while the Auric Bastion still stood.

'My lord...' urged Zintler, increasingly anxious to be gone.

Fury gripped Helborg. He still had the letter, crumpled up on the inside of his jerkin. The daemon's wounds, forgotten about in the heat of battle, suddenly spiked again, sending agonising bursts of pain flooding through his body.

Now his failure was complete. Now there could be nothing – *nothing* – preserved. He felt like screaming – balling his fists and raging at the heavens that had gifted him such an impossible task.

He gripped the runefang's hilt, and drew it shakily. He could still ride out, alone if need be, and bring vengeance to the slayer of his liege-lord. Slaying von Carstein would do nothing to arrest the collapse of the city's defences, but it would be a tiny piece of revenge, a morsel of sheer spite to mark the passing of the greatest realm of men between the mountains and sea.

Before he could kick his spurs in, though, his mind suddenly filled with a new voice, one he had never heard before but whose provenance was unmistakable. Von Carstein was addressing him from afar, projecting his mind-speech as amiably and evenly as if he had been standing right beside him, and the dry, strangely accented tones chilled him more than anything he had seen or heard until that moment.

'My dear Reiksmarshal,' the vampire said, somehow managing to sound both agreeable and utterly, utterly pitiless. 'It is time, I think, that you and I came to terms.'

TWENTY

Leoncoeur swooped low, plunging into the horde below and tearing it up. The hippogryph extended its claws, tearing the backs of the mutants that shambled to get out of its path. It picked up two, one in each foreclaw, ascending steeply, then flung them back to earth.

Leoncoeur watched the bodies tumble away before crashing into the seething mass of filth below. The pegasus riders were doing the same – tearing into the horde from the skies, skewering the enemy on lances or letting their steeds crush skulls with flailing hooves.

To the west, Jhared's cavalry had already struck, smashing hard into the main bulk of the enemy host. The Chaos forces had seen them approach too late, caught up in the slaughter ahead and desperate to reach the broken gates to the city. They were attempting to turn now, to form up in the face of the brutal assault from the south, but it was too little, too late. Jhared's knights ran amok, slaughtering freely.

Leoncoeur pulled Beaquis higher, angling across the battlefield and gaining loft. He hefted his bloodstained lance, still unbroken despite the kills he had made. Over to his right stood the towering mass of Altdorf, still deluged by the driving squalls and burning furiously from a thousand fires. The west gates had been driven in, overwhelmed by the concerted charge of hundreds of vast, plague-swollen horrors. The stones themselves seem to have been prised apart, and now boiled with tentacles and obscenely fast-growing fungi. The Chaos host was so vast that only the prized vanguard creatures had yet squeezed through the ruined gates, leaving the miles-long train of lesser warriors outside the stricken walls.

This was the filth that the Bretonnians now preyed upon, reaping a horrific harvest as their lances and blades rose and fell. Over to the extreme east of the battlefield, the second wave had already hit, with de Lyonesse leading a valiant charge into a shrieking mass of daemons and mutated soldiery. They were having equal success, cutting deep into the enemy and laying waste.

But the momentum of the charge could not last forever – the sheer numbers would slow them in time. Sensing the tide about to turn, Leoncoeur dived again, aiming for a great plague-ogre stumbling in a blind, spittle-flecked rage towards the breach. Beaquis folded its wings, plunging straight down like a falcon on the dive. The creature only pulled up at the last moment, sweeping low over the heads of the marching warriors and streaking towards the greater beast in their midst.

Leoncoeur leaned over in the saddle, gripping his lance tight. The plague-ogre turned to face him, swinging a heavy warhammer studded with smashed skull-fragments, and bellowed its challenge.

Beaquis adjusted course, darting up and out of reach. Leoncoeur adjusted his aim, going for the creature's throat. The lance-tip punched cleanly, severing arteries, before the hippogryph's momentum carried them swiftly out of reach of the whirling hammer-head.

The ogre clutched at its severed gullet, staggering on now-fragile legs, dropping its hammer from twitching fingers. Then it crashed onto its back, choking for air, crushing more than a dozen mutant warriors beneath it.

By then Leoncoeur was already searching for more prey. Riding through the foul mucus-rain was hard work, and it was difficult to see more than a few dozen yards in any direction. Beaquis's wings began to labour as the beast struggled to gain height.

'Stay strong,' urged Leoncoeur. He need a better vantage. Slaying mutant beasts was satisfying, but it would not halt the momentum of the assault – there were too many of them, and they were not in command.

The hippogryph beat harder, climbing high above the swirl and crash of combat. Leoncoeur twisted in the saddle, peering out over the beleaguered city, trying to make some sense of the pattern of battle.

He had expected to find the enemy hammering at the gates, expending its rage against the walls that had stood for over two thousand years, but it was clear that fighting was already rampant across the entire city. Whole sections were burning, collapsing in piles of stinking rotten timbers. He saw daemons swarming over the ruins, chasing down the last of the mortal defenders or fighting furiously with dwindling bands of battle wizards and priests. They were everywhere, as profligate as the rain-showers that splashed around them and covered the streets knee-deep in slime.

We come too late, he realised.

He drove Beaquis even higher, desperately searching for something to use to his advantage. The earthbound knights were committed now, locked in combat with a far greater foe, but he could still choose his prey.

The vast bulk of the Imperial Palace reared up out of the gloom. It was still immense – a mighty gothic pile of imposing stone and iron, ringed with huge statues to the Imperial gods – but already thick with corrosion and unnatural growth. Just as the forest had been, the Palace was raddled with foetid plant-matter, and the austere walls and domes were heaving with clinging grave-moss. The causeways leading to the Palace precincts were rammed tight with advancing warriors, led by a truly enormous troll-like creature bearing two lesser warriors on its back. The surviving defenders were doing what they could to halt it, firing the last of their blackpowder weapons from the high walls, but it would not be enough.

Leoncoeur considered swooping down on that horror. He might be able to pluck the riders from their mounts and break their backs. Then his gaze swept east, over the tight-packed roof-tops and towards the wan light of the rising sun.

The concentration of daemons was greatest there. They were streaming towards a lesser temple dome, one surrounded by the slumped hovels of the poor. A truly titanic greater daemon was lumbering directly for the temple, its echoing bellows of rage rising above the tumult.

As soon as he saw it, he knew that was the prize. Time seemed to slow down around him, isolating the creature of darkness as the true quarry of his long hunt.

He could not save the city – that was beyond any mortal now – but battles could still be won.

He wheeled back to where the pegasi still plunged and dived into the hordes below. Their attacks were lethal, but isolated, and they were doing little to blunt the momentum of the colossal army below.

'Brothers!' Leoncoeur bellowed, straining to make himself heard even as he raced back into their midst. 'The prize lies within the city! Follow me!'

He banked hard, dragging Beaquis back towards the burning walls. The pegasus riders immediately fell in behind him, and the sky-host shot over Altdorf's flaming walls.

Leoncoeur looked over his shoulder as he flew over the

shattered gates, over to where Jhared's knights fought on. They were still causing devastation, but the net was closing on them. It was only a matter of time before their unity was broken. A pang of guilt struck him, and he almost turned back.

They will die as they lived, came a familiar voice in his mind then. *As warriors. They slow the attack on the Palace, and thus their sacrifice will serve.*

Leoncoeur flew on, and Altdorf blurred below as Beaquis picked up speed. The pegasus riders caught up, and the phalanx burned towards its target.

And me? he asked, almost without meaning to. Just to hear Her voice in his mind again gave him comfort.

But She did not speak again. Beaquis started to plunge earthwards, and the grotesque daemon lurched up to meet them, still unaware of the danger from the skies. Lesser daemons rampaged around it, tearing at the walls of the temple and beating on the locked gates. The dome itself seemed to have some power to resist them, and alone of all the structures in that quarter of the city remained free of the creeping vines and grave-moss.

Leoncoeur fixed his eyes on the daemon, trying not to fixate on its sheer size and aura of terror. This was what he had come to slay – just one contribution amid a host of other duels that would seal the fate of humanity. Next to that, the loss of kingship felt like a trivial thing indeed.

'Follow me down!' he shouted to his fellow knights.

Then he shook the blood from his lance, crouched for the strike, and spurred his steed down towards the horror waiting below.

On a blasted hill to the north of the burning city, Kurt Helborg and Vlad von Carstein stood alone. Helborg's bodyguard, fewer than a dozen mounted knights, waited further down the slope on the Altdorf-facing side. The vast army of the undead waited to the north, arrayed for the advance but still making no move. In the distance, Altdorf's spires stood starkly against the plague-rain, now lit grey by the slowly strengthening light of the sun. Spidering strands of dark-green could be made out across the stone, strangling and crushing the ancient structures. Cannon-fire still boomed, and the crackle of magic could be made out sporadically, but the main sounds were the cries of the dying and the guttural chants of the victors.

'You never replied to my letter,' said Vlad.

Helborg felt light-headed and nauseous. Days of no sleep and constant toil had finally caught up with him, and simply to be in the presence of a vampire lord would have crushed the spirits of a lesser man. As he gazed up at von Carstein's spectral face, he saw something like eternity reflected back at him. The dark orbs of the creature's eyes barely flickered. In an instant, Helborg recognised the gulf in years between them – it was like staring down a god, one who had trodden the paths between the worlds and who had returned to usher in the destruction of them all.

At least the pain had faded. In the vampire's presence, the legacy of the daemon's claws seemed to lose its potency.

'What was there to reply to?' asked Helborg, trying to muster at least a show of belligerence.

'That you recognised the wisdom of my offer,' said Vlad, as smoothly as if he cared little one way or the other. 'I have gone to some trouble to assemble the army you see before you. It will march on my command.'

Helborg smiled cynically. 'And your price?'

'You know it. I wish to be Elector of Sylvania. I wish to preside over my people in peace. I wish to look you in the eye as...' He returned a colder smile. '...an equal.'

Helborg could still hear the sounds of battle. They were impossible to blot out, like constant reminders of everything he had done wrong.

'That power lies with the Emperor,' he said.

'He is here?'

'You know he is not.'

Vlad raised an eyebrow. 'You credit me with too much foresight. Harkon has been disciplined for what he did – I had no part of it. As to Karl Franz's survival or otherwise, a veil remains over it. Even my Master does not know his fate.'

Helborg wished he had something to lean on, to prop up his failing strength, but dared not show the slightest shred of weakness. Everything began to blur, like some nightmare that he had been plunged into. Contempt filled him, both for himself and for the creature he spoke to. That he had been reduced to negotiating with such a horror was humiliation enough, and he sensed there was more to come.

'Why *ask*, von Carstein?' Helborg asked, bitterly. 'You have your armies.'

For a moment, fleetingly, Vlad looked genuinely hurt. 'You always saw us as merely adversaries. You never stopped to ask what might be accomplished, were certain truths acknowledged.' He shrugged. 'The northern gate is the only one you still control. Allow me to enter it, and it will be enough. You will have *invited* me. That is important. I can aid you, but you must say the words.'

Helborg blurted out a sour, disbelieving laugh. 'You... *prey* on us! You drag the dead from their graves and make them march beneath your banners. If Karl Franz were here–'

'Which he is not, Reiksmarshal, and more's the pity, because his wisdom is greater than yours.' The vampire drew a little closer, and Helborg smelled the dry aroma from his armour. 'You are a fighter, Kurt. Your soul is not made for governing. Already you have erred – the storm that tears your city from within could have been prevented. Do not let this thick neck lead you into more error.' His dust-pale face creased in what might have passed for kindness, though it exposed wickedly long fangs. 'Your time is up. I bring you power beyond your wildest hopes. Give me the word, and I will deliver your city.'

Helborg found he could not rip his gaze away from the vampire's. There was no insulating himself from the sounds of destruction, though, nor the acrid smell of burning that drifted across the whole landscape.

Part of him burned to reach for his sword, just as he had planned. If he were quick enough, a single strike might suffice – the runefang had slain mightier creatures that this.

For some reason, he found himself thinking of Schwarzhelm. The gruff old warrior would never have got this close – the very prospect of *talking* to such a foul creature would have enraged him. Huss would have been the same. Helborg felt their eyes on him then, the great and the exalted of the Empire he venerated, judging him, accusing him.

But they were not there. They did not have to endure the screams, nor witness the slow destruction of all he had lived to preserve. He was alone and exhausted, and defeated.

There was nothing else. There were no other roads to take, no other allies to call on.

He looked into the darkness of the vampire's eyes, and felt the footsteps of damnation catch up at last.

'Then you will have what you demand,' Helborg said, the words dragged out from his lips and tainted with loathing. 'Save my city.'

The effect was immediate. All across the city, from the burning tenements to the moss-strangled walls of the Imperial Palace, the slime-covered soils started to shift. Just as at Wurtbad, at Kemperbad, and at every other staging-post along the great rivers, Vlad's command of the Wind of Shyish was total. Whatever lingering power of faith that had existed over Altdorf had long been shattered by the Leechlord's spells, and so the very fabric of Chaos came to the vampire's aid.

The first to lift themselves were those slain in the night's fighting. Cadavers rose from the mud, shaking off the wounds that had ended them and lurching instinctively towards the unwary servants of the plague-god. Huge piles of the dead had been dragged together before the two occupied gates, all of which suddenly began to twitch and stir.

The newly-killed were soon joined by those who had been in the cold earth for far longer. Forgotten graveyards trembled and shifted, their soils broken by dozens of clawed hands. With a sigh of ghostly half-breath, a new army arose amid the terror of the plague-rain, unaffected by fear and undaunted by the driving torrents of pus. They locked blank eyes onto the daemons, and marched towards them. All but the weakest of the aethyrborn were able to dispatch them easily, but the numbers soon rose, clogging the already claustrophobic streets with gangs of silent, eerily calm fighters.

Altdorf had been settled since the time of Sigmar, and had roots going back to the very dawn of human civilisation. With every passing moment, older warriors emerged from the slurry underfoot, tunnelling up from deep catacombs beneath lost chapels and warrior-temples. Armour that had not been seen for generations was exposed again to the uncertain light, and long-lost sigils of fallen houses were illuminated by the ravening flames.

Last of all, dredged up from the river itself, came the first inhabitants of the old Reik homesteads, the tribesmen who had marched with Sigmar himself as he forged his empire in blood. They crawled out of the stinking muds of the viscous waters, clutching onto the chains that still hung across the great wharfs. They emerged into the open, grim-faced, shaggy with stiff beards and long hair, their arms marked with bronze rings and their weapons beaten from iron. Unlike the later generations that had been raised, these looked as hale and strong as they had in life, save for the dull lack of awareness in their faces. They did not gaze in amazement at the enormous structures around them, despite their last living view of the city as a tiny fortress of wooden walls and stockades. All they had retained from their former existence was a primordial hatred of the enemies of mankind, and they raised their blades against the daemons without a moment's hesitation. The blades that had once been borne alongside the living god retained more potency against the daemonic than any others, and soon the fighting was joined all along the riverbanks. Implacable undead took on the foul denizens of the Other Realm in bloodless, bitter combat.

The ranks of living corpses were quickly joined by Vlad's host, which marched through the North Gate in triumph, dipping their sable banners under the portcullis and heading straight into the depths of the inner city. The surviving mortal defenders fell back to allow them passage, staring in horror at the ranks of vampires, ghouls and crypt horrors as they loped through walls that had defied them for a hundred lifetimes of men. For some, the sight was too much, and their will broke at last. They cast aside their weapons and fell to the ground, weeping with despair.

For others, though, the sight of such unnatural allies came as cause for sudden hope. Though the sight of the living dead may have turned their stomachs, witnessing them taking on the vast hordes of corrupted savages was enough to prove their worth. Those defenders remained at their posts, carving out a defence of the North Gate, hanging grimly on to the one slice of territory they had been able to keep unsullied.

Of Helborg himself, though, there was no sign. Leaving the command of the North Gate, the Reiksmarshal headed towards the river, his face a picture of harrowed resolve. Nor did Vlad von Carstein stay with the bulk of his host for long. Like the shades he commanded, the vampire melted into the shadows, leaving the prosecution of the battle to Mundvard and his other lieutenants. The bulk of the undead fanned out into Altdorf's vast hinterland of criss-crossing alleys and thoroughfares, and soon the entire city was gripped by the murderous conflict of perverse life against preternatural death.

Margrit was unaware of all of this as it happened. With the last of the sacred waters sprinkled about the perimeter of the temple, she had taken up arms at last, determined to fight for as long as her strength allowed her. Mumbling litanies over and over, she had joined the remnants of Gerhard's temple guard in the courtyard inside the gates. No more than three-dozen guards remained, the rest having succumbed at last to the contagions that now ran rampant even in the infirmaries. Fewer than a hundred sisters were still able to stand with them unaided, and they clustered close behind Margrit, each bearing whatever weapons had been to hand.

Before them, the inner wall's gates shivered as the creature beyond them hammered on the wood. The defenders inched back across the courtyard, assembling on the stairs leading up to the garden colonnade.

'Courage,' urged Margrit, despite the fear that rose up in her gorge and nearly throttled her.

They all felt fear. They were all trembling. The difference lay in how they dealt with that.

'Can it cross the threshold?' asked Elia, her hands visibly shaking.

Margrit did not know. The line of sacred water snaked across the courtyard in front of them, barely a hand's width wide. It looked so completely insubstantial – a child could have skipped across it without ever noticing it.

And yet, the temple endured while everything around had been reduced to smouldering, slime-boiling rubble. She had held her faith for her whole life, and the precepts had never failed her. The great and the good of the Empire had always looked down on the Sisters of Shallya, seeing them as matronly mystics and little more. And yet the proud Colleges of Magic were now shattered haunts of the daemonic, and the mighty Engineering School was a smoking crater.

'The threshold will endure,' Margrit said, trying to sound like she meant it.

The doors shuddered again, and a gurgling roar echoed out. The creature was becoming frustrated, and its maddened fury was spilling over into raw mania. The stones of the outer wall were rocked, sending trails of dust spiralling down to the earth. Another blow came in, almost snapping the main brace across the doors.

More blows came in, faster and heavier. A crack ran down the oak, splitting it into a lattice of splinters. A clawed fist punched clean through, breaking the heavy beams at last and rocking the iron hinges.

A sister screamed. Margrit turned on her. 'No retreat!' she shouted. 'We stand *here!* We are the blessed ones, the chosen of the Earth Goddess! No creature of the Outer Dark may–'

Her words were obscured by a huge *crack* as the gates gave way at last. With a throaty bellow of triumph, the greater daemon smashed its way through the remains, hurling aside the severed residue and sending the ragged-ended spars spinning.

Margrit shrunk back, her defiance dying in her throat. The creature was *enormous* – far bigger than it had seemed when she had first caught sight of it from the walls. Surely nothing could stop it – no power of magic, no power of faith. She looked up at it as the monster swaggered and hauled itself through the gap, and its enormous shadow fell over her.

Some of her sisters vomited, overcome by the incredible stench. Temple guards dropped their blades, staring slack-jawed at the vision of hell approaching. The behemoth rolled towards them, shedding slime down its flanks as the foul rain washed it into the mire beneath.

It took all her courage, but Margrit managed a single step forward, her blade clutched in two shaking hands. She glared up at the creature of Chaos, planting her feet firmly.

'Go back!' she cried. 'Take one more step, and, by the goddess, it will be your last!'

The daemon looked down at her, and laughed. Huge yellow eyes rolled with mirth, and drool the length of a man's arm spilled from its gaping maw. Moving deliberately, with an exaggerated, mocking studiousness, it lifted a cloven hoof and placed it, heavily, over the line of sacred water.

The liquid steamed and hissed as it was defiled, and Margrit smelled rotten flesh burning. For a moment, she dared to hope that the slender barrier would be enough.

Then the daemon chortled again, and hauled itself closer, dragging its flab through the smeared puddles of water.

Margrit stood her ground, her heart thumping, her last hope gone. Sliding like oil on water, the putrid shadow of the daemon fell across her once more.

TWENTY-ONE

Ghurk galloped onward, smashing his way up the long causeway to the Palace. Resistance was crumbling now.

Atop his habitual perch, Otto urged his outsize sibling harder, cracking the heel of his scythe across Ghurk's scaly neck.

'No time!' he blurted, feeling a mix of exhilaration and consternation. 'No time at all! Smash and break! Crush and stamp!'

The battle for the West Gate had been a frustratingly slow business, with the defenders lingering at their posts far longer than they had any right to. The cannons had caused havoc with his best troops until Ethrac had finally got close enough to burst their barrels with a few choice spells. Even then, the mortals had stupidly and annoyingly remained in place for much too long. They were led by a redoubtable captain wearing white and black who had roused them to almost insane levels of bravado. Otto had been forced to kill that one himself, leaping from Ghurk's back and going at him with his scythe. They had traded blows on the summit of the gates with green lightning crackling around them. The human had fought well, wielding his broadsword two-handed with both speed and power.

It had done him little good in the end. Otto may have looked bloated in comparison, but his muscles were infused with the raging power of the Urfather. He did not even need Ghurk to come to his aid this time, and his scythe ripped through the knight's stomach, slicing through the breastplate as if being dipped into water.

Once that warrior was thrown down, the defenders' resolve melted, and the resistance began to crack. The gates were broken and the biggest and best of Otto's serried host had flowed into the walls of the city. Just as at Marienburg, the glorious blossoming of the Urfather's pestilential delights followed them in. The place was ripe for it – half-consumed by spores and moss-growths already, it was fertile ground for Ethrac's conjurings.

Otto clambered back onto Ghurk's shoulders, and the onslaught continued. Columns of chanting Norscans surged up the twisting streets, torching the overhanging houses as they went. Bands of marauders broke from the main charge and rampaged through the whole district, greeted with joy by the gangs of petty daemons squatting and slavering on the eaves.

The remaining defenders were driven back, slain in swathes every time they attempted to mount a resistance. Reserves were called up, and were swept away. Lines of artillery, placed in the courtyards on the approach to the Palace, were briefly effective but soon overwhelmed.

It would have been faster if the damned horsemen had not appeared and dragged half his army away into a desperate battle outside the walls. Ghurk had wanted to turn back and take them on himself, and only Ethrac threatening to shrink his stomach to the size of a walnut had persuaded him to keep going. Combat could rage for as long they liked on the plain west of the walls, and it would still not suffice to keep them from their true goal. They would approach the inner city with diminished numbers, it was true, but they still had enough to accomplish their divine task.

Now it approached. The Palace itself reared up into the flame-streaked murk, already covered in a creeping jacket of twisting fibres. Its vast gates were cracked and thrown down, its mighty domes gaping like smashed eggshells, its immense towers burning. Daemons leapt and scampered across its long, rangy battlements, pursuing the few living defenders with commendably spiteful zeal. Lightning snapped and twisted across its shattered vistas, licking like whips along the ragged profile.

'There it lies, o my brother!' shouted Otto, standing up on Ghurk's heaving shoulders. 'You see it? There it lies!'

Even Ethrac was grinning then. He stood too, leaning on his staff. The Imperial Palace – the very heart of the mortals' realm – lay broken before them. No invading army had ever come this far. This was the throne of the boy-god, the very heart of his foul and decadent kingdom, and they were on the cusp of it. They had slain and slain and slain until the mud-mires of the streets were the colours of spoiled wine, and this was the reward.

Otto looked up at the colossal edifice, and began to laugh. The laughter split his lips, burbling like a torrent from his mouth. His ribs ached, his shoulders shook. There was nothing left – they had *done* it.

Ghurk cantered happily up the long straight road towards the Palace, crashing into the statues of old heroes that lined the processional. Behind him came the tribesmen of the wilds, driven into a frenzy by the savage joy of sacking the home of their ancestral enemies.

Otto was the first to spot the newcomers. In defiance of all reason, more defenders were clustering around the Palace's outer walls. As if plucked from the air, they were lining what remained of the parapets and waiting for the onslaught. At first, he could not believe it – thinking it a trick of the flickering half-light.

Then, slowly, he realised the truth.

'The dead,' he muttered.

By then, Ethrac had sensed it, too. 'I knew it!' the sorcerer snapped. 'Did I not warn you?'

Otto glowered at him. More skeletons and living cadavers were taking up position across the Palace approaches, blocking the head of the processional in ever greater numbers. Unlike the mortals they replaced, they showed nothing but implacable dedication, standing silently before the oncoming horde, their pale faces empty and their eyes unblinking.

'Do they fight us for the carcass of this Empire?' blurted Otto, furiously. 'Is that it? We must lay low *two* armies this day?'

Ethrac spat messily onto his brother's hide and started shaking his staff. 'They have joined against us, o my brother. They are united in weakness.' The sorcerer smiled grimly. 'But two rotten planks do not make a life-raft. They will *both* be swept away.'

At that, he brandished the staff two-handed, and the bells clanged wildly. More forks of aethyr-tempest slammed down, breaking up the cobbles and sending the stones flying. The Leechlord's vortex accelerated further, hurling great slaps of mucus into the waiting ranks of undead. The vines and grave-moss that had shot up from every mortar-joint writhed out like snakes.

Ghurk bellowed, pawing the ground like a giant bull. The Norscans at his feet roared in hatred, furious that an easy prize had been snatched away at the last moment.

'We broke the mortals!' cried Otto, his face purple with rage. 'Now we break the immortals!'

And with that, the horrific vanguard of the plague-god surged up the processional, beating for the Palace gates like a sluice of boiled blood flung down an abattoir's drain. With a final roar, the host of the Glottkin charged against the gathering might of the undead, and unholy battle was joined at last in the grounds of Sigmar's Palace.

The scale of the catastrophe had been apparent for miles. As Deathclaw had neared the Reik valley, the column of fire and storm-wind had loomed ever vaster, climbing like a mountain into the skies. It was twisting in a vast, glacial rotation, as if an immense vice were being applied to the city below, gradually squeezing the life out of it like a wine-press eking out the blood of the grapes.

Neither Martak nor Karl Franz said anything for a long time. There were no words to describe the sheer size of it. The heavens themselves were being ripped open, and the fury of the Other Realm poured down onto the land below. Nothing, surely, could stand against that degree of power. Whatever spells had been recited to unleash such devastation must have been beyond any that had been spoken before.

The world was indeed changed. Martak could sense it in his blood – the Laws that governed his art were twisting, buckled under enormous pressure. They had whispered this past year that the bonds of Shyish had been loosened, thinning the boundaries between life and death, but now it seemed that all the Eight Winds were running amok.

'This cannot be halted, lord!' Martak blurted out at last, unable to contain his frustration at what they were doing. He felt insignificant – a mere speck against an infinite sky, hurtling headlong into a maelstrom of terrifying size and power.

The Emperor did not reply. As the scale of the plague-storm had become steadily apparent, he had retreated into himself, driving Deathclaw hard. The griffon still bore the wounds it had taken at Heffengen, and was clearly losing strength, but Karl Franz gave the beast no respite.

Below them, the forest was scored with the paths of mighty armies. Whole swathes had been trampled down, betraying the routes the enemy had taken to beat down Altdorf's gates. The river itself was a thick, olive-green sliver of mud, its energy stripped from it. Even up high, the stench was incredible – an overpowering melange of death, sickness and mortal fear.

'You said you dreamed of this?' shouted Karl Franz at last.

Martak nodded grimly. Everything was as he had foreseen – the flames running riot through the lower portions of the city, the terrible slaughter all around the walls, the burgeoning vegetation rearing up against the Palace walls and breaking them open. As they neared, he could see pitched battles spreading out across the entire valley. To the west and east, mounted horsemen were fighting a desperate rearguard defence against a sea of Chaos infantry. At the North Gate, Empire troops were grimly holding onto a narrow stretch of territory against a tide of war-maddened beastmen. Inside the walls, the fighting was more confused, and appeared to be a messy three-way tussle between corrupted Chaos warriors, the hemmed-in remnants of Empire soldiery, and a host of undead, who had taken whole chunks of the poor quarter and were advancing, street by street, across the city.

The entire world, it seemed, had come to Altdorf – Sigmar's city had sucked them in, from Bretonnia, from Sylvania, from the Wastes of the north and the depths of the forest. All had come to feast on the Empire's harrowed corpse.

'I dreamed of more than this,' Martak cried back. 'You know of what I speak.'

Karl Franz maintained the pace, forcing Deathclaw lower. The city swept closer, spread out below them in all its ravaged glory. 'And yet you tell me the Law of Death is weakened.'

'It is,' replied Martak, struggling to make his own wilful steed follow the Emperor closely. 'But what of it? I am no necromancer – we cannot raise the slain.'

Karl Franz looked up then, a strange expression on his face. Martak had never seen a look quite like it – there was no fear, not even anger, just a kind of resignation.

'Surely even you see it now,' said the Emperor, gesturing towards the heavens.

Martak followed his gaze. Above them, still shrouded by the turning gyre of the heavens, a new light was now visible. Shorn of the competing glow of Morrslieb, the twin-tailed star could be made out, riding high above the drifting filth of the world below. Martak watched it burn, captivated by its strange, otherworldly light.

It was not a comforting light. There was nothing homely or warming about it – Sigmar's star had ever been a harbinger of great trials, and of the changing of ways, and of the passing of one age into another. The flames rippled along behind it, hard to focus on yet impossible to ignore.

Martak felt his heart miss its beat. All citizens of the Empire had been raised on tales of the comet. Men made its sign against their breast before going into battle; mothers made the gesture over the cots of the newborn, warding them against the terrors of the night. It was *their* sign, the mark of humanity, lodged amid a world of war and madness that had hated them for all eternity.

'What does it mean?' Martak asked.

Karl Franz flew on. The city was approaching quickly now. Below them, the gaping great dome of the Palace drew into focus. Vast forces were converging on it now, fighting against one another for the prize. Deathclaw began to plummet.

'That death is not to be feared,' said the Emperor, his voice trailing off as he descended.

Martak hovered above him for a moment longer, unwilling to commit to the dive. Everything below him reeked of corruption and insanity. Screams still mingled with the howl of the plague-wind, and the burning pyre of Altdorf loomed ahead like a festering scar on the hide of a gods-forsaken world.

'What does *that* mean?' he muttered, holding position, unable to share the blithe conviction displayed by his master. 'What has he seen?'

He could still get out. He had delivered the Emperor to the city, just as he had promised, and that was where his duty ended. Even if Altdorf were to be scrubbed from the earth, there might still be places to hide, refuges in the mountains where a man like him could scratch some kind of a living.

He laughed at himself harshly. They really had appointed a terrible Supreme Patriarch.

'I broke you out of that cage,' he said to his griffon, grimacing wryly. 'Time I took you back.'

He gave the command, and the griffon cawed wildly, before furling its wings and following the Emperor down into the inferno below.

Just as the daemon reached out for Margrit, something moving incredibly fast shot out of the skies, streaking like lightning from the storm. She had the vague impression of wings, blurred with speed, and the cry of a human voice speaking a language she did not understand. She scrambled backward, out of the path of the clutching claws, and saw what looked like a massive eagle diving straight at the daemon's face.

But it was not an eagle – it was a beast out of legends, a *hippogryph*, part-horse, part bird, with griffon-like claws and a long, lashing tail. Its rider thrust his long lance straight into the daemon's heart, and its hide broke open with a hideous rip.

The daemon screamed, and clutched at the lance. The rider's momentum carried him onward, and the steel tip drove in deeper, causing black blood to fountain along its length.

The daemon ripped the lance out, hurling both rider and steed clear. With a crash of armour, the hippogryph slammed into the courtyard wall, cracking the stone. The daemon reeled, the skin of its vast chest hanging open in strips. Blood continued to gush freely, pouring like an inky cataract down its sloping stomach and fizzing where it spread across the ground.

Possessed by a sudden impulse to come to the rider's aid, Margrit rushed forward, whirling the blunt blade in her hand. She stabbed it into the daemon's hoof. It took all her strength just to pierce the thick layers of hide encrusting the cloven foot, and she heaved down on the hilt to drive the rusting sword home.

To such an immense creature, the blow must have been little more than a scratch, but it brought fresh bellows nonetheless. The daemon leaned forward, bending double to clutch at her. Margrit staggered out of its reach again, feeling raw fear bubble up inside her. Her attack now seemed more an act of incredible rashness than bravery. Up close, the incapacitating stench was even worse than before, and she nearly retched as the claws reached out for her.

She felt the first talons scrape down her back, dragging at her sweat-stained robes, and prepared for death.

At least I bloodied it, she thought vindictively as she was hauled back.

But then the grip released, and she was dumped to the stone again. Twisting around, she saw the reason – the hippogryph rider had charged back into the fray, his lance gone but now bearing a broadsword.

Even amid all the terror and all the filth, Margrit was struck by his sheer beauty. His blond hair seemed to shimmer like gold, and his armour, though streaked with blood, still glittered with a high sheen. He charged straight at the daemon, spitting words of challenge that sounded like some strange music, working his blade in blistering arcs and hacking into its loose flesh. He moved so *fast*, shrugging off wounds and taking the fight straight to the creature that loomed over him in an almost comical mismatch of sizes. He had to leap into the air even to land a blow, driving his sword once more into the daemon's ribs and twisting the blade as gravity wrenched it out again.

The daemon, howling in rage and frustration, swept its sword at him in a massive, earth-breaking lunge. The knight, incredibly, met the strike with his shield, though the *clang* of metal-on-metal thrust him back six paces and nearly crushed him back against the wall.

Margrit shuffled further out of reach, on her knees, frantically searching for another weapon – something she could use to aid the knight. More cries of battle rang out from elsewhere in the courtyard, and she had the vague, blurred impression of other daemons racing through the broken gates, joining in combat with the rest of the sisters and their guards.

The greater daemon, though, consumed all her attention. It traded huge blows with the knight. Each one, by rights, ought to have broken him, but he just kept on fighting, hammering back with wild strokes, making up in speed and guile what he lacked in stature. He seemed to dance around the daemon's lumbering frame, giving it no time to crush him under its massive fists. The lance-wound in the daemon's chest still pumped blood, visibly draining it as the fight went on.

The monster howled with fury, and launched a backhanded swipe straight at the knight's chest. He managed to get his shield in the way, but the force of the impact slammed him to his knees. The daemon, sensing a kill, raised its other fist high and prepared to slam it down.

With a savage scream, the hippogryph hurtled across the courtyard, flying straight into the daemon's face and lashing out with its claws. The two creatures grappled with one another, gouging and tearing, and the daemon was once more rocked back onto its bloated haunches.

Eventually the daemon managed to scythe its heavy blade around, catching the hippogryph on its wing-shoulder and sending it tumbling back against the courtyard floor. Its wings broken and its chest leaking blood, the beast hit the stone with a wet snap, crumpled to the ground, and moved no more.

But it had given the knight time to recover. He rose again, blade in hand, and cast his battered shield to one side.

As Margrit looked on, both rapt and horrified by the spectacle, her roving hands finally closed on something. She looked down to see an earthenware pot, of the kind used by the sisters to carry the sacred water up from the wells. By some strange chance it was half-full, somehow overlooked when the rest had been poured around the perimeter. She grabbed it and dragged herself to her feet again.

'Master knight!' she cried, then threw it to him.

He caught the pot in his shield hand, more by instinct than anything else. He had no time to guess what it was, nor to protest, for the horribly wounded daemon bore down on him, reaching out to throttle him where he stood.

The knight lashed out with his blade, severing the hooked fingers as they closed, then raced forward, grabbing on to the daemon's slabbed stomach and climbing up its ravaged chest.

The daemon tried to rip the knight away, but was hampered by its own clumsy blade. The knight hurled the pot at the ragged wound-edge, where it smashed open, dousing the bloody flesh-pulp with sacred water.

Huge gouts of steam immediately erupted, engulfing both combatants. The daemon's screams were deafening now, and it clawed at itself in agony, opening up the flesh-rent further and exposing a huge, black heart within.

The knight took up his sword two-handed, holding it point-down above his head, bracing against the sway and twist of the daemon's writhing. With a cry of vindication, he plunged it straight down, bursting the creature's heart open in an explosion of boiling ichor.

The daemon thrashed and bucked, its entire body convulsing in a rippling wave of fat and torn muscle. Its horned head swung from side to side, narrowly missing goring the knight, who clung on somehow, twisting the sword in deeper, ramming it in up to the hilt and pressing it home.

With a horrific shudder, the daemon's struggles gradually gave out. Aethyr-lightning burst into life across its body, snapping and tearing at the fabric of reality. It bellowed again, a sound of pure spite, but now its frame was unravelling fast, dissipating back into the realm from whence it had been summoned.

Still the knight clung on, never letting go of his sword. A huge *bang* resounded across the courtyard, shattering stone and making the earth ripple like water. Margrit was thrown onto her back, and she hit the ground hard. There was a rush of wind, hot as flame, and a long, agonised shriek.

The wind blew out, tearing itself into oblivion almost as soon as it had arrived. Margrit looked up, feeling blood in her mouth. The courtyard was half-demolished, with the bodies of men, women and daemons lying prone in the rubble. A huge slime-crusted crater had opened up where the daemon had been. In the centre of it stood the knight, his shoulders bowed, keeping his feet with difficulty, his armour coated in gobbets of thick black slime.

He limped over to her, pushing his visor up, a weary smile on his drawn face. He bowed low, displaying more courtesy in that one gesture than any Empire soldier had ever given her across a lifetime of service, and addressed her in broken, heavily accented Reikspiel.

'My good lady,' he gasped, breathing heavily, 'you have the thanks of a king. By all that is holy, that was *well done*.'

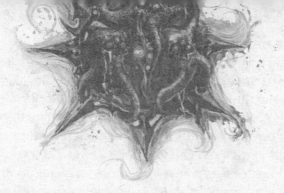

TWENTY-TWO

Helborg ran through the burning streets, fighting when he had to, hugging the shadows and sprinting hard when he did not. Only Zintler and nine of his most trusted Reiksguard had come with him; the rest had been left to hold the precarious line to the north.

Altdorf was now more populated than it had been for generations. A bizarre mix of Empire citizens, state troops, northmen, daemons and undead warriors fought one another in a bitter and fractured melee, breaking down into a thousand little battles over every scrap of unclaimed terrain. The arrival of von Carstein's army had thrown everything into confusion, locking the previously unstoppable march of the Chaos armies into a grinding stalemate. Across the devastated townscape, the various factions lost, gained and held ground, all under the continuing howl of the plague-storm.

In truth, the petty defeats and conquests now mattered little to Helborg. The city was lost, either to the still-massive hosts of the Ruinous Powers, or to the similarly gigantic force of raised slain that marched against them. Each enemy was as horrifying as the other. The daemons retained their unearthly powers, able to leap and shimmer through reality before bringing their spell-wound weapons to bear, while the dead had terrible strengths of their own. Helborg had seen the wight-kings tear into battle wearing the armour of ages and carrying blades forged at the very birth of the Empire. Ghosts and crypt horrors threw themselves into the fray, each capable of causing terrible damage before being dragged down. They were met by tallymen and plaguebearers, just as dire in combat and with the same lack of fear and pre-ternatural devotion to their cause.

The result was that the mortals were being pushed to one side. Exhausted by weeks of plague, fatigued by the long siege prepa-rations, shocked by the ferocity of the initial assault, the surviving Empire troops clung on to what little ground they could, increas-ingly only spectators before the real battles between the Fallen and the dead.

That was not enough for Helborg. He had not suffered so long to see his city torn apart by rival invaders. Vlad could protest as much as he liked – there was no honour in the scions of Sylva-nia, and as soon as the battle was done the vampire lord would revert to type. Even amid all that had taken place, there were still things that had to be accomplished.

He had to get to the Palace. That had not yet fallen in its entirety, despite the forces that fought their way towards it, street by street, kill by single kill.

So the Reiksguard ran hard. Helborg's face streamed with blood, and the pain spurred him on. He fought with an angry, vicious fury now, forgetting any pretensions at strategy or finesse and giving in to the raw violence that had threatened to over-whelm him for so long.

As they raced across the Griffon Bridge, its wide span crawling with whole clusters of desperate duels, he kicked and hacked his way through the throngs. The *Klingerach* lashed out, taking the head clean off a leering plaguebearer, before he spun on his heel and smashed the hilt into the face of an oncoming marauder. Then he was running again, his brother-knights hard on his heels.

Ahead of them, the Palace reared up into the storm, now covered in a thick layer of corrupted growths, its outline obscured and its lines tainted. White-edged flames licked across its broken back, fuelled and perverted by the poisons now freely coursing through the vegetation. Laughter still resounded in the storm-wind – the laughter of an amused, sadistic god that cared little how the battle fared so long as misery and misfortune continued to spread thickly.

'My lord!' cried Zintler, panting hard. 'The skies!'

Helborg looked up sharply, loath to be distracted from the chase. When he did so, however, his heart leapt.

A star burned brightly in the morning sky, only partly obscured by the roiling clouds. Its light was austere and hard to look at – a shifting flicker of pale flame. Behind it trailed two lines of fire, snapping and twisting like streamers.

He halted, suddenly held rapt by the vision.

The twin-tailed star.

'What does it mean?' asked Zintler.

Helborg laughed. 'I have no idea. But it is *here.*'

As he stared at it, it seemed to him that two tiny specks of darkness fell from the skies, racing out of the light of the star one after the other, plummeting like peregrines on the hunt-dive.

He blinked, trying to clear his sweat-blurred vision, and they were gone. For a moment, it had looked like two mighty eagles had dropped from the heavens, falling fast towards the open carcass of the Imperial Palace.

'We have to get there,' he said, snapping back into focus. The bridge terminated less than fifty yards ahead, after which the land rose sharply, crowned with the mansions and counting-houses of the nobility. Most were aflame, or slumped into rubble, or blazed with unnatural light, and what little remained was now contested by the two ancient enemies of mankind who now struggled for mastery.

It would be hellish. They would have to fight their way through a mile of steep, switchbacked roads before reaching the processional leading towards the gates. That was where the concentration of Chaos warriors was greatest, and where even the undead had toiled to make progress. They would be lucky to make it halfway, and unless the twin-tailed star looked kindly on them, they might not even get that far.

Helborg found himself grinning with a kind of fey madness. Everything he cherished was already gone. All that remained was the last, desperate sprint towards the heart of it all, to where he had always been destined to meet his end. The comet showed the way, lighting up the path with its flickering, gold-edged light.

The End Times, he thought to himself grimly as he broke into a run once more. *So this is what they look like.*

Leoncoeur did not have time to speak to the priestess for long – the courtyard was still crawling with plaguebearers. Many had been banished by the shock wave of the greater daemon's departure, but others lingered, re-knitting their aethyr-spun bodies together and advancing once more towards the huddled group of guardsmen and priestesses.

He could barely stand. The fight against the creature of Chaos had drained him to the core, and even with the timely aid of the blessed water he had scarcely prevailed. He backed away from the daemons' advance, gathering his strength for renewed fighting.

The priestess came with him, unarmed now but unwilling to leave his side.

'What is your name, lord?' she asked, her eyes never leaving the hordes of daemons creeping through the ruined outer wall.

'What does that matter now, sister?' Leoncoeur replied. 'We are all fighters.'

She looked satisfied by that. 'I was hoping for an Emperor,' she said dryly. 'Perhaps a king will do.'

Then, barging aside the lesser creatures of Chaos, the obese and horrific scythe-bearer clambered over the wreckage of the gates and fixed them both with a gaze of pure loathing. Though dwarfed by the slain greater daemon, this new creature was scarce less foul, and he stank just as badly. His jowls wobbled as he raised an accusing finger.

'*You*,' the monster drawled through bloody lips. 'You *killed* it.'

'As I will you,' warned Leoncoeur, remaining inside the line of the water. 'You have seen it already – come no closer.'

From outside the walls, sounds of battle had broken out again. Leoncoeur could hear the unearthly cries of the plaguebearers as they took on an unseen enemy. Perhaps some of the pegasus riders still fought on, though he guessed there were few of them left now. He caught the faint whiff of something sepulchral on the air, vying with the stench of decay, and wondered what it meant.

'You *killed* it!' screamed the Leechlord, advancing across the line of sacred water as if it were not there. Though it had proved a barrier against the least of the Chaos warriors, it did nothing to halt those most steeped in the twisting powers of the aethyr. 'Such *beauty*, gone from the world!'

Leoncoeur pushed the priestess behind him, shielding her with his body. The tumult of combat from beyond the walls grew louder. With a sudden realisation, Leoncoeur knew the reason for the creature's fury – the tide had turned. Against all hope, his army of fleshy horrors was being driven back, though by whom or what he could not yet see.

He allowed himself a smile of dark contentment. He had done what he had come for. The temple was secure, and a chink of light would endure amid the darkness. Whatever happened now, the journey had not been in vain.

'Your spells unravel themselves,' Leoncoeur taunted, edging warily closer. 'You will not take this place now, and it turns your mind to see it.'

That proved the final straw. The Leechlord lumbered towards him, raving and spitting, his flabby arms cartwheeling. Leoncoeur raised his sword, and their weapons clashed – steel against iron. They traded blows in a furious whirl. Leoncoeur shattered the creature's scythe with a single swipe, then pressed the attack by driving his blade deep into his overspilled stomach. Entrails flopped out, hanging like strings from the burst skin-sac.

Somehow, that did not stop him. The Leechlord swayed back into the attack, pulling a bone-saw from his belt and slashing wildly. Every blow that landed felt like a warhammer-strike – heavy and deadening. Leoncoeur could feel his arms ache. The long ride, followed by the battle at the gates, then the grinding duel against the greater daemon – the toll was too heavy.

'For the Lady!' he cried, redoubling the blows from his blood-smeared broadsword. He managed to drive another thrust deep into the creature's midriff, further opening the wound and showering the flagstones with speckled gore.

But the Leechlord was immune to pain, and his raddled body could absorb the most horrific levels of punishment. Unlike the daemon, he was a creation of flesh and blood, and would not be banished back to the aethyr. He opened his vast maw and vomited straight at Leoncoeur's chest.

The deluge was horrific, splattering into his eyes and making him gag. He staggered away, blinded by the foul matter. Unable to defend himself, he felt the sharp cut of the bone-saw as it punched into his throat.

He jerked away, flailing wildly with his sword, but he could already feel the hot cascade down his chest. The cut was mortal, and black stars spun before his eyes.

He crashed to the ground, fighting hard to stay conscious. The Leechlord towered over him triumphantly, his whole body sagging open from the wounds he had taken, but with the vicious light of victory in his porcine eyes.

Leoncoeur's blurred gaze wandered over to where the priestess stood, watching in horror, unable to intervene with no weapon to hand.

But she had done enough. The gift of water had proved sufficient, and the irony only then occurred to him.

Look for me in pure waters.

'She has blessed you indeed,' he murmured, just as the Leechlord brought the saw down and cut deep into his chest.

Leoncoeur's back arced in agony. He felt his ribs sever and his muscles part. Fighting back against the pain, he stared straight into the face of his killer, and cracked a grin.

That enraged the Leechlord further, but before he could twist the saw in deeper, he suddenly went rigid. A look of panic flashed across his features, and his arms thrust out, shivering. He tried to turn, but his body was rapidly turning into something else – hard, bark-like matter that burst out from under his pustulent hide.

'What... is...' he stammered, but then his tongue solidified and his whole body shuddered into rigidity.

His awareness slipping away, Leoncoeur just had enough time to see the cause. A tall warrior wearing crimson armour stepped from the shadow of the Leechlord, a bloody stake in his hand and a smoking ring on his pale finger. The two of them looked at one another, and the crimson-armoured lord inclined an ice-white, long-maned head.

With his last sight, Leoncoeur saw the remainder of the daemons being driven from the courtyard, pursued by grey-skinned warriors in archaic armour. With the Leechlord's downfall, there was nothing to bind them together – a new force had arrived, one with the power and the will to take them on.

Leoncoeur's head lolled. When it hit the stone, it felt almost like the feather bolsters of his old cot in Couronne's castle. An overwhelming feeling of numbness shot up his limbs, stifling the pain.

The priestess was at his side then, cradling him. He managed to shoot her a final smile.

'My lady,' he whispered.

So it was that, courteous to the last, Louen Leoncoeur died in the precincts of the Temple of Shallya, ringed by the living and the dead.

The Glottkin tore up to the Palace gates, surging like the unleashed force of nature they had always been. Undead warriors tried to block their path, forming a cordon before the open doorway, but they were swept away like chaff. Ghurk picked up several with one sweep of his fist. Disgusted that he could not eat them, he hurled their bony bodies away.

The cavernous interior of the Palace beckoned. Once it would have stood proudly, a masterpiece of baroque excess, soaring into the skies and ringed by graven images of gods and heroes. Now, mere hours after their arrival, the entire complex ran wild with an overabundance of reeking foliage. Mosses, vines and weeds sprouted from every crevice, prising apart the stone and bringing down pillars and buttresses. The entire structure now listed uneasily on its slime-glossed foundations, and entire wings had collapsed under the weight of the mucus-deluge and the burgeoning plague-growths.

Otto beat Ghurk's hide harder, forcing him to gallop into the heart of the great sprawl of ruination. The undead were everywhere now, spilling from balconies and clawing up from the sewers underfoot. Festus's plague-rain was already beginning to lessen, and the assault teetered on a knife-edge. Seizing the Palace was now imperative – the scryers had all foretold that the end would come there, and that *he*, Otto Glott, paramount servant of the Plaguefather, would be the one to land the killing blow. It would take place at the very centre, the oldest and the grandest edifice of humanity on earth, and no sudden apparitions nor ghosts from the blasted wilds could be allowed to halt that now. They had destroyed the undead at Heffengen, they had destroyed them at Marienburg, and now they would destroy them at Altdorf.

'Onward, on, o my brother!' Otto commanded, thrashing Ghurk madly with his scythe-butt.

Ghurk chortled happily, and crashed through a whole string of vine-strewn courtyards, lashing out with his tentacle-arm and crunching apart any skeletons unwary enough to oppose him.

Ethrac was busy too, hurling blast after blast of aethyr-lightning from his staff. Revenants were blown into slivers of spinning bone, their armour shattered and their swords crushed into spiralling shards. He had seen the twin-tailed star again, and this time the omen seemed to trouble him. He uttered no cries of victory, but mumbled an endless series of cantrips and summonings, ringing them all in a lattice of writhing witch-light.

The hosts of Chaos that had accompanied them on the long charge into the Palace grounds now fanned out, taking the fight to the scions of Sylvania. Every corridor, every passageway and bridge-span was clogged with struggling warriors, locked in a pitiless struggle for mastery. The storm raced above them, lashing the combatants in the plague-rain and drenching the few remaining open spaces. Everywhere else, the foul garden bloomed, spreading its poisons into the very depths of the city vaults.

'I saw them come down,' muttered Ethrac, hurling more green-laced fire from his staff-tip.

'Who?' asked Otto, preoccupied with directing Ghurk towards the centres of resistance.

'The fallen king. I saw him, under the light of the comet. He will be there.'

Otto let a grin slide across his sore-thick lips. 'We knew he would. That is the sacrifice, the one to usher in the end.'

'Cut him deep, o my brother,' said Ethrac, letting rip with a blast of aethyr-energy that blazed across the rain-thick air and exploded in virulent swirls against a formation of wights. 'Cut him so deep that the world beneath him is severed. Nothing else matters.'

The Glott siblings broke into a wide muster-yard just under the shadow of the Palace's colossal main dome. It was less than two hundred yards towards the smashed doorway inside, beyond which they could already see the marble and gold interior glinting.

Before them, though, was arranged the last defence. No living soldiers still guarded the inner Palace, but they were no longer needed. A whole army of zombies waited for them, clambering over one another in a press of squirming limbs. They seemed to be swarming out of the ground itself, piled up in a heap of wriggling, necrotic flesh that looked more like a single organism than a mob of hundreds.

Ghurk barrelled onwards, undeterred. Ethrac began to shriek new chants, and Otto built up momentum with his scythe. The Army of Corruption charged along beside them, pouring into the muster-yard.

With a high-pitched scream, the glut of zombies burst outward, cascading like a lanced boil. The tangled web of undead stumbled and staggered towards them, as thick as the slime-rain, a whole forest of grasping fingers and rusting blades. The two armies slammed into one another, and the muster-yard was immediately filled with the scrabbling, sickening sounds of dry flesh tearing and plague-riddled sinews ripping.

Ghurk waded into the melee, lashing out with his tentacle-arm and scooping up dozens of zombies. Ethrac blasted more of them, infesting their dead hides with virulent parasites that punched out from within, crippling them and leaving them writhing on the stone.

Nothing stopped them completely, though – they came on with inexorable purpose, groaning and reaching, ignoring blows that would have ended a mortal warrior. Zombies latched on to Ghurk's legs and began to climb. Many were kicked away, but others quickly took their place. Soon Ghurk was wading waist-deep in a morass of undead, and still they came on, clambering over one another to get at the creatures riding on his back.

Ethrac began to spit out his frustration, burning the undead with balefire, torching whole bands of them as they reached out to pull up higher. Otto reached down, swinging his long scythe to dislodge those who had dragged themselves into range. A tumbling rain of severed limbs clattered down to the seething mass of bodies below, eliciting not a sound from their stricken owners.

But that was not the worst – the zombie plague was just a fore-taste. With an ear-splitting scream, the vampire the triplets had fought – and defeated – at Marienburg flew down from the high parapet of the looming dome, his arms stretched wide and lined with tattered batwings. Other fell creatures came in his wake – a vast winged horror with a skeletal ribcage and bony claws – a *terrorgheist* – egged on by three shrieking ladies in bone-white lace. Clouds of corpse-gas billowed out as they swooped in, reacting with the plague-growths and hissing like snakes.

Ghurk instantly lunged for the winged creature, whipping his tentacle-arm up to haul it down from the skies. He connected, wrapping his arm around the beast's spiny neck, but had underestimated its strength. The terrorgheist remained aloft, and began to drag Ghurk across the ground, pulling him further into the writhing knots of zombies.

The first of the undead clambered onto Ghurk's back, and soon Otto and Ethrac were both fighting them off. They became separated from their own warriors, pulled by the terrorgheist deeper into the scrabbling pall of flesh-eaters.

'*Wither* them!' cried Otto, hacking his scythe down with frantic abandon.

Ethrac obliged, turning a whole gang of zombies into crackling torches of emerald flame, but it was not nearly enough. The terrorgheist continued to haul Ghurk along, forcing the compressed crowds of zombies up to chest-level.

Otto looked up, seeing the vampire lord preparing a spell of his own. Dark shadows began to crystallise around him, sucked out of the air and transfused into the Wind of Death.

'The vampire!' Otto shrieked, too far away to prevent it. 'He is the master! Snap his neck! Blind his eyes! Crack his bones!'

Ethrac, riding Ghurk's lurching back with difficulty, immediately saw the truth of it. The sorcerer lashed out with his staff, making the bells clang wildly. He spat out words of power, and the vampire's spell immediately inverted, turning on its owner in a vortex of ragged shadow. The vampire, taken by surprise, cried out in alarm, suddenly feeling the cold touch of his own magicks, but Ethrac was now in control, and the Chaos sorcerer shook his staff again with real venom.

Mundvard the Cruel's body exploded, flying outward in a welter of tattered strips. His skeleton hung together for an instant, then clattered down to the muster-yard's surface. As soon as the bones hit, they were crushed into the stone by the hundreds of criss-crossing boots. Once the vampire's grip was broken, the terrorgheist immediately lost its momentum, and the pressure on Ghurk abated.

Ghurk hauled back hard with his tentacle, digging his hooves in and tugging. The terrorgheist's bony neck broke, and the creature gasped out a glut of corpse-gas from its gaping jaws. Its sinewy wings flapped pathetically, and it thudded to the ground. With the creature's momentum broken, the mob of zombies collapsed around Ghurk, scattering in twisted piles of confusion at his feet.

'There is no *time* for this!' hissed Otto, using his scythe to clear the last of the clinging zombies from Ghurk's hide. 'Clear them out!'

Ghurk obeyed, bounding after the remaining enemy, swinging both arms like jackhammers.

The three women in lace leapt down from their vantage then, spitting curses. Ethrac was too busy breaking the remainder of the zombies to respond, so Otto hauled his scythe back, swung it around three times, then let go. The blade flew towards the leader of the trio, rotating in a blur of speed. Before she could evade the missile, it sliced clean across her neck, decapitating her in a single strike and spraying blood in broad spatters against the walls of the yard.

'Return!' cried Otto, reaching out with his right claw.

The scythe immediately swung around again, still spinning, and dropped back into his waiting palm.

That broke the spirit of the remaining undead horde. Bereft of the guiding will of their vampiric masters, the zombies lost all cohesion, and were soon mopped up by the oncoming tribesmen. The two remaining ladies fled back into the Palace depths, wailing like infants. Ghurk rampaged through the remaining throng, treading the last survivors into the stone underfoot. He crashed over the carcass of the terrorgheist and repeatedly stamped on it, powdering the bones and trampling the meagre scraps of sinew that still clung to them.

'Is this really the best they can do?' muttered Otto, still busy with his scythe.

'We killed the master,' said Ethrac, hurling more plague-slime about him with great heaves. 'Why do *any* still stand? The dead return to death when the master is killed.'

Otto shrugged. The Palace now lay before them, its doors gaping open and its riches clustered within, and lust was already overtaking his fury. 'Who knows? Perhaps there is another to be found.'

Ethrac kept up the barrage of raw sorcery, exploding zombies at a terrific rate. The broken dome of the Palace loomed up massively, a cyclopean structure even in its ruin. Flames still guttered around it, fuelled by the unleashed lethal energies, and the storm-pattern of clouds formed an immense cupola over the whole scene.

The devastation was now total. Every building in the city had been demolished or dragged into ruins. The death-toll was incalculable, and would never be recovered from. In a sense, it mattered not what happened now – they had done what no warlord of the north had ever done. They had broken Sigmar's city, wreathing it in fell sorcery and drenching it in the blood of the slain.

But there was still the final blow to be struck. The human Emperor still lived, and had come back to his den in time for the denouement. Such had always been predicted, and the Plague-father had never guided them awry.

'He is *in* there,' said Ethrac, barely noticing as his troops slaughtered and smashed the last remnants of the defence. 'I can *smell* him.'

Otto grinned back at him, his face sticky with blood.

'Then we go inside,' he said triumphantly. 'And bring this dance to its end.'

Margrit looked up at the vampire, not knowing whether to thank him or curse him. His fell warriors had cleared the courtyard of daemons and were now pursuing the remaining Chaos forces out of the square beyond. The surviving humans emerged from whatever places they had managed to barricade themselves behind, mistrust etched on their faces.

Vlad von Carstein was still gazing at the body of Leoncoeur. There was a sadness on the vampire's face.

For all that, the creature's aura still made Margrit shudder. For her whole life, she had been taught to fear and hate the grave-stealers. If any force of the world was truly anathema to hers, it was the bringers of everlasting death.

'And what of us, lord?' she asked, staring up at him defiantly. 'Now you have your victory, what is your purpose?'

Vlad turned to her, as if seeing her for the first time. Margrit could not help noticing that his gaze flickered instinctively down to her throat.

'If there were time, lady, I might show you all manner of wonders,' he said. 'You can see for yourself, though, that none remains.'

He looked up, past the temple dome and towards the Palace hilltop. His eyes narrowed, as if he were focusing on things far away.

'This is your temple again, for a time,' he said, coldly. 'Bury your dead and look to your walls. If all goes well, I *will* be back.'

Then his whole body seemed to shimmer like a shadow in sunlight. The ring on his finger briefly flared with crimson light, and his gaunt frame dissolved into a flock of squealing bats. They fluttered skywards, spiralling into the rain-lashed skies.

Margrit watched the bats go, slumped against the stone of the courtyard with the dead knight leaning against her. The noises of combat were falling away as the undead drove the daemons back from the temple's environs and into the maze of the burning poor quarter.

She looked up. The plague-rain was beginning to lessen, as was the tearing wind. Though the slimy droplets still cascaded, their force was already beginning to fade.

'But what is left?' she murmured to herself, looking around her destroyed temple, at the pools of blood on the stone, at the corroded and gaping rooftops beyond her little kingdom. 'What is there to be salvaged now?'

No answers came. She smoothed the bloodied hair from the knight's brow, and closed his eyes. It would have been nice to have known his name.

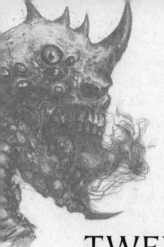

TWENTY-THREE

Deathclaw landed on the marble floor, its claws skittering on the polished surface. Karl Franz dismounted just as Martak's beast landed on the far side of the chamber.

The place had once been a chapel to Sigmar the Uniter. In its prime, a hundred priests a day would perform rites of absolution and petition, processing up the long aisles with burning torches in hand. The high altar was draped in gold and surrounded by the spoils of war – trophies from a hundred realms of the earth, the bleached and polished skulls of greenskins, the wargear of the northmen's many tribes.

Now all was in disarray. The chapel's arched roof had collapsed under the weight of pulsating mosses, and loops of pus-glistening tendrils hung from the ragged edges. The chequerboard floor had been driven up, exposing masses of writhing maggots beneath. The altar itself was broken, cracked in two by a creaking thorn-stump, and blowflies swarmed and buzzed over every exposed surface.

Karl Franz pulled the reins from around Deathclaw's neck and cast them aside. The very action of laying eyes on the devastation was enough to make him feel nauseous, but there was no time to linger over the desecration. From beyond the listing doorway at the rear of the long central aisle, he could already hear the echoes of fighting. The Palace was rife with it, from the high towers to the deepest dungeons. Even from the air he had seen how complete the defeat was – a huge army of Chaos tribesmen and mutated beasts had cut its way deep into the heart of the complex, resisted only by a motley mix of Palace guards and warriors of Sylvania's cursed moors.

It was just as it had been in Heffengen – the dead fighting with the living. How such allies came to be within the sanctity of the Palace grounds, though, was a question for another time.

'Now what?' asked Martak, dismounting clumsily and skidding on the polished floor.

'The Chamber of the Hammer,' replied Karl Franz, striding out towards the doors with Deathclaw in tow.

Martak took a little more time to persuade his steed to follow suit, and had to haul on its halter to bring it along. 'What of the Menagerie, lord?' he asked. 'The dragon! Can you not rouse the dragon?'

Karl Franz kept walking. He could have done that. He could have opened all the cages and let the beasts loose, but it would not accomplish anything now. There was only one course open to him, one he barely understood, one that could only bring him pain.

'Time is short, wizard,' he said, reaching the doors and peering out through their wreckage. A long corridor stretched away, empty of enemies for the moment and ankle-thick with fungus spores. 'You will have to trust me.'

Martak hurried to catch up. '*Trust* you? You have told me nothing! You saw the armies, you know how close they are.' He fixed the Emperor with a look of pure exasperation. 'What will this *serve?*'

Karl Franz looked back at him with some sympathy. There were no easy answers, and it was not as if his own intentions filled him with any certainty. All he had now were feelings, stirred by the sight of the comet and prompted by vague premonitions and old whisperings.

It could all be futile – everything, every step he had taken since the disaster at the Auric Bastion. But, he reflected, was that not the essence of *faith*? To trust in the promptings of the soul in the face of all evidence to the contrary?

He would have to dig deeper, to drag some surety from somewhere. In the meantime, there was little he could do to assuage the wizard's doubts.

'If you wish to rouse the beasts, then I will not prevent you,' said Karl Franz. 'You have delivered me to this place, and for that alone I remain in your debt. But I will not join you – the time is drawing closer, and I must be under the sign of Ghal Maraz when the test comes.'

He forced a smile. The wizard would have to follow his own path now.

'You may join me or leave me – such is your fate – but do not try to prevent me.' He started walking again, and Deathclaw followed close behind, ducking under the lintel of the chapel doors. 'This is the end of all things, and when all is gone – all magic, all strength, all hope – then only faith remains.'

The spell guttered out, and Vlad reconstituted deep in the heart of the Imperial Palace.

For a moment, it was all he could do not to stare. He had dreamed of being in this place for so long – more than the lifetime of any mortal. The yearning had stretched through the aeons, as bitter and unfulfilled as the love he had once borne for her. For Isabella. He had often imagined how it would be, to tread the halls as a victor, drinking in the splendour of aeons. Long ago, so long that even he struggled to retain the memory, he had imagined himself on the throne itself, presiding over a whispering court of black-clad servants, the candles burning low in their holders and the music of Old Sylvania echoing in the shadowed vaults.

To have accomplished those long hopes should have made him glad. In the event, all he felt was a kind of confusion. Nagash had given him what he needed to get here at last, but it turned out that all that remained was a ruin of foliage-smothered stonework and gaping, eyeless halls. It would never be rebuilt, not now. He had accomplished his goal, only to find that he was a master of ashes.

'My lord,' came a familiar voice.

Vlad turned to see Herrscher and a band of wight-warriors in the armour of the Palace. They must have been raised recently, for their greaves and breastplates were still mottled with soil. Further back stood silent ranks of the undead, interspersed with ragged-looking groups of zombies.

'Where are the rest?' asked Vlad.

'Mundvard and the ladies rode out to halt the plague-host before it reached the Palace,' said Herrscher. 'They did not come back.'

Vlad nodded. Perhaps he should have expected it – the Ruinous Powers had always been too strong for his servants to take on.

'Then their commanders will be within the walls now,' said Vlad.

'They have taken the southern entrance,' said Herrscher. 'They are heading for the centre, and we are in their path. If we leave now–'

'Leave?'

Herrscher looked confused. 'We cannot stay here, lord,' he protested. 'Your army is spread throughout the city, but they have broken into the Palace in force. They cannot be stopped, not by us, not without summoning reinforcements.'

Vlad smiled tolerantly. Herrscher looked genuinely perturbed at the prospect of harm coming to him, which was as good a sign as any that his transformation was complete.

'You are right, witch hunter,' said Vlad. 'The longer this goes on, the worse things will go for us. To bring this beast low, we must sever it at the head.' He smiled thinly. 'The savages of the north lead their armies from the front. If we wish to find the authors of this plague, look to the vanguard.'

Herrscher looked doubtful. 'We are so few,' he muttered.

'Ah, but you have *me* with you now.' Vlad glanced up and down the corridor, trying to get his bearings. 'I wonder, do any of your old kind still live, or do we have this place to ourselves?'

As if in answer, there was a huge, resounding bang from the corridor running away to the south, like a massive door had been flung back on its hinges. Following that came the sound of a low, slurring panting. The floor shook, trembling with the impact of heavy footfalls.

Herrscher drew his blade, as did the wights, and they fell into a defensive ring around their master.

Vlad unsheathed his own sword with a flourish, finding himself looking forward to what was to come. The footfalls grew louder as the beast smashed its way towards them.

'So the hunt is unnecessary – they have come to us.' Vlad raised his sword to his face, noting the lack of reflection in the steel. 'Now look and learn, witch hunter – this is how a mortarch skins his prey.'

With some regret, both Otto and Ethrac had to dismount from Ghurk as he barrelled on into the Palace interior. Their huge steed now scraped the roof of the corridors, bringing down chandeliers and ceiling-panels as he lumbered ever closer to the goal.

Otto and Ethrac ran alongside him now, both panting hard from the exertion. Ghurk himself seemed as infinitely strong as ever, his bulging muscles still rippling under his mottled hide. The vanguard of their suppurating horde came on behind, wheezing through closed-face helms and carrying their axes two-handed before their bodies.

As they came, they destroyed. Paintings were torn from their frames and ripped to pieces, statues were cast down and shattered. Ghurk's hooves tore up the marble flooring, and his flailing fists dragged whole sections of wall panels along with him. They were like a hurricane streaking into the heart of the enemy's abode, breaking it down, brick by brick, into a heap of mouldering refuse.

As they rounded a narrow corner, Otto was the first to catch sight of fresh enemies. A thrill ran through him, and he picked up the pace. 'Shatter them!' he cried, his voice cracking with enthusiasm. '*Smash* them!'

Just as at the Palace gates, the warriors lined up against them were no mortals, but more of the undead that had dogged their passage ever since the breaking of the walls. Otto began to feel genuine anger – they just *could not* be eradicated. They were like a... *plague.*

Ghurk bounded ahead, and Ethrac matched pace, his staff already shimmering with gathering witch-light. The undead wights rushed down the wide passageway to meet them, racing into battle with their unearthly silence. Soon the corridor was filled with the echoing *clang* of blades clashing. Zombies and skeletons went up against marauders and tribesmen in a mirror of the desperate combat still scored across the entire cityscape.

There was only one opponent worthy of Otto's attention, though – a crimson-armoured vampire lord bearing a longsword and wearing a long sable cloak. That one towered over even the mightiest of his servants, and swept arrogantly into battle with the poise of a true warrior-artisan.

Otto swung his scythe, clattering it into the vampire's oncoming blade even as Ghurk and Ethrac blundered onwards, reaping a swathe through the undead ranks beyond.

'You are the master, then,' Otto remarked, parrying a counter-blow before trying to skewer the vampire with his blade's point. 'Do you have a name?'

'My name is known from Kislev to Tilea,' replied the vampire distastefully. 'Vlad von Carstein, Elector Count of Sylvania. You, though, are unknown to me.'

Otto laughed, whirling the scythe faster. 'We are the Glottkin. We come to bury the Empire in its own filth. Why not let us?'

Vlad sneered, trying to find a way through Otto's whirling defence. The vampire carried himself with an almost unconscious arrogance – the bearing of a creature born to rule, and one who knew how to use a sword. 'You would cover the whole world in your stink. That will not be allowed to happen.'

'It cannot be stopped now. You surely know that.'

Vlad hammered his blade into the attack. 'Nothing is certain. Not even death – I should know.'

Otto laughed out loud, enjoying the artistry of the combat. Ghurk would never have understood it, nor Ethrac, but their gifts had always been different. 'You are rather good, vampire,' he observed.

'And you... fight with a scythe,' replied Vlad, contemptuously.

As if to demonstrate the weapon's uselessness, the vampire suddenly changed the angle of his sword-swipe, catching the hook of the blade and pulling it out of Otto's hands. Otto lunged to reclaim it, but it fell, clanking, to the floor. The vampire trod on the blade, advancing on his prey with a dark satisfaction in his unblinking eyes.

Otto let fly with a punch, hoping to rock the vampire, but Vlad was far too quick – he caught Otto's clenched fist in his own gauntlet, and twisted the wrist back on itself. Caught prone, Otto was forced round, his spine twisted.

Before he could do anything else, the vampire's blade punched up through his ribcage, sliding through his encrusted skin with a slick hiss. Vlad lifted him bodily from the floor, held rigid by the length of steel protruding from his torso. The pain was excruciating.

'And so it ends, creature of the Outer Dark,' said Vlad, bringing his sword-tip up to his lips. As was his wont with the defeated, he licked along the sword's edge, drinking deep of the blood that ran freely along the cutting edge.

As soon as he had gulped it down, though, he released his grip. His hands flew to his throat, and his eyes bulged.

Otto laughed, freeing himself of the blade and sauntering over to his scythe to retrieve it. The pain was already passing, thanks to the gifts of the Urfather. 'Drink my blood, eh?' he asked. 'Now, I wonder, have you the stomach for it?'

By now Vlad was retching. He staggered against the wall of the corridor, his cheeks red, bile trickling down his chin. A look of horror flashed across his tortured face as he realised what he had imbibed. 'You... are...' he gasped.

'*Very* unpalatable,' said Otto, reaching for his blade. 'My lord, I fear your appetites have undone you.'

Vlad gazed back at him, all the arrogance bled from his face. He vomited, hurling up a torrent of stinking black ichor. In his eyes was the full realisation of what he had done. He was poisoned to the core. He had taken in not blood but raw pollution, the very essence of plague, and now it was eating him from the inside. Once that finished him, all the souls raised by his arts would collapse back into their state of true death – every wight, zombie, skeleton and ghoul would shiver away, their reanimated corpses disintegrating back into the essence of dust.

Otto raised the scythe, appreciating the imagery of the reaper ending the necromancer. 'That was enjoyable, vampire,' he said, taking aim. 'Almost a shame it has to end.'

With a snarl, the shivering Vlad crossed his shaking arms over his chest, still retching uncontrollably. There was a flash of dark matter, and his body disintegrated into a cloud of fluttering bats.

Otto swiped, but his scythe passed harmlessly through the flock, scraping against the floor in a shower of sparks. He laughed again, admiring the vampire's art. He really had been a worthy opponent. The bats lurched and flapped down the corridor, heading for the outside and too flighty to catch.

With Vlad gone, the rest of his forces melted away. Otto turned to see the skeletons collapsing and the wights slumping to the floor. Ghurk paused in his rampage, his fists stuffed with bones, his mighty head swaying back and forth in confusion as his enemies clattered into tiny heaps around him.

The last to remain on his feet was an oddly mortal-looking warrior in a long coat and with a pair of pistols strapped to his waist. He stared at the spot where Vlad had been, his face a mix of loathing and regret. For a moment, he appeared to fight the inevitable, as if, having been reacquainted with unlife he was now loath to leave it.

But the end had to come. The man's jaw fell open with a sigh, his eyes rolled up into their sockets, and he collapsed to the floor. Once he was down, his body withered quickly, reverting to its true state in seconds.

Otto looked up at Ethrac, and grinned. The vampire's wound had already closed over, sealed with a line of glistening bile. There were advantages to being constituted of such glorious poisons.

'Then we are almost done, o my brother,' Otto remarked, brandishing his scythe.

Ethrac nodded. 'One by one, we devour them all. Now for the final meal.'

TWENTY-FOUR

Karl Franz and Martak entered the Chamber of Ghal Maraz. It had been abandoned long ago as the battle for the Palace was lost, and now stood as silent and as corroded as every other hall in the colossal complex.

The walls were weeping now, dripping with thick white layers of pus that fell in clots from the domed ceiling. The supporting pillars were covered in a hide of matted plant-matter, all of it shedding virulent pods that glowed and pulsed in the semi-dark. The great cupola over the circular space was half-ruined, with ivy tresses suspended like nooses from the broken stonework. Rain still spattered down through the gap, adding to the slick of mucus that swam across the chamber floor.

The two men both hurried to the high altar, the only structure to have remained relatively unscathed. The two empty chain-lengths still swayed from their bearings, hanging over the heavy iron table below.

Martak had no idea why they were there. The Imperial Palace had hundreds of chambers, many of them grander and more ornate that this one. If they had to select a place to die, why opt for the ancient resting place of the warhammer, a weapon that was now lost in the north and borne, if at all, by the boy-champion?

Karl Franz drew his runefang and backed up towards the altar's edge. Deathclaw remained protectively by his side, growling all the while from its huge barrel chest. Martak took up position at the other end of the iron structure, his own griffon remaining close by and snarling with customary spite.

'I do not–' he began, but then the words died in his mouth. Whether they were being tracked, or whether fate had simply decreed that the end would come then, the doors at the far end of the chamber slammed open, ripped from their hinges and flung aside like matchwood.

Three grotesque creatures burst inside, each one a distorted corruption of a man. The first was a slack-fleshed warrior bearing a scythe in two claw-like hands. His green skin, criss-crossed with bleeding sores and warty growths, glinted dully under the reflected glare of the pus-cascades.

The second was a similarly wizened creature clad in dirty patched robes and brandishing a staff nearly as gnarled as Martak's own.

The third was a true giant, barely able to shove itself through the huge double doors. Once inside the chamber he stood erect, one tentacled arm slack at his side, the other clenched into a hammer-like fist. His greasy, stupid face was deformed into a loathsome grin, and long trails of blood ran down from his mouth like warpaint.

Behind them, jostling for position, came more Chaos warriors, some in the furred garb of the far north, some bearing the mutated marks of more recent conversion. Their three leaders all bled horrific amounts of power from their addled frames. They were living embodiments of corruption, as vile and virulent as the Rot itself.

Karl Franz, unfazed, stepped forward, his blade raised towards them as if in grim tribute.

'I will not repeat this warning,' he said, and his calm voice echoed around the chamber. 'Leave this place now, or your souls will be bound to it forever. The spirit of almighty Sigmar runs deep here, and His sign shines above us. You do not know your danger.'

There was something about the deep authority in that voice, the measured expression, which gave even the three creatures of madness pause. They held back, and the huge one looked uncertainly at his companions.

The sorcerer was the first to laugh, though, breaking the moment. The warrior with the scythe joined in quickly.

'You did not need to be here, Emperor,' said the scythe-bearer, bowing floridly before him. 'We could have destroyed your city well enough on our own, but your death makes the exercise just a little more rewarding.'

The sorcerer bowed in turn, a mocking smile playing across his scarred face. 'We are the Glottkin, your excellency, once as mortal and as sickly as you, now filled with the magnificence of the Urfather. Know our names, before we slay you. I am Ethrac, this is my brother Otto, and this, the greatest of us all, is the mighty Ghurk.'

Ghurk emitted a wheezing *hhur* as his name was recited, then crackled the knuckles of his one true hand.

Martak clutched his staff a little tighter, allowing the Wind of Ghur to flow along its length. The chamber was electric with tension, just waiting for the false war of words to conclude – nothing would be settled now by rhetoric.

Karl Franz's face remained stony. His self-control was complete. Even in the heart of his annihilated kingdom, his visage never so much as flickered.

'I do not need to know your names,' he said, letting a shade of contempt dance around the edge of his speech. 'You will die just as all your breed will die – beyond the light of redemption, forever condemned to howl your misery to the void.'

Otto glanced over at Ethrac, amused, and shrugged. 'Then there is nothing to say to him, o my brother,' he remarked.

Ethrac nodded. 'It seems not, o my brother.'

They both turned back to face the altar, and the three of them burst into movement.

Otto was quickest, sprinting over to Karl Franz with his scythe whirring around his head. Ethrac was next, his staff alight with black energy, all aimed at Martak. Ghurk lumbered along in the rear, backed up by the charge of the northmen.

Deathclaw pounced in response, using a single thrust of its huge wings to power straight into Ghurk's oncoming charge. The griffon latched onto the huge monster, lashing out with its claws and tearing with its open beak. The two of them fell into a brutal exchange of blows, rocking and swaying as they ripped into one another.

Ethrac launched a barrage of plague-magic straight at Martak, aiming to deluge him in a wave of thick, viscous choke-slime. Martak countered with a blast from his own staff, puncturing the wave of effluent and sending it splattering back to its sender. Ethrac lashed his staff around, rousing the vines and creepers hanging from the chamber vaults into barbed flails. Martak cut them down as they emerged, summoning spectral blades that cartwheeled through the air.

Martak's own griffon took on the bulk of the tribesmen, bounding amongst them, goring and stabbing, leaving Otto and the Emperor to their combat undisturbed. The chamber rang with the sound and fury of combat, the runefang glittering as it was swung against the rusted scythe-blade.

'I saw you come back,' said Otto, letting a little admiration creep into his parched voice. 'Why did you do that? You know you cannot beat us.'

Karl Franz said nothing, but launched into a disciplined flurry with his blade, matching the blistering sweeps of the scythe.

Martak, kept busy with his own magical duel, only caught fragmentary glimpses of the combat, but he could hear the taunting words of the Glotts well enough. The mucus-rain continued to fall, tumbling down from the gaping roof and bouncing messily on the torn-up marble.

By then Ghurk was getting the better of Deathclaw. The griffon savaged its opponent, but the vast creature of Chaos was immune to pain and virtually indestructible. With a sickening snap, the griffon's wings were broken again. Deathclaw screamed, and was hurled aside, skidding into the chamber walls.

Martak backed away from Ethrac, fighting off fresh flurries of dark magic. The sorcerer was far more potent than he was, able to pull the very stuff of Chaos from the aethyr and direct it straight at him. With growing horror, Martak saw the first pustules rise on his forearms, and felt his staff begin to twist out of shape. His essence was being corrupted, turned against him and driven into the insane growths that had blighted the Empire from Marienburg to Ostermark.

Karl Franz fought on undeterred, matching Otto's blows with careful precision. He carried himself with all the elegance of an expertly-trained sword-master, adopting the proper posture and giving himself room to counter every blade movement. Otto, by contrast, came at him in a whirl of wild strokes, trying to unnerve him by flinging the scythe out wide before hauling it back in close. In a strange way, they were oddly matched, rocking to and fro before the altar, hacking and blocking under the shadow of the swinging chains.

Martak fell back further, bludgeoned by the superior magic of Ethrac. The pustules on his skin burst open, drenching him in foul-smelling liquids. He unleashed a flock of shadow-crows, which flew into Ethrac's face and pecked at his eyes, but the sorcerer whispered a single word, bursting their bellies and causing them to flop, lifeless, onto the chamber floor. More globules of burning slime were flung at Martak, and he barely parried them, feeling their acidic bite as they splashed across his face.

With a sick feeling in the pit of his stomach, Martak knew he was overmatched. Nothing he summoned troubled the sorcerer, and he could barely keep the counter-blasts from goring straight into him. Even as he retreated further, driven away from the altar and towards the chamber's east door, he saw the futility of it all, just as he had warned the Emperor.

There is no glory in dying here, and he wants *to die.*

Martak found himself snarling at the stupidity of it all. Noble gestures were for the aristocracy, for those with knightly blood or jewels spilling from their fingers. There were still other ways, still other weapons. If the Emperor would not give him leave, then he would go himself. The Menagerie was so *close*, and stocked with creatures that would chew through even the greatest of Chaos-spawned horrors.

His griffon, now bleeding heavily from a dozen wounds, suddenly turned and launched itself at Ethrac. The sorcerer, caught off-balance, had to work furiously not to be sliced apart, and for an instant turned away from Martak.

Seeing the chance, the Supreme Patriarch glanced a final time over at Karl Franz, uncertain whether his instincts were right. The Emperor fought on blindly, hugging the shadow of the altar. He was consumed by the duel, and Martak saw the look of utter conviction on his face. Karl Franz would not leave now, and nor could Martak reach him to drag him out.

Martak turned, and fled the chamber. Once outside, he tore down the narrow corridor beyond, his robes flapping about him. Soon he heard the sounds of pursuit as the northmen followed him, and he picked up the pace.

At least I have drawn them away, he though grimly, battling with incipient guilt at his desertion even as he struggled to remember the quickest way down to the cages. *That will buy him a little more time, and I* will *return.*

Otto watched the wizard flee with a smirk on his face. Given the choice, mortals always took the easier path. That was what made them so easy to turn, and so easy to kill. They had no proper comprehension of hard choices, the kind that would lead a tribesman to give up everything in the service of higher powers.

Sacrifice was the key. Learning to submit before the strenuous demands of uncompromising gods was the first step on the road to greatness. As he slammed the scythe towards the human Emperor's face, he began to feel excitement building.

He would be the one to end the dreams of humanity. *He* would be the one who would bring the City of Sigmar down, its every stone cracked and frozen by the abundance of the plague-forest, its every tower squeezed into cloying dust by the strangle-vines and barb-creepers. Soon all that would be left would be the Garden, the infinite expression of the Urfather's genius, swamping all else and extending infinitely towards all the horizons.

Heady with glee, he cracked the scythe down further, now aiming for the Emperor's chest. Karl Franz blocked the blow, but he seemed to be going through the motions now. A strange expression remained on his haggard face – a kind of serenity.

That bothered Otto, and he pressed harder. With a wild swipe, he managed to knock the runefang aside. He pounced, driving a long gouge down the Emperor's arm and eliciting a stark cry of pain.

Karl Franz staggered back against the altar, half-falling to his knees. Otto rose up triumphantly, holding his scythe high.

'And so it ends!' he screamed, and dragged the blade down.

Just before it connected, though, a sword-edge interposed itself, locking with the curved scythe-edge and holding it fast. Otto looked down to see an Empire warrior in the way, his blade held firm and his eyes blazing with fury. He wore elaborate plate armour, and his hawk-like face was half-hidden by a voluminous moustache.

For a second, Otto was transfixed with shock. All the mortals were supposed to be dead or driven far away from the Palace. He turned to see other armoured Empire warriors charge into the chamber and launch themselves at the remaining northmen.

So there were some humans with the spine to fight on.

Otto twisted his mouth into a smirking leer, and yanked the scythe free. The Emperor, bleeding profusely, fell to his knees, his place taken by the newcomer.

'You come here,' snarled the moustached warrior through gritted teeth, drawing himself up to his full height. 'You bring the plague, you bring the fires, you bring the pain.' His scarred face creased into an expression of pure, unadulterated hatred. 'Now *I* bring the reckoning.'

Martak panted as he ran, feeling his battered body protest. They were already on his heels, and he could almost taste their foul breath on his neck.

He careered down the spiralling stairs, hoping that he had remembered the way, trying to *think* and not to panic. He ought to have been able to smell the beasts by now, but the festering mess in the Palace made it hard to tell the stinks apart.

He reached the base of the stairs, almost slipping on the tiles but managing to push on. He shoved through a thick wooden door, and at last heard the sounds he had been hoping to pick up.

The beasts were roused – they were pawing in their pens, driven mad by the spoor of Chaos within the Palace. The griffons would be tearing at their cages, the demigryphs and manticores would be slavering with fury. And down at the very heart of it all, the mightiest of creatures, the one that only Karl Franz had ever been able to tame, would be waiting, its old, cold mind roused to thoughts of murder.

Martak felt something whirr past his ear, and veered sharply to one side. A throwing-axe clanged from the wall ahead of him, missing by a finger's breadth.

He kept going, trying to keep his shoulders lower. A pair of iron gates loomed before him, still locked and looped with chains.

It was all he could do to blurt out a spell of opening before he stumbled into them, pushing through and staggering into the darkness beyond.

From all around him, he suddenly heard the snarls and growls of the caged animals. It was uniquely comforting – he had spent his whole life among beasts, and now they surrounded him once more.

He smiled, and kept running. He knew where he was going now, and there was no hope of stopping him. He could already smell the embers, and hear the dry hiss of scales moving over stone.

Almost there.

Karl Franz watched helplessly as Helborg took the fight to Otto Glott. He had been cut deep, and felt his arm hanging uselessly at his side. The Reiksguard knights Helborg had brought with him threw themselves into battle with the sorcerer and the behemoth, roaring the name of Sigmar as they wheeled their blades about.

Karl Franz could only look on. It was staggeringly brave. He had last seen Helborg on the eve of Heffengen, and could only imagine what trials he had faced in the meantime. He looked a shadow of his earlier, ebullient self – his face was lean, disfigured by long gouges and etched with fatigue. It looked like he could barely walk, let alone fight, but somehow he worked his blade with all the old arrogant flair, driving Otto back with every blurred arc of steel, giving him no room to respond.

Karl Franz wanted to speak out, then – to tell him that he had got it wrong, and that no force of arms could possibly make a difference now. If the Glotts were slain in this chamber, nothing would change – the armies of Chaos would still run rampant, the city would still be lost, the Reik would still be corrupted. For his whole life, Karl Franz had drilled into his subjects the need to fight on, to never give in, to reach for the blade as a first resort. He could hardly tell them any different now, but as he watched his chosen Reiksguard being hacked to pieces by the dread power of Ethrac and the sheer brute force of Ghurk, it made him want to weep.

Moving stiffly, he shoved himself onto one elbow, panting hard as the pain kicked in. He could not move from the altar. That was the key – the great sacrificial slab that had been placed under the dome for a reason. The light of the comet streamed down through the gap, bathing everything in a candle-yellow sheen. He had learned to accept that only *he* could see the light properly, that even Martak had not been able to perceive it truly, and that to others it was a pale flicker in a scoured sky. To him, it was the light of the sun and the moon combined, a brilliant star amid the sour corruption of the earth. It was calling to him even now, reminding him of the great trial, whispering words of power that only he could hear.

Karl Franz stood up, wincing against the pain. It was as Helborg had told him – he was not a man like any other, one whose soul was bound by mortal limits. He had always been set apart, devoted to a purer calling.

You are the Empire.

Helborg was tiring now. He could not sustain the fury, and Otto was beating him back. Karl Franz looked on grimly, knowing that Helborg *had* to be beaten, but nonetheless barely able to watch it unfold.

The Reiksmarshal launched into a final series of devastating strikes, throwing everything into them. The way he moved the runefang then was magnificent, as good as he had ever been, and against any other foe it would surely have brought the kill he was so desperate for. For an instant, Helborg threw off his long weariness, his disappointments and his inadequacies, and became the perfect swordsman again, a vision of pure speed and power. It was all Otto could do to avoid being smashed aside and hacked to pieces, and for the first time a sheen of sweat burst out across his calloused brow.

Karl Franz could have joined him then. He could have limped over, adding his runefang to his Reiksmarshal's, and perhaps together they could have slain the beast. Instead, he remained bathed in the light of the comet, loathing every moment of inaction but staying true to the duty that compelled him.

When the end came, it was swift. Helborg overreached himself, leaving his defence open. Otto pounced, jabbing the point of the scythe down hard. The wickedly curved edge bit deep, cracking Helborg's breastplate and driving into the flesh beneath. With unnatural strength, Otto dragged Helborg off his feet and hurled him to one side, ripping out his heart as he did so.

Helborg skidded across the marble before crashing into the altar, his chest torn open. With his final breath, he looked up at Karl Franz, and there was still a wild hope in those pain-wracked eyes. He shivered, his arms clutching, his body rigid and his back arched.

'Fight... *on*,' he gasped.

Then he went limp, slumped against the altar's edge, his armour drenched in blood. The last defender of Altdorf died at the heart of his city, gazing up at the empty dome above, his haunted features at last free from the pain that had consumed him for so long.

With Helborg slain, Otto advanced on Karl Franz once more, a wide grin on his face. In the background, the Reiksguard were being cut down, one by one.

'You people do not know when to give in,' said Otto. 'It becomes tiresome.'

Karl Franz watched him approach, preparing himself, knowing how painful the transition would be, dreading it and yet yearning for it to come.

'But surely you can see that this thing is over now,' said Otto, drawing back the scythe. His green eyes glittered with triumph.

'There is nothing more to be done, heir of the boy-god. Listen to the truth: the reign of man is ended.'

He swung the blade, and the tip, still hot from Helborg's blood, sliced into the Emperor's chest.

Karl Franz staggered backward, his breath taken away by the agony of it, struggling to keep his vision. Otto ripped the scythe-blade free, tearing up muscle and sinew and leaving a long bloody trail across the altar's side.

The Emperor slid further down, his body pressed against the altar-top, the runefang falling uselessly from his open palm. Each of the three Glott brothers, their enemies destroyed now, shuffled closer, peering with morbid curiosity as the life ebbed out of their victim.

Karl Franz looked up at them, gasping for air, feeling the blood clog in his throat.

They were not even gloating. They suddenly looked like children, shocked at what they had done, as if only now could they contemplate what it might mean.

That made him want to smile. He gripped the altar's edge, and ceased fighting. Everything went cold, then black, and then became nothing. It was like tipping over the edge of a precipice, then falling fast.

And so it was that, under the shattered dome of the Chamber of Ghal Maraz, Karl Franz, Elector Count of Reikland, Prince of Altdorf, Bearer of the Silver Seal and the holder of the *Drachenzahn* runefang, Emperor of all Sigmar's holy inheritance between the Worlds Edge Mountains and the Great Sea, died.

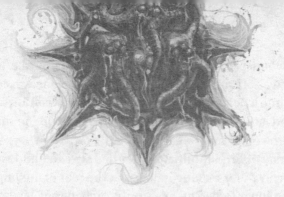

TWENTY-FIVE

Martak reached the very base of the Menagerie's dungeons, his breath heaving and his lungs burning. The last cage was buried deep, surrounded by huge walls of stone and ringed with iron chains. The air stank of flame and charring, and every surface had been burned as black as coal.

He could hear the footfalls at the top of the stairs. They had almost caught him, right at the end, and he could sense their bloodlust burning like a beacon in the darkness.

He reached the iron lattice, slamming into it and fumbling for the great lock. It was the size of his chest, and took a key the length of his forearm, but that would not be necessary now. Stammering over the words, he spoke the spell of unbinding, and the lock fell apart.

Heavy clangs rang out as iron-shod boots thudded down the steep stairs, and Martak barely pushed his way into the cage before metal gauntlets reached out to haul him back.

He wrenched himself free, skidding over to one side as he scrambled for safety. For a terrible moment, grovelling in the dark, he wondered if he had made some awful mistake, and the vast cage was already empty. If so, all he had done was lead his pursuers into a dead end, one from which there was no escaping.

A second later, though, twin gouts of flame lit up the shadows, and he allowed himself a gasp of relief.

The bursts of fire illuminated a curled, twisted and writhing mass of scaly hide, snaking in loops at the rear of the huge pen. Enormous wings folded up against the arched roof, leathery and as thick as a man's hand. Two great eyes, slit-pupilled like a cat's, blinked in the dark, exposing yellow depths that seemed to go on forever.

Blind to the danger, the warriors of Chaos blundered into the cage after Martak, only realising their error too late.

The Imperial dragon opened its vast jaws, sending a stream of crimson flame roaring into them. The marauders screamed, clawing at their own flesh as the dragon's fire tore through them. Those that could tried to retreat, but the curtains of immolation overtook them all, ripping the armour from their backs and melting it across their blistered skin.

Martak pressed himself flat against the cage's curving inner wall, feeling the furious heat surge across his face. He screwed his eyes shut, barely enduring the ferocious blaze even as it thundered past.

After only a few moments, the torrent guttered out. Martak coughed and gasped, falling to his knees as smoke billowed out from the dragon's jaws. He glanced back to the cage entrance, where dozens of bodies lay gently steaming, as black as burned offerings.

He allowed himself a twisted grin, and shuffled up to the dragon's great iron collar.

'That was well done, dragon,' he said, reaching up for the mighty lock.

The dragon hissed at him, sending a fresh burst of flame-laced hot air blasting into his flushed face. Martak whispered words for the quieting of the animal spirits, drawing on the Wind of Ghur that eddied throughout the whole Menagerie. He had no chance of truly mastering a dragon's mind, but he could do just enough to persuade it that *he* was no threat, and that freedom was a small step away, and that the horrors running amok in the Palace above were the real prey.

He placed his hands over the massive padlock, and exerted his will. The lock clicked open, and the iron chains fell to the ground with a resounding clang. Though still hampered by the confines of the cell, the great creature stretched out, its head rising up to the roof and its wings unfurling around the walls. A grating, iron-hard growl emerged from its chest, and its clawed forelegs pawed at the straw.

'Now, take the fight to *them!*' urged Martak gazing up at the creature's snake-like neck and marvelling at just how huge it was. 'You are free – let me guide you.'

The dragon did not move. Though released from its chains, it remained where it was, curled up in a dungeon at the very base of the vast Palace. Its old, old face seemed lost in thought, its eyes narrowing and its nostrils flared.

Martak began to lose patience. If the Emperor still lived, there would be little time to save him. Every moment saw more of the city destroyed, and more lives lost.

'Come *on!*' he commanded, infusing his voice with as much beast-mastery as he could. 'What are you waiting for?'

As soon as he uttered those words, though, he realised what was happening. The dragon *was* waiting for something. It had no intention at all of leaving its cell, and its huge head remained motionless, slightly inclined, as if listening.

It was only then that Martak felt it himself. He had been so preoccupied with survival, so fixed on his goal of releasing the dragon, that the tremors had passed him by completely, but now, with his hunters slain and the mighty beast standing before him, he wondered how he had missed them.

The ground was vibrating. Not strongly, as if in an earthquake, but with a steady, persistent harmonic. The straws under his feet were trembling, and lines of dust were falling from the brick-work roof. A low hum filled the chamber, reverberating just on the edge of hearing. It sounded like it was coming from every-where – the stone, the earth, the air itself.

Martak backed away from the dragon. Whatever he sensed was nothing like the sorcery that had infused the city since the beginning of the siege. It felt... *older*, somehow, as if it belonged to Altdorf's very bones. After witnessing the dead raised and the order of nature turned against itself, it should have been impos-sible to conceive of more potent magic coming to the Reik, but Martak was enough of a mage to recognise true power when he felt it.

'What *is* this?' he murmured, looking up at the roof of the dragon's cage, any thought of trying to use the creature now abandoned. 'What comes now?'

For a moment, nothing changed.

Then the first shafts of light angled down from the open dome, harsh and piercing. The Glottkin looked up, as did their surviving troops in the chamber. More shafts lanced through the gaping breach, shimmering like spun gold. They focussed on the altar, seeming to soak into the iron.

Otto started to back away. Ethrac stared at the growing pool of gold, a gathering unease on his face.

'And what?' Otto demanded. 'What is this?'

Spinning points of gold coalesced over the altar-top, clustering together and glittering like stars. Far above, the clouds broke at last, burned away by the lone star riding the high airs. Across the city, beleaguered defenders suddenly stared up into the heavens, noticing the strange play of light dancing across the shattered townscape. The marauders paused in their plunder, and daemons shrunk back, their laughter halted.

'Just a star!' protested Ethrac, outraged. 'You told me – it was just a star!'

The light kept growing, building up into a column of iridescence that hurt the eyes to look upon. A column of pure gold shot down onto the altar where Karl Franz's body lay like the sacrifice it had been. Shimmering luminescence shot out in all directions, trembling with a blaze of metallic light.

Otto was forced back from the altar, his eyes streaming. Ethrac's staff shattered in his hands, and its bells rolled across the marble.

With a roar like distant thunder, the rain of gold turned into a torrent, cascading down from the comet and smashing against the altar-top. Rays of severe iridescence radiated outward, refracting and spinning, making the columns around them glisten as if newly gilded. The stained-glass windows blew out, sending shards of diamond-like glass flying into the plague-storm beyond.

Bathed now in a pillar of shifting gold, the Emperor's body began to change. The harrowed expression left his face and the lines of care smoothed out. His corpse rose, suspended in an aegis of fire. The chains above the altar thrashed and twisted, buffeted by a new wind.

His eyes opened, and golden brilliance flared from the sockets. He righted himself, now floating directly over the altar, and swept his blinding gaze across the cowering mutants below. He seemed to augment, to grow, becoming far more than a man. The last of his armour fell away, exposing a shifting phantasm of pure coruscation beneath. Shafts of gold danced around him, reflecting from the now-dazzling surfaces of the chamber.

It was hard to make out what manner of being now hung above the black iron. Karl Franz's face could be made out amid the sparkling clouds of light, blurred and fractured, but older faces were there too, coexisting in a merger of souls. A series of Emperors gazed serenely out from the blistering fires, unharmed by them, sustained by them, before the vision shifted once more.

Otto's flesh began to burn, curling away from the bone in crisping flaps. Ethrac and Ghurk followed, their withered muscles scorched by the rays of light surging from the gathering inferno of gold. The being that had once been the Emperor continued to expand, until an argent titan hung in the chamber's heart, blazing like the dawn rising.

A voice echoed around the shimmering space, redolent of the old Emperors, but containing a choir of others with it, all speaking in a harmony of different accents and timbres.

'The Law of Death is broken,' it announced, and the words echoed among the roar of golden flames. 'All worlds are now open.'

The titan's face began to flicker, changing from one to another, now bearded, now smooth, now old, now young. A new visage came to the fore – a ruddy-cheeked youth with a mane of long blond hair, laughing with warrior's eyes. The intensity of the golden aura became truly blinding, spreading out across the entire chamber in shimmering curtains of brilliance.

'We are the Empire,' announced the flickering avatar, its flaming eyes sweeping across the burning vista. 'We have always been the Empire.'

It raised its hands high, and it seemed that a mighty warhammer now hung from the clanking chains. The titan took it up, and the weapon blazed with the same intense light that filled the chamber.

'And now,' it said, portentously, 'let *all things change*.'

A hard *bang* rang out, blowing what remained of the glass out of the windows and making the earth shake. The heart of the golden being exploded, filling the vaults with white-hot illumination. A racing wave of energy surged out from the epicentre, sweeping and ethereal, consuming all before it. The burning bodies of the Glotts were devoured, seared to ash and blown away by the racing storm-front.

A radial wave smashed through the walls of the chapel, rising up in a dome of unleashed power. The hemisphere, swimming with translucence, spread across the entire city, a wall of gold, tearing out from the Palace at its heart and scouring everything it touched. The scorching barrage of flame destroyed every lingering creature of Chaos as it thundered outward, stripping the layers of slime and filth clean from the stone beneath and immolating them into nothingness. The fallen undead were blasted apart, their dry bones turned to powder and thrown into the wind.

Above the city, the last of the plague-storm clouds were torn away, exposing a clear sky above. The comet burned vividly now, linked to the earth by the roaring column of gold. The expanding fire-dome ground its way outward across the entire valley, rising into the heavens and encompassing the fields of war below. At its edge, the corrupted forest burst and burned, and its foul taints were stripped clear of the raw earth.

For a moment longer, the entire Palace shimmered from the golden storm within, its every portal bleeding pure comet-fire. The dome of Sigmar's temple flared in answer, reflecting mesmerising rays across a glittering sky. The Reik, for so long a turgid well of slime, burst into cleansing flame, revealing pure waters boiling under the skin of filth. Aeons of grime were scrubbed from the ancient stone walls, revealing Altdorf as in the days of old – the city of white stone, the home of kings, the birthplace of Emperors.

And then, with a final roar, the dome of light shimmered out. The city below it seemed to shudder, and then fall still.

The dead were gone. The corrupted were consumed. Amid the wreckage and the ruins, the surviving human defenders crept out of whatever cover they had found, shading their eyes against the glare that still lingered on the waters.

The air was cold and clear. For the first time in months, the wind tasted fresh. The spores were gone, the cankers had been stripped away.

With a growing sense of awe, they began to realise what had happened. The enemy was destroyed, burned on the altar of wrath, its limitless powers exposed for the sham and trickery they were. Something new had emerged, something unprecedented.

The Palace still glowed from within. Whatever had been unleashed there still lingered, though none dared approach its burning precincts.

All they could do was stare up at the listing battlements and the broken towers, and guess at what new and terrible god now dwelt amid the graven images of the old.

EPILOGUE

Early winter 2525

As the storm clouds gradually headed north, their heavy aegis broken, the rising sun illuminated a scene of gently steaming devastation.

Everything was gone. The mighty walls had been reduced to rubble, and smoke still curled from the charred remains of the great buildings. The temples, the counting-houses, the merchants' mansions, the beggars' hovels – all had disappeared, withered by the fury of the North, rendered down to whitened dust.

The few that had survived lingered in the ruins only for want of somewhere better to go. The remnants of Helborg's command fanned out from their North Gate fastness, blinking in the suddenly pure light. Bretonnian knights stumbled under the gaping arch of the West Gate, already resigned to the loss of their leader but determined to seek him out. Exhausted townsfolk all across the city fell to their knees, gazing around them in blank amazement.

No victory songs were sung, for every living throat was parched raw. A pall of shock had seeped into the earth. None had the words for what they had seen, and none tried to find any.

Slowly, though, the instincts of survival took over. Men and women began to seek one another out, searching through the rubble for survivors. Under the fractured shadow of the still-huge Palace walls, the few living commanders started to try to impose some sense of order on what remained. Food would have to be found from somewhere, and water drawn, and fires lit, and searches launched. Perhaps Helborg still lived. Perhaps some of the electors still lived.

In the city's poorest quarter, at the very centre of where the daemon-storms had been greatest, it took a long time for Margrit to do anything other than stare up into the cleared heavens, her heart beating heavily. Eventually her senses returned to her, though the world around seemed as blurred as a badly-remembered dream.

Her fellow sisters pulled themselves up from the stone, their faces drained with shock, their hands still trembling. From within the temple, weak voices could already be heard, crying out, pleading to know what had taken place.

She had no idea what to tell them. It took her a long time to get up, first gently shifting the body of the slain king from her lap. When she stood, she felt light-headed. She tried to remember how the old tenements surrounding the temple had appeared in the past. Now the dome of Shallya was the only thing still standing, and beyond it stretched an empty landscape of smouldering rubble.

But Margrit was a practical woman, and there were already tasks at hand. The temple had to be secured. They had to look to the gardens, to try to salvage anything that might help with the wounded, for there were sure to be thousands of them. She started moving again, speaking to the others, who trod amid the detritus just as numbly as her.

'There will be answers,' she told them, not knowing if that were true but needing something to say. 'For now, remember your vows.'

Once they had something to do, to occupy them, things became easier. The hours passed again, filled with the old tasks of care. A group of knights found their way to the temple, and bore away the body of their king in reverence. Margrit watched them go, making no attempt to lay claim to him. The warriors barely noticed her.

They would not have spoken to her, in any case. They were men of war, and so few of them had ever paid any attention to the women in their midst, unless they were bejewelled queens or ethereal goddesses, and Margrit was neither.

By the time Martak found her, the sun was high in the sky, and a warm wind had started blowing from the south. The wizard looked as filthy as ever, though his long beard looked to have been singed half away.

As he picked his way towards her through the wreckage, Margrit crossed her arms, and waited.

'You never got me those soldiers,' she said.

Martak shot her an apologetic look. 'He was a hard man to persuade.'

'Was?'

Martak nodded, and Margrit sighed. She had heard men curse Kurt Helborg to damnation during the days of toil, but the Reiksmarshal had stood beside them at the end, and that was worth something.

'You promised me an Emperor, too,' she said.

The wizard looked bone-weary. With a grunt, he sat down on a broad stone step. Margrit joined him, and together they looked out across the rubble-strewn courtyard. For a while, neither of them spoke.

'I do not know what happened,' said Martak eventually.

'If you do not, then no one will.'

Martak looked at her. All his earlier gruffness had been ripped from him. His voice was still as earthy as the mulch under the forest floor, but something had changed. He looked... humbled.

'I brought him back,' he said, looking unsure how to feel about that. 'Do not misunderstand me – it was *his* choice. I tried to get him to escape it, but he wouldn't listen.'

Margrit placed a calloused palm on Martak's wringing hands. 'When you told me he would come back, I believed you.'

'I was telling you what you wanted to hear.'

'It doesn't matter.' She summoned a weak smile. 'The *words* mattered.'

Martak looked sceptical, but said nothing. He made no attempt to shift her hand from his, and the two of them stayed where they were. Crouched at the edge of ruin, a ragged, dirt-streaked pedlar from the lowliest of colleges and a portly old woman from the most disregarded of temples.

Not much to be proud of, but they were alive.

'So, what now?' she asked him.

Martak shook his head, a wry expression playing across his wrinkled brow. She could tell what he was thinking. Plans would have to be made. Schwarzhelm might yet live. Valten might still carry Ghal Maraz. There were mysteries to delve into, and at some stage someone would have to go back into the Palace, searching for any remains of the... event. They had all seen the tides of gold, and they had all heard the roar of the storm, and they all knew that it had changed everything, and that a new power had been birthed in Altdorf beneath the comet's glare.

For now, though, it was too soon.

'I do not know, sister,' Martak said, clutching her hand tight.

The two of them sat next to one another after that, looking out onto the aftermath of the apocalypse, sharing silence.

Altdorf was destroyed, shriven to its foundations, and there would be no rebuilding. The old city was gone – its garrisons, its theatres, its chapels, its taverns and its storehouses, swept into nothingness.

The End Times had come, but they had not brought the utter destruction the gods of the North desired.

The old stories had ended, their power gone and their magic decayed. Now new stories would be told, but where they would lead, and who would tell them, even the wisest could not tell.

ABOUT THE AUTHOR

Chris Wraight is the author of the Horus Heresy novel *Scars*, the novella *Brotherhood of the Storm* and the audio drama *The Sigillite*. For Warhammer 40,000 he has written the Space Wolves novels *Blood of Asaheim* and *Stormcaller*, and the short story collection *Wolves of Fenris*, as well as the Space Marine Battles novels *Wrath of Iron* and *Battle of the Fang*. Additionally, he has many Warhammer novels to his name, including the Time of Legends novel *Master of Dragons*, which forms part of the War of Vengeance series. Chris lives and works near Bristol, in south-west England.

WARHAMMER
THE END TIMES

THE CURSE OF
KHAINE

GAV THORPE

An extract from The Curse of Khaine,
Book III of Warhammer: The End Times
by Gav Thorpe

It was not the first attack Eagle Gate had weathered since the
druchii had arrived, but Malekith was determined that it would
not stand against him this time. He had given the honour, dubious though it was, to Malus Darkblade, but it was not to the
warriors of Hag Graef nor the knights of the Tyrant that the Witch
King truly entrusted victory. It was a simple fact that from the
moment the immense druchii fleet had landed on the shores of
Nagarythe and disgorged its hosts towards Ellyrion, the fate of
Eagle Gate had been sealed, and the efforts of Darkblade and
his regiments was simply a bloody teaser of the violence to come
– a test of Malus's dedication to maintaining his veneer of loyalty to Malekith.

Malus was doomed to failure from the outset, and probably
knew as much. He had saved his most precious troops, protecting
them like a dwarf king hoards his gold, but the time had rapidly
come when the first assaults had failed and the Tyrant was forced
to commit his household troops: the knights of Burning Dark.

He led them now on a desperate charge through the defenders, assisted by Drusala and her sorceresses.

No doubt the sight of Malekith standing beside Seraphon watching the proceedings did little to hearten the Tyrant. The Witch King was content to observe the lord of Hag Graef while he expended his forces, weakening his power with every failed attack, unable to defy his king. And the true beauty was that the attacks of Malus served Malekith's purpose in another fashion, drawing the eye of the enemy outwards to the Shadowlands, bringing in more of their reserves and forces from across the nearby kingdoms. Malus did not know that knights from Ellyrion had arrived, and dismounted they waited now amongst the bolstered ranks of the defenders. Flame-winged phoenixes drove away the harpies that had been scavenging the dead in the upper towers and then swooped upon the vanguard of Malus's latest assault threatening to scatter them as the early attacks had been thwarted. Every elf that died defending the Gate was one less Malekith would face when he finally made his move, or one less to support Malus should he survive the encounter and make a claim for the crown.

Despite the forlorn situation, Malekith admired the knights and warriors bearing down upon the defenders. It was rare for him to contemplate such lowly subjects but he took a moment to acknowledge the unswerving dedication and bravery demonstrated by their sacrifice below. Many of them would die, of course, without knowing such regard existed, but the fortunate few that survived to see the dusk Malekith would reward for their endeavour, further undermining Malus's power. He was, after all, a magnanimous ruler when required. That which could not be coerced with dread was easily bought with gold and favour, and in the new world they would carve on these shores the druchii knew only a few would rise to the top of society and would happily betray each other for such position.

There was a great commotion at the front of the assault, but Malekith could not see clearly what passed. He saw an explosion of daemonic energy and the asur army was in disarray for a while. No doubt Malus had unleashed whatever power it was Malekith had sensed at the council. It mattered little, the assault was grinding to its inevitable stop.

The mountains rang then with deafening roars, followed by a tumult of cheering from the ramparts of the Gate. A palpable aura of despair engulfed the druchii host pressing into the valley, from spearmen to knights, sorceresses to the beastmasters that drove Malus's two monstrous hydras into battle. Malekith turned to the south, knowing what it was that had caused such consternation so quickly, broken lips twisted into a smile.

Dragons.

There were dozens of the immense creatures, each ridden by one of the proud knights of Caledor. A rainbow of colours against the summer sky, a glittering chromatic display of raw strength. The surprise and delight of the defenders was all the greater for recent events. Imrik of Caledor had declined to help Tyrion against the daemon assault and had withdrawn his forces to the borders of his kingdom.

His aid had been unlooked for, but now it seemed the tide would be turned by Imrik's intervention.

Such relief and joy was untimely.

Malekith pulled himself up into Seraphon's saddle-throne and picked up the iron chains of her reins.

'Go,' he whispered. 'Go to your cousins.'

Shouts of encouragement from the druchii followed Malekith into the sky as those below thought he sought to take on the squadrons of Caledor single-handed. Jeers rang out from the defenders, mocking his arrogance.

The jeers faded and the praise of the druchii fell to silence as Malekith and Imrik guided their monstrous mounts towards each other, weapons bared. As he closed with the Caledorian prince, Malekith was surprised by just how alike he was to his ancestor whose name he had taken.

He fixed this new Imrik with his dread gaze and lifted *Urithain*.

Cries of surprise and dismay sounded from the mountainsides as Imrik saluted with his lance and the two dragonriders turned towards Eagle Gate, the lord of Caledor following behind the Witch King of Naggaroth. In their wake came the gold and silver and red and blue scales of Caledorian mounts, but amongst them more ebon-hued beasts raised by the masters of Clar Karond and Karond Kar.

There was already fighting on the walls as Caledorian knights that had been part of the garrison revealed their true loyalty. Even as the dragons descended with claws and deadly breath the great portal of Eagle Gate's seventh wall was opening.

The druchii roar of glee was almost as thunderous as the cries of the dragons as Malekith's followers surged into the pass, intent on the doomed fortification.

Available from *blacklibrary.com*
and

GAMES WORKSHOP®

Hobby Centres.